The Hurly Burly

AND OTHER STORIES

ECCO ART OF THE STORY

The Hurly Burly

AND OTHER STORIES

A. E. COPPARD

HarperCollins books may be purchased for educational, business, or sales promotional use. For information, please email the Special Markets Department at SPsales@harpercollins.com.

Ecco® and HarperCollins® are trademarks of HarperCollins Publishers.

FIRST EDITION

Designed by Michelle Crowe

Library of Congress Cataloging-in-Publication Data has been applied for.

ISBN 978-0-06-305416-5

21 22 23 24 25   LSC   10 9 8 7 6 5 4 3 2 1

CONTENTS

Preface

by Russell Banks

HOW IS IT POSSIBLE THAT AN ACCLAIMED TWENTIETH-century master of the English short story, his work loved and admired by critics and writers as different and demanding as Ford Madox Ford, Malcolm Cowley, Frank O'Connor, and Doris Lessing, turns up all but lost to us today? From the start of his career, he was compared favorably to Hardy, Kipling, and D. H. Lawrence, and was viewed as Chekhov's and Maupassant's legitimate British heir. Between 1921 and his death in 1957, he published more than twenty short story collections. *The Collected Tales of A. E. Coppard* was published in the US by Knopf in 1949, and, thanks to a letter-writing campaign led by Eudora Welty, Elizabeth Bowen, Robert Frost, and Carl Sandburg, was the Book of the Month Club headliner in 1951—a very big deal at the time, critically and commercially, rare for a non-American writer and rarer still for a book of short stories.

Yet, until the early 1980s, I myself had read only one of Coppard's stories when I taught a seminar on the modern American short story in the Columbia Graduate Writing Program and assigned Frank O'Connor's *The Lonely Voice: A Study of the Short Story* to help guide the students through the bodies of work of writers like Flannery O'Connor, J. D. Salinger, Grace Paley, Donald Barthelme, James Alan McPherson, Raymond Carver, John Cheever, and so on. At that time, there was a short-lived renaissance in writing, publishing, and reading short stories, and students in creative writing workshops were eager to learn how it was done.

The Lonely Voice gives high praise and an entire chapter over to the work of A. E. Coppard. "Coppard was a Georgian in the same way that Robert Frost, Edward Thomas, Edmund Blunden, and a score of others were Georgians, and he shared their obsession with personal freedom—freedom from responsibilities; freedom from conventions, particularly sexual conventions; freedom from duties to state and church; above all, freedom from the tyranny of money." Elsewhere, O'Connor says, "He was fascinated primarily by women's secretiveness: it is the theme of most of his great stories." These were themes that my students and the American writers on their syllabus were obsessed with, too. It was time to read some A. E. Coppard, I decided.

Easier said than done. Most of his books were long out of print, even in England, and his *Collected Tales* could be found only as an abused copy at the legendary Strand Bookstore (this was pre-eBay, Amazon, and quickie print-on-demand facsimile editions of out-of-copyright books). Eventually I got my hands on the *Collected Tales*, which is more "selected" than "collected," the stories chosen and briefly introduced by Coppard himself, and a tattered copy of *The Black Dog and Other Stories*, published in the US in 1923 by Knopf. Between the two volumes, I had access to most of his best stories, early and late. It's from these two collections that I've chosen the fifteen that follow, five from *The Black Dog and Other Stories* and ten from *The Collected Tales of A. E. Coppard*.

Reading them for the first time was a revelation. The best of the stories, like "The Black Dog," "The Higgler," and "The Field of Mustard," are as fine as anything in the English language. In almost all his stories, even the ones I was obliged to leave out, the influence of Hardy and Maupassant is wide and deep, especially in the dark ironies and unintended consequences that upend the quiet lives of desperation led by ordinary workingmen and -women, and their sad-eyed children trailing behind. Like Maupassant, Coppard was a careful, affectionate, compassionate observer of the lives of women: mostly poor, abandoned, or "fallen" women, young and old. And like Hardy, and to a lesser degree Lawrence, he took pure delight in the English countryside. A true countryman, he possessed a vast and deep personal knowledge of all of England's green. As Lessing noted, "Coppard knew England through walking over it," and he was, indeed, in the tradition of Coleridge and Wordsworth, a tireless, lifelong tramper.

But there was something uniquely characteristic of Coppard's stories that I'd rarely seen in male writers, especially of his generation—perhaps of any generation. Yes, he was, as O'Connor said, "fascinated by women's secretiveness," although I would put it rather differently. In many, if not most of Coppard's best stories, the protagonist is a man or boy whose life is confounded by his inability to see into the heart and mind of the woman or girl he loves. But it's not because of her "secretiveness." It's because the male is too obtuse, self-absorbed, overloaded with fantasy and projection, dishonest and insecure, or merely too professionally and financially ambitious to see what's before his clouded eyes. Coppard himself, however (and thus the reader), sees clearly into the hidden depths of the beloved woman's vulnerable heart and mind. It's his male protagonists, the lovestruck suitor or the befuddled husband or the overprotective father or the dismissive brother or son, who cannot catch a glimpse until it's too late, and both lover and beloved must go their separate ways. As a result, at the center of these stories there is a profound, heartbreaking loneliness for all—male and female alike. A loneliness, one senses, that is shared by the author.

Alfred Edgar Coppard was born into extreme poverty in 1878 in Folkestone, Kent, the eldest of four children. His mother was a housemaid; his father, a tailor, deserted the family when Coppard was six, forcing his mother to support the family by herself as a presser and with parish relief. His was a Dickensian childhood: Taken from school at the age of nine and apprenticed to a paraffin oil vendor, he was later shipped off to live with an uncle in London, where he worked at a series of jobs as a messenger boy and eventually as a clerk for small businesses and manufacturing firms. At fifteen he was earning side money as a professional sprinter and using it to buy books. The boy with three years of formal education had fallen in love with literature—specifically, he wrote in his autobiography, with Keats's "La Belle Dame sans Merci," Hardy's *Life's Little Ironies*, and the poems of Robert Bridges and Walt Whitman. He read voraciously and indiscriminately, and memorized whole swaths of poetry in English that he could, and would, recite for the rest of his life.

In 1905 he married and in his late twenties was at Oxford, but not as a student. He was employed there as a clerk—an irascible autodidact with nascent literary ambitions and all the usual insecurities and defenses, elbows sharpened, no doubt, by his friendships with the collegiate literary intellectuals. In his autobiography, he confesses, "Here were all these boys, boys! with their poems and tales already in being . . . some even in real books. Straightway I was fired, though not by any more worthy muse than the spirit of rivalry." He wrote his first story at thirty-four—twelve thousand words—called "Fleet," which was rejected by *The English Review* for being too long. But the floodgate had opened, and soon he was publishing poetry and stories, among them some of his best, like "Dusky Ruth" and "The Wife of Ted Wickham," in the most prestigious English and American journals of the day, including *The Double Dealer*, *The Dial*, and *The Saturday Review*. He may have come late to the party, but he had definitely arrived. Ford Madox Ford remembered that "the first English writer to whom I wrote for a contribution to *The Transatlantic Review* was Mr. Coppard."

Each of the fifteen stories included here is emotionally stirring in its own way, sometimes unexpectedly, as in "The Black Dog," when, halfway into the story, the locus for our sympathy shifts from the besotted middle-aged bachelor, the Honorable Gerald Loughlin, over to the young woman he's obsessed with, "a mere girl, just twenty-three or twenty-four," and then near the end shifts yet again to the older woman whom the "mere girl" has roughly displaced. The movement incriminates the reader: we see that we have granted our sympathy too casually to the two characters who don't deserve it and overlooked the fate of the one who does. It leaves one feeling almost ashamed. Or similarly in "The Higgler," our sympathies and easy identification are first attached to the lonely, impecunious young peddler who, suspicious of his good fortune when a widowed, dying mother offers him her prosperous farm and the hand of her daughter, rejects both and settles for much less. In the end, it's the lovelorn daughter we most care about. It's her fate that moves us. The higgler's fate is merely absurd and somehow deserved.

Characteristically, these two masterpieces, like most of Coppard's stories, or "tales," as he insisted on calling them, are told in the close third-person, past-tense point of view. Yet we are constantly aware of a personalized, confiding narrator who is telling the story, someone not in any way a player in the tale or a witness to its unfolding—just someone who has drawn his chair close to ours by the fire and has begun to speak in a most interesting way about a surprising thing that happened to someone else. In his introduction to *Collected Tales*, Coppard argues that the short story, unlike the novel, "is an ancient art originating in the folk tale, which was a thing of joy even before writing, not to mention printing, was invented. . . . The folk tale ministered to an apparently inborn and universal desire to hear tales, and it is my feeling that the closer the modern short story conforms to that ancient tradition of being spoken to you, rather than being read at you, the more acceptable it becomes." These stories, then, are *told* and not written, *heard* and not read.

They are artfully told, and they seduce the reader's ear with great skill. The diction and tone are not archaic or exotic, but there is a distinctly Gaelic twist and inversion to the grammar and phrasing, and a warm appreciation for the English country-man's and countrywoman's colloquialisms, with a striking lyrical flare to the descriptive passages. Ford Madox Ford says Coppard's language is "Celto-British," and that seems right. But Coppard deploys it with amazing grace and transparency—it never sounds like dialect or impersonation. Ford goes further and says that Coppard "is almost the first English writer to get into English prose the peculiar quality of English lyric verse. I do not mean that he is metrical; I mean that hitherto no English prose writer has had the fancy, the turn of imagination, the wisdom, the as it were piety and the beauty of the great seventeenth-century lyricists like Donne or Herbert—or even Herrick." That, too, seems about right.

I like knowing what writers from the past looked like, especially writers whose work I love. I wonder what it was like to be in the room with them. There are few photographs of Coppard, and no film footage that I'm aware of. He seems to have kept himself out of the camera's way, no doubt deliberately. I'm grateful, therefore, for Doris Lessing's word-portrait, made after a sponsored journey with Coppard and several other leftist English writers to Russia in 1950: "He was a small man, light in build. At that time he was seventy-two, but looked sixty, and with a boyish face. Characteristically he would stand to one side of a scene, in observation of it, or quietly stroll around it, his face rather lifted, as it were leading with his chin, his nose alert for humbug, or for the pretensions of the rich or the powerful—about which he was not passionate but mildly derisive. . . ."

One has to wonder how and why, barely seventy-five years

after his death, a writer of Coppard's widely acclaimed ability and with his significant body of work is so little known today, even among writers. No doubt it has something to do with the erroneous, market-driven view of the short story as the illegitimate stepchild of the novel, a kind of practice field for the apprentice writer training to play in the big leagues of novel writing, rather than a literary form as distinct from the novel as poetry or drama or film. It may also be partially blamed on the fact that Coppard lived most of his life in country villages far from literary or academic nexuses, avoiding coteries, claques, and cliques. As Lessing observed, "What came out strong in him was his inability to play the role 'writer.' He didn't like making speeches, he didn't like formal occasions, or conferences or big statements about literature. He did like talking half the night to an old pre-revolutionary waiter about Tolstoy, or examining plants that grew beside the field in a collective farm. He liked flirting in a gentle, humorous way with the beautiful girl doctor at the children's holiday camp." Indeed, just the sort of man we would expect to have written these fifteen marvelous stories.

The Hurly Burly

AND OTHER STORIES

The Black Dog

❧

Having pocketed his fare the freckled rustic took himself and his antediluvian cab back to the village limbo from which they had briefly emerged. Loughlin checked his luggage into the care of the porter, an angular man with one eye who was apparently the only other living being in this remote minute station, and sat down in the platform shade. July noon had a stark eye-tiring brightness, and a silence so very deep—when that porter ceased his intolerable clatter—that Loughlin could hear footsteps crunching in the road half a mile away. The train was late. There were no other passengers. Nothing to look at except his trunks, two shiny rails in the grim track, red hollyhocks against white palings on the opposite bank.

The holiday in this quiet neighbourhood had delighted him, but its crowning experience had been too brief. On the last day but one the loveliest woman he had ever known had emerged almost as briefly as that cabman. Some men are constantly meeting that woman. Not so the Honourable Gerald Loughlin, but no man turns his back tranquilly on destiny even if it is but two days old and already some half-dozen miles away. The visit had come to its end, Loughlin had come to his station, the cab had gone back to its lair, but on reflection he could find no other reasons for going away and denying himself the delight of this proffered experience. Time was his own, as much as he could buy of it, and he had an income that enabled him to buy a good deal.

Moody and hesitant he began to fill his pipe when the one-eyed porter again approached him.

"Take a pipe of that?" said Loughlin, offering him the pouch.

"Thanky, sir, but I can't smoke a pipe; a cigarette I take now and again, thanky, sir, not often, just to keep me from cussing and damming. My wife buys me a packet sometimes, she says I don't swear so much then, but I don't know, I has to knock 'em off soon's they make me feel bad, and then, dam it all, I be worsen ever . . ."

"Look here," said the other, interrupting him, "I'm not going by this train after all. Something I have forgotten. Now look after my bags and I'll come along later, this afternoon." He turned and left the station as hurriedly as if his business was really of the high importance the porter immediately conceived it to be.

The Honourable Gerald, though handsome and honest, was not a fool. A fool is one who becomes distracted between the claims of instinct and common sense; the larger foolishness is the peculiar doom of imaginative people, artists and their kind, while the smaller foolishness is the mark of all those who have nothing but their foolishness to endorse them. Loughlin responded to this impulse unhesitatingly but without distraction, calmly and directly as became a well-bred bachelor in the early thirties. He might have written to the young beauty with the

queer name, Orianda Crabbe, but that course teemed with absurdities and difficulties for he was modest, his romantic imagination weak, and he had only met her at old Lady Tillington's
a couple of days before. Of this mere girl, just twenty-three or
twenty-four, he knew nothing save that they had been immediately and vividly charming to each other. That was no excuse for
presenting himself again to the old invalid of Tillington Park,
it would be impossible for him to do so, but there had been one
vague moment of their recalled intercourse, a glimmering inti-
mation, which just now seemed to offer a remote possibility of
achievement, and so he walked on in the direction of the park.

Tillington was some miles off and the heat was oppressive.
At the end of an hour's stroll he stepped into "The Three Pigeons" at Denbury and drank a deep drink. It was quiet and deliciously cool in the taproom there, yes, as silent as that little
station had been. Empty the world seemed to-day, quite empty;
he had not passed a human creature. Happily bemused he took
another draught. Eighteen small panes of glass in that long window and perhaps as many flies buzzing in the room. He could
hear and see a breeze saluting the bright walled ivy outside and
the bushes by a stream. This drowsiness was heaven, it made
so clear his recollection of Orianda. It was impossible to par-
ticularize but she was in her way, her rather uncultured way,
just perfection. He had engaged her upon several themes, music,
fishing (Loughlin loved fishing), golf, tennis, and books; none
of these had particularly stirred her but she had brains, quite
an original turn of mind. There had been neither time nor opportunity to discover anything about her, but there she was,
staying there, that was the one thing certain, apparently indefi-
nitely, for she described the park in a witty detailed way even to

a certain favourite glade which she always visited in the afternoons. When she had told him that, he could swear she was not finessing; no, no, it was a most engaging simplicity, a frankness that was positively marmoreal.

He would certainly write to her; yes, and he began to think of fine phrases to put in a letter, but could there be anything finer, now, just at this moment, than to be sitting with her in this empty inn. It was not a fair place, though it was clean, but how she would brighten it, yes! there were two long settles and two short ones, two tiny tables and eight spittoons (he *had* to count them), and somehow he felt her image flitting adorably into this setting, defeating with its native glory all the scrupulous beer-smelling impoverishment. And then, after a while, he would take her, and they would lie in the grass under a deep-bosomed tree and speak of love. How beautiful she would be. But she was not there, and so he left the inn and crossed the road to a church, pleasant and tiny and tidy, whitewalled and clean-ceilinged. A sparrow chirped in the porch, flies hummed in the nave, a puppy was barking in the vicarage garden. How trivial, how absurdly solemn, everything seemed. The thud of the great pendulum in the tower had the sound of a dead man beating on a bar of spiritless iron. He was tired of the vapid tidiness of these altars with their insignificant tapestries, candlesticks of gilded wood, the bunches of pale flowers oppressed by the rich glow from the windows. He longed for an altar that should be an inspiring symbol of belief, a place of green and solemn walls with a dark velvet shrine sweeping aloft to the peaked roof unhindered by tarnishing lustre and tedious linen. Holiness was always something richly dim. There was no more holiness here than in the tough hassocks and rush-bottomed chairs; not here, surely, the apple of Eden flourished. And yet, turning to the lectern, he noted the large prayer book open at the office of marriage. He idly read over the words of the ceremony, filling in at the gaps the names of Gerald Wilmot Loughlin and Orianda Crabbe.

What a fool! He closed the book with a slam and left the church. Absurd! You *couldn't* fall in love with a person as sharply as all that, could you? But why not? Unless fancy was charged with the lightning of gods it was nothing at all.

Tramping away still in the direction of Tillington Park he came in the afternoon to that glade under a screen of trees spoken of by the girl. It was green and shady, full of scattering birds. He flung himself down in the grass under a deep-bosomed tree. She had spoken delightfully of this delightful spot.

When she came, for come she did, the confrontation left him very unsteady as he sprang to his feet. (Confound that potation at "The Three Pigeons"! Enormously hungry, too!) But he was amazed, entranced, she was so happy to see him again. They sat down together, but he was still bewildered and his confusion left him all at sixes and sevens. Fortunately her own rivulet of casual chatter carried them on until he suddenly asked: "Are you related to the Crabbes of Cotterton—I fancy I know them?"

"No, I think not, no, I am from the south country, near the sea, nobody at all, my father keeps an inn."

"An inn! How extraordinary! How very . . . very . . ."

"Extraordinary?" Nodding her head in the direction of the hidden mansion she added: "I am her companion."

"Lady Tillington's?"

She assented coolly, was silent, while Loughlin ransacked his brains for some delicate reference that would clear him over this . . . this . . . cataract. But he felt stupid—that confounded potation at "The Three Pigeons"! Why, that was where he had thought of her so admirably, too. He asked if she cared for the position, was it pleasant, and so on. Heavens, what an astonishing creature for a domestic, quite positively lovely, a compendium of delightful qualities, this girl, so frank, so simple!

"Yes, I like it, but home is better. I should love to go back to my home, to father, but I can't, I'm still afraid—I ran away from home three years ago, to go with my mother. I'm like my mother, she ran away from home too."

Orianda picked up the open parasol which she had dropped, closed it in a thoughtful manner, and laid its crimson folds beside her. There was no other note of colour in her white attire; she was without a hat. Her fair hair had a quenching tinge upon it that made it less bright than gold, but more rare. Her cheeks had the colour of homely flowers, the lily and the pink. Her teeth were as even as the peas in a newly opened pod, as clear as milk.

"Tell me about all that. May I hear it?"

"I have not seen him or heard from him since, but I love him very much now."

"Your father?"

"Yes, but he is stern, a simple man, and he is so just. We live at a tiny old inn at the end of a village near the hills. 'The Black Dog.' It is thatched and has tiny rooms. It's painted all over with pink, pink whitewash."

"Ah, I know."

"There's a porch, under a sycamore tree, where people sit, and an old rusty chain hanging on a hook just outside the door."

"What's that for?"

"I don't know what it is for, horses, perhaps, but it is always there, I always see that rusty chain. And on the opposite side of the road there are three lime trees and behind them is the yard where my father works. He makes hurdles and ladders. He is the best hurdle maker in three counties, he has won many prizes at the shows. It is splendid to see him working at the willow wood, soft and white. The yard is full of poles and palings, spars and fagots, and long shavings of the thin bark like seaweed. It smells so nice. In the spring the chaffinches and wrens are singing about him all day long; the wren is lovely, but in the summer of course it's the whitethroats come chippering, and yellow-hammers."

"Ah, blackbirds, thrushes, nightingales!"

"Yes, but it's the little birds seem to love my father's yard."

"Well then, but why did you, why did you run away?"

"My mother was much younger, and different from father; she was handsome and proud too, and in all sorts of ways superior to him. They got to hate each other; they were so quiet about it, but I could see. Their only common interest was me, they both loved me very much. Three years ago she ran away from him. Quite suddenly, you know; there was nothing at all leading up to such a thing. But I could not understand my father, not then, he took it all so calmly. He did not mention even her name to me for a long time, and I feared to intrude; you see, I did not understand, I was only twenty. When I did ask about her he told me not to bother him, forbade me to write to her. I didn't know where she was, but he knew, and at last I found out too."

"And you defied him, I suppose?"

"No, I deceived him. He gave me money for some purpose— to pay a debt—and I stole it. I left him a letter and ran away to my mother. I loved her."

"O well, that was only to be expected," said Loughlin. "It was all right, quite right."

"She was living with another man. I didn't know. I was a fool."

"Good lord! That was a shock for you," Loughlin said. "What did you do?"

"No, I was not shocked, she was so happy. I lived with them for a year . . ."

"Extraordinary!"

"And then she died."

"Your mother died!"

"Yes, so you see I could not stop with my . . . I could not stay where I was, and I couldn't go back to my father."

"I see, no, but you want to go back to your father now."

"I'm afraid. I love him, but I'm afraid. I don't blame my mother, I feel she was right, quite right—it was such happiness. And yet I feel, too, that father was deeply wronged. I can't understand that, it sounds foolish. I should so love to go home again. This other kind of life doesn't seem to eclipse me—things have been extraordinary kind—I don't feel out of my setting, but still it doesn't satisfy, it is polite and soft, like silk, perhaps it isn't barbarous enough, and I want to live, somehow—well, I have not found what I wanted to find."

"What did you want to find?"

"I shan't know until I have found it. I do want to go home now, but I am full of strange feelings about it. I feel as if I was bearing the mark of something that can't be hidden or disguised of what my mother did, as if I were all a burning recollection for him that he couldn't fail to see. He is good, a just man. He . . . he is the best hurdle maker in three counties."

While listening to this daughter of a man who made ladders the Honourable Gerald had been swiftly thinking of an intriguing phrase that leaped into his mind. Social plesiomorphism, that was it! Caste was humbug, no doubt, but even if it was conscious humbug it was there, really there, like the patterned frost upon a window pane, beautiful though a little incoherent, and conditioned only by the size and number of your windows. (Eighteen windows in that pub!) But what did it amount to, after all? It was stuck upon your clear polished outline for every eye to see, but within was something surprising as the sight of a badger in church—until you got used to the indubitable relation of such badgers to such churches. Fine turpitudes!

"My dear girl," he burst out, "your mother and you were right, absolutely. I am sure life is enhanced not by amassing conventions, but by destroying them. And your feeling for your father is right, too, rightest of all. Tell me . . . let me . . . may I take you back to him?"

The girl's eyes dwelt upon his with some intensity.

"Your courage is kind," she said, "but he doesn't know you, nor you him." And to that she added, "You don't even know me."

"I have known you for ten thousand years. Come home to him with me, we will go back together. Yes, you can explain. Tell him"—the Honourable Gerald had got the bit between his teeth now—"Tell him I'm your sweetheart, will you—will you?"

"Ten thousand . . . ! Yes, I know; but it's strange to think you have only seen me just once before!"

"Does that matter? Everything grows from that one small moment into a world of . . . well of . . . boundless admiration."

"I don't want," said Orianda, reopening her crimson parasol, "to grow into a world of any kind."

"No, of course you don't. But I mean the emotion is irresistible, 'the desire of the moth for the star,' that sort of thing, you know, and I immolate myself, the happy victim of your attractions."

"All that has been said before." Orianda adjusted her parasol as a screen for her raillery.

"I swear," said he, "I have not said it before, never to a living soul."

Fountains of amusement beamed in her brilliant eyes. She was exquisite; he was no longer in doubt about the colour of her eyes—though he could not describe them. And the precise shade of her hair was—well, it was extraordinarily beautiful.

"I mean—it's been said to me!"

"O damnation! Of course it's been said to you. Ah, and isn't that my complete justification? But you agree, do you not? Tell me if it's possible. Say you agree, and let me take you back to your father."

"I think I would like you to," the jolly girl said, slowly.

II

On an August morning a few weeks later they travelled down together to see her father. In the interim Orianda had resigned her appointment, and several times Gerald had met her secretly in the purlieus of Tillington Park. The girl's cool casual nature fascinated him not less than her appearance. Admiration certainly outdistanced his happiness, although that also increased; but the bliss had its shadow, for the outcome of their friendship seemed mysteriously to depend on the outcome of the proposed return to her father's home, devotion to that project forming the first principle, as it were, of their intercourse. Orianda had not dangled before him the prospect of any serener relationship; she took his caresses as naturally and undemonstratively as a pet bird takes a piece of sugar. But he had begun to be aware of a certain force behind all her charming naivete; the beauty that exhaled the freshness, the apparent fragility, of a drop of dew had none the less a savour of tyranny which he vowed should never, least of all by him, be pressed to vulgar exercise.

When the train reached its destination Orianda confided calmly that she had preferred not to write to her father. Really she did not know for certain whether he was alive or even living on at the old home she so loved. And there was a journey of three miles or more which Orianda proposed to walk. So they walked.

The road lay across an expanse of marshy country and approached the wooded uplands of her home only by numerous eccentric divagations made necessary by culverts that drained the marsh. The day was bright; the sky, so vast an arch over this flat land, was a very oven for heat; there were cracks in the earth, the grass was like stubble. At the mid journey they crossed a river by its wooden bridge, upon which a boy sat fishing with stick and string. Near the water was a long white hut with a flag; a few tethered boats floated upon the stream. Gerald gave a shilling to a travelling woman who carried a burden on her back and shuffled slowly upon the harsh road sighing, looking neither to right nor left; she did not look into the sky, her gaze was fastened upon her dolorous feet, one two, one two, one two; her shift, if she had such a garment, must have clung to her old body like a shrimping net.

In an hour they had reached the uplands and soon, at the top of a sylvan slope where there was shade and cooling air, Gerald saw a sign hung upon a sycamore tree, *The Black Dog by Nathaniel Crabbe*. The inn was small, pleasant with pink wash and brown paint, and faced across the road a large yard encircled by hedges, trees, and a gate. The travellers stood peeping into the enclosure which was stocked with new ladders, hurdles, and poles of various sizes. Amid them stood a tall burly man at a block, trimming with an axe the butt of a willow rod. He was about fifty, clad in rough country clothes, a white shirt, and a soft straw hat. He had mild simple features coloured, like his arms and neck, almost to the hue of a bay horse.

"Hullo!" called the girl. The man with the axe looked round at her unrecognizingly. Orianda hurried through the gateway. "Father!" she cried.

"I did not know. I was not rightly sure of ye," said the man, dropping the axe, "such a lady you've grown."

As he kissed his daughter his heavy discoloured hands rested on her shoulders, her gloved ones lay against his breast. Orianda took out her purse.

"Here is the money I stole, father."

She dropped some coins one by one into his palm. He counted them over, and saying simply "Thank you, my dear," put them into his pocket.

"I'm dashed!"—thought Loughlin, who had followed the girl—"It's exactly how *she* would take it; no explanation, no apology. They do not know what reproach means. Have they no code at all?"

She went on chatting with her father, and seemed to have forgotten her companion.

"You mean you want to come back!" exclaimed her father eagerly, "come back here? That would be grand, that would. But look, tell me what I am to do. I've—you see—this is how it is—"

He spat upon the ground, picked up his axe, rested one foot upon the axe-block and one arm upon his knee. Orianda sat down upon a pile of the logs.

"This is how it is . . . be you married?"

"Come and sit here, Gerald," called the girl. As he came forward Orianda rose and said: "This is my very dear friend, father, Gerald Loughlin. He has been so kind. It is he who has given me the courage to come back. I wanted to for so long. O, a long time, father, a long time. And yet Gerald had to drag me here in the end."

"What was you afraid of, my girl?" asked the big man.

"Myself."

The two visitors sat upon the logs. "Shall I tell you about mother?" asked the girl.

Crabbe hesitated; looked at the ground.

"Ah, yes, you might," he said.

"She died, did you know?"

The man looked up at the trees with their myriads of unmoving leaves; each leaf seemed to be listening.

"She died?" he said softly. "No, I did not know she died."

"Two years ago," continued the girl, warily, as if probing his mood.

"Two years!" He repeated it without emotion. "No, I did not know she died. 'Tis a bad job." He was quite still, his mind seemed to be turning over his own secret memories, but what he bent forward and suddenly said was: "Don't say anything about it in there." He nodded towards the inn.

"No?" Orianda opened her crimson parasol.

"You see," he went on, again resting one foot on the axe-block and addressing himself more particularly to Gerald: "I've . . . this is how it is. When I was left alone I could not get along here, not by myself. That's for certain. There's the house and the bar and the yard—I'd to get help, a young woman from Brighton. I met her at Brighton." He rubbed the blade of the axe reflectively across his palm—"And she manages house for me now, you see."

He let the axe fall again and stood upright. "Her name's Lizzie."

"O, quite so, you could do no other," Gerald exclaimed cheerfully, turning to the girl. But Orianda said softly: "What a family we are! He means he is living with her. And so you don't want your undutiful daughter after all, father?" Her gaiety was a little tremulous.

"No, no!" he retorted quickly, "you must come back, you must come back, if so be you can. There's nothing I'd like better, nothing on this mortal earth. My God, if something don't soon happen I don't know what *will* happen." Once more he stooped for the axe. "That's right, Orianda, yes, yes, but you've no call to mention to her"—he glared uneasily at the inn doorway—"That . . . that about your mother."

Orianda stared up at him though he would not meet her gaze.

"You mean she doesn't know?" she asked, "you mean she would want you to marry her if she did know?"

"Yes, that's about how it is with us."

Loughlin was amazed at the girl's divination. It seemed miraculous, what a subtle mind she had, extraordinary! And how casually she took the old rascal's—well, what could you call it?—effrontery, shame, misdemeanour, helplessness. But was not her mother like it too? He had grasped nothing at all of the situation yet, save that Nathaniel Crabbe appeared to be netted in the toils of this housekeeper, this Lizzie from Brighton. Dear Orianda was "dished" now, poor girl. She could not conceivably return to such a menage.

Orianda was saying: "Then I may stay, father, mayn't I, for good with you?"

Her father's eyes left no doubt of his pleasure.

"Can we give Gerald a bedroom for a few days? Or do we ask Lizzie?"

"Ah, better ask her," said the shameless man. "You want to make a stay here, sir?"

"If it won't incommode you," replied Loughlin.

"O, make no doubt about that, to be sure no, I make no doubt about that."

"Have you still got my old bedroom?" asked Orianda, for the amount of dubiety in his air was in prodigious antagonism to his expressed confidence.

"Why yes, it may happen," he replied slowly.

"Then Gerald can have the spare room. It's all wainscot and painted dark blue. It's a shrimp of a room, but there's a preserved albatross in a glass case as big as a van."

"I make no doubt about that," chimed in her father, straightening himself and scratching his chin uneasily, "you must talk to Lizzie."

"Splendid!" said Gerald to Orianda, "I've never seen an albatross."

"We'll ask Lizzie," said she, "at once."

Loughlin was experiencing not a little inward distress at this turn in the affair, but it was he who had brought Orianda to her home, and he would have to go through with the horrid business.

"Is she difficult, father?"

"No, she's not difficult, not difficult, so to say, you must make allowance."

The girl was implacable. Her directness almost froze the blood of the Hon. Loughlin.

"Are you fond of her? How long has she been here?"

"O, a goodish while, yes, let me see—no, she's not difficult, if that's what you mean—three years, perhaps."

"Well, but that's long enough!"

(Long enough for what—wondered Loughlin?)

"Yes, it is longish."

"If you really want to get rid of her you could tell her . . ."

"Tell her what?"

"You know what to tell her!"

But her father looked bewildered and professed his ignorance.

"Take me in to her," said Orianda, and they all walked across to "The Black Dog." There was no one within; father and daughter went into the garden while Gerald stayed behind in a small parlour. Through the window that looked upon a grass plot he could see a woman sitting in a deck chair under a tree. Her face was turned away so that he saw only a curve of pink cheek and a thin mound of fair hair tossed and untidy. Lizzie's large red fingers were slipping a sprig of watercress into a mouth that was hidden round the corner of the curve. With her other hand she was caressing a large brown hen that sat on her lap. Her black skirt wrapped her limbs tightly, a round hip and a thigh being rigidly outlined, while the blouse of figured cotton also seemed strained upon her buxom breast, for it was torn and split in places. She had strong white arms and holes in her stockings. When she turned to confront the others it was easy to see that she was a foolish, untidy, but still a rather pleasant woman of about thirty.

"How do you do, Lizzie?" cried Orianda, offering a cordial hand. The hen fluttered away as, smiling a little wanly, the woman rose.

"Who is it, 'Thaniel?" she asked.

Loughlin heard no more, for some men came noisily into the bar and Crabbe hurried back to serve them.

III

In the afternoon Orianda drove Gerald in the gig back to the station to fetch the baggage.

"Well, what success, Orianda?" he asked as they jogged along.

"It would be perfect but for Lizzie—that *was* rather a blow. But I should have foreseen her—Lizzies are inevitable. And she *is* difficult—she weeps. But, O I am glad to be home again. Gerald, I feel I shall not leave it, ever."

"Yes, Orianda," he protested, "leave it for me. I'll give your nostalgia a little time to fade. I think it was a man named Pater said: 'All life is a wandering to find home.' You don't want to omit the wandering?"

"Not if I have found my home again?"

"A home with Lizzie!"

"No, not with Lizzie." She flicked the horse with the whip. "I shall be too much for Lizzie; Lizzie will resume her wandering. She's as stupid as a wax widow in a show. Nathaniel is tired of Lizzie, and Lizzie of Nathaniel. The two wretches! But I wish she did not weep."

Gerald had not observed any signs of tearfulness in Lizzie at the midday dinner; on the contrary, she seemed rather a jolly creature, not that she had spoken much beyond "Yes, 'Thaniel, No, 'Thaniel," or Gerald, or Orianda, as the case had been. Her use of his Christian name, which had swept him at once into the bosom of the family, shocked him rather pleasantly. But he did not know what had taken place between the two women; perhaps Lizzie had already perceived and tacitly accepted her displacement.

He was wakened next morning by unusual sounds, chatter of magpies in the front trees, and the ching of hammers on a bulk of iron at the smithy. Below his window a brown terrier stood on its barrel barking at a goose. Such common simple things had power to please him, and for a few days everything at "The Black Dog" seemed planned on this scale of novel enjoyment. The old inn itself, the log yard, harvesting, the chatter of the evening topers, even the village Sunday delighted him with its parade of Phyllis and Corydon, though it is true Phyllis wore a pink frock, stockings of faint blue, and walked like a man, while Corydon had a bowler hat and walked like a bear.

He helped 'Thaniel with axe, hammer, and plane, but best of all was to serve mugs of beer nightly in the bar and to drop the coins into the drawer of money. The rest of the time he spent with Orianda whom he wooed happily enough, though without establishing any marked progress. They roamed in fields and in copses, lounged in lanes, looking at things and idling deliciously, at last returning home to be fed by Lizzie, whose case somehow hung in the air, faintly deflecting the perfect stream of felicity.

In their favourite glade a rivulet was joined by a number of springs bubbling from a pool of sand and rock. Below it the enlarged stream was dammed into a small lake once used for turning a mill, but now, since the mill was dismantled, covered with arrow heads and lily leaves, surrounded by inclining trees, bushes of rich green growth, terraces of willow herb, whose fairy-like pink steeples Orianda called "codlins and cream," and catmint with knobs of agreeable odour. A giant hornbeam tree had fallen and lay half buried in the lake. This, and the black poplars whose vacillating leaves underscored the solemn clamour of the outfall, gave to it the very serenity of desolation.

Here they caught sight of the two woodpeckers bathing in the springs, a cock and his hen, who had flown away yaffling, leaving a pretty mottled feather tinged with green floating there. It was endless pleasure to watch each spring bubble upwards from a pouch of sand that spread smoke-like in the water, turning each cone into a midget Vesuvius. A wasp crawled laboriously along a flat rock lying in the pool. It moved weakly, as if, marooned like a mariner upon some unknown isle, it could find no way of escape; only, this isle was no bigger than a dish in an ocean as small as a cartwheel. The wasp seemed to have forgotten that it had wings, it creepingly examined every inch of the rock until it came to a patch of dried dung. Proceeding still as wearily it paused upon a dead leaf until a breeze blew leaf and insect into the water. The wasp was overwhelmed by the rush from the bubbles, but at last it emerged, clutching the woodpecker's floating feather and dragged itself into safety as a swimmer heaves himself into a boat. In a moment it preened its wings, flew back to the rock, and played at Crusoe again. Orianda picked the feather from the pool.

"What a fool that wasp is," declared Gerald, "I wonder what it is doing?"

Orianda, placing the feather in his hat, told him it was probably wandering to find home.

One day, brightest of all days, they went to picnic in the marshes, a strange place to choose, all rank with the musty smell of cattle, and populous with grasshoppers that burred below you and millions, quadrillions of flies that buzzed above. But Orianda loved it. The vast area of coarse pasture harboured not a single farmhouse, only a shed here and there marking a particular field, for a thousand shallow brooks flowed like veins from all directions to the arterial river moving through its silent leagues. Small frills of willow curving on the river brink, and elsewhere a temple of lofty elms, offered the only refuge from sun or storm. Store cattle roamed unchecked from field to field, and in the shade of gaunt rascally bushes sheep were nestling. Green reeds and willow herb followed the watercourses with endless efflorescence, beautiful indeed.

In the late afternoon they had come to a spot where they could see their village three or four miles away, but between them lay the inexorable barrier of the river without a bridge. There was a bridge miles away to the right, they had crossed it earlier in the day; and there was another bridge on the left, but that also was miles distant.

"Now what are we to do?" asked Orianda. She wore a white muslin frock, a country frock, and a large straw hat with poppies, a country hat. They approached a column of trees. In the soft smooth wind the foliage of the willows was tossed into delicate greys. Orianda said they looked like cockshy heads on spindly necks. She would like to shy at them, but she was tired. "I know what we *could* do." Orianda glanced around the landscape, trees, and bushes; the river was narrow, though deep, not more than forty feet across, and had high banks.

"You can swim, Gerald?"

Yes, Gerald could swim rather well.

"Then let's swim it, Gerald, and carry our own clothes over."

"Can you swim, Orianda?"

Yes, Orianda could swim rather well.

"All right then," he said. "I'll go down here a little way."

"O, don't go far, I don't want you to go far away, Gerald," and she added softly, "my dear."

"No, I won't go far," he said, and sat down behind a bush a hundred yards away. Here he undressed, flung his shoes one after the other across the river, and swimming on his back carried his clothes over in two journeys. As he sat drying in the sunlight he heard a shout from Orianda. He peeped out and saw her sporting in the stream quite close below him. She swam with a graceful overarm stroke that tossed a spray of drops behind her and launched her body as easily as a fish's. Her hair was bound in a handkerchief. She waved a hand to him. "You've done it! Bravo! What courage! Wait for me. Lovely." She turned away like an eel, and at every two or three strokes she spat into the air a gay little fountain of water. How extraordinary she was. Gerald wished he had not hurried. By and by he slipped into the water again and swam upstream. He could not see her.

"Have you finished?" he cried.

"I have finished, yes." Her voice was close above his head. She was lying in the grass, her face propped between her palms, smiling down at him. He could see bare arms and shoulders.

"Got your clothes across?"

"Of course."

"All dry?"

She nodded.

"How many journeys? I made two."

"Two," said Orianda briefly.

"You're all right then." He wafted a kiss, swam back, and dressed slowly. Then as she did not appear he wandered along to her humming a discreet and very audible hum as he went. When he came upon her she still lay upon the grass most scantily clothed.

"I beg your pardon," he said hastily, and full of surprise and modesty walked away. The unembarrassed girl called after him: "Drying my hair."

"All right"—he did not turn round—"No hurry."

But what sensations assailed him. They aroused in his decent gentlemanly mind not exactly a tumult, but a flux of emotions, impressions, and qualms; doubtful emotions, incredible impressions, and torturing qualms. That alluring picture of Orianda, her errant father, the abandoned Lizzie! Had the water perhaps heated his mind though it had cooled his body? He felt he would have to urge her, drag her if need be, from this "Black Dog." The setting was fair enough and she was fair, but lovely as she was not even she could escape the brush of its vulgarity, its plebeian pressure.

And if all this has, or seems to have, nothing, or little enough to do with the drying of Orianda's hair, it is because the Honourable Gerald was accustomed to walk from grossness with an averted mind.

"Orianda," said he, when she rejoined him, "when are you going to give it up. You cannot stay here . . . with Lizzie . . . can you?"

"Why not?" she asked, sharply tossing back her hair. "I stayed with my mother, you know."

"That was different from this. I don't know how, but it must have been."

She took his arm. "Yes, it was. Lizzie I hate, and poor stupid father loves her as much as he loves his axe or his handsaw. I hate her meekness, too. She has taken the heart out of everything. I must get her away."

"I see your need, Orianda, but what can you do?"

"I shall lie to her, lie like a libertine. And I shall tell her that my mother is coming home at once. No Lizzie could face that."

He was silent. Poor Lizzie did not know that there was now no Mrs. Crabbe.

"You don't like my trick, do you?" Orianda shook his arm caressingly.

"It hasn't any particular grandeur about it, you know."

"Pooh! You shouldn't waste grandeur on clearing up a mess. This is a very dirty Eden."

"No, all's fair, I suppose."

"But it isn't war, you dear, if that's what you mean. I'm only doing for them what they are naturally loth to do for themselves." She pronounced the word "loth" as if it rimed with moth.

"Lizzie," he said, "I'm sure about Lizzie. I'll swear there is still some fondness in her funny little heart."

"It isn't love, though; she's just sentimental in her puffy kind of way. My dear Honourable, you don't know what love is." He hated her to use his title, for there was then always a breath of scorn in her tone. Just at odd times she seemed to be—not vulgar, that was unthinkable—she seemed to display a contempt for good breeding. He asked with a stiff smile "What *is* love?"

"For me," said Orianda, fumbling for a definition, "for me it is a compound of anticipation and gratitude. When either of these two ingredients is absent love is dead."

Gerald shook his head, laughing. "It sounds like a malignant bolus that I shouldn't like to take. I feel that love is just self-sacrifice. Apart from the taste of the thing or the price of the thing, why and for what this anticipation, this gratitude?"

"For the moment of passion, of course. Honour thy moments of passion and keep them holy. But O, Gerald Loughlin," she added mockingly, "this you cannot understand, for you are not a lover; you are not, no, you are not even a good swimmer." Her mockery was adorable, but baffling.

"I do not understand you," he said. Now why in the whole world of images should she refer to his swimming? He *was* a good swimmer. He was silent for a long time and then again he began to speak of marriage, urging her to give up her project and leave Lizzie in her simple peace.

Then, not for the first time, she burst into a strange perverse intensity that may have been love but might have been rage, that was toned like scorn and yet must have been a jest.

"Lovely Gerald, you must never marry, Gerald, you are too good for marriage. All the best women are already married, yes, they are—to all the worst men." There was an infinite slow caress in her tone but she went on rapidly. "So I shall never marry you, how should I marry a kind man, a good man? I am a barbarian, and want a barbarian lover, to crush and scarify me, but you are so tender and I am so crude. When your soft eyes look on me they look on a volcano."

"I have never known anything half as lovely," he broke in.

Her sudden emotion, though controlled, was unconcealed and she turned away from him.

"My love is a gentleman, but with him I should feel like a wild bee in a canary cage."

"What are you saying!" cried Gerald, putting his arms around her. "Orianda!"

"O yes, we do love in a mezzotinted kind of way. You could do anything with me short of making me marry you, anything, Gerald." She repeated it tenderly. "Anything. But short of marrying me I could make you do nothing." She turned from him again for a moment or two. Then she took his arm and as they walked on she shook it and said chaffingly, "And what a timid swimmer my Gerald is."

But he was dead silent. That flux of sensations in his mind had taken another twist, fiery and exquisite. Like rich clouds they shaped themselves in the sky of his mind, fancy's bright towers with shining pinnacles.

Lizzie welcomed them home. Had they enjoyed themselves—

yes, the day had been fine—and so they had enjoyed themselves—well, well, that was right. But throughout the evening Orianda hid herself from him, so he wandered almost distracted about the village until in a garth he saw some men struggling with a cow. Ropes were twisted around its horns and legs. It was flung to the earth. No countryman ever speaks to an animal without blaspheming it, although if he be engaged in some solitary work and inspired to music, he invariably sings a hymn in a voice that seems to have some vague association with wood pulp. So they all blasphemed and shouted. One man, with sore eyes, dressed in a coat of blue fustian and brown cord trousers, hung to the end of a rope at an angle of forty-five degrees. His posture suggested that he was trying to pull the head off the cow. Two other men had taken turns of other rope around some stout posts, and one stood by with a handsaw.

"What are you going to do?" asked Gerald.

"Its harns be bent, yeu see," said the man with the saw, "they be going into its head. 'Twill blind or madden the beast."

So they blasphemed the cow, and sawed off its crumpled horns.

When Gerald went back to the inn Orianda was still absent. He sat down but he could not rest. He could never rest now until he had won her promise. That lovely image in the river spat fountains of scornful fire at him. "Do not leave me, Gerald," she had said. He would never leave her, he would never leave her. But the men talking in the inn scattered his flying fiery thoughts. They discoursed with a vacuity whose very endlessness was transcendent. Good God! Was there ever a living person more magnificently inane than old Tottel, the registrar. He would have inspired a stork to protest. Of course, a man of his age should not have worn a cap, a small one especially; Tottel himself was small, and it made him look rumpled. He was bandy: his intellect was bandy too.

"Yes," Mr. Tottel was saying, "it's very interesting to see interesting things, no matter if it's man, woman, or an object. The most interesting man as I ever met in my life I met on my honeymoon. Years ago. He made a lifelong study of railways, that man, knew 'em from Alpha to . . . to . . . what is it?"

"Abednego," said someone.

"Yes, the trunk lines, the fares, the routs, the junctions of anywheres in England or Scotland or Ireland or Wales. London, too, the Underground. I tested him, every station in correct order from South Kensington to King's Cross. A strange thing! Nothing to do with railways in 'imself, it was just his 'obby. Was a Baptist minister, really, but still a most interesting man."

Loughlin could stand it no longer, he hurried away into the garden. He could not find her. Into the kitchen—she was not there. He sat down excited and impatient, but he must wait for her, he wanted to know, to know at once. How divinely she could swim! What was it he wanted to know? He tried to read a book there, a ragged dusty volume about the polar regions. He learned that when a baby whale is born it weighs at least a ton. How horrible!

He rushed out into the fields full of extravagant melancholy and stupid distraction. That! All that was to be her life here! This was your rustic beauty, idiots and railways, boors who could choke an ox and chop off its horns—maddening doubts, maddening doubts—foul-smelling rooms, darkness, indecency. She held him at arm's length still, but she was dovelike, and he was grappled to her soul with hoops of steel, yes, indeed.

But soon this extravagance was allayed. Dim loneliness came imperceivably into the fields and he turned back. The birds piped oddly; some wind was caressing the higher foliage, turning it all one way, the way home. Telegraph poles ahead looked like half-used pencils; the small cross on the steeple glittered with a sharp and shapely permanence.

When he came to the inn Orianda was gone to bed.

IV

The next morning an air of uneasy bustle crept into the house after breakfast, much going in and out and up and down in restrained perturbation.

Orianda asked him if he could drive the horse and trap to the station. Yes, he thought he could drive it.

"Lizzie is departing," she said, "there are her boxes and things. It is very good of you, Gerald, if you will be so kind. It is a quiet horse."

Lizzie, then, had been subdued. She was faintly affable during the meal, but thereafter she had been silent; Gerald could not look at her until the last dreadful moment had come and her things were in the trap.

"Good-bye, 'Thaniel," she said to the innkeeper, and kissed him.

"Good-bye, Orianda," and she kissed Orianda, and then climbed into the trap beside Gerald, who said "Click click," and away went the nag.

Lizzie did not speak during the drive—perhaps she was in

tears. Gerald would have liked to comfort her, but the nag was unusually spirited and clacked so freshly along that he did not dare turn to the sorrowing woman. They trotted down from the uplands and into the windy road over the marshes. The church spire in the town ahead seemed to change its position with every turn of that twisting route. It would have a back-ground now of high sour-hued down, now of dark woodland, anon of nothing but sky and cloud; in a few miles farther there would be the sea. Hereabout there were no trees, few houses, the world was vast and bright, the sky vast and blue. What was prettiest of all was a windmill turning its fans steadily in the draught from the sea. When they crossed the river its slaty slow-going flow was broken into blue waves.

At the station Lizzie dismounted without a word and Gerald hitched the nag to a tree. A porter took the luggage and labelled it while Gerald and Lizzie walked about the platform. A calf with a sack over its loins, tied by the neck to a pillar, was bellow-ing deeply; Lizzie let it suck at her finger for a while, but at last she resumed her walk and talked with her companion.

"She's a fine young thing, clever, his daughter; I'd do anything for her, but for him I've nothing to say. What can I say? What could I do? I gave up a great deal for that man, Mr. Loughlin— I'd better not call you Gerald any more now—a great deal. I knew he'd had trouble with his wicked wife, and now to take her back after so many years, eh! It's beyond me, I know how he hates her. I gave up everything for him, I gave him what he can't give back to me, and he hates her; you know?"

"No, I did not know. I don't know anything of this affair."

"No, of course, you would not know anything of this affair," said Lizzie with a sigh. "I don't want to see him again. I'm a fool, but I got my pride, and that's something to the good, it's almost satisfactory, ain't it?"

As the train was signalled she left him and went into the booking office. He marched up and down, her sad case affecting him with sorrow. The poor wretch, she had given up so much and could yet smile at her trouble. He himself had never surrendered to anything in life—that was what life demanded of you—surrender. For reward it gave you love, this swarthy, skin-deep love that exacted remorseless penalties. What German philosopher was it who said Woman pays the debt of life not by what she does, but by what she suffers? The train rushed in. Gerald busied himself with the luggage, saw that it was loaded, but did not see its owner. He walked rapidly along the carriages, but he could not find her. Well, she was sick of them all, probably hiding from him. Poor woman. The train moved off, and he turned away.

But the station yard outside was startlingly empty, horse and trap were gone. The tree was still there, but with a man leaning against it, a dirty man with a dirty pipe and a dirty smell. Had he seen a horse and trap?

"A brown mare?"

"Yes."

"Trap with yaller wheels?"

"That's it."

"O ah, a young ooman druv away in that . . ."

"A young woman!"

"Ah, two minutes ago." And he described Lizzie. "Out yon," said the dirty man, pointing with his dirty pipe to the marshes.

Gerald ran until he saw a way off on the level winding

road the trap bowling along at a great pace; Lizzie was lashing the cob.

"The damned cat!" He puffed large puffs of exasperation and felt almost sick with rage, but there was nothing now to be done except walk back to "The Black Dog," which he began to do. Rage gave place to anxiety, fear of some unthinkable disaster, some tragic horror at the inn.

"What a clumsy fool! All my fault, my own stupidity!" He groaned when he crossed the bridge at the half distance. He halted there: "It's dreadful, dreadful!" A tremor in his blood, the shame of his foolishness, the fear of catastrophe, all urged him to turn back to the station and hasten away from these miserable complications.

But he did not do so, for across the marshes at the foot of the uplands he saw the horse and trap coming back furiously towards him. Orianda was driving it.

"What has happened?" she cried, jumping from the trap. "O, what fear I was in, what's happened?" She put her arms around him tenderly.

"And I was in great fear," he said with a laugh of relief. "What has happened?"

"The horse came home, just trotted up to the door and stood still. Covered with sweat and foam, you see. The trap was empty. We couldn't understand it, anything, unless you had been flung out and were bleeding on the road somewhere. I turned the thing back and came on at once." She was without a hat; she had been anxious and touched him fondly. "Tell me what's the scare?"

He told her all.

"But Lizzie was not in the trap," Orianda declared excitedly.

"She has not come back. What does it mean, what does she want
to do? Let us find her. Jump up, Gerald."

Away they drove again, but nobody had seen anything of
Lizzie. She had gone, vanished, dissolved, and in that strong
warm air her soul might indeed have been blown to Paradise.
But they did not know how or why. Nobody knew. A vague
search was carried on in the afternoon, guarded though fruit-
less enquiries were made, and at last it seemed clear, tolerably
clear, that Lizzie had conquered her mad impulse or intention
or whatever it was, and walked quietly away across the fields
to a station in another direction.

V

For a day or two longer time resumed its sweet slow delight-
fulness, though its clarity was diminished and some of its enjoyment dimmed. A village woman came to assist in the mornings,
but Orianda was now seldom able to leave the inn; she had come
home to a burden, a happy, pleasing burden, that could not
often be laid aside, and therefore a somewhat lonely Loughlin
walked the high and the low of the country by day and only
in the evenings sat in the parlour with Orianda. Hope too was
slipping from his heart as even the joy was slipping from his
days, for the spirit of vanished Lizzie, defrauded and indicting,
hung in the air of the inn, an implacable obsession, a triumphant
foreboding that was proved a prophecy when some boys fishing in the mill dam hooked dead Lizzie from the pool under the
hornbeam tree.

Then it was that Loughlin's soul discovered to him a mass

of feelings—fine sympathy, futile sentiment, a passion for righteousness, morbid regrets—from which a tragic bias was born. After the dread ordeal of the inquest, which gave a passive verdict of Found Drowned, it was not possible for him to stem this disloyal tendency of his mind. It laid that drowned figure accusatively at the feet of his beloved girl, and no argument or sophistry could disperse the venal savour that clung to the house of "The Black Dog." "To analyse or assess a person's failings or deficiencies," he declared to himself, "is useless, not because such blemishes are immovable, but because they affect the mass of beholders in divers ways. Different minds perceive utterly variant figures in the same being. To Brown Robinson is a hero, to Jones a snob, to Smith a fool. Who then is right? You are lucky if you can put your miserable self in relation at an angle where your own deficiencies are submerged or minimized, and wise if you can maintain your vision of that interesting angle." But embedded in Loughlin's modest intellect there was a stratum of probity that was rock to these sprays of the casuist; and although Orianda grew more alluring than ever, he packed his bag, and on a morning she herself drove him in the gig to the station.

Upon that miserable departure it was fitting that rain should fall. The station platform was piled with bushel baskets and empty oil barrels. It rained with a quiet remorselessness. Neither spoke a word, no one spoke, no sound was uttered but the faint flicking of the raindrops. Her kiss to him was long and sweet, her good-bye almost voiceless.

"You will write?" she whispered.

"Yes, I will write."

But he does not do so. In London he has not forgotten, but

he cannot endure the thought of that countryside—to be far from the madding crowd is to be mad indeed. It is only after some trance of recollection, when his fond experience is all delicately and renewingly there, that he wavers; but time and time again he relinquishes or postpones his return. And sometimes he thinks he really will write a letter to his friend who lives in the country.

But he does not do so.

The Handsome Lady

TOWARDS THE CLOSE OF THE NINETEENTH CENTURY the parish of Tull was a genial but angular hamlet hung out on the north side of a midland hill, with scarcely renown enough to get itself marked on a map. Its felicities, whatever they might be, lay some miles distant from a railway station, and so were seldom regarded, being neither boasted of by the inhabitants nor visited by strangers.

But here as elsewhere people were born and, as unusual, unconspicuously born. John Pettigrove made a note of them then, and when people came in their turns to die Pettigrove made a note of that too, for he was the district registrar. In between whiles, like fish in a pond, they were immersed in labour until the Divine Angler hooked them to the bank, and then, as is the custom, they were conspicuously buried and laboured presumably no more.

The registrar was perhaps the one person who had love and praise for the simple place. He was born and bred in Tull, he had never left Tull, and at forty years of age was as firmly attached to it as the black clock to the tower of Tull Church, which never recorded anything but twenty minutes past four. His wife, Carrie, a delicate woman, was also satisfied with Tull, but as she owned two or three small pieces of house property there her fancy may not have been entirely beyond suspicion; possession, as you might say, being nine points of the prejudice just as it is of the law. A year or two after their marriage Carrie began to suffer from a complication of ailments that turned her into a permanent invalid; she was seldom seen out of the house and under her misfortunes she peaked and pined, she was troublesome, there was no pleasing her. If Pettigrove went about unshaven she was vexed; it was unclean, it was lazy, disgusting; but when he once appeared with his moustache shaven off she was exceedingly angry; it was scandalous, it was shameful, maddening. There is no pleasing some women—what is a man to do? When he began to let it grow again and encouraged a beard she was more tyrannical than ever.

The grey church was small and looked shrunken, as if it had sagged; it seemed to stoop down upon the green yard, but the stones and mounds, the cypress and holly, the strangely faded blue of a door that led through the churchyard wall to the mansion of the vicar, were beautiful without pretence, and though as often as not the parson's goats used to graze among the graves and had been known to follow him into the nave, there was about the ground, the indulgent dimness under the trees, and the tower with its unmoving clock, the very delicacy of solitude. It inspired compassion and not cynicism as, peering as it were through the glass of antiquity, the stranger gazed upon its mortal register. In its peace, its beauty, and its age, all those pious records and hopes inscribed upon its stones, seemed not uttered in pride nor all in vain. But to speak truth the church's grace was partly the achievement of its lofty situation. A road climbing up from sloping fields turned abruptly and traversed the village, sidling up to the church; there, having apparently satisfied some itch of curiosity, it turned abruptly again and trundled back another way into that northern prospect of farms and forest that lay in the direction of Whitewater Copse, Hangman's Corner, and One O'clock.

It was that prospect which most delighted Pettigrove, for he was a simple-minded countryman full of ambling content. Not even the church allured him so much, for though it pleased him and was just at his own threshold, he never entered it at all. Once upon a time there had been talk of him joining the church choir, for he had a pleasant singing voice, but he would not go.

"It's flying in the face of Providence," cried his exasperated wife—her mind, too, was a falsetto one: "You've as strong a voice as anyone in Tull, in fact stronger, not that that is saying much, for Tull air don't seem good for songsters if you may judge by that choir. The air is too thick maybe, I can't say, it certainly oppresses my own chest, or perhaps it's too thin, I don't thrive on it myself; but you've the strength and it would do you credit; you'd be a credit to yourself and it would be a credit to me. But that won't move you! I can't tell what you'd be at; a drunken man 'ull get sober again, but a fool . . . well, there!"

John, unwilling to be a credit, would mumble an objection to being tied down to that sort of thing. That was just like him, no spontaneity, no tidiness in his mind. Whenever he addressed himself to any discussion he had, as you might say, to tuck up his intellectual sleeves, give a hitch to his argumentative trousers. So he went on singing, just when he had a mind to it, old country songs, for he disliked what he called "gimcrack ballads about buzzums and roses."

Pettigrove's occupation dealt with the extreme features of existence, but he himself had no extreme notions. He was a good medium type of man mentally and something more than that physically, but nevertheless he was a disappointment to his wife—he never gave her any opportunity to shine by his reflected light. She had nurtured foolish ideas of him first as a figure of romance, then of some social importance; he ought to be a parish councillor or develop eminence somehow in their way of life. But John was nothing like this, he did not develop, or shine, or offer counsel, he was just a big, solid, happy man. There were times when his childless wife hated every ounce and sign of him, when his fair clipped beard and hair, which she declared were the colour of jute, and his stolidity, sickened her.

"I do my duty by him and, please God, I'll continue to do it. I'm a humble woman and easily satisfied. An afflicted woman has no chance, no chance at all," she said. After twelve years of wedded life Pettigrove sometimes vaguely wondered what it would have been like not to have married anybody.

One Michaelmas a small house belonging to Mrs. Pettigrove was let to a widow from Eastbourne. Mrs. Cronshaw was a fine upstanding woman, gracefully grave and, as the neighbours said, clean as a pink. For several evenings after she had taken possession of the house Pettigrove, who was a very handy sort of man, worked upon some alterations to her garden, and at the end of the third or fourth evening she had invited him into her bower to sip a glass of some cordial, and she thanked him for his labours.

"Not at all, Mrs. Cronshaw." And he drank to her very good fortune. Just that and no more.

The next evening she did the same, and the very next evening to that again. And so it was not long before they spoke of themselves to each other, turn and turn about as you might say. She was the widow of an ironmonger who had died two years before, and the ironmonger's very astute brother had given her an annuity in exchange for her interest in the business. Without family and with few friends she had been lonely.

"But Tull is such a hearty place," she said. "It's beautiful. One might forget to be lonely."

"Be sure of that," commented Pettigrove. They had the light of two candles and a blazing fire. She grew kind and more communicative to him; a strangely, disturbingly attractive woman, dark, with an abundance of well-dressed hair and a figure of charm. She had carpet all over her floor; nobody else in Tull dreamed of such a thing. She did not cover her old dark table with a cloth as everybody else habitually did. The pictures on the wall were real, and the black-lined sofa had cushions on it of violet silk which she sometimes actually sat upon. There was a dainty dresser with china and things, a bureau, and a tall clock that told the exact time. But there was no music, music made her melancholy. In Pettigrove's home there were things like these but they were not the same. His bureau was jammed in a corner with flowerpots upon its top; his pictures comprised two photo prints of a public park in Swansea—his wife had bought them at an auction sale. Their dresser was a cumbersome thing with knobs and hooks and jars and bottles, and the tall clock never chimed the hours. The very armchairs at Mrs. Cronshaw's were wells of such solid comfort that it made him feel uncomfortable to use them.

"Ah, I should like to be sure of it!" she continued. "I have not found kindly people in the cities—they do not even seem to notice a fine day!—I have not found them anywhere, so why should they be in Tull? You are a wise man, tell me, is Tull the exception?"

"Yes, Mrs. Cronshaw. You must come and visit us whenever you've a mind to; have no fear of loneliness."

"Yes, I will come and visit you," she declared, "soon, I will."

"That's right, you must visit us."

"Yes, soon, I must."

But weeks passed over and the widow did not keep her promise although she only lived a furlong from his door. Pettigrove made no further invitation for he found excuses on many evenings to visit her. It was easy to see that she did not care for his wife, and he did not mind this for neither did he care for her now. The old wish that he had never been married crept back into his mind, a sly, unsavoury visitant; it was complicated by a thought that his wife might not live long, a dark, shameful thought that nevertheless trembled into hope. So on many of the long winter evenings, while his wife dozed in her bed, he sat in the widow's room talking of things that were strange and agreeable. She could neither understand nor quite forgive his parochialism; this was sweet flattery to him. He had scarcely ever set foot outside a ten-mile radius of Tull, but he was an intelligent man, and all her discourse was of things he could perfectly understand! For the first time in his life Pettigrove found himself lamenting the dullness of existence. He tried to suppress this tendency, but words would come and he was distressed. He had always been in love with things that lasted, that had stability, that gave him a recognition and guidance, but now his feelings were flickering like grass in a gale.

"How strange that is," she said, when he told her this, "we seem to have exchanged our feelings. I am happy here, but I know that dark thought, yes, that life is a dull journey on which the mind searches for variety, unvarying variety."

"But what for?" he cried.

"It is constantly seeking change."

"But for why? It seems like treachery to life."

"It may be so, but if you seek, you find."

"What?"

"Whatever you are seeking."

"What am I seeking?"

"Not to know that is the blackest treachery to life. We are growing old," she added inconsequently, stretching her hands to the fire. She wore black silk mittens.

"Perhaps that's it," he allowed, with a laugh. "Childhood's best."

"Surely not," she protested.

"Ah, but I was gay enough then. I'm not a religious man, you know—and perhaps that's the reason—but however—I can remember things of great joy and pleasure then."

And it seemed from his recollections that not the least pleasant and persistent was his memory of the chapel, a Baptist hall long since closed and decayed, to which his mother had sent him on Sunday afternoons. It was a plain, tough, little tabernacle, with benches of deal, plain deal, very hard, covered with a clear varnish that smelled pleasant. The platform and its railing, the teacher's desk, the pulpit were all of deal, the plainest deal, very hard and all covered with the clear varnish that smelled very pleasant. And somehow the creed and the teacher and the attendants were like that too, all plain and hard, covered with a varnish that was pleasant. But there was a way in which the afternoon sun beamed through the cheap windows that lit up for young Pettigrove an everlasting light. There were hymns with tunes that he hoped would be sung in Paradise. The texts, the stories, the admonitions of the teachers, were vivid and evidently beautiful in his memory. Best of all was the privilege of borrowing a book at the end of school time—*Pilgrim's Progress* or *Uncle Tom's Cabin*.

For a while his recollections restored him to cheerfulness, but his dullness soon overcame him again.

"I have been content all my life. Never was a man more content. And now! It's treachery if you like. My faith's gone, content gone, for why?"

He rose to go, and as he paused at the door to bid her goodnight she took his hand and softly and tenderly said: "Why are you depressed? Don't be so. Life is not dull, it is only momentarily unkind."

"Ah, I'll get used to it."

"John Pettigrove, you must never get used to dullness, I forbid you."

"But I thought Tull was beautiful," he said as he paused upon the doorsill. "I thought Tull was beautiful . . ."

"Until I came?" It was so softly uttered and she closed the door so quickly upon him. They called "Good-night, good-night" to each other through the door.

He went away through the village, his mind streaming with strange emotions. He exulted, and yet he feared for himself and for the widow, but he could not summon from the depths of his mind what it was he feared. He passed a woman in the darkness who, perhaps mistaking him for another, said "Good-night, my love."

The next morning he sat in the kitchen after breakfast. It wanted but a few days to Christmas. There was no frost in the air; the wind roared, but the day, though grey, was not gloomy; only the man was gloomy.

"Nothing ever happens," he murmured. "True, but what would you want to happen?"

Out in the scullery a village girl was washing dishes; as she rattled the ware she hummed a song. From his back window Pettigrove could see a barn in a field, two broken gates, a pile of logs, faggots, and a single pollarded willow whose head was strangled under a hat of ivy. Beside a barley stack was a goose with a crooked neck; it stood sulking. High aloft in the sky thousands of blown rooks wrangled like lost men. And Pettigrove vowed he would go no more to the widow—not for a while. Something inside him kept asking, Why not? And he as quickly replied to himself: "You know, you know. You'll find it all in God-a-mighty's own commandments. Stick to them, you can't do more—at least, you might, but what would be the good?"

So that evening he went along to the Christmas lottery held in a vast barn, dimly lit and smelling of vermin. A rope hung over each of its two giant beams, dangling smoky lanterns. There was a crowd of men and boys inspecting the prizes in the gloomy corners, a pig sulking in a pen of hurdles, sacks of wheat, live hens in coops, a row of dead hares hung on the rail of a wagon.

Amid silence a man plunged his hand into a corn measure and drew forth a numbered ticket; another man drew from a similar measure a blank ticket or a prize ticket. Each time a prize was drawn a hum of interest spread through the onlookers, but when the chief prize, the fat pig, was drawn against number seventy-nine there was agitation, excitement even.

"Who be it?" cried several. "Who be number seventy-nine for the fat pig?"

A man consulted a list and said doubtfully: "Miss Subey Jones—who be she?"

No one seemed to know until a husky alto voice from a corner piped: "I know her. She's from Shottsford way, over by Squire Marchand's."

"Oh," murmured the disappointed men; the husky voice continued: "Day afore yesterday she hung herself."

For a few seconds there was a pained silence, until a powerful voice cried: "It's a mortal shame, chaps."

The ceremony proceeded until all the tickets were drawn and all the prizes won and distributed. The cackling hens were seized from the pens by their legs and handed upside down to their new owners. The pig was bundled squealing into a sack. Bags of wheat were shouldered and the white-bellied hares were held up to the light. Everybody was animated and chattered loudly.

"I had number thirty in the big chance and I won nothing. And I had number thirty-one in the little chance and I won a duck. Number thirty-one was my number, and number thirty in the big draw; I won nothing in that, but in the little draw I won a duck. Well, there's flesh for you."

Some of those who had won hens held them out to a white-faced youth who smoked a large rank pipe; he took each fowl quietly by the neck and twisted it till it died. A few small feathers stuck to his hands or wavered to the floor, and even after the bird was dead and carried away it continued slowly and vaguely to flap its big wings and scatter its lorn feathers.

Pettigrove spent most of the next day in the forest plantation south of Tull Great Wood, where a few chain of soil had been cultivated and reserved for seedlings, trees of larch and pine no bigger than potted geraniums, groves of oaks with stems slender as a cockerel's leg and most of the stiff brown leaves still clinging to the famished twigs; or sycamores, thin but tall, flourishing in a mat of their own dropped foliage that was the colour of butter fringed with blood and stained with black gouts like a child's copy-book. It was a toy forest, dense enough for the lair of a beast, and dim enough for an anchorite's meditations, but a dog could leap over it, and a boy could stand amid its growth and look like Gulliver in Lilliput.

"May I go into the wood?" a voice called to Pettigrove. Looking sharply up he saw Mrs. Cronshaw, clad in a long dark blue cloak with a fur necklet, a grey velvet hat trimmed with a pigeon's wing confining her luxuriant hair.

"Ah, you may," he said, stalking to her side, "but you'd best not, 'tis a heavy marshy soil within and the ways are stabbled by the hunters' horses. Better keep out till summer comes, then 'tis dry and pleasant-like."

She sat down awkwardly on a heap of faggots, her feet turned slightly inwards, but her cheeks were dainty pink in the cold air. What a smart lady! He stood telling her things about the wood, its birds and foxes; deep in the heart of it all was a lovely open space covered with the greenest grass and a hawthorn tree in the middle of that. It bloomed in spring with heavy creamy blossom. No, he had never seen any fairies there. Come to that, he did not expect to, he had never thought of it.

"But there are fairies, you know," cried the widow. "O yes, in old times, I mean very old times, before the Romans, in fact before Abraham, Isaac, and Jacob then, the Mother of the earth had a big family, thousands, something like the old woman who lived in a shoe she was. And one day God sent word to say he was coming to visit her. Well, then! She was so excited—the Mother of the earth—that she made a great to do you may be sure, and after she had made her house sparkle with cleanliness and had baked a great big pie she began to wash her children. All of a sudden she heard the trumpets blow—God was just a-coming! So as she hadn't got time to finish them all, she hid those unwashed ones away out of sight, and bade them to remain there and make no noise or she would be angry and punish them. But you can't conceal anything from the King of All and He knew of those hidden children, and he caused them to be hidden from mortal eyes for ever, and they are the fairies, O yes!"

"No, nothing can be concealed," Pettigrove admitted in his slow grave fashion, "murder will out, as they say, but that's a tough morsel if you're going to swallow it all."

"But I like to believe in those things I wish were true."

"Ah, so, yes," said Pettigrove.

It was an afternoon of damp squally blusters, uncheering, with slaty sky; the air itself seemed slaty, and though it had every opportunity and invitation to fall, the rain, with strange perversity, held off. In the oddest corners of the sky, north and east, a miraculous glow could be seen, as if the sun in a moment of aberration had determined to set just then and just there. The wind made a long noise in the sky, the smell of earth rose about them, of timber and of dead leaves; except for rooks, or a wren cockering itself in a bush, no birds were to be seen.

Letting his spade fall Pettigrove sat down beside the widow and kissed her. She blushed red as a cherry and he got up quickly.

"I ought not to ha' done it, I ought not to ha' done that, Mrs. Cronshaw!"

"Caroline!" said she, smiling the correction at him.

"Is that your name?" He sat down by her again. "Why, it is the same as my wife's."

And Caroline said "Humph! You're a strange man, but you are wise and good. Tell me, does she understand you?"

"What is there to understand? We are wed and we are faithful to each other, I can take my oath on that to God or man."

"Yes, yes, but what is faith—without love between you? You see? You have long since broken your vows to love and cherish, understand that, you have broken them in half."

She had picked up a stick and was drawing patterns of cubes and stars in the soil.

"But what is to be done, Caroline? Life is good, but there is good living and there is bad living, there is fire and there is water. It is strange what the Almighty permits to happen."

A slow-speaking man; scrupulous of thought and speech he weighed each idea before its delivery as carefully as a tobacconist weighs an ounce of tobacco.

"Have some cake?" said Caroline, drawing a package from a pocket. "Will you have a piece . . . John?"

She seemed to be on the point of laughing aloud at him. He took the fragment of cake but he did not eat it as she did. He held it between finger and thumb and stared at it.

"It's strange how a man lets his tongue wag now and again as if he'd got the universe stuck on the end of a common fork."

"Or at the end of a knitting needle, yes, I know," laughed Caroline, brushing the crumbs from her lap. Then she bent her head, patted her lips, and regurgitated with a gesture of apology—just like a lady. "But what are you saying? If there is love between you there is faithfulness, if there is no love there is no fidelity."

He bit a mouthful off the cake at last.

"Maybe true, but you must have respect for the beliefs of others . . ."

"How can you if they don't fit in with your own?"

"Or there is sorrow." He bolted the rest of his cake. "O you are right, I daresay, Caroline, no doubt; it's right, I know, but is it reasonable?"

"There are afflictions," she said, "which time will cure, so they don't matter; but there are others which time only aggravates, so what can we do? I daresay it's different with a man, but a woman, you know, grasps at what she wants. That sounds reasonable, but you don't think it's right?"

In the cold whistling sky a patch of sunset had now begun to settle in its proper quarter, but as frigid and unconvincing as a stage fireplace. Pettigrove sat with his great hands clasped between his knees. Perhaps she grew tired of watching the back of him; she rose to go, but she said gently enough: "Come in tonight, I want to tell you something."

"I will, Caroline."

Later, when he reached home, he found two little nieces had

arrived, children of some relatives who lived a dozen miles away. A passing farmer had dropped them at Tull; their parents were coming a day later to spend Christmas with the Pettigroves.

They sat up in his wife's room after tea, for Carrie left her bed only for an hour or two at noon. She dozed against her pillows, a brown shawl covering her shoulders, while the two children played by the hearth. Pettigrove sat silent, gazing in the fire.

"What a racket you are making, Polly and Jane!" quavered Carrie.

The little girls thereupon ceased their sporting and took a picture book to the hearthrug where they examined it in awed silence by the firelight. After some minutes the invalid called out: "Don't make such a noise turning over all them leaves."

Polly made a grimace and little Jane said: "We are looking at the pictures."

"Well," snapped Mrs. Pettigrove, "why can't you keep to the one page!"

John sat by the fire vowing to himself that he would not go along to the widow, and in the very act of vowing he got up and began putting on his coat.

"Are you going out, John?"

"There's a window catch to put right along at Mrs. Cronshaw's," he said. At other times it had been a pump to mend, a door latch to adjust, or a jamb to ease.

"I never knew things to go like it before—I can't understand it," his wife commented. "What with windows and doors and pumps and bannisters anyone would think the house had got the rot. It's done for the purpose, or my name's not what it is."

"It won't take long," he said as he went.

The wind had fallen away, but the sky, though clearer, had a dull opaque mean appearance, and the risen moon, without glow, without refulgence, was like a brass-headed nail stuck in a kitchen wall.

The yellow blind at the widow's cot was drawn down and the candles within cast upon the blind a slanting image of the birdcage hanging at the window; a fat dapper bird appeared to be snoozing upon its rod; a tiny square was probably a lump of sugar; the glass well must have been half full of water, it glistened and twinkled on the blind. The shadowy bird shifted one foot, then the other, and just opened its beak as Pettigrove tapped at the door.

They did not converse very easily, there was constraint between them, Pettigrove's simple mind had a twinge of guilt.

"Will you take lime juice or cocoa?" asked the widow, and he said: "Cocoa."

"Little or large?"

And he said: "Large."

While they sat sipping the cocoa Caroline began: "Well, I am going away, you know. No, not for good, just a short while, for Christmas only, or very little longer. I must go."

She nestled her blue shawl more snugly round her shoulders. A cough seemed to trouble her. "There are things you can't put on one side for ever . . ."

"Even if they don't fit in with your own ideas!" he said slyly.

"Yes, even then."

He put down his cup and took both her hands in his own. "How long?"

"Not long, not very long, not long enough . . ."

"Enough for what?" He broke up her hesitation. "For me to

forget you? No, no, not in the fifty-two weeks of the whole world of time."

"I did want to stay here," she said, "and see all the funny things country people do now." She was rather vague about those funny things. "Carols, mumming, visiting; go to church on Christmas morning, though how I should get past those dreadful goats, I don't know; why are they always in the churchyard?"

"Teasy creatures they are! Followed parson into service one Sunday, indeed, ah! one of 'em did. Jumped up in his pulpit, too, so 'tis said. But when are you coming back?"

She told him it was a little uncertain, she was not sure, she could not say, it was a little uncertain.

"In a week, maybe?"

Yes, a week; but perhaps it would be longer, she could not say, it was uncertain.

"So. Well, all right then, I shall watch for you."

"Yes, watch for me."

They gave each other good wishes and said good-bye in the little dark porch. The shadowy bird on the blind stood up and shrugged itself. Pettigrove's stay had scarcely lasted an hour, but in that time the moon had gone, the sky had cleared, and in its ravishing darkness the stars almost crackled, so fierce was their mysterious perturbation. The village man felt Caroline's arms about him and her lips against his mouth as she whispered a "God bless you." He turned away home, dazed, entranced, he did not heed the stars. In the darkness a knacker's cart trotted past him with a dim lantern swinging at its tail and the driver bawling a song. In the keen air the odour from the dead horse sickened him.

Pettigrove passed Christmas gaily enough with his kindred,

and even his wife indulged in brief gaieties. Her cousin was one of those men full of affable disagreements; an attitude rather than an activity of mind. He had a curious face resembling an owl's except in its colour (which was pink) and in its tiny black moustache curling downwards like a dark ring under his nose. If Pettigrove remarked upon a fine sunset the cousin scoffed, scoffed benignantly; there was a sunset every day, wasn't there?—common as grass, weren't they? As for the farming hereabouts, nothing particular in it was there? The scenery was, well, it was just scenery, a few hills, a few woods, plenty of grass fields. No special suitability of soil for any crop; corn would be just average, wasn't that so? And the roots, well, on his farm at home he could show mangolds as big as young porkers, forty to the cartload, or thereabouts. There weren't no farmers round here making a fortune, he'd be bound, and as for their birds, he should think they lived on rook pie.

Pettigrove submitted that none of the Tull farmers looked much the worse for farming.

"Well, come," said the other, "I hear your work-houses be middling full. Now an old neighbour of mine, old Frank Stinsgrove, was a man as *could* farm, any mortal thing. He wouldn't have looked at this land, not at a crown an acre, and he was a man as *could* farm, any mortal thing, oranges and lemons if he'd a mind to it. What a head that man had, God bless, his brain was stuffed! Full! He'd declare black was white, and what's more he could prove it. I like a man like that."

The cousin's wife was a vast woman, shaped like a cottage loaf. For some reason she clung to her stays: it could not be to disguise or curb her bulk, for they merely put a gloss upon it. You could only view her as a dimension, think of her as a circumference, and wonder grimly what she looked like when she prepared for the bath. She devoured turkey and pig griskin with such audible voracity that her husband declared that he would soon be compelled to wear corks in his earholes at meal times, yes, the same as they did in the artillery. She was quite unperturbed by this even when little Jane giggled, and she avowed that good food was a great enjoyment to her.

"O 'tis a good thing and a grand thing, but take that child now," said her father. Resting his elbow on the table he indicated with his fork the diminutive Jane; upon the fork hung a portion of meat large enough to half-sole a lady's shoe. "She's just the reverse, she eats as soft as a fly, a spillikin a day, and not a mite more; no, very dainty is our Jane." Here he swallowed the meat and treated four promising potatoes with very great savagery. "Do you know our Jane is going to marry a house-painter, yah, a house-painter, or is it a coach-painter? 'Tis smooth and gentle work, she says, not like rough farmers or chaps that knock things pretty hard, smiths and carpenters, you know. O Lord! eight years old, would you believe it? The spillikin! John, this griskin's a lovely bit of meat."

"Beautiful meat," chanted his wife, "like a pig we killed a month ago. That was a nice pig, fat and contented as you'd find any pig, 'twould have been a shame to keep him alive any longer. It dressed so well, a picture it was, the kidneys shun like gold."

"That reminds me of poor old Frank Stinsgrove," said her husband. "He'd a mint of money, a very wealthy man, but he didn't like parting with it. He'd got oldish and afraid of his death, must have a doctor calling to examine him every so often. Didn't mind spending a fortune on doctors, but every other way he'd skin a flint. And there was nought wrong with him, 'cept age. So his daughter ups and says to him one day—You are wasting your money on all these doctors, father, they do you no good, what you must have is nice, dainty, nourishing food. Now what about some of these new laid eggs? How much are they fetching now? old Frank says. A penny farthing, says she. A penny farthing! I cannot afford it. And there was that man with a mint of money, a mint, could have bought Buckingham Palace—you understand me—and yet he must go on with his porridge and his mustard plasters and his syrup of squills, until at last a smartish doctor really did find something the matter with him, in his kidneys. They operated, mark you, and they say—but I never quite had the rights of it—they say they gave him a new kidney made of wax; a new wax kidney, ah, and I believe it was successful, only he had not to get himself into any kind of a heat, of course, nor sit too close to the fire. 'Stonishing what they doctors can do with your innards. But of course he was too old, soon died. Left a fortune, a mint of money, could have bought the crown of England. Staunch old chap, you know."

Throughout the holidays John sang his customary ballads, "The Bicester Ram," "The Unquiet Grave," and dozens of others. After songs there would be things to eat. Then a game of cards, and after that things to eat. Then a walk to the inn, to the church, to a farm, or to a friend's where, in all jollity, there would be things to eat and drink. They went to a meet of the hounds, a most successful outing for it gave them ravening appetites. In short, as the cousin's wife said when bidding farewell, it was a time of great enjoyment.

And Pettigrove said so too. He believed it, and yet was glad to be quit of his friends in order to contemplate the serene dawn that was to come at any hour now. By New Year's Day Mrs. Cronshaw had not returned, but the big countryman was patient, his mind, though not at rest, was confident. The days passed as invisibly as warriors in a hostile country, and almost before he had begun to despair February came, a haggard month to follow a frosty January. Mist clung to the earth as tightly as the dense grey fur on the back of a cat, ice began to uncongeal, adjacent lands became indistinct, and distant fields could not be seen at all. The banks of the roads and the squat hedges were heavily dewed. The cries of invisible rooks, the bleat of unseen sheep, made yet more gloomy the contours of motionless trees wherefrom the slightest movement of a bird fetched a splatter of drops to the road, cold and uncheering.

All this inclemency crowded into the heart of the waiting man, a distress without a gleam of anger or doubt, but only a fond anxiety. Other anxieties came upon him which, without lessening his melancholy, somewhat diverted it: his wife suffered a sudden grave decline in health, and on calling in the doctor Pettigrove was made aware of her approaching end. Torn between a strange recovered fondness for his sinking wife and the romantic adventure with the widow, which, to his mind at such a juncture, wore the sourest aspect of infidelity, Pettigrove dwelt in remorse and grief until the night of St. Valentine's Day, when he received a letter. It came from a coast town in Norfolk, from a hospital; Caroline, too, was ill. She made light of her illness, but it was clear to him now that this and this alone was the urgent reason of her retreat from Tull at Christmas. It was old tubercular trouble (that was consumption, wasn't it?) which had driven her into sanatoriums on several occasions in recent years. She was getting better now, she wrote, but it would be months before she would be allowed to return. It had been rather a bad attack, so sudden. Now she had no other thought or desire in the world but to be back at Tull with her friend, and in time to see that fairy may tree at bloom in the wood—he had promised to show it to her—they would often go together, wouldn't they—and she signed herself his, "with the deepest affection."

He did not remember any promise to show her the tree, but he sat down straightway and wrote her a letter of love, incoherently disclosed and obscurely worded for any eyes but hers. He did not mention his wife; he had suddenly forgotten her. He sealed the letter and put it aside to be posted on the morrow. Then he crept back to his wife's room and continued his sick vigil.

But in that dim room, lit by one small candle, he did not heed the invalid. His mind, feverishly alert, was devoted to thoughts of that other who also lay sick, and who had intimidated him. He had feared her, feared for himself. He had behaved like a lost wanderer who at night, deep in a forest, had come upon the embers of a fire left mysteriously glowing, and had crept up to it frightened, without stick or stone: if only he had conquered his fear he might have lain down and rested by its strange comfort. But now he was sure of her love, sure of his own, he was secure, he would lay down and rest. She would come with all the sweetness of her passion and the valour of her frailty, stretching smooth, quiet wings over his lost soul.

Then he began to be aware of a soft, insistent noise, tapping, tapping, tapping, that seemed to come from the front door below. To assure himself he listened intently, and soon it became almost the only sound in the world, clear but soft, sharp and thin, as if struck with the finger nails only, tap, tap, tap, quickly on the door. When the noise ceased he got up and groped stealthily down his narrow crooked staircase. At the bottom he waited in an uncanny pause until just beyond him he heard the gentle urgency again, tap, tap, and he flung open the door. There was enough gloomy light to reveal the emptiness of the porch; there was nothing there, nothing to be seen, but he could distinctly hear the sound of feet being vigorously shuffled on the doormat below him, as if the shoes of some light-foot visitor were being carefully cleaned before entry. Then it stopped. Beyond that—nothing. Pettigrove was afraid, he dared not cross the startling threshold, he shot back the door, bolted it in a fluster, and blundered away up the stairs.

And there was now darkness, the candle in his wife's room having spent itself, but as a glow from the fire embers remained he did not hasten to light another candle. Instead, he fastened the bedroom door also, and stood filled with wondering uneasiness, dreading to hear the tap, tap, tap come again, just there, behind him. He listened for it with stopped breath, but he could hear nothing, not the faintest scruple of sound, not the beat of his own heart, not a flutter from the fire, not a rustle of feet, not a breath—no! not even a breathing! He rushed to the bed and struck a match: that was a dead face . . . Under the violence of his sharpening shock he sank upon the bed beside dead Carrie and a faint crepuscular agony began to gleam over the pensive darkness of his mind, with a promise of mad moonlight to follow.

Two days later a stranger came to the Pettigrove's door, a short, brusque, sharp-talking man with iron-grey hair and iron-rimmed spectacles. He was an ironmonger.

"Mr. Pettigrove? My name is Cronshaw, of Eastbourne, rather painful errand, my sister-in-law, Mrs. Cronshaw, tenant of yours, I believe."

Pettigrove stiffened into antagonism: what the devil was all this? "Come in," he remarked grimly.

"Thank you," said Cronshaw, following Pettigrove into the parlour where, with many sighs and much circumstance, he doffed his overcoat and stood his umbrella in a corner. "Had to walk from the station, no conveyances; that's pretty stiff, miles and miles."

"Have a drop of wine?" invited Pettigrove.

"Thank you," said the visitor.

"It's dandelion."

"Very kind of you, I'm sure." Cronshaw drew a chair up to the fireplace, though the fire had not been lit, and the grate was full of ashes, and asked if he might smoke. Pettigrove did not mind; he poured out a glass of the yellow wine while Cronshaw lit his pipe. The room smelled stuffy, heavy noises came from overhead as if men were moving furniture. The stranger swallowed a few drops of the wine, coughed, and said: "My sister-in-law is dead, I'm sorry to say. You had not heard, I suppose?"

"Dead!" whispered Pettigrove. "Mrs. Cronshaw! No, no, I had not, I had not heard that, I did not know. Mrs. Cronshaw dead—is it true?"

"Ah," said the stranger with a laboured sigh. "Two nights ago in a hospital at Mundesley. I've just come on from there. It was very sudden, O, frightfully sudden, but it was not unexpected, poor woman, it's been off and on with her for years. She was very much attached to this village, I suppose, and we're going to bury her here, it was her last request. That's what I want to do now. I want to arrange about the burial and the disposal of her things and to give up possession of your house. I'm very sorry for that."

"I'm uncommon grieved to hear this," said Pettigrove. "She was a handsome lady."

"O yes," the ironmonger took out his pocket-book and prepared to write in it.

"A handsome lady," continued the countryman tremulously, "handsome, handsome."

At that moment someone came heavily down the stairs and knocked at the parlour door.

"Come in," cried Pettigrove. A man with red face and white hair shuffled into the room; he was dressed in a black suit that had been made for a man not only bigger, but probably different in other ways.

"We shall have to shift her down here now," he began. "I was sure we should, the coffin's too big to get round that awkward crook in these stairs when it's loaded. In fact, 'tis impossible. Better have her down now afore we put her in, or there'll be an accident on the day as sure as judgment." The man, then noticing Cronshaw, said: "Good-morning, sir, you'll excuse me."

The ironmonger stared at him with horror, and then put his notebook away.

"Yes, yes, then," mumbled Pettigrove. "I'll come up in a few minutes."

The man went out and Cronshaw jumped up and said: "You'll pardon me, Mr. Pettigrove, I had no idea that you had had a bereavement too."

"My wife," said Pettigrove dully, "two nights ago."

"Two nights ago! I am very sorry, most sorry," stammered the other, picking up his umbrella and hat. "I'll go away. What a sad coincidence!"

"There's no call to do that; what's got to be done must be done."

"I'll not detain you long then, just a few details: I am most sorry, very sorry, it's extraordinary."

He took out his notebook again—it had red edges and a fat elastic band—and after conferring with Pettigrove for some time the stranger went off to see the vicar, saying, as he shook hands: "I shall of course see you again when it is all over. How bewildering it is, and what a shock it is; from one day to another, and then nothing; and the day after to-morrow they'll be buried beside one another. I am very sorry, most sorry. I shall of course come and see you again when it is all over."

After he had gone Pettigrove walked about the room murmuring: "She was a lady, a handsome lady," and then, still murmuring, he stumbled up the stairs to the undertakers. His wife lay on the bed in a white gown. He enveloped her stiff thin body in a blanket and carried it downstairs to the parlour; the others, with much difficulty, carried down the coffin and when they had fixed it upon some trestles they unwrapped Carrie from the blankets and laid her in it.

Caroline and Carrie were buried on the same day in adjoining graves, buried by the same men, and as the ironmonger was prevented by some other misfortune from attending the obsequies there were no other mourners than Pettigrove. The workshop sign of the Tull carpenter bore the following notice:

COMPLETE UNDERTAKER
SMALL HEARSE KEPT.

and therefore it was he who ushered the handsome lady from the station on that bitter day. Frost was so heavy that the umbrage of pine and fir looked woolly, thick grey swabs. Horses stood miserably in the frozen fields, breathing into any friendly bush. Rooks pecked industriously at the tough pastures, but wiser fowls, unlike the fabulous good child, could be neither seen nor heard. And all day someone was grinding corn at the millhouse; the engine was old and kept on emitting explosions that shook the neighbourhood like a dreadful bomb. Pettigrove, who had not provided himself with a black overcoat and therefore wore none at all, shivered so intensely during the ceremony that the keen edge of his grief was dulled, and indeed from that time onwards his grief, whatever its source, seemed deprived of all keenness: it just dulled him with a permanent dullness.

He caused to be placed on his wife's grave a headstone, quite small, not a yard high, inscribed to

CAROLINE
THE BELOVED WIFE
OF
JOHN PETTIGROVE

Some days after its erection he was astonished to find the headstone had fallen flat on its face. It was very strange, but after all it was a small matter, a simple affair, so in the dusk he himself took a spade and set it up again. A day or two later it had fallen once more. He was now inclined to some suspicion, he fancied that mischievous boys had done it; he would complain to the vicar. But Pettigrove was an easy-going man, he did not complain; he replaced the stone, setting it more deeply in the earth and padding the turf more firmly around it.

When it fell the third time he was astonished and deeply moved, but he was no longer in doubt, and as he once more made a good upheaval by the grave in the dusk he said in his mind, and he felt too in his heart, that he understood.

"It will not fall again," he said, and he was right: it did not.

Pettigrove himself lived for another score of years, during which the monotony of his life was but mildly varied; he just went on registering births and deaths and rearing little oaks and pines, firs and sycamores. Sentimental deference to the oft-repeated wish of his wife led him to join the church choir and sing its anthems and hymns with a secular blitheness that was at least mellifluous. Moreover, after a year or two, he *did* become a parish councillor and in a modest way was something of a "shining light."

"If I were you," observed an old countryman to him, "and I had my way, I know what I would do: I would live in a little house and have a quiet life, and I wouldn't care the toss of a ha'penny for nothing and nobody!"

In the time of May, always, Pettigrove would wander in Tull Great Wood as far as the hidden pleasaunce where the hawthorn so whitely bloomed. None but he knew of that, or remembered it, and when its dying petals were heaped upon the grass he gathered handfuls to keep in his pocket till they rotted. Sometimes he thought he would leave Tull and see something of the world; he often thought of that, but it seemed as if time had stabilized and contracted round his heart and he did not go. At last, after twenty years of widowhood, he died and was buried, and this was the manner of that.

Two men were digging his grave on the morning of the interment, a summer's day so everlasting beautiful that it was incredible anyone should be dead. The two men, an ancient named Jethro and a younger whom he called Mark, went to sit in the cool porch for a brief rest. The work on the grave had been very much delayed, but now the old headstone was laid on one side, and most of the earth that had covered his wife's body was heaped in untidy mounds upon the turf close by. Otherwise there was no change in the yard or the trees that grew so high, the grass that grew so greenly, the dark brick wall, or the door of fugitive blue; there was even a dappled goat quietly cropping. A woman came into the porch, remarked upon the grand day, and then passed into the church to her task of tidying up for the ceremony. Jethro took a swig of drink from a bottle and handed it to his mate.

"You don't remember old Fan as used to clean the church, do you? No, 'twas 'fore you come about these parts. She was a smartish old gal. Bother me if one of they goats didn't follow her into the darn church one day, ah, and wouldn't be drove out on it, neither, no, and she chasing of it from here to there and one place and another but out it would not go, that goat. And at last it act-u-ally marched up into the pulpit and putt its two forelegs on the holy book and said 'Baa-a-a!'" Here Jethro gave a prolonged imitation of a goat's cry. "Well, old Fan had been a bit skeered but she was so overcome by that bit of piety that, darn me, if she didn't sit down and play the organ for it!"

Mark received this narration with a lack-lustre air and at

once the two men resumed their work. Meanwhile a man ascended the church tower; other men had gone into the home of the dead man. Soon the vicar came hurrying through the blue door in the wall and the bell gave forth its first solemn toll.

"Hey, Jethro," called Mark from the grave. "What d'you say's the name of this chap?"

"Pettigrove. Hurry up, now."

Mark, after bending down, whispered from the grave: "What was his wife's name?"

"Why, man alive, that 'ud be Pettigrove, too."

The bell in the tower gave another profoundly solemn beat.

"What's the name on that headstone?" asked Mark.

"Caroline Pettigrove. What be you thinking on?"

"We're in the wrong hole, Jethro; come and see for yourself, the plate on this old coffin says Caroline Cronshaw, see for yourself, we're in the wrong hole."

Again the bell voiced its melancholy admonition.

Jethro descended the short ladder and stood in the grave with Mark just as the cortège entered the church by the door on the opposite side of the yard. He knelt down and rubbed with his own fingers the dulled inscription on the mouldering coffin; there was no doubt about it, Caroline Cronshaw lay there.

"Well, may I go to glory," slowly said the old man. It may have occurred to Mark that this was an extravagantly remote destination to prescribe; at any rate he said: "There ain't no time, now, come on."

"Who the devil be she? However come that wrong headstone to be putt on this wrong grave?" quavered the kneeling man.

"Are you coming out?" growled Mark, standing with one

foot on the ladder, "or ain't you? They'll be chucking him on top of you in a couple o' minutes. There's no time, I tell you."

"'Tis a strange come-up as ever I see," said the old man; striking one wall of the grave with his hand: "that's where we should be, Mark, next door, but there's no time to change it and it must go as it is, Mark. Well, it's fate; what is to be must be whether it's good or right and you can't odds it, you darn't go against it, or you be wrong." They stood in the grave muttering together. "Not a word, Mark, mind you!" At last they shovelled some earth back upon the tell-tale name-plate, climbed out of the grave, drew up the ladder, and stood with bent heads as the coffin was borne from the church towards them. It was lowered into the grave, and at the "earth to earth" Jethro, with a flirt of his spade dropped in a handful of sticky marl, another at "ashes to ashes," and again at the "dust to dust." Finally, when they were alone together again, they covered in the old lovers, dumping the earth tightly and everlastingly about them, and reset the headstone, Jethro remarking as they did so: "That headstone, well, 'tis a mystery, Mark! And I can't bottom it, I can't bottom it at all, 'tis a mystery."

And indeed, how should it not be, for the secret had long since been forgotten by its originator.

The Wife of Ted Wickham

PERHAPS IT IS A MERCY WE CAN'T SEE OURSELVES AS others see us. Molly Wickham was a remarkable pretty woman in days gone by; maybe she is wiser since she has aged, but when she was young she was foolish. She never seemed to realize it, but I wasn't deceived.

So said the cattle-dealer, a healthy looking man, massive, morose, and bordering on fifty. He did not say it to anybody in particular, for it was said—it was to himself he said it—privately, musingly, as if to soothe the still embittered recollection of a beauty that was foolish, a fondness that was vain.

Ted Wickham himself was silly, too, when he married her. Must have been extraordinarily touched to marry a little soft, religious, teetotal party like her, and him a great sporting cock of a man, just come into a public-house business that his aunt had left him, "The Half Moon," up on the Bath Road. He always ate like an elephant, but she'd only the appetite of a scorpion. And what was worse, he was a true blood conservative while all her family were a set of radicals that you couldn't talk sense to: if you only so much as mentioned the name of Gladstone they would turn their eyes up to the ceiling as if he was a saint in glory. Blood is thicker than water, I know, but it's unnatural stuff to drink so much of. Grant their name was. They christened her Pamela, and as if that wasn't cruel enough they messed her initials up by giving her the middle name of Isabel.

But she was a handsome creature, on the small side but sound as a roach and sweet as an apple tree in bloom. Pretty enough to convert Ted, and I thought she would convert him, but she was a cussed woman—never did what you would expect of her—and so she didn't even try. She gave up religion herself, gave it up altogether and went to church no more. That was against her inclination, but of course it was only right, for Ted never could have put up with that. Wedlock's one thing and religion's two: that's odd and even: a little is all very well if it don't go a long ways. Parson Twamley kept calling on her for a year or two afterwards, trying to persuade her to return to the fold—he couldn't have called oftener if she had owed him a hundred pound—but she would not hear of it, she would not go. He was not much of a parson, not one to wake anybody up, but he had a good delivery, and when he'd the luck to get hold of a sermon of any sense his delivery was very good, very good indeed. She would say: "No, sir, my feelings arn't changed one bit, but I won't come to church any more, I've my private reasons." And the parson would glare across at old Ted as if he were a Belzeboob, for Ted always sat and listened to the parson chattering to her. Never said a word himself, always kept his pipe stuck in his jaw. Ted never persuaded her in the least, just left it to her, and she would come round to his manner of thinking in the end, for though he never actually said it, she always knew what his way of thinking was. A strange thing, it takes a real woman to do that, silly or no! At election times she would plaster the place all over with tory bills, do it with her own hands!

Still, there's no stability in meekness of that sort, a weather-vane can only go with wind and weather, and there was no sense in her giving in to Ted as she did, not in the long run, for he couldn't help but despise her. A man wants something or other to whet the edge of his life on; and he did despise her, I know.

But she was a fine creature in her way, only her way wasn't his. A beautiful woman, too, well-limbered up, with lovely hair, but always a very proper sort, a milksop—Ted told me once that he had never seen her naked. Well, can you wonder at the man? And always badgering him to do things that could not be done at the time. To have "The Half Moon" painted, or en-larged, or insured: she'd keep on badgering him, and he could not make her see that any god's amount of money spent on paint wouldn't improve the taste of liquor.

"I can see as far into a quart pot as the King of England," he says, "and I know that if this bar was four times as big as 'tis a quart wouldn't hold a drop more then than it does now."

"No, of course," she says.

"Nor a drop less neither," says Ted. He showed her that all the money expended on improvements and insurance and such things were so much off something else. Ted was a generous chap—liked to see plenty of everything, even though he had to give some of it away. But you can't make some women see some things.

"Not a roof to our heads, nor a floor to our feet, nor a pound to turn round on if a fire broke out," Molly would say.

"But why should a fire break out?" he'd ask her. "There never has been a fire here, there never ought to be a fire here, and what's more, there never will be a fire here, so why should there be a fire?"

And of course she let him have his own way, and they never had a fire there while he was alive, though I don't know that any great harm would have been done anyways, for after a few years trade began to slacken off, and the place got dull, and what with the taxes it was not much more than a bread and cheese business. Still, there's no matter of that: a man don't ask for a bed of roses: a world without some disturbance or anxiety would be like a duckpond where the ducks sleep all day and are carried off at night by the foxes.

Molly was like that in many things, not really contrary, but not tact. After Ted died she kept on at "The Half Moon" for a year or two by herself, and regular as clockwork every month Pollock, the insurance manager, would drop in and try for to persuade her to insure the house or the stock or the furniture, any mortal thing. Well, believe you, when she had only got herself to please in the matter that woman wouldn't have anything to say to that insurance—she never did insure, and never would.

"I wouldn't run such a risk; upon my soul it's flying in the face of possibilities, Mrs. Wickham"—he was a palavering chap, that Pollock; a tall fellow with sandy hair, and he always stunk of liniment for he had asthma on the chest—"A very grave risk, it is indeed," he would say, "the Meazer's family was burnt clean out of hearth and home last St. Valentine's day, and if they hadn't taken up a policy what would have become of those Meazers?"

"I dunno," Molly says—that was the name Ted give her—"I dunno, and I'm sorry for unfortunate people, but I've my private reasons."

She was always talking about her private reasons, and they must have been devilish private, for not a soul on God's earth ever set eyes on them.

"Well, Mrs. Wickham," says Pollock, "they'd have been a tidy ways up Queer Street, and ruin's a long-lasting affair," Pollock says. He was a rare palavering chap, and he used to talk about Gladstone, too, for he knew her family history; but that didn't move her, and she did not insure.

"Yes, I quite agree," she says, "but I've my private reasons."

Sheer female cussedness! But where her own husband couldn't persuade her Pollock had no chance at all. And then, of course, two years after Ted died she did go and have a fire there. "The Half Moon" was burnt clean out, rafter and railings, and she had to give it up and shift into the little bullseye business where she is now, selling bullseyes to infants and ginger beer to boy scholars on bicycles. And what does it all amount to? Why, it don't keep her in hairpins. She had the most beautiful hair once. But that's telling the story back foremost.

Ted was a smart chap, a particular friend of mine (so was Molly), and he could have made something of himself and of his business, perhaps, if it hadn't been for her. He was a sportsman to the backbone; cricket, shooting, fishing, always game for a bit of life, any mortal thing—what was there he couldn't do? And a perfect demon with women, I've never seen the like. If there was a woman for miles around as he couldn't come at, then you could bet a crown no one else could. He had the gift. Well, when one woman ain't enough for a man, twenty ain't too many. He and me were in a tight corner together more than once, but he never went back on a friend, his word was his Bible oath. And there was he all the while tied up to this soft wife of his, who never once let on she knew of it at all, though she knowed much. And never would she cast the blink of her eyes—splendid eyes they were, too—on any willing stranger, nor even a friend, say, like myself; it was all Ted this and Ted that, though I was just her own age and Ted was twelve years ahead of us both. She didn't know her own value, wouldn't take her opportunities, hadn't the sense, as I say, though she had got everything else. Ah, she was a woman to be looking at once, and none so bad now; she wears well.

But she was too pious and proper, it aggravated him, but Ted never once laid a finger on her and never uttered one word of reproach though he despised her; never grudged her a thing in reason when things were going well with him. It's God Almighty's own true gospel—they never had a quarrel in all the twelve years they was wed, and I don't believe they ever had an angry word, but how he kept his hands off her I don't know. I couldn't have done it, but I was never married—I was too independent for that work. He'd contradict her sometimes, for she *would* talk, and Ted was one of your silent sorts, but *she*—she would talk for ever more. She was so artful that she used to invent all manners of tomfoolery on purpose to make him contradict her; believe you, she did, even on his death-bed.

I used to go and sit with him when he was going, poor Ted, for I knew he was done for; and on the day he died, she said to him—and I was there and I heard it: "Is there anything you would like me to do, dear?" And he said, "No." He was almost at his last gasp, he had strained his heart, but she was for ever on at him, even then, an unresting woman. It was in May, I remember it, a grand bright afternoon outside, but the room itself was dreadful, it didn't seem to be afternoon at all; it was unbearable for a strong man to be dying in such fine weather, and the carts going by, and though we were a watching him, it seemed more as if something was watching us.

And she says to him again: "Isn't there anything you would like me to do?"

Ted says to her: "Ah! I'd like to hear you give one downright good damn curse. Swear, my dear!"

"At what?" she says.

"Me, if you like."

"What for?" she says. I can see her now, staring at him.

"For my sins."

"What sins?" she says.

Now did you ever hear anything like that? What sins! After a while she began at him once more.

"Ted, if anything happens to you I'll never marry again."

"Do what you like," says he.

"I'll not do that," she says, and she put her arms round him, "for you'd not rest quiet in your grave, would you, Ted?"

"Leave me alone," he says, for he was a very crusty sick man, very crusty, poor Ted, but could you wonder? "You leave me alone and I'll rest sure enough."

"You can be certain," she cries, "that I'd never, never do that, I'd never look at another man after you, Ted, never; I promise it solemnly."

"Don't bother me, don't bother at all." And poor Ted give a grunt and turned over on his side to get away from her.

At that moment some gruel boiled over on the hob—gruel

and brandy was all he could take. She turned to look after it, and just then old Ted gave a breath and was gone, dead. She turned like a flash, with the steaming pot in her hand, bewildered for a moment. She saw he had gone. Then she put the pot back gently on the fender, walked over to the window and pulled down the blind. Never dropped a tear, not one tear.

Well, that was the end of Ted. We buried him, one or two of us. There was an insurance on his life for fifty pounds, but Ted had long before mortgaged the policy and so there was next to nothing for her. But what else could the man do? (Molly always swore the bank defrauded her!) She put a death notice in the paper, how he was dead, and the date, and what he died of: "after a long illness, nobly and patiently borne." Of course, that was sarcasm, she never meant one word of it, for he was a terror to nurse, the worst that ever was; a strong man on his back is like a wasp in a bottle. But every year, when the day comes round—and it's ten years now since he died—she puts a memorial notice in the same paper about her loving faithful husband and the long illness nobly and patiently borne!

And then, as I said, the insurance man and the parson began to call again on that foolish woman, but she would not alter her ways for any of them. Not one bit. The things she had once enjoyed before her marriage, the things she had wanted her own husband to do but were all against his grain, these she could nohow bring herself to do when he was dead and gone and she was alone and free to do them. What a farce human nature can be! There was an Italian hawker came along with rings in his ears and a coloured cart full of these little statues of Cupid, and churches with spires a yard long and red glass in them, and heads of some of the great people like the Queen and General Gordon.

"Have you got a head of Lord Beaconsfield?" Molly asks him.

He goes and searches in his cart and brings her out a beautiful head on a stand, all white and new, and charges her half a crown for it. Few days later the parson calls on the job of persuading her to return to his flock now that she was free to go once more. But no. She says: "I can never change now, sir, it may be all wrong of me, but what my man thought was good enough for me, and I somehow cling to that. It's all wrong, I suppose, and you can't understand it, sir, but it's all my life."

Well, Twamley chumbled over an argument or two, but he couldn't move her; there's no mortal man could ever more that woman except Ted—and he didn't give a damn.

"Well," says parson, "I have hopes, Mrs. Wickham, that you will come to see the matter in a new light, a little later on perhaps. In fact, I'm sure you will, for look, there's that bust," he says, and he points to it on the mantelpiece. I thought you and he were all against Gladstone, but now you've got his bust upon your shelf; it's a new one, I see."

"No, no, that isn't Gladstone," cried Molly, all of a tremble, "that isn't Gladstone, it's Lord Beaconsfield!"

"Indeed, but pardon me, Mrs. Wickham, that is certainly a bust of Mr. Gladstone."

So it was. This Italian chap had deceived the silly creature and palmed her off with any bust that come handy, and it happened to be Gladstone. She went white to the teeth, and gave a sort of scream, and dashed the little bust in a hundred pieces on the hearth in front of the minister there. O, he had a very vexing time with her.

That was years ago. And then came the fire, and then the bullseye shop. For ten years now I've prayed that woman to marry me, and she just tells me: No. She says she pledged her solemn word to Ted as he lay a-dying that she would not wed again. It was his last wish—she says. But it's a lie, a lie, for I heard them both. Such a lie! She's a mad woman, but fond of him still in her way, I suppose. She liked to see Ted make a fool of himself, liked him better so. Perhaps that's what she don't see in me. And what I see in her—I can't imagine. But it's a something, something in her that sways me now just as it swayed me then, and I doubt but it will sway me for ever.

The Poor Man

❦

ONE OF THE COMMONEST SIGHTS IN THE VALE WAS A
certain man on a bicycle carrying a bag full of newspapers. He
was as much a sound as a sight, for what distinguished him from
all other men to be encountered there on bicycles was not his
appearance, though that was noticeable; it was his sweet tenor
voice, heard as he rode along singing each morning from Cobbs
Mill, through Kezzal Predy Peter, Thasper, and Buzzlebury, and
so on to Trinkel and Nuncton. All sorts of things he sang, ballads, chanties, bits of glees, airs from operas, hymns, and sa-
cred anthems—he was leader of Thasper church choir—but he
seemed to observe some sort of rotation in their rendering. In
the forepart of the week it was hymns and anthems; on Wednesday he usually turned to modestly secular tunes; he was rolling
on Thursday and Friday through a gamut of love songs and ballads undoubtedly secular and not necessarily modest, while on
Saturday—particularly at eve, spent in the tap of "The White
Hart"—his programme was entirely ribald and often a little

improper. But always on Sunday he was the most decorous of men, no questionable liquor passed his lips, and his comportment was a credit to the church, a model even for soberer men.

Dan Pavey was about thirty-five years old, of medium height and of medium appearance except as to his hat (a hard black bowler which seemed never to belong to him, though he had worn it for years) and as to his nose. It was an ugly nose, big as a baby's elbow; he had been born thus, it had not been broken or maltreated, though it might have engaged in some pre-natal conflict when it was malleable, since when nature had healed, but had not restored it. But there was ever a soft smile that covered his ugliness, which made it genial and said, or seemed to say: Don't make a fool of me, I am a friendly man, this is really my hat, and as for my nose—God made it so.

The six hamlets which he supplied with newspapers lie along the Icknield Vale close under the ridge of woody hills, and the inhabitants adjacent to the woods fell the beech timber and, in their own homes, turn it into rungs or stretchers for chair manufacturers who, somewhere out of sight beyond the hills, endlessly make chair, and nothing but chair. Sometimes in a wood itself there may be seen a shanty built of faggots in which sits a man turning pieces of chair on a treadle lathe. Tall, hollow, and greenly dim are the woods, very solemn places, and they survey the six little towns as a man might look at six tiny pebbles lying on a green rug at his feet.

One August morning the newspaper man was riding back to Thasper. The day was sparkling like a diamond, but he was not singing, he was thinking of Scroope, the new rector of Thasper parish, and the thought of Scroope annoyed him. It was not only the tone of the sermon he had preached on Sunday,

"The poor we have always with us," though that was in bad taste from a man reputed rich and with a heart—people said—as hard as a door-knocker; it was something more vital, a congenital difference between them as profound as it was disagreeable. The Rev. Faudel Scroope was wealthy, he seemed to have complete confidence in his ability to remain so, and he was the kind of man with whom Dan Pavey would never be able to agree. As for Mrs. Scroope, gloom pattered upon him in a strong sighing shower at the least thought of her.

At Larkspur Lane he came suddenly upon the rector talking to an oldish man, Eli Bond, who was hacking away at a hedge. Scroope never wore a hat, he had a curly bush of dull hair. Though his face was shaven clean it remained a regular plantation of ridges and wrinkles; there was a stoop in his shoulders, a lurch in his gait, and he had a voice that howled.

"Just a moment, Pavey," he bellowed, and Dan dismounted.

"All those years," the parson went on talking to the hedger; "all those years, dear me!"

"I were born in Thasper sixty-six year ago, come the twenty-third of October, sir, the same day—but two years before—as Lady Hesseltine eloped with Rudolf Moxley. I was reared here and I worked here sin' I were six year old. Twalve children I have had (though five on 'em come to naught and two be in the army) and I never knowed what was to be out of work for one single day in all that sixty year. Never. I can't thank my blessed master enough for it."

"Isn't that splendidly feudal," murmured the priest, "who is your good master?"

The old man solemnly touched his hat and said: "God."

"O, I see, yes, yes," cried the Rev. Scroope. "Well, good health and constant, and good work and plenty of it, are glorious things. The man who has never done a day's work is a dog, and the man who deceives his master is a dog too."

"I never donn that, sir."

"And you've had happy days in Thasper, I'm sure?"

"Right-a-many, sir."

"Splendid. Well . . . um . . . what a heavy rain we had in the night."

"Ah, that *was* heavy! At five o'clock this morning I daren't let my ducks out—they'd a bin drownded, sir."

"Ha, now, now, now!" warbled the rector as he turned away with Dan.

"Capital old fellow, happy and contented. I wish there were more of the same breed. I wish . . ." The parson sighed pleasantly as he and Dan walked on together until they came to the village street where swallows were darting and flashing very low. A small boy stood about, trying to catch them in his hands as they swooped close to him. Dan's own dog pranced up to his master for a greeting. It was black, somewhat like a greyhound, but stouter. Its tail curled right over its back and it was cocky as a bird, for it was young; it could fight like a tiger and run like the wind—many a hare had had proof of that.

Said Mr. Scroope, eyeing the dog: "Is there much poaching goes on here?"

"Poaching, sir?"

"I am told there is. I hope it isn't true for I have rented most of the shooting myself."

"I never heard tell of it, sir. Years ago, maybe. The Buzzle-bury chaps one time were rare hands at taking a few birds, so

I've heard, but I shouldn't think there's an onlicensed gun for miles around."

"I'm not thinking so much of guns. Farmer Prescott had his warren netted by someone last week and lost fifty or sixty rabbits. There's scarcely a hare to be seen, and I find wires wherever I go. It's a crime like anything else, you know," Scroope's voice was loud and strident, "and I shall deal very severely with poaching of any kind. O yes, you have to, you know, Pavey. O yes. There was a man in my last parish was a poacher, cunning scoundrel of the worst type, never did a stroke of work, and *he* had a dog, it wasn't unlike your dog—this *is* your dog, isn't it? You haven't got your name on its collar, you should have your name on a dog's collar—well, he had a perfect brute of a dog, carried off my pheasants by the dozen; as for hares, he exterminated them. Man never did anything else, but we laid him by the heels and in the end I shot the dog myself."

"Shot it?" said Dan. "No, I couldn't tell a poacher if I was to see one. I know no more about 'em than a bone in the earth."

"We shall be," continued Scroope, "very severe with them. Let me see—are you singing the Purcell on Sunday evening?"

"*He Shall Feed His Flock*—sir—*like a Shepherd.*"

"Splendid! *Good*-day, Pavey."

Dan, followed by his bounding, barking dog, pedalled home to a little cottage that seemed to sag under the burden of its own thatch; it had eaves a yard wide, and birds' nests in the roof at least ten years old. Here Dan lived with his mother, Meg Pavey, for he had never married. She kept an absurd little shop for the sale of sweets, vinegar, boot buttons and such things, and was a very excellent old dame, but as naive as she was vague. If you went in to her counter for a newspaper and banged down a half-crown she would as likely as not give you change for sixpence—until you mentioned the discrepancy, when she would smilingly give you back your half-crown again.

Dan passed into the back room where Meg was preparing dinner, threw off his bag, and sat down without speaking. His mother was making a heavy succession of journeys between the table and a larder.

"Mrs. Scroope's been here," said Meg, bringing a loaf to the table.

"What did *she* want?"

"She wanted to reprimand me."

"And what have *you* been doing?"

Meg was in the larder again. "'Tis not me, 'tis you."

"What do you mean, mother?"

"She's been a-hinting," here Meg pushed a dish of potatoes to the right of the bread, and a salt-cellar to the left of the yawning remains of a rabbit pie, "about your not being a teetotal. She says the boozing do give the choir a bad name and I was to persuade you to give it up."

"I should like to persuade her it was time she is dead. I don't go for to take any pattern from that rich trash. Are we the grass under their feet? And can you tell me why parsons' wives are always so much more awful than the parsons themselves? I never shall understand that if I lives a thousand years. Name o' God, what next?"

"Well, 'tis as she says. Drink is no good to any man, and she can't say as I ain't reprimanded you."

"Name o' God," he replied, "do you think I booze just for the sake o' the booze, because I like booze? No man does that. He drinks so that he shan't be thought a fool, or rank himself better than his mates—though he knows in his heart he might be if he weren't so poor or so timid. Not that one would mind to be poor if it warn't preached to him that he must be contented. How can the poor be contented as long as there's the rich to serve? The rich we have always with *us*, that's *our* responsibility, we are the grass under their feet. Why should we be proud of that? When a man's poor the only thing left him is hope—for something better: and that's called envy. If you don't like your riches you can always give it up, but poverty you can't desert, nor it won't desert you."

"It's no good flying in the face of everything like that, Dan, it's folly."

"If I had my way I'd be an independent man and live by myself a hundred miles from anywheres or anybody. But that's madness, that's madness, the world don't expect you to go on like that, so I do as other folks do, not because I want to, but because I a'nt the pluck to be different. You taught me a good deal, mother, but you never taught me courage and I wasn't born with any, so I drinks with a lot of fools who drink with me for much the same reason, I expect. It's the same with other things besides drink."

His indignation lasted throughout the afternoon as he sat in the shed in his yard turning out his usual quantity of chair. He sang not one note, he but muttered and mumbled over all his anger. Towards evening he recovered his amiability and began to sing with a gusto that astonished even his mother. He went out into the dusk humming like a bee, taking his dog with him. In the morning the Rev. Scroope found a dead hare tied by the neck to his own door-knocker, and at night (it being Saturday)

Dan Pavey was merrier than ever in "The White Hart." If he was not drunk he was what Thasper calls "tightish," and had never before sung so many of those ribald songs (mostly of his own composition) for which he was noted.

A few evenings later Dan attended a meeting of the Church Men's Guild. A group of very mute countrymen sat in the village hall and were goaded into speech by the rector.

"Thasper," declared Mr. Scroope, "has a great name for its singing. All over the six hamlets there is surprising musical genius. There's the Buzzlebury band—it is a capital band."

"It is that," interrupted a maroon-faced butcher from Buzzlebury, "it can play as well at nine o'clock in the morning as it can at nine o'clock at night, and that's a good band as can do it."

"Now I want our choir to compete at the county musical festival next year. Thasper is going to show those highly trained choristers what a native choir is capable of. Yes, and I'm sure our friend Pavey can win the tenor solo competition. Let us all put our backs into it and work agreeably and consistently. Those are the two main springs of good human conduct—consistency and agreeability. The consistent man will always attain his legitimate ends, always. I remember a man in my last parish, Tom Turkem, known and loved throughout the county; he was not only the best cricketer in our village, he was the best for miles around. He revelled in cricket, and cricket only; he played cricket and lived for cricket. The years went on and he got old, but he never dreamed of giving up cricket. His bowling average got larger every year and his batting average got smaller, but he still went on, consistent as ever. His order of going in dropped down to No. 6 and he seldom bowled; then he got down to No. 8 and never bowled. For a season or two the once famous Tom

Turkem was really the last man in! After that he became um-
pire, then scorer, and then he died. He had got a little money,
very little, just enough to live comfortably on. No, he never married. He was a very happy, hearty, hale old man. So you see? Now
there is a cricket club at Buzzlebury, and one at Trinkel. Why
not a cricket club at Thasper? Shall we do that? . . . Good!"

The parson went on outlining his projects, and although it
was plain to Dan that the Rev. Scroope had very little, if any,
compassion for the weaknesses natural to mortal flesh, and attached an extravagant value to the virtues of decency, sobriety,
consistency, and, above all, loyalty to all sorts of incomprehensible notions, yet his intentions were undeniably agreeable and
the Guild was consistently grateful.

"One thing, Pavey," said Scroope when the meeting had dis-
persed, "one thing I will not tolerate in this parish, and that is
gambling."

"Gambling? I have never gambled in my life, sir. I couldn't
tell you hardly the difference between spades and clubs."

"I am speaking of horse-racing, Pavey."

"Now that's a thing I never see in my life, Mr. Scroope."

"Ah, you need not go to the races to bet on horses; the slips
of paper and money can be collected by men who are agents for
racing bookmakers. And that is going on all round the six hamlets, and the man who does the collecting, even if he does not
bet himself, is a social and moral danger, he is a criminal, he is
against the law. Whoever he is," said the vicar, moderating his
voice, but confidently beaming and patting Dan's shoulder, "I
shall stamp him out mercilessly. *Good*-night, Pavey."

Dan went away with murder in his heart. Timid strangers
here and there had fancied that a man with such a misshapen

face would be capable of committing a crime, not a mere peccadillo—you wouldn't take notice of that, of course—but a solid substantial misdemeanour like murder. And it was true, he *was* capable of murder—just as everybody else is, or ought to be. But he was also capable of curbing that distressing tendency in the usual way, and in point of fact he never did commit a murder.

These rectorial denunciations troubled the air but momentarily, and he still sang gaily and beautifully on his daily ride from Cobbs Mill along the little roads to Trinkel and Nuncton. The hanging richness of the long woods yellowing on the fringe of autumn, the long solemn hills themselves, cold sunlight, coloured berries in briary loops, the brown small leaves of hawthorn that had begun to drop from the hedge and flutter in the road like dying moths, teams of horses sturdily ploughing, sheepfolds already thatched into little nooks where the ewes could lie—Dan said—as warm as a pudding: these things filled him with tiny ecstasies too incoherent for him to transcribe—he could only sing.

On Bonfire Night the lads of the village lit a great fire on the space opposite "The White Hart." Snow was falling; it was not freezing weather, but the snow lay in a soft thin mat upon the road. Dan was returning on his bicycle from a long journey and the light from the bonfire was cheering. It lit up the courtyard of the inn genially and curiously, for the recumbent hart upon the balcony had a pad of snow upon its wooden nose, which somehow made it look like a camel, in spite of the huddled snow on its back which gave it the resemblance of a sheep. A few boys stood with bemused wrinkled faces before the roaring warmth.

Dan dismounted very carefully opposite the blaze, for a tiny boy rode on the back of the bicycle, wrapped up and tied to the frame by a long scarf; very small, very silent, about five years old. A red wool wrap was bound round his head and ears and chin, and a green scarf encircled his neck and waist, almost hiding his jacket; gaiters of grey wool were drawn up over his knicker-bockers. Dan lifted him down and stood him in the road, but he was so cumbered with clothing that he could scarcely walk. He was shy; he may have thought it ridiculous; he moved a few paces and turned to stare at his footmarks in the snow.

"Cold?" asked Dan.

The child shook its head solemnly at him and then put one hand in Dan's and gazed at the fire that was bringing a bright-ness into the longlashed dark eyes and tenderly flushing the pale face.

"Hungry?"

The child did not reply. It only silently smiled when the boys brought him a lighted stick from the faggots. Dan caught him up into his arms and pushed the cycle across the way into his own home.

Plump Meg had just shredded up two or three red cabbages and rammed them into a crock with a shower of peppercorns and some terrible knots of ginger. There was a bright fire and a sharp odour of vinegar—always some strange pleasant smell in Meg Pavey's home—she had covered the top of the crock with a shield of brown paper, pinioned that with string, licked a label: "Cabege Novenbr 5t," and smoothed it on the crock, when the latch lifted and Dan carried in his little tiny boy.

"Here he is, mother."

Where Dan stood him, there the child remained; he did not seem to see Mother Pavey, his glance had happened to fall on the big crock with the white label—and he kept it there.

"Whoever's that?" asked the astonished Meg with her arms akimbo as Dan began to unwrap the child.

"That's mine," said her son, brushing a few flakes of snow from the curls on its forehead.

"Yours! How long have it been yours?"

"Since 'twas born. No, let him alone, I'll undo him, he's full up wi' pins and hooks. I'll undo him."

Meg stood apart while Dan unravelled his offspring.

"But it is not your child, surely, Dan?"

"Ay, I've brought him home for keeps, mother. He can sleep wi' me."

"Who's its mother?"

"'Tis no matter about that. Dan Cupid did it."

"You're making a mock of me. Who is his mother? Where is she? You're fooling, Dan, you're fooling!"

"I'm making no mock of anyone. There, there's a bonny grandson for you!"

Meg gathered the child into her arms, peering into its face, perhaps to find some answer to the riddle, perhaps to divine a familiar likeness. But there was nothing in its soft smooth features that at all resembled her rugged Dan's.

"Who are you? What's your little name?"

The child whispered: "Martin."

"It's a pretty, pretty thing, Dan."

"Ah!" said her son, "that's his mother. We were rare fond of each other—once. Now she's wedd'n another chap and I've took the boy, for it's best that way. He's five year old. Don't ask me about her, it's *our* secret and always has been. It was a good secret and a grand secret, and it was well kept. That's her ring."

The child's thumb had a ring upon it, a golden ring with a small green stone. The thumb was crooked, and he clasped the ring safely.

For a while Meg asked no more questions about the child. She pressed it tenderly to her bosom.

But the long-kept secret, as Dan soon discovered, began to bristle with complications. The boy was his, of course it was his—he seemed to rejoice in his paternity of the quiet, pretty, illegitimate creature. As if that brazen turpitude was not enough to confound him he was taken a week later in the act of receiving betting commissions and heavily fined in the police court, although it was quite true that he himself did not bet, and was merely a collecting agent for a bookmaker who remained discreetly in the background and who promptly paid his fine.

There was naturally a great racket in the vestry about these things—there is no more rhadamanthine formation than that which can mount the ornamental forehead of a deacon—and Dan was bidden to an interview at the "Scroopery." After some hesitation he visited it.

"Ah, Pavey," said the rector, not at all minatory but very subdued and unhappy. "So the blow has fallen, in spite of my warning. I am more sorry than I can express, for it means an end to a very long connection. It is very difficult and very disagreeable for me to deal with the situation, but there is no help for it now, you must understand that. I offer no judgment upon these unfortunate events, no judgment at all, but I can find no way of avoiding my clear duty. Your course of life is incompatible with your position in the choir, and I sadly fear it reveals not only a social misdemeanour but a religious one—it is a mockery, a mockery of God."

The rector sat at a table with his head pressed on his hands. Pavey sat opposite him, and in his hands he dangled his bowler hat.

"You may be right enough in your way, sir, but I've never mocked God. For the betting, I grant you. It may be a dirty job, but I never ate the dirt myself, I never betted in my life. It's a way of life, a poor man has but little chance of earning more than a bare living, and there's many a dirty job there's no prosecution for, leastways not in this world."

"Let me say, Pavey, that the betting counts less heavily with me than the question of this unfortunate little boy. I offer no judgment upon the matter, your acknowledgment of him is only right and proper. But the fact of his existence at all cannot be disregarded; that at least is flagrant, and as far as concerns your position in my church, it is a mockery of God."

"You may be right, sir, as far as your judgment goes, or you may not be. I beg your pardon for that, but we can only measure other people by our own scales, and as we can never understand one another entirely, so we can't ever judge them rightly, for they all differ from us and from each other in some special ways. But as for being a mocker of God, why it looks to me as if you was trying to teach the Almighty how to judge me."

"Pavey," said the rector with solemnity, "I pity you from the bottom of my heart. We won't continue this painful discussion, we should both regret it. There was a man in the parish where I came from who was an atheist and mocked God. He subsequently became deaf. Was he convinced? No, he was not—because the punishment came a long time after his offence. He mocked God again, and became blind. Not at once: God has eternity to work in. Still he was not convinced. That," said the rector ponderously, "is what the Church has to contend with; a failure to read the most obvious signs, and an indisposition even to remedy that failure. Klopstock was that poor man's name. His sister—you know her well, Jane Klopstock—is now my cook."

The rector then stood up and held out his hand. "God bless you, Pavey."

"I thank you, sir," said Dan. "I quite understand."

He went home moodily reflecting. Nobody else in the village minded his misdeeds, they did not care a button, and none condemned him. On the contrary, indeed. But the blow had fallen, there was nothing that he could now do, the shock of it had been anticipated, but it was severe. And the pang would last, for he was deprived of his chief opportunity for singing, that art in which he excelled, in that perfect quiet setting he so loved. Rancour grew upon him, and on Saturday he had a roaring audacious evening at "The White Hart" where, to the tune of "The British Grenadiers," he sung a doggerel:

Our parson loves his motor car
His garden and his mansion,
And he loves his beef for I've remarked
His belly's brave expansion;
He loves all mortal mundane things
As he loved his beer at college,
And so he loves his housemaid (not
With Mrs. parson's knowledge).

Our parson lies both hot and strong,
It does not suit his station,

But still his reverend soul delights
In much dissimulation;
Both in and out and roundabout
He practises distortion,
And he lies with a public sinner when
Grass widowhood's his portion.

All of which was a savage libel on a very worthy man, composed in anger and regretted as soon as sung.

From that time forward Dan gave up his boozing and devoted himself to the boy, little Martin, who, a Thasper joker suggested, might have some kinship with the notorious Betty of that name. But Dan's voice was now seldom heard singing upon the roads he travelled. They were icy wintry roads, but that was not the cause of his muteness. It was severance from the choir; not from its connoted spirit of religion—there was little enough of that in Dan Pavey—but from the solemn beauty of the chorale, which it was his unique gift to adorn, and in which he had shared with eagerness and pride since his boyhood. To be cast out from that was to be cast from something he held most dear, the opportunity of expression in an art which he had made triumphantly his own.

With the coming of spring he repaired one evening to a town some miles away and interviewed a choirmaster. Thereafter Dan Pavey journeyed to and fro twice every Sunday to sing in a church that lay seven or eight miles off, and he kept it all a profound secret from Thasper until his appearance at the county musical festival, where he won the treasured prize for tenor soloists. Then Dan was himself again. To his crude apprehension he had been vindicated, and he was heard once more carolling in the lanes of the Vale as he had been heard any time for these twenty years.

The child began its schooling, but though he was free to go about the village little Martin did not wander far. The tidy cluster of hair about his poll was of deep chestnut colour. His skin—Meg said—was like "ollobarster": it was soft and unfreckled, always pale. His eyes were two wet damsons—so Meg declared: they were dark and ever questioning. As for his nose, his lips, his cheeks, his chin, Meg could do no other than call it the face of a blessed saint; and indeed, he had some of the bearing of a saint, so quiet, so gentle, so shy. The golden ring he no longer wore; it hung from a tintack on the bedroom wall.

Old John, who lived next door, became a friend of his. He was very aged—in the Vale you got to be a hundred before you knew where you were—and he was very bent; he resembled a sickle standing upon its handle. Very bald, too, and so very sharp.

Martin was staring up at the roof of John's cottage.

"What you looking at, my boy?"

"Chimbley," whispered the child.

"O ah! that's crooked, a'nt it?"

"Yes, crooked."

"I know 'tis, but I can't help it; my chimney's crooked, and I can't putt it straight, neither, I can't putt it right. My chimney's crooked, a'nt it, ah, and I'm crooked, too."

"Yes," said Martin.

"I know, but I can't help it. It *is* crooked, a'nt it?" said the old man, also staring up at a red pot tilted at an angle suggestive of conviviality.

"Yes."

"That chimney's crooked. But you come along and look at my beautiful bird."

A cock thrush inhabited a cage in the old gaffer's kitchen. Martin stood before it.

"There's a beautiful bird. Hoicks!" cried old John, tapping the bars of the cage with his terrible finger-nail. "But he won't sing."

"Won't he sing?"

"He donn make hisself at home. He donn make hisself at home at all, do 'ee, my beautiful bird? No, he donn't. So I'm a-going to chop his head off," said the laughing old man, "and then I shall bile him."

Afterwards Martin went every day to see if the thrush was still there. And it was.

Martin grew. Almost before Dan was aware of it the child had grown into a boy. At school he excelled nobody in anything except, perhaps, behaviour, but he had a strange little gift for unobtrusively not doing the things he did not care for, and these were rather many unless his father was concerned in them. Even so, the affection between them was seldom tangibly expressed, their alliance was something far deeper than its expression. Dan talked with him as if he were a grown man, and perhaps he often regarded him as one; he was the only being to whom he ever opened his mind. As they sat together in the evening while Dan put in a spell at turning chair—at which he was astoundingly adept—the father would talk to his son, or rather he would heap upon him all the unuttered thoughts that had accumulated in his mind during his adult years. The dog would loll with its head on Martin's knees; the boy would sit nodding gravely, though seldom speaking: he was an untiring listener. "Like sire, like son," thought Dan, "he will always coop his thoughts up within himself." It was the one characteristic of the boy that caused him anxiety.

"Never take pattern by me," he would adjure him, "not by me. I'm a fool, a failure, just grass, and I'm trying to instruct you, but you've no call to follow in my fashion; I'm a weak man. There's been thoughts in my mind that I daren't let out. I wanted to do things that other men don't seem to do and don't want to do. They were not evil things—and what they were I've nigh forgotten now. I never had much ambition, I wasn't clever, I wanted to live a simple life, in a simple way, the way I had a mind to—I can't remember that either. But I did not do any of those things because I had a fear of what other people might think of me. I walked in the ruck with the rest of my mates and did the things I didn't ever want to do—and now I can only wonder why I did them. I sung them the silly songs they liked, and not the ones I cherished. I agreed with most everybody, and all agreed with me. I'm a friendly man, too friendly, and I went back on my life, I made nought of my life, you see, I just sat over the job like a snob codgering an old boot."

The boy would sit regarding him as if he already understood. Perhaps that curious little mind did glean some flavour of his father's tragedy.

"You've no call to follow me, you'll be a scholar. Of course I know some of those long words at school take a bit of licking together—like elephant and saucepan. You get about half-way through 'em and then you're done, you're mastered. I was just the same (like sire, like son), and I'm no better now. If you and me was to go to yon school together, and set on the same stool together, I warrant you would win the prize and I should wear the dunce's cap—all except sums, and there I should beat ye. You'd have all the candy and I'd have all the cane, you'd be king and I'd be the dirty rascal, so you've no call to follow me. What you want is courage, and to do the things you've a mind to. I never had any and I didn't."

Dan seldom kissed his son, neither of them sought that tender expression, though Meg was for ever ruffling the boy for these pledges of affection, and he was always gracious to the old woman. There was a small mole in the centre of her chin, and in the centre of the mole grew one short stiff hair. It was a surprise to Martin when he first kissed her.

Twice a week father and son bathed in the shed devoted to chair. The tub was the half of a wooden barrel. Dan would roll up two or three buckets of water from the well, they would both strip to the skin, the boy would kneel in the tub and dash the water about his body for a few moments. While Martin towelled himself Dan stepped into the tub, and after laving his face and hands and legs he would sit down in it. "Ready?" Martin would ask, and scooping up the water in an iron basin he would pour it over his father's head.

"Name o' God, that's sharpish this morning," Dan would say, "it would strip the bark off a crocodile. Broo-o-o-oh! But there: winter and summer I go up and down the land and there's not—Broo-o-o-oh!—a mighty difference between 'em, it's mostly fancy. Come day, go day, frost or fair doings, all alike I go about the land, and there's little in winter I havn't the heart to rejoice in. (On with your breeches or I'll be at the porridge pot afore you're clad.) All their talk about winter and their dread of it shows poor spirit. Nothing's prettier than a fall of snow, nothing more grand than the storms upending the woods. There's no more rain in winter than in summer, you can be shod for it, and there's a heart back of your ribs that's proof against any blast. (Is this my shirt or yours? Dashed if they buttons a'nt the plague of my life.) Country is grand year's end to year's end, whether or no. I once lived in London—only a few weeks—and for noise, and for terror, and for filth—name o' God, there was bugs in the butter there, once there was!"

But the boy's chosen season was that time of year when the plums ripened. Pavey's garden was then a tiny paradise.

"You put a spell on these trees," Dan would declare to his son every year when they gathered the fruit. I planted them nearly twenty years ago, two 'gages and one magny bonum, but they never growed enough to make a pudden. They always bloomed well and looked well. I propped 'em and I dunged 'em, but they wouldn't beer at all, and I'm a-going to cut 'em down—when, along comes you!"

Well, hadn't those trees borne remarkable ever since he'd come there?

"Of course, good luck's deceiving, and it's never bothered our family overmuch. Still, bad luck is one thing and bad life's another. And yet—I dunno—they come to much the same in the end, there's very little difference. There's so much misunderstanding, half the folks don't know their own good intentions, nor all the love that's sunk deep in their own minds."

But nothing in the world gave (or could give) Dan such flattering joy as his son's sweet treble voice. Martin could sing! In the dark months no evening passed without some instruction by the proud father. The living room at the back of the shop was the tiniest of rooms, and its smallness was not lessened, nor its tidiness increased, by the stacks of merchandise that had strayed from Meg's emporium into every corner, and overflowed every shelf in packages, piles, and bundles. The metalliferous categories—iron nails, lead pencils, tintacks, zinc ointment, and brass hinges—were there. Platoons of bottles were there, bottles of blue-black writing fluid, bottles of scarlet—and presumably plebeian—ink, bottles of lollipops and of oil (both hair and castor). Balls of string, of blue, of peppermint, and balls to bounce were adjacent to an assortment of prim-looking books—account memorandum, exercise, and note. But the room was cosy, and if its inhabitants fitted it almost as closely as birds fit their nests they were as happy as birds, few of whom (save the swallows) sing in their nests. With pitchpipe to hand and a bundle of music before them Dan and Martin would begin. The dog would snooze on the rug before the fire; Meg would snooze amply in her armchair until roused by the sudden terrific tinkling of her shopbell. She would waddle off to her dim little shop—every step she took rattling the paraffin lamp on the table, the coal in the scuttle, and sometimes the very panes in the window—and the dog would clamber into her chair. Having supplied an aged gaffer with an ounce of carraway seed, or some gay lad with a packet of cigarettes, Meg would waddle back and sink down upon the dog, whereupon its awful indignation would sound to the very heavens, drowning the voices even of Dan and his son.

"What shall we wind up with?" Dan would ask at the close of the lesson, and as often as not Martin would say: "You must sing 'Timmie.'"

This was "Timmie," and it had a tune something like the chorus to "Father O'Flynn."

O Timmie my brother,
Best son of our mother,
Our labour it prospers, the mowing is done;
A holiday take you,
The loss it won't break you,
A day's never lost if a holiday's won.

We'll go with clean faces
To see the horse races,
And if the luck chances we'll gather some gear;
But never a jockey
Will win it, my cocky,
Who catches one glance from a girl I know there.

There's lords and there's ladies
Wi' pretty sunshadies,
And farmers and jossers and fat men and small,
But the pride of these trips is
The scallywag gipsies
Wi' not a whole rag to the backs of 'em all.

There's cokernut shying,
And devil defying,
And a racket and babel to hear and to see,
Wi' boxing and shooting,
And fine high faluting
From chaps wi' a table and thimble and pea.

My Nancy will be there,
The best thing to see there,

She'll win all the praises wi' ne'er a rebuke;
And she has a sister—
I wonder you've missed her—
As sweet as the daisies and fit for a duke.

Come along, brother Timmie,
Don't linger, but gimme
My hat and my purse and your company there;
For sporting and courting,
The cream of resorting,
And nothing much worse, Timmie—Come to the fair.

On the third anniversary of Martin's homecoming Dan rose up very early in the dark morn, and leaving his son sleeping he crept out of the house followed by his dog. They went away from Thasper, though the darkness was profound and the grass filled with dew, out upon the hills towards Chapel Cheary. The night was starless, but Dan knew every trick and turn of the paths, and after an hour's walk he met a man waiting by a signpost. They conversed for a few minutes and then went off together, the dog at their heels, until they came to a field gate. Upon this they fastened a net and then sent the dog into the darkness upon his errand, while they waited for the hare which the dog would drive into the net. They waited so long that it was clear the dog had not drawn its quarry. Dan whistled softly, but the dog did not return. Dan opened the gate and went down the fields himself, scouring the hedges for a long time, but he could not find the dog. The murk of the night had begun to lift, but the valley was filled with mist. He went back to the gate: the net had been taken down, his friend had departed—perhaps he had been disturbed? The dog had now been missing for an hour. Dan still hung about, but neither friend nor dog came back. It grew grey and more grey, though little could be distinguished, the raw mist obscuring everything that the dawn uncovered. He shivered with gloom and dampness, his boots were now as pliable as gloves, his eyebrows had grey drops upon them, so had his moustache and the backs of his hands. His dark coat looked as if it was made of grey wool; it was tightly buttoned around his throat and he stood with his chin crumpled, unconsciously holding his breath until it burst forth in a gasp. But he could not abandon his dog, and he roamed once more down into the misty valley towards woods that he knew well, whistling softly and with great caution a repetition of two notes.

And he found his dog. It was lying on a heap of dead sodden leaves. It just whimpered. It could not rise, it could not move, it seemed paralysed. Dawn was now really upon them. Dan wanted to get the dog away, quickly, it was a dangerous quarter, but when he lifted it to his feet the dog collapsed like a scarecrow. In a flash Dan knew he was poisoned, he had probably picked up some piece of dainty flesh that a farmer had baited for the foxes. He seized a knob of chalk that lay thereby, grated some of it into his hands, and forced it down the dog's throat. Then he tied the lead to its neck. He was going to drag the dog to its feet and force it to walk. But the dog was past all energy, it was limp and mute. Dan dragged him by the neck for some yards as a man draws behind him a heavy sack. It must have weighed three stone, but Dan lifted him on to his own shoulders and staggered back up the hill. He carried it thus for half a mile, but then he was still four miles from home, and it was daylight, at any moment he might meet somebody he would not care to meet. He entered a ride opening into some coverts, and, bending down, slipped the dog over his head to rest upon the ground. He was exhausted and felt giddy, his brains were swirling round—trying to slop out of his skull—and—yes—the dog was dead, his old dog dead. When he looked up, he saw a keeper with a gun standing a few yards off.

"Good morning," said Dan. All his weariness was suddenly gone from him.

"I'll have your name and address," replied the keeper, a giant of a man, with a sort of contemptuous affability.

"What for?"

"You'll hear about what for," the giant grinned. "I'll be sure to let ye know, in doo coorse." He laid his gun upon the ground and began searching in his pockets, while Dan stood up with rage in his heart and confusion in his mind. So the Old Imp was at him again!

"Humph!" said the keeper. "I've alost my notebook somewheres. Have you got a bit of paper on ye?"

The culprit searched his pockets and produced a folded fragment.

"Thanks." The giant did not cease to grin. "What is it?"

"What?" queried Dan.

"Your name and address."

"Ah, but what do you want it for. What do you think I'm doing?" protested Dan.

"I've a net in my pocket which I took from a gate about an hour ago. I saw summat was afoot, and me and a friend o' mine have been looking for 'ee. Now let's have your name and no nonsense."

"My name," said Dan, "my name? Well, it is . . . Piper."

"Piper is it, ah! Was you baptized ever?"

"Peter," said Dan savagely.

"Peter Piper! Well, you've picked a tidy peppercarn this time."

Again he was searching his pockets. There was a frown on his face. "You'd better lend me a bit o' pencil too."

Dan produced a stump of lead pencil and the gamekeeper, smoothing the paper on his lifted knee, wrote down the name of Peter Piper.

"And where might you come from?" He peered up at the miserable man, who replied: "From Leasington"—naming a village several miles to the west of his real home.

"Leasington!" commented the other. "You must know John Eustace, then?" John Eustace was a sporting farmer famed for his stock and his riches.

"Know him!" exclaimed Dan. "He's my uncle!"

"O ah!" The other carefully folded the paper and put it into his breast pocket. "Well, you can trot along home now, my lad."

Dan knelt down and unbuckled the collar from his dead dog's neck. He was fond of his dog, it looked piteous now. And kneeling there it suddenly came upon Dan that he had been a coward again, he had told nothing but lies, foolish lies, and he had let a great hulking flunkey walk roughshod over him. In one astonishing moment the reproving face of his little son seemed to loom up beside the dog, the blood flamed in his brain.

"I'll take charge of that," said the keeper, snatching the collar from his hand.

"Blast you!" Dan sprang to his feet, and suddenly screaming like a madman: "I'm Dan Pavey of Thasper," he leapt at the keeper with a fury that shook even that calm stalwart.

"You would, would ye?" he yapped, darting for his gun. Dan

also seized it, and in their struggle the gun was fired off harmlessly between them. Dan let go.

"My God!" roared the keeper, "you'd murder me, would ye? Wi' my own gun, would ye?" He struck Dan a swinging blow with the butt of it, yelling: "Would ye? Would ye? Would ye?" And he did not cease striking until Dan tumbled senseless and bloody across the body of the dog.

Soon another keeper came hurrying through the trees.

"Tried to murder me—wi' me own gun, he did," declared the big man, "wi' me own gun!"

They revived the stricken Pavey after a while and then conveyed him to a policeman, who conveyed him to a gaol.

The magistrates took a grave view of the case and sent it for trial at the assizes. They were soon held, he had not long to wait, and before the end of November he was condemned. The assize court was a place of intolerable gloom, intolerable formality, intolerable pain, but the public seemed to enjoy it. The keeper swore Dan had tried to shoot him, and the prisoner contested this. He did not deny that he was the aggressor. The jury found him guilty. What had he to say? He had nothing to say, but he was deeply moved by the spectacle of the Rev. Scroope standing up and testifying to his sobriety, his honesty, his general good repute, and pleading for a lenient sentence because he was a man of considerable force of character, misguided no doubt, a little unfortunate, and prone to recklessness.

Said the judge, examining the papers of the indictment: "I see there is a previous conviction—for betting offences."

"That was three years ago, my lord. There has been nothing of the kind since, my lord, of that I am sure, quite sure."

Scroope showed none of his old time confident aspect, he

was perspiring and trembling. The clerk of the assize leaned up and held a whispered colloquy with the judge, who then addressed the rector.

"Apparently he is still a betting agent. He gave a false name and address, which was taken down by the keeper on a piece of paper furnished by the prisoner. Here it is, on one side the name of Peter Pope (Piper, sir!) Piper: and on the other side this is written;

3 o/c race. Pretty Dear, 5/-to win. F. Klopstock.

Are there any Klopstocks in your parish?"

"Klopstock!" murmured the parson, "it is the name of my cook."

What had the prisoner to say about that? The prisoner had nothing to say, and he was sentenced to twelve months' imprisonment with hard labour.

So Dan was taken away. He was a tough man, an amenable man, and the mere rigours of the prison did not unduly afflict him. His behaviour was good, and he looked forward to gaining the maximum remission of his sentence. Meg, his mother, went to see him once, alone, but she did not repeat the visit. The prison chaplain paid him special attention. He, too, was a Scroope, a huge fellow, not long from Oxford, and Pavey learned that he was related to the Thasper rector. The new year came, February came, March came, and Dan was afforded some privileges. His singing in chapel was much admired, and occasionally he was allowed to sing to the prisoners. April came, May came, and then his son Martin was drowned in a boating accident, on a lake, in a park. The Thasper children had been

taken there for a holiday. On hearing it, Pavey sank limply to
the floor of his cell. The warders sat him up, but they could
make nothing of him, he was dazed, and he could not speak.
He was taken to the hospital wing. "This man has had a stroke,
he is gone dumb," said the doctor. On the following day he appeared to be well enough, but still he could not speak. He went
about the ward doing hospital duty, dumb as a ladder; he could
not even mourn, but a jig kept flickering through his voiceless
mind:

> In a park there was a lake,
> On the lake there was a boat,
> In the boat there was a boy.

Hour after hour the stupid jingle flowed through his con-
sciousness. Perhaps it kept him from going mad, but it did not
bring him back his speech, he was dumb, dumb. And he remembered a man who had been stricken deaf, and then blind—
Scroope knew him too, it was some man who had mocked God.

> In a park there was a lake,
> On the lake there was a boat,
> In the boat there was a boy.

On the day of the funeral Pavey imagined that he had been
let out of prison; he dreamed that someone had been kind and
set him free for an hour or two to bury his dead boy. He seemed
to arrive at Thasper when the ceremony was already begun,
the coffin was already in the church. Pavey knelt down beside
his mother. The rector intoned the office, the child was taken to

its grave. Dumb dreaming Pavey turned his eyes from it. The day was too bright for death, it was a stainless day. The wind seemed to flow in soft streams, rolling the lilac blooms. A small white feather, blown from a pigeon on the church gable, whirled about like a butterfly. "We give thee hearty thanks," the priest was saying, "for that it hath pleased thee to deliver this our brother out of the miseries of this sinful world." At the end of it all Pavey kissed his mother, and saw himself turn back to his prison. He went by the field paths away to the railway junction. The country had begun to look a little parched, for rain was wanted—vividly he could see all this—but things were growing, corn was thriving greenly, the beanfields smelled sweet. A frill of yellow kilk and wild white carrot spray lined every hedge. Cattle dreamed in the grass, the colt stretched itself unregarded in front of its mother. Larks, wrens, yellow-hammers. There were the great beech trees and the great hills, calm and confident, overlooking Cobbs and Peter, Thasper and Trinkel, Buzzlebury and Nuncton. He sees the summer is coming on, he is going back to prison. "Courage is vain," he thinks, "we are like the grass underfoot, a blade that excels is quickly shorn. In this sort of a world the poor have no call to be proud, they had only need be penitent."

> In the park there was a lake,
> On the lake. . . . . . boat,
> In the boat. . . . .

Luxury

〜

EIGHT O'CLOCK OF A FINE SPRING MORNING IN THE HAM-
let of Kezzal Predy Peter, great horses with chains clinking
down the road, and Alexander Finkle rising from his bed singing: "O lah soh doh, soh lah me doh," timing his notes to the
ching of his neighbour's anvil. He boils a cupful of water on
an oil stove, his shaving brush stands (where it always stands)
upon the window-ledge ("Soh lah soh do-o-o-oh, soh doh soh
la-a-a-ah!") but as he addresses himself to his toilet the clamour
of the anvil ceases and then Finkle too becomes silent, for the
unresting cares of his life begin again to afflict him.

"This cottage is no good," he mumbles, "and I'm no good.
Literature is no good when you live too much on porridge. Your
writing's no good, sir, you can't get any glow out of oatmeal.
Why did you ever come here? It's a hopeless job and you know
it!" Stropping his razor petulantly as if the soul of that frus-
trating oatmeal lay there between the leather and the blade, he
continues: "But it isn't the cottage, it isn't me, it isn't the writing—

it's the privation. I must give it up and get a job as a railway porter."

And indeed he was very impoverished, the living he derived from his writings was meagre; the cottage had many imperfections, both its rooms were gloomy, and to obviate the inconvenience arising from its defective roof he always slept downstairs.

Two years ago he had been working for a wall-paper manufacturer in Bethnal Green. He was not poor then, not so very poor, he had the clothes he stood up in (they were good clothes) and fifty pounds in the bank besides. But although he had served the wall-paper man for fifteen years that fifty pounds had not been derived from clerking, he had earned it by means of his hobby, a little knack of writing things for provincial newspapers. On his thirty-first birthday Finkle argued—for he had a habit of conducting long and not unsatisfactory discussions between himself and a self that apparently wasn't him—that what he could do reasonably well in his scanty leisure could be multiplied exceedingly if he had time and opportunity, lived in the country, somewhere where he could go into a garden to smell the roses or whatever was blooming and draw deep draughts of happiness, think his profound thoughts and realize the goodness of God, and then sit and read right through some long and difficult book about Napoleon or Mahomet. Bursting with literary ambition Finkle had hesitated no longer: he could live on nothing in the country—for a time. He had the fifty pounds, he had saved it, it had taken him seven years, but he had made it and saved it. He handed in his notice. That was very astonishing to his master, who esteemed him, but more astonishing to Finkle was the parting gift of ten pounds which the master had given him. The workmen, too, had collected more money for him, and bought for him a clock, a monster, it weighed twelve pounds and had a brass figure of Lohengrin on the top, while the serene old messenger man who cleaned the windows and bought surreptitious beer for the clerks gave him a prescription for the instantaneous relief of a painful stomach ailment. "It might come in handy," he had said. That was two years ago, and now just think! He had bought himself an inkpot of crystalline glass—a large one, it held nearly half a pint—and two pens, one for red ink and one for black, besides a quill for signing his name with. Here he was at "Pretty Peter" and the devil himself was in it! Nothing had ever been right, the hamlet itself was poor. Like all places near the chalk hills its roads were of flint, the church was of flint, the farms and cots of flint with brick corners. There was an old milestone outside his cot, he was pleased with that, it gave the miles to London and the miles to Winchester, it was nice to have a milestone there like that—your very own.

He finished shaving and threw open the cottage door; the scent of wallflowers and lilac came to him as sweet almost as a wedge of newly cut cake. The may bloom on his hedge drooped over the branches like crudded cream, and the dew in the gritty road smelled of harsh dust in a way that was pleasant. Well, if the cottage wasn't much good, the bit of a garden was all right.

There was a rosebush too, a little vagrant in its growth. He leaned over his garden gate; there was no one in sight. He took out the fire shovel and scooped up a clot of manure that lay in the road adjacent to his cottage and trotted back to place it in a little heap at the root of those scatter-brained roses, pink and bulging, that never seemed to do very well and yet were so satisfactory.

"Nicish day," remarked Finkle, lolling against his doorpost, "but it's always nice if you are doing a good day's work. The garden is all right, and literature is all right, and life's all right—only I live too much on porridge. It isn't the privation itself, it's the things privation makes a man do. It makes a man do things he ought not want to do, it makes him mean, it makes him feel mean, I tell you, and if he feels mean and thinks mean he writes meanly, that's how it is."

He had written topical notes and articles, stories of gay life (of which he knew nothing), of sport (of which he knew less), a poem about "hope," and some cheerful pieces for a girls' weekly paper. And yet his outgoings still exceeded his income, painfully and perversely after two years. It was terrifying. He wanted success, he had come to conquer—not to find what he *had* found. But he would be content with encouragement now even if he did not win success; it was absolutely necessary, he had not sold a thing for six months, his public would forget him, his connection would be gone.

"There's no use though," mused Finkle, as he scrutinized his worn boots, "in looking at things in detail, that's mean; a large view is the thing. Whatever is isolated is bound to look alarming."

But he continued to lean against the doorpost in the full blaze of the stark, almost gritty sunlight, thinking mournfully until he heard the porridge in the saucepan begin to bubble. Turning into the room he felt giddy, and scarlet spots and other phantasmagoria waved in the air before him.

Without an appetite he swallowed the porridge and ate some bread and cheese and watercress. Watercress, at least, was plentiful there, for the little runnels that came down from the big hills expanded in the Predy Peter fields and in their shallow bottoms the cress flourished.

He finished his breakfast, cleared the things away, and sat down to see if he could write, but it was in vain—he could not write. He could think, but his mind would embrace no subject, it just teetered about with the objects within sight, the empty, disconsolate grate, the pattern of the rug, and the black butterfly that had hung dead upon the wall for so many months. Then he thought of the books he intended to read but could never procure, the books he had procured but did not like, the books he had liked but was already, so soon, forgetting. Smoking would have helped and he wanted to smoke, but he could not afford it now. If ever he had a real good windfall he intended to buy a tub, a little tub it would have to be of course, and he would fill it to the bung with cigarettes, full to the bung, if it cost him pounds. And he would help himself to one whenever he had a mind to do so.

"Bah, you fool!" he murmured, "you think you have the whole world against you, that you are fighting it, keeping up your end with heroism! Idiot! What does it all amount to? You've withdrawn yourself from the world, run away from it, and here you sit making futile dabs at it, like a child sticking pins into a pudding and wondering why nothing happens. What *could* happen? What? The world doesn't know about you, or care, you are useless. It isn't aware of you any more than a chain of mountains is aware of a gnat. And whose fault is that—is it the mountains' fault? Idiot! But I can't starve and I must go and get a job as a railway porter, it's all I'm fit for."

Two farmers paused outside Finkle's garden and began a solid conversation upon a topic that made him feel hungry indeed. He listened, fascinated, though he was scarcely aware of it.

"Six-stone lambs," said one, "are fetching three pounds apiece."

"Ah!"

"I shall fat some."

"Myself I don't care for lamb, never did care."

"It's good eating."

"Ah, but I don't care for it. Now we had a bit of spare rib last night off an old pig. 'Twas cold, you know, but beautiful. I said to my dame: 'What can mortal man want better than spare rib off an old pig? Tender and white, ate like lard.'"

"Yes, it's good eating."

"Nor veal, I don't like—nothing that's young."

"Veal's good eating."

"Don't care for it, never did, it eats short to my mind."

Then the school bell began to ring so loudly that Finkle could hear no more, but his mind continued to hover over the choice of lamb or veal or old pork until he was angry. Why had he done this foolish thing, thrown away his comfortable job, reasonable food, ease of mind, friendship, pocket money, tobacco? Even his girl had forgotten him. Why had he done this impudent thing, it was insanity surely? But he knew that man has instinctive reasons that transcend logic, what a parson would call the superior reason of the heart.

"I wanted a change, and I got it. Now I want another change, but what shall I get? Chance and change, they are the sweet features of existence. Chance and change, and not too much prosperity. If I were an idealist I could live from my hair upwards."

The two farmers separated. Finkle staring haplessly from his window saw them go. Some schoolboys were playing a game of marbles in the road there. Another boy sat on the green bank quietly singing, while one in spectacles knelt slyly behind him trying to burn a hole in the singer's breeches with a magnifying glass. Finkle's thoughts still hovered over the flavours and satisfactions of veal and lamb and pig until, like mother Hubbard, he turned and opened his larder.

There, to his surprise, he saw four bananas lying on a saucer. Bought from a travelling hawker a couple of days ago they had cost him threepence halfpenny. And he had forgotten them! He could not afford another luxury like that for a week at least, and he stood looking at them, full of doubt. He debated whether he should take one now, he would still have one left for Wednesday, one for Thursday, and one for Friday. But he thought he would not, he had had his breakfast and he had not remembered them. He grew suddenly and absurdly angry again. That was the worst of poverty, not what it made you endure, but what it made you *want* to endure. Why shouldn't he eat a banana—why shouldn't he eat all of them? And yet bananas always seemed to him such luxuriant, expensive things, so much peel, and then two, or not more than three, delicious bites. But if he fancied a banana—there it was. No, he did not want to destroy the blasted thing! No reason at all why he should not, but that was what continuous hardship did for you, nothing could stop this miserable feeling for economy now. If he had a thousand pounds at this moment he knew he would be careful about bananas and about butter and about sugar and things like that; but he would never have a thousand pounds, nobody had ever had it, it was impossible to believe that anyone had ever had wholly and entirely to themselves a thousand pounds. It could not be believed. He was like a man dreaming that he had the hangman's noose around his neck; yet the drop did not take place, it did not take place, and it would not take place. But the noose was still there. He picked up the bananas one by one, the four bananas, the whole four. No other man in the world, surely, had ever had four such fine bananas as that and not wanted to eat them? O, why had such stupid, mean scruples seized him again? It was disgusting and ungenerous to himself, it made him feel mean, it *was* mean! Rushing to his cottage door he cried: "Here y'are!" to the playing schoolboys and flung two of the bananas into the midst of them. Then he flung another. He hesitated at the fourth, and tearing the peel from it he crammed the fruit into his own mouth. wolfing it down and gasping: "So perish all such traitors."

When he had completely absorbed its savour, he stared like a fool at the empty saucer. It was empty, the bananas were gone, all four irrecoverably gone.

"Damned pig!" cried Finkle.

But then he sat down and wrote all this, just as it appears.

The Higgler

❧

I

On a cold April afternoon a higgler was driving across Shag
Moor in a two-wheeled cart.

H. WITLOW
DEALER IN POULTRY
DINNOP

was painted on the hood; the horse was of mean appearance
but notorious ancestry. A high upland common was this moor,
two miles from end to end, and full of furze and bracken. There
were no trees and not a house, nothing but a line of telegraph
poles following the road, sweeping with rigidity from north to
south; nailed upon one of them a small scarlet notice to stone-
throwers was prominent as a wound. On so high and wide a
region as Shag Moor the wind always blew, or if it did not quite
blow there was a cool activity in the air. The furze was always
green and growing, and, taking no account of seasons, often

golden. Here in summer solitude lounged and snoozed; at other times, as now, it shivered and looked sinister.

Higglers in general are ugly and shrewd, old and hard, crafty and callous, but Harvey Witlow though shrewd was not ugly; he was hard but not old, crafty but not at all unkind. If you had eggs to sell he would buy them, by the score he would, or by the long hundred. Other odds and ends he would buy or do, paying good bright silver, bartering a bag of apples, carrying your little pig to market, or fetching a tree from the nurseries. But the season was backward, eggs were scarce, trade was bad—by crumps, it was indeed!—and as he crossed the moor Harvey could not help discussing the situation with himself.

"If things don't change, and change for the better, and change soon, I can't last and I can't endure it; I'll be damned and done, and I'll have to sell," he said, prodding the animal with the butt of his whip, "this cob. And," he said, as if in afterthought, prodding the footboard, "this cart, and go back to the land. And I'll have lost my fifty pounds. Well, that's what war does for you. It does it for you, sir," he announced sharply to the vacant moor, "and it does it for me. Fifty pounds! I was better off in the war. I was better off working for farmers; much; but it's no good chattering about it, it's the trick of life; when you get so far, then you can go and order your funeral. Get along, Dodger!"

The horse responded briskly for a few moments.

"I tell ye," said Harvey adjuring the ambient air, "you can go and order your funeral. Get along, Dodger!"

Again Dodger got along.

"Then there's Sophy, what about Sophy and me?"

He was not engaged to Sophy Daws, not exactly, but he was keeping company with her. He was not pledged or affianced, he was just keeping company with her. But Sophy, as he knew, not only desired a marriage with Mr. Witlow, she expected it, and expected it soon. So did her parents, her friends, and everybody in the village, including the postman, who didn't live in it but wished he did, and the parson, who did live in it but wished he didn't.

"Well, that's damned and done, fair damned and done now, unless things take a turn, and soon, so it's no good chattering about it."

And just then and there things did take a turn. He had never been across the moor before; he was prospecting for trade. At the end of Shag Moor he saw standing back in the common, fifty yards from the road, a neat square house set in a little farm. Twenty acres, perhaps. The house was girded by some white palings; beside it was a snug orchard in a hedge covered with blackthorn bloom. It was very green and pleasant in front of the house. The turf was cleared and closely cropped, some ewes were grazing and under the blackthorn, out of the wind, lay half a dozen lambs, but what chiefly moved the imagination of Harvey Witlow was a field on the far side of the house. It had a small rickyard with a few small stacks in it; everything here seemed on the small scale, but snug, very snug; and in that field and yard were hundreds of fowls, hundreds of good breed, and mostly white. Leaving his horse to sniff the greensward, the higgler entered a white wicket gateway and passed to the back of the house, noting as he did so a yellow wagon inscribed

ELIZABETH SADGROVE
PRATTLE CORNER

At the kitchen door he was confronted by a tall gaunt woman of middle age with a teapot in her hands.

"Afternoon, ma'am. Have you anything to sell?" began Harvey Witlow, tilting his hat with a confident affable air. The tall woman was cleanly dressed, a superior person; her hair was grey. She gazed at him.

"It's cold," he continued. She looked at him as uncomprehendingly as a mouse might look at a gravestone.

"I'll buy any mottal thing, ma'am. Except trouble; I'm full up wi' that already. Eggs? Fowls?"

"I've not seen you before," commented Mrs. Sadgrove a little bleakly, in a deep husky voice.

"No, 'tis the first time as ever I drove in this part. To tell you the truth, ma'am, I'm new to the business. Six months. I was in the war a year ago. Now I'm trying to knock up a connection. Difficult work. Things are very quiet."

Mrs. Sadgrove silently removed the lid of the teapot, inspected the interior of the pot with an intense glance, and then replaced the lid as if she had seen a black-beetle there.

"Ah, well," sighed the higgler. "You've a neat little farm here, ma'am."

"It's quiet enough," said she.

"Sure it is, ma'am. Very lonely."

"And it's difficult work, too." Mrs. Sadgrove almost smiled.

"Sure it is, ma'am; but you does it well, I can see. Oh, you've some nice little ricks of corn, ah! I does well enough at the dealing now and again, but it's teasy work, and mostly I don't earn enough to keep my horse in shoe leather."

"I've a few eggs, perhaps," said she.

"I could do with a score or two, ma'am, if you could let me have 'em."

"You'll have to come all my way if I do."

"Name your own price, ma'am, if you don't mind trading with me."

"Mind! Your money's as good as my own, isn't it?"

"It must be, ma'am. That's meaning no disrespects to you," the young higgler assured her hastily, and was thereupon invited to enter the kitchen.

A stone floor with two or three mats; open hearth with burning logs; a big dresser painted brown, carrying a row of white cups on brass hooks, and shelves of plates overlapping each other like the scales of fish. A dark settle half hid a flight of stairs with a small gate at the top. Under the window a black sofa, deeply indented, invited you a little repellingly, and in the middle of the room stood a large table, exquisitely scrubbed, with one end of it laid for tea. Evidently a living-room as well as kitchen. A girl, making toast at the fire, turned as the higgler entered. Beautiful she was: red hair, a complexion like the inside of a nut, blue eyes, and the hands of a lady. He saw it all at once, jacket of bright green wool, black dress, grey stockings and shoes, and forgot his errand, her mother, his fifty pounds, Sophy—momentarily he forgot everything. The girl stared strangely at him. He was tall, clean-shaven, with a loop of black hair curling handsomely over one side of his brow.

"Good afternoon," said Harvey Witlow, as softly as if he had entered a church.

"Some eggs, Mary," Mrs. Sadgrove explained. The girl laid down her toasting-fork. She was less tall than her mother, whom she resembled only enough for the relationship to be noted. Silently she crossed the kitchen and opened a door that led into a dairy. Two pans of milk were creaming on a bench there, and on the flags were two great baskets filled with eggs.

"How many are there?" asked Mrs. Sadgrove, and the girl replied: "Fifteen score, I think."

"Take the lot, higgler?"

"Yes, ma'am," he cried eagerly, and ran out to his cart and fetched a number of trays. In them he packed the eggs as the girl handed them to him from the baskets. Mrs. Sadgrove left them together. For a time the higgler was silent.

"No," at length he murmured, "I've never been this road before."

There was no reply from Mary. Sometimes their fingers touched, and often, as they bent over the eggs, her bright hair almost brushed his face.

"It is a loneish spot," he ventured again.

"Yes," said Mary Sadgrove.

When the eggs were all transferred her mother came in again.

"Would you buy a few pullets, higgler?"

"Any number, ma'am," he declared quickly. Any number; by crumps, the tide was turning. He followed the mother into the yard, and there again she left him, waiting. He mused about the girl and wondered about the trade. If they offered him ten thousand chickens, he'd buy them, somehow, he would. She had stopped in the kitchen. Just in there she was, just behind him, a few feet away. Over the low wall of the yard a fat black pony was strolling in a field of bright greensward. In the yard, watching him, was a young gander, and on a stone staddle beside it lay a dead thrush on its back, its legs stiff in the air. The girl stayed in the kitchen; she was moving about, though, he could hear her; perhaps she was spying at him through the window. Twenty million eggs he would buy if Mrs. Sadgrove had got them. She was gone a long time. It was very quiet. The gander began to comb its white breast with its beak. Its three-toed feet were a most tender pink, shaped like wide diamonds, and at each of the three forward points here was a toe like a small blanched nut. It lifted one foot, folding the webs, and hid it under its wing and sank into a resigned meditation on one leg. It had a blue eye that was meek—it had two, but you could only see one at a time—a meek blue eye, set in a pink rim that gave it a dissolute air, and its beak had raw red nostrils as though it suffered from the damp. Altogether a beautiful bird. And in some absurd way it resembled Mrs. Sadgrove.

"Would you sell that young gollan, ma'am?" Harvey inquired when the mother returned.

Yes, she would sell him, and she also sold him two dozen pullets. Harvey packed the fowls in a crate.

"Come on," he cried cuddling the squalling gander in his arms, "you needn't be afeared of me, I never kills anything afore Saturdays."

He roped it by its leg to a hook inside his cart. Then he took out his bag of money, paid Mrs. Sadgrove her dues, said: "Good day, ma'am, good day" and drove off without seeing another sign or stitch of that fine young girl.

"Get along, Dodger, get along wi' you." They went bowling along for nearly an hour, and then he could see the landmark on Dan'el Green's Hill, a windmill that never turned though it looked a fine competent piece of architecture, just beyond Dinnop.

Soon he reached his cottage and was chaffing his mother, a hearty buxom dame, who stayed at home and higgled with any chance callers. At this business she was perhaps more enlightened than her son. It was almost a misfortune to get into her clutches.

"How much you give for this?" he cried, eyeing with humorous contempt an object in a coop that was neither flesh nor rude red herring.

"Oh crumps," he declared when she told him, "I am damned and done!"

"Go on with you, that's a good bird, I tell you, with a full heart, as will lay in a month."

"I doubt it's a hen at all," he protested. "Oh what a ravenous beak! Damned and done I am."

Mrs. Witlow's voice began indignantly to rise.

"Oh well," mused her son, "it's thrifty perhaps. It ain't quite right, but it's not so wrong as to make a fuss about, especially as I be pretty sharp set. And if it's hens you want," he continued triumphantly, dropping the crate of huddled fowls before her, "there's hens for you; and a gander! There's a gander for you, if it's a gander you want."

Leaving them all in his cottage yard he went and stalled the horse and cart at the inn, for he had no stable of his own. After supper he told his mother about the Sadgroves of Prattle Corner. "Prettiest girl you ever seen, but the shyest mottal alive. Hair like a squirrel, lovely."

"An't you got to go over and see Sophy tonight," inquired his mother, lighting the lamp.

"Oh lord, if I an't clean forgot that. Well, I'm tired, shan't go tonight. See her tomorrow."

II

Mrs. Sadgrove had been a widow for ten years—and she was glad of it. Prattle Corner was her property, she owned it and farmed it with the aid of a little old man and a large lad. The older this old man grew, and the less wages he received (for Elizabeth Sadgrove was reputed a "grinder"), the more ardently he worked; the older the lad grew, the less he laboured and the more he swore. She was thriving. She was worth money, was Mrs. Sadgrove. Ah! And her daughter Mary, it was clear, had received an education fit for a lord's lady; she had been at a seminary for gentlefolk's females until she was seventeen. Well, whether or no, a clock must run as you time it; but it wronged her for the work of a farm, it spoiled her, it completely deranged her for the work of a farm; and this was a pity and foolish, because some day the farm was coming to her as didn't know hay from a bull's foot.

All this, and more, the young higgler quickly learned, and plenty more he soon divined. Business began to flourish with him now; his despair was gone, he was established, he could look forward, to whatever it was he wanted to look forward, with equanimity and such pleasurable anticipation as the chances and charges of life might engender. Every week, and twice a week, he would call at the farm, and though these occasions had their superior business inducements they often borrowed a less formal tone and intention.

"Take a cup of tea, higgler?" Mrs. Sadgrove would abruptly invite him; and he would drink tea and discourse with her for half an hour on barndoor ornithology, on harness, and markets, the treatment of swine, the wear and tear of gear. Mary, always present, was always silent, seldom uttering a word to the higgler; yet a certain grace emanated from her to him, an interest, a light, a favour, circumscribed indeed by some modesty, shyness, some inhibition, that neither had the wit or the opportunity to overcome.

One evening he pulled up at the white palings of Prattle Corner. It was a calm evening in May, the sun was on its downgoing, chaffinches and wrens sung ceaselessly. Mary in the orchard was heavily veiled; he could see her over the hedge, holding a brush in her gloved hands, and a bee skep. A swarm was clustered like a great gnarl on the limb of an apple tree. Bloom was thickly covering the twigs. She made several timid attempts to brush the bees into the skep but they resented this.

"They knows if you be afraid of 'em," bawled Harvey. "I better come and give you a hand."

When he took the skep and brush from her she stood like one helpless, released by fate from a task ill-understood and gracelessly waived. But he liked her shyness, her almost uncouth immobility.

"Never mind about that," said Harvey, as she unfastened her veil, scattering the white petals that had collected upon it; "when they kicks they hurts; but I've been stung so often that I'm 'noculated against 'em. They knows if you be afraid of 'em."

Wearing neither veil nor gloves he went confidently to the tree and collected the swarm without mishap.

"Don't want to show no fear of them," said Harvey. "Nor of anything else, come to that," he added with a guffaw, "nor anybody."

At that she blushed and thanked him very softly, and she did look straight and clearly at him.

Never anything beyond a blush and a thank-you. When in the kitchen, or the parlour, Mrs. Sadgrove sometimes left them alone together Harvey would try a lot of talk, blarneying talk or sensible talk, or talk about events in the world that was neither the one nor the other. No good. The girl's responses were ever brief and confused. Why was this? Again and again he asked himself that question. Was there anything the matter with her? Nothing that you could see; she was a bright and beautiful being. And it was not contempt, either, for despite her fright, her voicelessness, her timid eyes, he divined her friendly feeling for himself; and he would discourse to his own mother about her and her mother:

"They are well-up people, you know, well off, plenty of money and nothing to do with it. The farm's their own, freehold. A whole row of cottages she's got, too, in Smoorton Comfrey, so I heard; good cottages, well let. She's worth a few thousands, I warrant. Mary's beautiful. I took a fancy to that girl the first moment I see her. But she's very highly cultivated—and, of course, there's Sophy."

To this enigmatic statement Mrs. Witlow offered no response; but mothers are inscrutable beings to their sons, always.

Once he bought some trees of cherries from Mrs. Sadgrove, and went on a July morning to pick the fruit. Under the trees Mary was walking slowly to and fro, twirling a clapper to scare away the birds. He stood watching her from the gateway. Among the bejewelled trees she passed, turning the rattle with a listless air, as if beating time to a sad music that only she could hear. The man knew that he was deeply fond of her. He passed into the orchard, bade her good morning, and lifting his ladder into one of the trees nearest the hedge began to pluck cherries. Mary moved slimly in her white frock up and down a shady avenue in the orchard, waving the clapper. The brightness of sun and sky was almost harsh; there was a little wind that feebly lifted the despondent leaves. He had doffed his coat; his shirt was white and clean. The lock of dark hair drooped over one side of his forehead; his face was brown and pleasant, his bare arms were brown and powerful. From his high perch among the leaves Witlow watched for the girl to draw near to him in her perambulation. Knavish birds would scatter at her approach, only to drop again into the trees she had passed. His soul had an immensity of longing for her, but she never spoke a word to him. She would come from the shade of the little avenue, through the dumb trees that could only bend to greet her, into the sunlight whose dazzle gilded her own triumphant bloom. Fine! Fine! And always as she passed his mind refused to register a single thought he could offer her, or else his tongue would refuse to utter it. But his glance never left her face until she had passed out of sight again, and then he would lean against the ladder in the tree, staring down at the ground, seeing nothing or less than nothing, except a field mouse climbing to the top of a coventry bush in the hedge below him, nipping off one thick leaf and descending with the leaf in its mouth. Sometimes Mary rested at the other end of the avenue; the clapper would be silent and she would not appear for—oh, hours! She never rested near the trees Witlow was denuding. The mouse went on ascending and descending, and Witlow filled his basket, and shifted his stand, and wondered.

At noon he got down and sat on the hedge bank to eat a snack of lunch. Mary had gone indoors for hers, and he was alone for a while. Capriciously enough, his thoughts dwelt upon Sophy Daws. Sophy was a fine girl too; not such a lady as Mary Sadgrove—oh lord, no! her father was a gamekeeper!—but she was jolly and ample. She had been a little captious lately, said he was neglecting her. That wasn't true; hadn't he been busy? Besides, he wasn't bound to her in any sort of way, and of course he couldn't afford any marriage yet awhile. Sophy hadn't got any money, never had any. What she did with her wages—she was a parlour-maid—was a teaser! Harvey grunted a little, and said "Well!" And that is all he said, and all he thought about Sophy Daws then, for he could hear Mary's clapper begin again in a corner of the orchard. He went back to his work. There at the foot of the tree were the baskets full of cherries, and those yet to be filled.

"Phew, but that's hot!" commented the man, "I'm as dry as a rattle."

A few cherries had spilled from one basket and lay on the ground. The little furry mouse had found them and was industriously nibbling at one. The higgler nonchalantly stamped his foot upon it, and kept it so for a moment or two. Then he looked at the dead mouse. A tangle of entrails had gushed from its whiskered muzzle.

He resumed his work and the clapper rattled on throughout the afternoon, for there were other cherry trees that other buyers would come to strip in a day or two. At four o'clock he was finished. Never a word had he spoken with Mary, or she with him. When he went over to the house to pay Mrs. Sadgrove Mary stopped in the orchard scaring the birds.

"Take a cup of tea, Mr. Witlow," said Mrs. Sadgrove; and then she surprisingly added: "Where's Mary?"

"Still a-frightening the birds, and pretty well tired of that, I should think, ma'am."

The mother had poured out three cups of tea.

"Shall I go and call her in?" he asked, rising.

"You might," said she.

In the orchard the clappering had ceased. He walked all round, and in among the trees, but saw no sign of Mary; nor on the common, nor in the yard. But when he went back to the house Mary was there already, chatting at the table with her mother. She did not greet him, though she ceased talking to her mother as he sat down. After drinking his tea he went off briskly to load the baskets into the cart. As he climbed up to drive off, Mrs. Sadgrove came out and stood beside the horse.

"You're off now?" said she.

"Yes, ma'am; all loaded, and thank you."

She glanced vaguely along the road he had to travel. The afternoon was as clear as wine, the greensward itself dazzled him; lonely Shag Moor stretched away, humped with sweet yellow furze and pilastered with its telegraph poles. No life there, no life at all. Harvey sat on his driving board, musingly brushing the flank of his horse with the trailing whip.

"Ever round this way on Sundays?" inquired the woman, peering up at him.

"Well, not in a manner of speaking, I'm not, ma'am," he answered her.

The widow laid her hand on the horse's back, patting vaguely. The horse pricked up its ears, as if it were listening.

"If you are, at all, ever, you must look in and have a bit of dinner with us."

"I will, ma'am, I will."

"Next Sunday?" she went on.

"I will, ma'am, yes, I will," he repeated, "and thank you."

"One o'clock?" The widow smiled up at him.

"At one o'clock, ma'am; next Sunday; I will, and thank you," he said.

She stood away from the horse and waved her hand. The first tangible thought that floated mutely out of the higgler's mind as he drove away was: "I'm damned if I ain't a-going it, Sophy!"

He told his mother of Mrs. Sadgrove's invitation with an air of curbed triumph. "Come round—she says. Yes—I says—I 'ull. That's right—she says—so do."

III

On the Sunday morn he dressed himself gallantly. It was again a sweet unclouded day. The church bell at Dinnop had begun to ring. From his window, as he fastened his most ornate tie, Harvey could observe his neighbour's two small children in the next garden, a boy and girl clad for church-going and each carrying a clerical book. The tiny boy placed his sister in front of a hen-roost and, opening his book, began to pace to and fro before her, shrilly intoning: "Jesus is the shepherd, ring the bell. Oh lord, ring the bell, am I a good boy? Amen. Oh lord, ring the bell." The little girl bowed her head piously over her book. The lad then picked up from the ground a dish that had contained the dog's food, and presented it momentarily before the lilac bush, the rabbit in a hutch, the axe fixed in a chopping block, and then before his sister. Without lifting her peering gaze from her book she meekly dropped two pebbles in the plate, and the boy passed on, lightly moaning, to the clothes-line post and a cock scooping in some dust.

"Ah, the little impets!" cried Harvey Witlow. "Here, Toby! Here, Margaret!" He took two pennies from his pocket and lobbed them from the window to the astonished children. As they stooped to pick up the coins Harvey heard the hoarse voice of neighbour Nathan, their father, bawl from his kitchen: "Come on in, and shut that bloody door, d'y'ear!"

Harnessing his moody horse to the gig Harvey was soon bowling away to Shag Moor, and as he drove along he sung loudly. He had a pink rose in his buttonhole. Mrs. Sadgrove received him almost affably, and though Mary was more shy than ever before, Harvey had determined to make an impression. During the dinner he fired off his bucolic jokes, and pleasant tattle of a more respectful and sober nature; but after dinner Mary sat like Patience, not upon a monument but as if upon a rocking-horse, shy and fearful, and her mother made no effort to inspire her as the higgler did, unsuccessful though he was. They went to the pens to look at the pigs, and as they leaned against the low walls and poked the maudlin inhabitants, Harvey began: "Reminds me, when I was in the war . . ."

"Were you in the war!" interrupted Mrs. Sadgrove.

"Oh yes, I was in that war, ah, and there was a pig . . . Danger? Oh lord bless me it was a bit dangerous, but you never knew where it was or wat it 'ud be at next; it was like the sword of Damockels. There was a bullet once come 'ithin a foot of my head, and it went through a board an inch thick, slap through that board." Both women gazed at him apprehendingly. "Why, I might 'a' been killed, you know," said Harvey, cocking his eye musingly at the weather-vane on the barn. "We was in billets at St. Gratien, and one day a chasseur came up—a French yoossar, you know—and he began talking to our sergeant. That was Hubert Luxter, the butcher: died a month or two ago of measles. But this yoossar couldn't speak English at all, and none of us chaps could make sense of him. I never could understand that lingo somehow, never; and though there was half a dozen of us chaps there, none of us were man enough for it neither. 'Nil compree,' we says, 'non compos.' I told him straight: 'You ought to learn English,' I said, 'it's much easier than your kind of bally chatter.' So he kept shaping up as if he was holding a rifle, and then he'd say 'Fusee—bang!' and then he'd say 'cushion'—kept on saying 'cushion.' Then he gets a bit of chalk and draws on the wall something that looks like a horrible dog, and says 'cushion' again."

"Pig," interjected Mary Sadgrove, softly.

"Yes, yes!" ejaculated Harvey, "so 'twas! Do you know any French lingo?"

"Oh yes," declared her mother, "Mary knows it very well."

"Ah," sighed the higgler, "I don't, although I been to France. And I couldn't do it now, not for luck nor love. You learnt it, I suppose. Well, this yoossar wants to borrow my rifle, but of course I can't lend him. So he taps on this horrible pig he'd drawn, and then he taps on his own head, and rolls his eyes about dreadful! 'Mad?' I says. And that was it, that was it. He'd got a pig on his little farm there what had gone mad, and he wanted us to come and shoot it; he was on leave and he hadn't got any ammunition. So Hubert Luxter he says: 'Come on, some of you,' and we all goes with the yoossar and shot the pig for him. Ah, that was a pig! And when it died it jumped a somersault just like a rabbit. It had got the mange, and was mad as anything I ever see in my life; it was full of madness. Couldn't hit him at all at first, and it kicked up bobs-a-dying. 'Ready, present, fire!' Hubert Luxter says, and bang goes the six of us, and every time we missed him he spotted us and we had to run for our lives."

As Harvey looked up he caught a glance of the girl fixed on him. She dropped her gaze at once and, turning away, walked off to the house.

"Come and take a look at the meadow," said Mrs. Sadgrove to him, and they went into the soft smooth meadow where the black pony was grazing. Very bright and green it was, and very blue the sky. He sniffed at the pink rose in his buttonhole, and determined that come what may he would give it to Mary if he could get a nice quiet chance to offer it. And just then, while he and Mrs. Sadgrove were strolling alone in the soft smooth meadow, quite alone, she suddenly, startlingly, asked him: "Are you courting anybody?"

"Beg pardon, ma'am?" he exclaimed.

"You haven't got a sweetheart, have you?" she asked, most deliberately.

Harvey grinned sheepishly: "Ha ha ha," and then he said: "No."

"I want to see my daughter married," the widow went on significantly.

"Miss Mary!" he cried.

"Yes," said she; and something in the higgler's veins began

to pound rapidly. His breast might have been a revolving cage and his heart a demon squirrel. "I can't live for ever," said Mrs. Sadgrove, almost with levity, "in fact, not for long, and so I'd like to see her settled soon with some decent understanding young man, one that could carry on here, and not make a mess of things."

"But, but," stuttered the understanding young man, "I'm no scholar, and she's a lady. I'm a poor chap, rough, and no scholar, ma'am. But mind you . . ."

"That doesn't matter at all," the widow interrupted, "not as things are. You want a scholar for learning, but for the land . . ."

"Ah, that's right, Mrs. Sadgrove, but . . ."

"I want to see her settled. This farm, you know, with the stock and things are worth nigh upon three thousand pounds."

"You want a farmer for farming, that's true, Mrs. Sadgrove, but when you come to marriage, well, with her learning and French and all that . . ."

"A sensible woman will take a man rather than a box of tricks any day of the week," the widow retorted. "Education may be a fine thing, but it often costs a lot of foolish money."

"It do, it do. You want to see her settled?"

"I want to see her settled and secure. When she is twenty-five she comes into five hundred pounds of her own right."

The distracted higgler hummed and haaed in his bewilderment as if he had just been offered the purchase of a dubious duck. "How old is she, ma'am?" he at last huskily inquired.

"Two and twenty nearly. She's a good healthy girl for I've never spent a pound on a doctor for her, and very quiet she is, and very sensible; but she's got a strong will of her own, though you might not think it or believe it."

"She's a fine creature, Mrs. Sadgrove, and I'm very fond of her, I don't mind owning up to that, very fond of her I am."

"Well, think it over, take your time, and see what you think. There's no hurry I hope, please God."

"I shan't want much time," he declared with a laugh, "but I doubt I'm the fair right sort for her."

"Oh, fair days, fair doings!" said she inscrutably, "I'm not a long liver, I'm afraid."

"God forbid, ma'am!" His ejaculation was intoned with deep gravity.

"No, I'm not a long-living woman." She surveyed him with her calm eyes, and he returned her gaze. Hers was a long sallow face, with heavy lips. Sometimes she would stretch her features (as if to keep them from petrifying) in an elastic grin, and display her dazzling teeth; the lips would curl thickly, no longer crimson but blue. He wondered if there was any sign of a doom registered upon her gaunt face. She might die, and die soon.

"You couldn't do better than think it over, then, eh?" She had a queer frown as she regarded him.

"I couldn't do worse than not, Mrs. Sadgrove," he said gaily.

They left it at that. He had no reason for hurrying away, and he couldn't have explained his desire to do so, but he hurried away. Driving along past the end of the moor, and peering back at the lonely farm where they dwelled amid the thick furze snoozing in the heat, he remembered that he had not asked if Mary was willing to marry him! Perhaps the widow took her agreement for granted. That would be good fortune, for otherwise how the devil was he to get round a girl who had never spoken half a dozen words to him! And never would! She was a lady, a girl of fortune, knew her French; but there it was, the girl's own mother was asking him to wed her. Strange, very strange! He dimly feared something, but he did not know what it was he feared. He had still got the pink rose in his buttonhole.

IV

At first his mother was incredulous; when he told her of the astonishing proposal she declared he was a joker; but she was soon as convinced of his sincerity as she was amazed at his hesitation. And even vexed: "Was there anything the matter with this Mary?"

"No, no, no! She's quiet, very quiet indeed, I tell you, but a fine young woman, and a beautiful young woman. Oh, she's all right, right as rain, right as a trivet, right as ninepence. But there's a catch in it somewheres, I fear. I can't see through it yet, but I shall afore long, or I'd have the girl, like a shot I would. 'Tain't the girl, mother, it's the money, if you understand me."

"Well, I don't understand you, certainly I don't. What about Sophy?"

"Oh lord!" He scratched his head ruefully.

"You wouldn't think of giving this the go-by for Sophy, Harvey, would you? A girl as you ain't even engaged to, Harvey, would you?"

"We don't want to chatter about that," declared her son. "I got to think it over, and it's going to tie my wool, I can tell you, for there's a bit of craft somewheres, I'll take my oath. If there ain't, there ought to be!"

Over the alluring project his decision wavered for days, until his mother became mortified at his inexplicable vacillation.

"I tell you," he cried, "I can't make tops or bottoms of it all. I like the girl well enough, but I like Sophy, too, and it's no good beating about the bush. I like Sophy, she's the girl I love; but Mary's a fine creature, and money like that wants looking at before you throw it away, love or no love. Three thousand pounds! I'd be a made man."

And as if in sheer spite to his mother; as if a bushel of money lay on the doorstep for him to kick over whenever the fancy seized him in short (as Mrs. Witlow very clearly intimated) as if in contempt of Providence, he began to pursue Sophy Daws with a new fervour, and walked with that young girl more than he was accustomed to, more than ever before; in fact, as his mother bemoaned, more than he had need to. It was unreasonable, it was a shame, a foolishness; it wasn't decent and it wasn't safe.

On his weekly visits to the farm his mind still wavered. Mrs. Sadgrove let him alone; she was very good, she did not pester him with questions and entreaties. There was Mary with her white dress and her red hair and her silence; a girl with a great fortune, walking about the yard, or sitting in the room, and casting not a glance upon him. Not that he would have known it if she did, for now he was just as shy of her. Mrs. Sadgrove often left them alone, but when they were alone he could not dish up a word for the pretty maid; he was dumb as a statue. If either she or her mother had lifted so much as a finger, then there would have been an end to his hesitations or suspicions, for in Mary's presence the fine glory of the girl seized him incontinently; he was again full of a longing to press her lips, to lay down his doubts, to touch her bosom—though he could not think she would ever allow that! Not an atom of doubt about *her* ever visited him; she was unaware of her mother's queer project. Rather, if she became aware he was sure it would be the end of him. Too beautiful she was, too learned, and too rich. Decidedly it was his native cunning, and no want of love, that inhibited him. Folks with property did not often come along and bid you help yourself. Not very often! And throw in a grand bright girl, just for good measure as you might say. Not very often!

For weeks the higgler made his customary calls, and each time the outcome was the same; no more, no less. "Some dodge," he mused, "something the girl don't know and the mother does." Were they going bankrupt, or were they mortgaged up to the neck, or was there anything the matter with the girl, or was it just the mother wanted to get hold of him? He knew his own value if he didn't know his own mind, and his value couldn't match that girl any more than his mind could. So what *did* they want him for? Whatever it was, Harvey Witlow was ready for it whenever he was in Mary's presence, but once away from her his own craftiness asserted itself; it was a snare, they were trying to make a mock of him!

But nothing could prevent his own mother mocking him, and her treatment of Sophy was so unbearable that if the heart of that dusky beauty had not been proof against all impediments, Harvey might have had to whistle for her favour. But whenever he was with Sophy he had only one heart, undivided and true, and certain as time itself.

"I love Sophy best. It's true enough I love Mary, too, but I love Sophy better. I know it; Sophy's the girl I must wed. It might not be so if I weren't all dashed and doddered about the money; I don't know. But I do know that Mary's innocent of all this craftiness; it's her mother trying to mogue me into it."

Later he would be wishing he could only forget Sophy and do it. Without the hindrance of conscience he could do it, catch or no catch.

He went on calling at the farm, with nothing said or settled, until October. Then Harvey made up his mind, and without a word to the Sadgroves he went and married Sophy Daws and gave up calling at the farm altogether. This gave him some feeling of dishonesty, some qualm and a vague unhappiness; likewise he feared the cold hostility of Mrs. Sadgrove. She would be terribly vexed. As for Mary, he was nothing to her, poor girl; it was a shame. The last time he drove that way he did not call at the farm. Autumn was advancing, and the apples were down, the bracken dying, the furze out of bloom, and the farm on the moor looked more and more lonely, and most cold, though it lodged a flame-haired silent woman, fit for a nobleman, whom they wanted to mate with a common higgler. Crafty, you know, too crafty!

V

The marriage was a gay little occasion, but they did not go away for a honeymoon. Sophy's grandmother from a distant village, Cassandra Fundy, who had a deafness and a speckled skin, brought her third husband, Amos, whom the family had never seen before. Not a very wise man, indeed he was a common man, stooping like a decayed tree, he was so old. But he shaved every day and his hairless skull was yellow. Cassandra, who was yellow too, had long since turned into a fool; she did not shave, though she ought to have done. She was like to die soon, but everybody said old Amos would live to be a hundred; it was expected of him, and he, too, was determined.

The guests declared that a storm was threatening, but Amos Fundy denied it and scorned it.

"Thunder p'raps, but 'twill clear; 'tis only de pride o' der morning."

"Don't you be a fool," remarked his wife, enigmatically, "you'll die soon enough."

"You must behold der moon," continued the octogenarian; "de closer it is to der wheel, de closer der rain; de furder away it is, de furder der rain."

"You could pour that man's brain into a thimble," declared Cassandra of her spouse, "and they wouldn't fill it—he's deaf."

Fundy was right; the day did clear. The marriage was made and the guests returned with the man and his bride to their home. But Fundy was also wrong, for storm came soon after and rain set in. The guests stayed on for tea, and then, as it was no better, they feasted and stayed till night. And Harvey began to think they never would go, but of course they couldn't and so there they were. Sophy was looking wonderful in white stockings and shiny shoes and a red frock with a tiny white apron. A big girl she seemed, with her shaken dark hair and flushed face. Grandmother Fundy spoke seriously, but not secretly to her.

"I've had my fourteen touch of children," said Grandmother Fundy. "Yes, they were flung on the mercy of God—poor little devils. I've followed most of 'em to the churchyard. You go slow, Sophia."

"Yes, granny."

"Why," continued Cassandra, embracing the whole company, as it were, with her disclosure, "my mother had me by some gentleman!"

The announcement aroused no response except sympathetic, and perhaps encouraging, nods from the women.

"She had me by some gentleman—she ought to ha' had a twal' month, she did!"

"Wasn't she ever married?" Sophy inquired of her grandmother.

"Married? Yes, course she was," replied the old dame, "of course. But marriage ain't everything. Twice she was, but not to he, she wasn't."

"Not to the gentleman?"

"No! Oh no! He'd got money—bushels! Marriage ain't much, not with these gentry."

"Ho, ho, that's a tidy come-up!" laughed Harvey.

"Who was the gentleman?" Sophia's interest was deeply engaged. But Cassandra Fundy was silent, pondering like a china image. Her gaze was towards the mantelpiece, where there were four lamps—but only one usable—and two clocks—but only one going—and a coloured greeting card a foot long with large letters KEEP SMILING adorned with lithographic honeysuckle.

"She's hard of hearing," interpolated Grandfather Amos, "very hard, gets worse. She've a horn at home, big as that . . ." His eyes roved the room for an object of comparison, and he seized upon the fire shovel that lay in the fender. "Big as that shovel. Crown silver it is, and solid, a beautiful horn, but"—he brandished the shovel before them—"Her won't use 'en."

"Granny, who was that gentleman?" shouted Sophy. "Did you know him?"

"No! No!" declared the indignant dame. "I dunno ever his name, nor I don't want to. He took hisself off to Ameriky, and now he's in the land of heaven. I never seen him. If I had, I'd 'a' given it to him properly; oh, my dear, not blay-guarding him, you know, but just plain language! Where's your seven commandments?"

At last the rain abated. Peeping into the dark garden you could see the fugitive moonlight hung in a million raindrops in the black twigs of all sorts of bushes and trees, while along the cantle of the porch a line of raindrops hung, even and regular, as if they were nailheads made of glass. So all the guests departed, in one long staggering, struggling, giggling, guffawing body, into the village street. The bride and her man stood in the porch, watching, and waving hands. Sophy was momentarily grieving: what a lot of trouble and fuss when you announced that henceforward you were going to sleep with a man because you loved him true! She had said good-bye to her Grandmother Cassandra, to her father and her little sister. She had hung on her mother's breast, sighing an almost intolerable farewell to innocence—never treasured until it is gone—and thenceforward a pretty sorrow cherished more deeply than wilder joys.

Into Harvey's mind, as they stood there at last alone, momentarily stole an image of a bright-haired girl, lovely, silent, sad, whom he felt he had deeply wronged. And he was sorry. He had escaped the snare, but if there had been no snare he might this night have been sleeping with a different bride. And it would have been just as well. Sophy looked but a girl with her blown hair and wet face. She was wiping her tears on the tiny apron. But she had the breasts of a woman and decoying eyes.

"Sophy, Sophy!" breathed Harvey, wooing her in the darkness.

"It blows and it rains, and it rains and it blows," chattered the crumpled bride, "and I'm all so bescambled I can't tell wet from windy."

"Come, my love," whispered the bridegroom, "come in, to home."

VI

Four or five months later the higgler's affairs had again taken a rude turn. Marriage, alas, was not all it might be; his wife and his mother quarrelled unendingly. Sometimes he sided with the one, sometimes with the other. He could not yet afford to install his mother in a separate cottage, and therefore even Sophy had to admit that her mother-in-law had a right to be living there with them, the home being hers. Harvey hadn't bought much of it; and though he was welcome to it all now, and it would be exclusively his as soon as she died, still, it was her furniture and you couldn't drive any woman (even your mother) off her own property. Sophy, who wanted a home of her own, was vexed and moody, and antagonistic to her man. Business, too, had gone down sadly of late. He had thrown up the Shag Moor round months ago; he could not bring himself to go there again, and he had not been able to square up the loss by any substantial new connections. On top of it all his horse died. It stumbled on a hill one day and fell, and it couldn't get up, or it wouldn't—at any rate, it didn't. Harvey thrashed it and coaxed it, then he cursed it and kicked it; after that he sent for a veterinary man, and the

veterinary man ordered it to be shot. And it was shot. A great
blow to Harvey Witlow was that. He had no money to buy another horse; money was tight with him, very tight; and so he
had to hire at fabulous cost a decrepit nag that ate like a good
one. It ate—well, it would have astonished you to see what that
creature disposed of, with hay the price it was, and corn gone
up to heaven nearly. In fact Harvey found that he couldn't stand
the racket much longer, and as he could not possibly buy another it looked very much as if he was in queer street once more,
unless he could borrow the money from some friendly person.
Of course there were plenty of friendly persons but they had no
money, just as there were many persons who had the money
but were not what you might call friendly; and so the higgler
began to reiterate twenty times a day, and forty times a day, that
he was entirely and absolutely damned and done. Things were
thus very bad with him, they were at their worst—for he had a
wife to keep now, as well as a mother, and a horse that ate like
Satan, and worked like a gnat—when it suddenly came into his
mind that Mrs. Sadgrove was reputed to have a lot of money,
and had no call to be unfriendly to him. He had his grave doubts
about the size of her purse, but there could be no harm in trying so long as you approached her in a right reasonable manner.

For a week or two he held off from this appeal, but the grim
spectre of destitution gave him no rest, and so, near the close
of a wild March day he took his desperate courage and his cart
and the decrepit nag to Shag Moor. Wild it was, though dry, and
the wind against them, a vast turmoil of icy air strident and
baffling. The nag threw up its head and declined to trot. Evening was but an hour away, the fury of the wind did not retard
it, nor the clouds hasten it. Low down the sun was quitting the

wrack of storm, exposing a jolly orb of magnifying fire that shone flush under eaves and through the casements of cottages, casting a pattern of lattice and tossing boughs upon the interior walls, lovelier than dreamed-of pictures. The heads of mothers and old dames were also imaged there, recognizable in their black shadows; and little children held up their hands between window and wall to make five-fingered shapes upon the golden screen. To drive on the moor then was to drive into blasts more dire. Darkness began to fall, and bitter cold it was. No birds to be seen, neither beast nor man; empty of everything it was, except sound and a marvel of dying light, and Harvey Witlow of Dinnop with a sour old nag driving from end to end of it. At Prattle Corner dusk was already abroad: there was just one shaft of light that broached a sharp-angled stack in the rickyard, an ark of darkness, along whose top the gads and wooden pins and tilted straws were miraculously fringed in the last glare. Hitching his nag to the palings he knocked at the door, and knew in the gloom that it was Mary who opened it and stood peering forth at him.

"Good evening," he said, touching his hat.

"Oh!" the girl uttered a cry, "higgler! What do you come for?" It was the longest sentence she had ever spoken to him; a sad frightened voice.

"I thought," he began, "I'd call—and see Mrs. Sadgrove. I wondered . . ."

"Mother's dead," said the girl. She drew the door farther back, as if inviting him, and he entered. The door was shut behind him, and they were alone in darkness, together. The girl was deeply grieving. Trembling, he asked the question: "What is it you tell me, Mary?"

"Mother's dead," repeated the girl, "all day, all day, all day." They were close to each other, but he could not see her. All round the house the wind roved lamentingly, shuddering at doors and windows. "She died in the night. The doctor was to have come, but he has not come all day," Mary whispered, "all day, all day. I don't understand; I have waited for him, and he has not come. She died, she was dead in her bed this morning, and I've been alone all day, all day, and I don't know what is to be done."

"I'll go for the doctor," he said hastily, but she took him by the hand and drew him into the kitchen. There was no candle lit; a fire was burning there, richly glowing embers, that laid a gaunt shadow of the table across a corner of the ceiling. Every dish on the dresser gleamed, the stone floor was rosy, and each smooth curve on the dark settle was shining like ice. Without invitation he sat down.

"No," said the girl, in a tremulous voice, "you must help me." She lit a candle: her face was white as the moon, her lips were sharply red, and her eyes were wild. "Come," she said, and he followed her behind the settle and up the stairs to a room where there was a disordered bed, and what might be a body lying under the quilt. The higgler stood still, staring at the form under the quilt. The girl, too, was still and staring. Wind dashed upon the ivy at the window and hallooed like a grieving multitude. A crumpled gown hid the body's head, but thrust from under it, almost as if to greet him, was her naked lean arm, the palm of the hand lying uppermost. At the foot of the bed was a large washing-bowl, with sponge and towels.

"You've been laying her out! Yourself!" exclaimed Witlow. The pale girl set down the candle on a chest of drawers. "Help me now," she said, and moving to the bed she lifted the crumpled gown from off the face of the dead woman, at the same time smoothing the quilt closely up to the body's chin. "I cannot put the gown on, because of her arm, it has gone stiff." She shuddered, and stood holding the gown as if offering it to the man. He lifted that dead naked arm and tried to place it down at the body's side, but it resisted and he let go his hold. The arm swung back to its former outstretched position, as if it still lived and resented that pressure. The girl retreated from the bed with a timorous cry.

"Get me a bandage," he said, "or something we can tear up."

She gave him some pieces of linen.

"I'll finish this for you," he brusquely whispered, "you get along downstairs and take a swig of brandy. Got any brandy?"

She did not move. He put his arm around her and gently urged her to the door.

"Brandy," he repeated, "and light your candles."

He watched her go heavily down the stairs before he shut the door. Returning to the bed he lifted the quilt. The dead body was naked and smelt of soap. Dropping the quilt he lifted the outstretched arm again, like cold wax to the touch and unpliant as a sturdy sapling, and tried once more to bend it to the body's side. As he did so the bedroom door blew open with a crash. It was only a draught of the wind, and a loose latch—Mary had opened a door downstairs, perhaps—but it awed him, as if some invisible looker were there resenting his presence. He went and closed the door, the latch had a loose hasp, and tiptoeing nervously back, he seized the dreadful arm with a sudden brutal energy, and bent it by thrusting his knee violently into the hollow of the elbow. Hurriedly he slipped the gown over the head and inserted the arm in the sleeve. A strange impulse of modesty stayed him for a moment: should he call the girl and let her complete the robing of the naked body under the quilt? That preposterous pause seemed to add a new anger to the wind, and again the door sprang open. He delayed no longer, but letting it remain open, he uncovered the dead woman. As he lifted the chill body the long outstretched arm moved and tilted like the boom of a sail, but crushing it to its side he bound the limb fast with the strips of linen. So Mrs. Sadgrove was made ready for her coffin. Drawing the quilt back to her neck, with a gush of relief he glanced about the room. It was a very ordinary bedroom, bed, washstand, chest of drawers, chair, and two pictures—one of deeply religious import, and the other a little pink print, in a gilded frame, of a bouncing nude nymph recumbent upon a cloud. It was queer: a lot of people, people whom you wouldn't think it of, had that sort of picture in their bedrooms.

Mary was now coming up the stairs again, with a glass half full of liquid. She brought it to him.

"No, you drink it," he urged, and Mary sipped the brandy.

"I've finished—I've finished," he said as he watched her, "she's quite comfortable now."

The girl looked her silent thanks at him, again holding out the glass. "No, sup it yourself," he said; but as she stood in the dim light, regarding him with her strange gaze, and still offering the drink, he took it from her, drained it at a gulp, and put the glass upon the chest, beside the candle. "She's quite comfortable now. I'm very grieved, Mary," he said with awkward kindness, "about all this trouble that's come on you."

She was motionless as a wax image, as if she had died in her steps, her hand still extended as when he took the glass from it. So piercing was her gaze that his own drifted from her face and took in again the objects in the room, the washstand, the candle on the chest, the little pink picture. The wind beat upon the ivy outside the window as if a monstrous whip were lashing its slaves.

"You must notify the registrar," he began again, "but you must see the doctor first."

"I've waited for him all day," Mary whispered, "all day. The nurse will come again soon. She went home to rest in the night." She turned towards the bed. "She has only been ill a week."

"Yes?" he lamely said. "Dear me, it is sudden."

"I must see the doctor," she continued.

"I'll drive you over to him in my gig." He was eager to do that.

"I don't know," said Mary slowly.

"Yes, I'll do that, soon's you're ready. Mary," he fumbled with his speech, "I'm not wanting to pry into your affairs, or anything as don't concern me, but how are you going to get along now? Have you got any relations?"

"No," the girl shook her head, "no."

"That's bad. What was you thinking of doing? How has she left you—things were in a baddish way, weren't they?"

"Oh no." Mary looked up quickly. "She has left me very well off. I shall go on with the farm; there's the old man and the boy—they've gone to a wedding today; I shall go on with it. She was so thoughtful for me, and I would not care to leave all this, I love it."

"But you can't do it by yourself, alone?"

"No. I'm to get a man to superintend, a working bailiff," she said.

"Oh!" And again they were silent. The girl went to the bed and lifted the covering. She saw the bound arm and then drew the quilt tenderly over the dead face. Witlow picked up his hat and found himself staring again at the pink picture. Mary took the candle preparatory to descending the stairs. Suddenly the higgler turned to her and ventured: "Did you know as she once asked me to marry you?" he blurted.

Her eyes turned from him, but he guessed—he could feel that she *had* known.

"I've often wondered why," he murmured, "why she wanted that."

"She didn't," said the girl.

That gave pause to the man; he felt stupid at once, and roved his fingers in a silly way along the roughened nap of his hat.

"Well, she asked me to," he bluntly protested.

"She knew," Mary's voice was no louder than a sigh, "that you were courting another girl, the one you married."

"But, but," stuttered the honest higgler, "if she knew that, why did she want for me to marry you?"

"She didn't," said Mary again; and again, in the pause, he did silly things to his hat. How shy this girl was, how lovely in her modesty and grief!

"I can't make tops or bottoms of it," he said, "but she asked me, as sure as God's my maker."

"I know. It was me, I wanted it."

"You!" he cried, "you wanted to marry me!"

The girl bowed her head, lovely in her grief and modesty. "She was against it, but I made her ask you."

"And I hadn't an idea that you cast a thought on me," he murmured. "I feared it was a sort of trick she was playing on me.

I didn't understand, I had no idea that you knew about it even. And so I didn't ever ask you."

"Oh, why not, why not? I was fond of you then," whispered she. "Mother tried to persuade me against it, but I was fond of you—then."

He was in a queer distress and confusion: "Oh, if you'd only tipped me a word, or given me a sort of look," he sighed. "Oh, Mary!"

She said no more but went downstairs. He followed her and immediately fetched the lamps from his gig. As he lit the candles: "How strange," Mary said, "that you should come back just as I most needed help! I am very grateful."

"Mary, I'll drive you to the doctor's now."

She shook her head; she was smiling.

"Then I'll stay till the nurse comes."

"No, you must go. Go at once."

He picked up the two lamps and, turning at the door, said: "I'll come again tomorrow." Then the wind rushed into the room. "Good-bye," she cried, shutting the door quickly behind him.

He drove away in deep darkness, the wind howling, his thoughts strange and bitter. He had thrown away a love, a love that was dumb and hid itself. By God, he had thrown away a fortune, too! And he had forgotten all about his real errand until now, forgotten all about the loan! Well; let it go; give it up. He would give up higgling; he would take on some other job; a bailiff, a working bailiff, that was the job as would suit him, a working bailiff. Of course, there was Sophy; but still—Sophy!

Fishmonger's Fiddle (1925)

Dusky Ruth

❧

AT THE CLOSE OF AN APRIL DAY, CHILLY AND WET, THE traveller came to a country town. In the Cotswolds, though the towns are small and sweet and the inns snug, the general habit of the land is bleak and bare. He had newly come upon upland roads so void of human affairs, so lonely, that they might have been made for some forgotten uses by departed men, and left to the unwitting passage of such strangers as himself. Even the unending walls, built of old rough laminated rock, that detailed the far-spreading fields, had grown very old again in their courses; there were dabs of darkness, buttons of moss, and fossils on every stone. He had passed a few neighbourhoods, sometimes at the crook of a stream, or at the cross of debouching roads, where old habitations, their gangrenated thatch riddled with bird holes, had been not so much erected as just spattered about the places. Beyond these signs an odd lark or blackbird, the ruckle of partridges, or the nifty gallop of a hare had been the only mitigation of the living loneliness that was almost as profound by day as by night. But the traveller had a care for such times and places. There are men who love to gaze with the mind at things that can never be seen, feel at least the throb of a beauty that will never be known, and hear over immense bleak reaches the echo of that which is no celestial music, but only their own hearts' vain cries; and though his garments clung to him like clay it was with deliberate questing step that the traveller trod the single street of the town, and at last entered the inn, shuffling his shoes in the doorway for a moment and striking the raindrops from his hat. Then he turned into a small smoking-room. Leather-lined benches, much worn, were fixed to the wall under the window and in other odd corners and nooks behind mahogany tables. One wall was furnished with all the congenial gear of a bar, but without any intervening counter. Opposite, a bright fire was burning, and a neatly dressed young woman sat before it in a Windsor chair, staring at the flames. There was no other inmate of the room, and as he entered, the girl rose up and greeted him. He found that he could be accommodated for the night, and in a few moments his hat and scarf were removed and placed inside the fender, his wet overcoat was taken to the kitchen, the landlord, an old fellow, was lending him a roomy pair of slippers, and a maid was setting supper in an adjoining room.

He sat while this was doing and talked to the barmaid. She had a beautiful but rather mournful face as it was lit by the fire-light, and when her glance was turned away from it her eyes had a piercing brightness. Friendly and well spoken as she was, the melancholy in her aspect was noticeable—perhaps it was the dim room, or the wet day, or the long hours ministering a multitude of cocktails to thirsty gallantry.

When he went to his supper he found cheering food and drink, with pleasant garniture of silver and mahogany. There were no other visitors, he was to be alone; blinds were drawn, lamps lit, and the fire at his back was comforting. So he sat long about his meal until a white-faced maid came to clear the table, discoursing to him about country things as she busied about the room. It was a long, narrow room, with a sideboard and the door at one end and the fireplace at the other. A bookshelf, almost devoid of books, contained a number of plates; the long wall that faced the windows was almost destitute of pictures, but there were hung upon it, for some inscrutable but doubtless sufficient reason, many dish-covers, solidly shaped, of the kind held in such mysterious regard and known as "willow pattern"; one was even hung upon the face of a map. Two musty prints were mixed with them, presentments of horses having a stilted extravagant physique and bestridden by images of inhuman and incommunicable dignity, clothed in whiskers, coloured jackets, and tight white breeches.

He took down the books from the shelf, but his interest was speedily exhausted, and the almanacs, the county directory, and various guide-books were exchanged for the *Cotswold Chronicle*. With this, having drawn the deep chair to the hearth, he whiled away the time. The newspaper amused him with its advertisements of stock shows, farm auctions, travelling quacks and conjurers, and there was a lengthy account of the execution of a local felon, one Timothy Bridger, who had murdered an infant in some shameful circumstances. This dazzling crescendo proved rather trying to the traveller; he threw down the paper.

The town was all as quiet as the hills, and he could hear no sounds in the house. He got up and went across the hall to the smoke-room. The door was shut, but there was light within, and he entered. The girl sat there much as he had seen her on his arrival, still alone, with feet on fender. He shut the door behind him, sat down, and crossing his legs puffed at his pipe, admired the snug little room and the pretty figure of the girl, which he could do without embarrassment, as her meditative head, slightly bowed, was turned away from him. He could see something of her, too, in the mirror at the bar, which repeated also the agreeable contours of bottles of coloured wines and rich liqueurs—so entrancing in form and aspect that they seemed destined to charming histories, even in disuse—and those of familiar outline containing mere spirits or small beer, for which are reserved the harsher destinies of base oils, horse medicines, disinfectants, and cold tea. There were coloured glasses for bitter wines, white glasses for sweet, a tiny leaden sink beneath them, and the four black handles of the beer engines.

The girl wore a light blouse of silk, a short skirt of black velvet, and a pair of very thin silk stockings that showed the flesh of instep and shin so plainly that he could see they were reddened by the warmth of the fire. She had on a pair of dainty cloth shoes with high heels, but what was wonderful about her was the heap of rich black hair piled at the back of her head and shadowing the dusky neck. He sat puffing his pipe and letting the loud tick of the clock fill the quiet room. She did not stir and he could move no muscle. It was as if he had been willed to come there and wait silently. That, he felt now, had been his desire all the evening; and here, in her presence, he was more strangely stirred in a few short minutes than by any event he could remember.

In youth he had viewed women as futile, pitiable things that grew long hair, wore stays and garters, and prayed incomprehensible prayers. Viewing them in the stalls of the theatre from his vantage-point in the gallery, he always disliked the articulation of their naked shoulders. But still, there was a god in the sky, a god with flowing hair and exquisite eyes, whose one stride with an ardour grandly rendered took him across the whole round hemisphere to which his buoyant limbs were bound like spokes to the eternal rim and axle, his bright hair burning in the pity of the sunsets and tossing in the anger of the dawns.

Master traveller had indeed come into this room to be with this woman, and she as surely desired him, and for all its accidental occasion it was as if he, walking the ways of the world, had suddenly come upon what, what so imaginable with all permitted reverence as, well, just a shrine; and he, admirably humble, bowed the instant head.

Were there no other people within? The clock indicated a few minutes to nine. He sat on, still as stone, and the woman might have been of wax for all the movement or sound she made. There was allurement in the air between them; he had forborne his smoking, the pipe grew cold between his teeth. He waited for a look from her, a movement to break the trance of silence. No footfall in street or house, no voice in the inn but the clock, beating away as if pronouncing a doom. Suddenly it rasped out nine large notes, a bell in the town repeated them dolefully, and a cuckoo no farther than the kitchen mocked them with three times three. After that came the weak steps of the old landlord along the hall, the slam of doors, the clatter of lock and bolt, and then the silence returning unendurably upon them.

He rose and stood behind her; he touched the black hair. She made no movement or sign. He pulled out two or three combs and, dropping them into her lap, let the whole mass tumble about his hands. It had a curious harsh touch in the unravelling, but was so full and shining; black as a rook's wings it was. He slid his palms through it. His fingers searched it and fought with its fine strangeness; into his mind there travelled a serious thought, stilling his wayward fancy—this was no wayward fancy, but a rite accomplishing itself! (*Run, run, silly man, y'are lost!*) But having got so far, he burnt his boats, leaned over, and drew her face back to him. And at that, seizing his wrists, she gave him back ardour for ardour, pressing his hands to her bosom, while the kiss was sealed and sealed again. Then she sprang up and picking his scarf and hat from the fender said:

"I have been drying them for you, but the hat has shrunk a bit, I'm sure—I tried it on."

He took them from her and put them behind him; he leaned lightly back upon the table, holding it with both his hands behind him; he could not speak.

"Aren't you going to thank me for drying them?" she asked, picking her combs from the rug and repinning her hair.

"I wonder why we did that?" he asked, shamedly.

"It is what I'm thinking too," she said.

"You were so beautiful about—about it, you know."

She made no rejoinder, but continued to bind her hair, looking brightly at him under her brows. When she had finished she went close to him.

"Will that do?"

"I'll take it down again."

"No, no, the old man or the old woman will be coming in."

"What of that?" he said, taking her into his arms. "Tell me your name."

She shook her head, but she returned his kisses and stroked his hair and shoulders with beautifully melting gestures.

"What is your name? I want to call you by your name," he said. "I can't keep calling you Lovely Woman, Lovely Woman."

Again she shook her head and was dumb.

"I'll call you Ruth, then, Dusky Ruth, Ruth of the black, beautiful hair."

"That is a nice-sounding name—I knew a deaf and dumb girl named Ruth; she went to Nottingham and married an organ-grinder—but I should like it for my name."

"Then I give it to you."

"Mine is so ugly."

"What is it?"

Again the shaken head and the burning caress.

"Then you shall be Ruth; will you keep that name?"

"Yes, if you give me the name I will keep it for you."

Time had indeed taken them by the forelock, and they looked upon a ruddled world.

"I stake my one talent," he said jestingly, "and behold it returns me fortyfold; I feel like the boy who catches three mice with one piece of cheese."

At ten o'clock the girl said:

"I must go and see how *they* are getting on," and she went to the door.

"Are we keeping them up?"

She nodded.

"Are you tired?"

"No, I am not tired." She looked at him doubtfully.

"We ought not to stay in here; go into the coffee room and I'll come there in a few minutes."

"Right," he whispered gaily, "we'll sit up all night."

She stood at the door for him to pass out, and he crossed the hall to the other room. It was in darkness except for the flash of the fire. Standing at the hearth he lit a match for the lamp, but paused at the globe; then he extinguished the match.

"No, it's better to sit in the firelight."

He heard voices at the other end of the house that seemed to have a chiding note in them.

"Lord," he thought, "is she getting into a row?"

Then her steps came echoing over the stone floor of the hall; she opened the door and stood there with a lighted candle in her hand; he stood at the other end of the room, smiling.

"Good night," she said.

"Oh no, no! come along," he protested, but not moving from the hearth.

"Got to go to bed," she answered.

"Are they angry with you?"

"No."

"Well, then, come over here and sit down."

"Got to go to bed," she said again, but she had meanwhile put her candlestick upon the little sideboard and was trimming the wick with a burnt match.

"Oh, come along, just half an hour," he protested. She did not answer, but went on prodding the wick of the candle.

"Ten minutes, then," he said, still not going towards her.

"Five minutes," he begged.

She shook her head and, picking up the candlestick, turned to the door. He did not move, he just called her name: "Ruth!"

She came back then, put down the candlestick, and tiptoed across the room until he met her. The bliss of the embrace was so poignant that he was almost glad when she stood up again and said with affected steadiness, though he heard the tremor in her voice:

"I must get you your candle."

She brought one from the hall, set it on the table in front of him, and struck the match.

"What is my number?" he asked.

"Number-six room," she answered, prodding the wick vaguely with her match, while a slip of white wax dropped over the shoulder of the new candle. "Number six . . . next to mine."

The match burnt out; she said abruptly: "Good night," took up her own candle, and left him there.

In a few moments he ascended the stairs and went into his room. He fastened the door, removed his coat, collar, and slippers, but the rack of passion had seized him and he moved about with no inclination to sleep. He sat down, but there was no medium of distraction. He tried to read the newspaper that he had carried up with him, and without realizing a single phrase he forced himself to read again the whole account of the execution of the miscreant Bridger. When he had finished this he carefully folded the paper and stood up, listening. He went to the parting wall and tapped thereon with his fingertips. He waited half a minute, one minute, two minutes; there was no answering sign. He tapped again, more loudly, with his knuckles, but there was no response, and he tapped many times. He opened his door as noiselessly as possible; along the dark passage there were slips of light under the other doors, the one next his own, and the one beyond that. He stood in the corridor listening to the rumble of old voices in the farther room, the old man and his wife going to their rest. Holding his breath fearfully, he stepped to *her* door and tapped gently upon it. There was no answer, but he could somehow divine her awareness of him; he tapped again; she moved to the door and whispered: "No, no, go away." He turned the handle, the door was locked.

"Let me in," he pleaded. He knew she was standing there an inch or two beyond him.

"Hush," she called softly. "Go away, the old woman has ears like a fox."

He stood silent for a moment.

"Unlock it," he urged; but he got no further reply, and feeling foolish and baffled he moved back to his own room, cast his clothes from him, doused the candle and crept into the bed with soul as wild as a storm-swept forest, his heart beating a vagrant summons. The room filled with strange heat, there was no composure for mind or limb, nothing but flaming visions and furious embraces.

"Morality . . . what is it but agreement with your own soul?"

So he lay for two hours—the clocks chimed twelve—listening with foolish persistency for *her* step along the corridor, fancying every light sound—and the night was full of them—was her hand upon the door.

Suddenly, then—and it seemed as if his very heart would abash the house with its thunder—he could hear distinctly someone knocking on the wall. He got quickly from his bed and stood at his door, listening. Again the knocking was heard, and having half-clothed himself he crept into the passage, which was now in utter darkness, trailing his hand along the wall until he felt her door; it was standing open. He entered her room and closed the door behind him. There was not the faintest gleam of light, he could see nothing. He whispered: "Ruth!"

and she was standing there. She touched him, but not speaking. He put out his hands, and they met round her neck; her hair was flowing in its great wave about her; he put his lips to her face and found that her eyes were streaming with tears, salt and strange and disturbing. In the close darkness he put his arms about her with no thought but to comfort her; one hand had plunged through the long harsh tresses and the other across her hips before he realized that she was ungowned; then he was aware of the softness of her breasts and the cold naked sleekness of her shoulders. But she was crying there, crying silently with great tears, her strange sorrow stifling his desire.

"Ruth, Ruth, my beautiful dear!" he murmured soothingly. He felt for the bed with one hand, and turning back the quilt and sheets, he lifted her in as easily as a mother does her child, replaced the bedding, and, in his clothes, he lay stretched beside her, comforting her. They lay so, innocent as children, for an hour, when she seemed to have gone to sleep. He rose then and went silently to his room, full of weariness.

In the morning he breakfasted without seeing her, but as he had business in the world that gave him just an hour longer at the inn before he left it for good and all, he went into the smoke-room and found her. She greeted him with curious gaze, but merrily enough, for there were other men there now—farmers, a butcher, a registrar, an old, old man. The hour passed, but not these men, and at length he donned his coat, took up his stick, and said good-bye. Her shining glances followed him to the door, and from the window as far as they could view him.

Adam and Eve and Pinch Me (1921)

Ring the Bells of Heaven

~⁊~

To every man his proper gift
Dame Nature gives complete.

I

The sun was glaring over a Suffolk heath that spread on either side of a sandy road thick with dust. The heath had two prevailing colours—the hue of its bracken green and tall, the tint of its flowering ling. These colours were clearly denoted and merged in isolated tracts, as though in the comity of vegetation one had commanded: thus far the purple, and the other: thus far the green. At the edge of the green ferns, haunt of heath fleas and lady-birds, some brown skeletons of last year's foliage, blown there by mournful airs, lay clinging to their youthful offspring as if to say: "Dream not, but mourn for us." On this July afternoon the blue of the sky was swart and clear although some stray clouds, trussed like the wool on a sheep's back, soared over a few odd groups of pine and a white windmill turning on a knoll.

And along the road came padding a small black pony swishing its tail; wisps of dust puffed up from its hoofs, and bareback upon the pony sat a small uncomely boy about ten years old, carrying on his arm a bright tin bucket half full of red currants. The boy, who had the queer name of Blandford Febery, though he commonly answered to the call of "Cheery," was off to meet his father, who had gone to market. The pony pranced along the heath road for a mile or so until they came to the town and so into the market. Mr. Febery was sitting at a table in the cool courtyard of the Tumble Down Dick inn with a group of men clad in cutaway coats and gaiters. He got up, took the bucket of currants from his son, and set it down by the table. "That's my Cheery boy!" he cried gaily, lifting his son from the pony. "Now you jest slip along to Mrs. Farringay's and leave her those currants from me while I put pony in stall, and I'll wait here for you."

"They be large currants, Albert," said George Sands, as Blandford carried them away.

"A fairish sample, George," shouted Mr. Febery, leading the pony off; "but my stomach can't never abide such traffic, it turns on 'em, it do. And all our family be the same."

"Has he got a large family?" asked Henry Ottershaw, a man with a big rosy face and a black patch over one eye.

"He's got two boys," replied George; "two boys and a gal. That one's the oldest."

"He's the very image of his father, whether or no."

"Oh, ay," George answered; "Albert might have spit 'e out of his blessed mouth."

This was only externally true. Albert Febery was a small yeoman farmer of cheerful disposition, for in those days—the 1880's—farming was still a pretty business, and farmers, like his friends bluff George Sands and Henry Ottershaw, were spruce men whose wants were modest and their cares few. But his son was morose, and his wants were not modest.

The sky had grown overcast. Around the inn the air was full of protesting sounds and the smell of ordure, for the cattle were being routed out of the pens and screaming pigs were being lugged into carts. The market was over, though some stall-holders were still trading briskly in sweets and shoddy clothing.

The boy returned from his errand before his father had finished stalling the pony, and he sat himself silently down on the bench beside George Sands.

"I was a-going to begin cutting our oats tomorrow," said Henry Ottershaw, casting a glance at the sky, "but I don't like the look o' they raggedy clouds; they can't hold their water, we shall have a dirty Thursday. I think I do know when rain's about—I can smell it."

"Teasy weather," remarked Sands. "Weather is teasy, you can never be sure. I had ten pole of early potatoes this year in my kitchen garden; sweet and blooming they was. Come a frost in May and cut 'em off like a soot sack."

Ottershaw held up an admonishing finger. "We shall have a hard winter, George, mark you. Last week I was digging up a nut hazel bush and there was a frog and a toad under the root of it. 'Ho, ho,' I says, 'there's a hard weather brewing, you mark my words, people.' I recollect two year ago a man prophesying as this very winter before us now was going to be the worst known for two hundred year. 'Oh my,' I says to him, 'how ever can you recollect all that?' 'Never you mind,' he says, 'it's the God's truth I'm be telling you.'"

"Who was that, Henry?"

"Maybe you don't know him—Will Goodson?"

"Oh, ah! Went bankrupt, didn't he?"

"That's the chap. And owed me thirteen pound ten. He come and told me one day, leaned on the back of his cart and cried till the tears rolled all along the tailboard and dropped on to the road. I saw 'em, couldn't take my eyes off 'em, George."

"Cried! That man Goodson!"

"Like a girl, George."

Sands shook his head and pursed his lips derisively: "A must have put pepper in his eyes."

Young Blandford went into the inn to seek his father. The taproom was empty. On the wall hung a theatre poster:

THE MARKET HALL

TONIGHT

The boy went to it at once and stood intently transcribing its meaning. He made out that it was the bill of a benefit performance with all sorts of attractions for that night only, such as scenes from *The Lady of Lyons* and *The Dumb Man of Manchester*, including a recitation (illuminated with lantern slides) by the world-renowned tragedian, Caesar Truman (*Hamlet, Belphegor, The Duke's Motto*, etc., etc.). At the bottom of the bill was a small woodcut, the picture of a carter with a long whip pulling at a horse that looked tired, and a verse beginning:

"The curfew tolls the knell of parting day."

Mr. Febery came in. "Hallo!" he said. The boy did not answer, and his father peered over his shoulder at the bill.

"That's a nice bit of poetry. Yes, it is; and you'll be able to read it all if you live long enough."

The boy still silently studied it, while his father rambled on: "My! You could hear some grand reciting twenty years ago. You never hear anything like it now. They'd frighten you, they would! They'd make the tears pour out of your eyes, they would then."

"Father," said the boy, "it's tonight, let us go."

"Oh, we can't do that," his father gruffly answered. "No, no, we must have a cup of tea and then cut along home. It's going to rain, I think."

To his amazement his son's eyes were brimmed with tears!

"Oh, father, take me!" cried the boy. "Take me, I *must* go!"

"Hoi! hoi! What's amiss?" the elder sternly asked. "You're too young for that sort of canter, Cheery."

The youngster bent his head, drew his sleeve across his snivelling nose, and sobbed.

"Why, Blandford! What's this ado? Shut up, now, shut up and come and have your tea."

But the boy was inconsolable.

"I tell you we cannot go," the father angrily expostulated. "We cannot go. Your mother would die of fright not knowing where we were."

"I must! I must!" raged the unhappy boy.

George Sands came in and stared alternately at father and at son. "Why, what's he been up to?"

"This infant wants me to take him to the theayter!" Albert explained. "Crying fit to burst! Look at him. Did you ever?"

"Well," Mr. Sands commented, "what a God's the harm of it?"

"'Tain't the harm. Had I known on't I could 'a' told Susan this morning, but Susan don't know; she'd worry herself into her grave afore dark."

"You know," Mr. Sands said, "I like to see a bit of good play-acting myself. If you go I'll come with ye. You can send word to your missus—Jim Easby passes your door within a hundred yards almost. I'll be seeing him in a few minutes."

The elder Febery hovered exasperatingly over this simple solution, but at last gave way and consented.

"All right, George. If you do, see Jim and tell him to tell my missus, will you, as Cheery and me have gone to the performance and won't be home till late. Now dry up!" he exhorted the boy.

"Oh, father!" In a passion of thankfulness the youngster threw his arms around his father's hips.

"God bless my soul!" Mr. Febery was bewildered.

Father and son then went into the parlour and sat down to a tea served with ham and pickled cabbage, for the Tumble Down Dick was an ancient inn, lacy, leathery, and agreeably musty, famed for its good fare. If you halted there and for a moment doubted, you had but to open the precious album of beanfeast tributes that lay on the parlour table and you could doubt no longer. The very first page recorded the immense gratification of the Dredging Department of the London & So-&-So Railway, and not far off was the eulogy of the policemen from Plaistow: "To satisfy thirty-one policemen is no mean feat. We are confident there is no more comfortable hostel place to put up at than Tumble Down Dick's. Signed Sergeant Trepelcock. X Div."

The Feberys ate gustily until George Sands came back after

instructing Jim Easby, and then George Sands sat down to eat too. And he told Cheery what a lot of fine things and comic things and terrible things they would be sure to see at the play; murders and daggers and pistols going off bang, and strangulation and poison, and bushels of blood flowing, enough to perish his little bones; but it would not do for him to be frittened, there was no call to be frittened, for it was all false as the devil's heart. That was what everyone liked—the Lord knew why—it was a corker!

"But I do love a good drama, Albert. A good drama is what I do love."

"Oh, ah!" said Mr. Febery.

"It's education."

"That's it."

"And I reckon it 'ull do him a smartish bit of good. There's ghosts and what all, Cheery. Are you feared of ghosties?"

The boy shook his head, his mouth was full of onion.

"Nor me, neither," said Mr. Sands. "I likes to see a good ghost or two; it brings the hereafter before you, don't it?"

Mr. Febery averred that it certainly did that.

They went to the skittle alley at the back of the inn and the two men began to play a match, but Blandford soon tired of watching them heave the clumping cheeses at the fat ninepins and he stole away. When they had finished their game they found him standing in front of the theatre bill, moving his forefinger slowly along the words of the verse, spelling out those difficult lines about the curfew and the lowing herd. What *was* a curfew, or a knell? And those other words? His untutored mind was bothered, but none the less something had brushed his fancy with magic wings, had touched it indelibly. It set up some astonishing absurdities, and he could not ask his father to explain them.

"Let's be off," cried George, "there's bound to be a crowd if we want a good place."

Across the square they went to the Market Hall and stood for half a weary hour in a crowd clustered about the door, while everyone said jovial pleasant things until the doors were opened, but when the doors were opened all the men fought like tigers and swore and blasted and shoved and screamed. Somehow everybody got into the hall at last and although breathless and bruised they were jovial and pleasant once more. The hall had a bluewashed indigent interior, but there was a platform at one end hidden by curtains of real red velvet with golden tassels, and in front of that a smiling man with a melodeon, a man with a clarionet, and a boy with a triangle and a drum sat and played agreeable music. The boy was no bigger than Cheery, but he performed—as George Sands declared—remarkable well.

"Now you watch," Mr. Febery enjoined his son when the music ceased. "You mustn't say a word, and don't be scared, 'cause it is not real at all. Watch!"

The curtain rolled up. There was nothing to be scared about. It was a short play, all about a clergyman being lathered for a shave by a black footman with a whitewash brush out of a bucketful of soapy suds. The audience rocked with laughter.

"What d'ye think o' that?" panted Mr. Sands as the curtain descended.

The boy smiled a little wanly. "When will they do that bit about the curfew?"

"Curfew? Curfew? Oh, the curfew! Yes, that's the last of all; presently."

The next piece was all about a poor orphan boy named Frankie, and he was adopted by a rich lady and gentleman who had no children of their own. Frankie was not a bit bigger than Blandford Febery; this rich lady and gentleman treated him very, very kindly, and he was being educated for a higher station in life. One evening this rich lady and gentleman left him alone in the study doing his home lessons and went upstairs to their parlour to have a little music. And while he was studying his home lessons and counting on his fingers, a nasty burglar crept through a window behind Frankie and began crawling on his hands and knees towards the gentleman's safe where he kept all his gold and silver. This ugly burglar had a horrible knife in his hand and went crawling very quiet like a snake to steal all the gold and silver, but Frankie happened to catch sight of him and said: "Hoi!" The burglar sprang up. "Silence!" he hissed. But Frankie was too brave for him: "I cannot allow you to pass," he cried. "Silence!" the burglar hissed again, "or I shall cut your head off with my knife." "No," replied Frankie, "I shall not keep silent. You are on mischief bent. You are about to rob my benefactor, to whom I owe everything that is dear." And he called out: "Help! Police!"

Then the burglar jumped on him and stabbed him in the chest. Frankie fell down on the hearthrug, and the burglar felt rather sorry because it was only a child. He bent down and said: "You're not hurt, are you?" Just then the rich lady rushed in and flung herself on top of Frankie and screamed, and Frankie said he was dying and feeling very cold. So the lady said: "Help!" and her rich husband came hurrying in just as Frankie breathed his last. "Merciful Heaven!" moaned the rich man when he saw that all was over. He turned to the burglar, and pointing to the orphan's body on the hearthrug, he asked him very haughtily: "Was yours the hand that struck this innocent youth that deadly blow?" The burglar shuffled and snivelled and then he tearfully said: "I couldn't help it, guvnor; I couldn't, on my honour." But that was not good enough for the rich gentleman; he went to the window and shut it down with a bang. Then he latched it. Then, in a terrible voice, he said to the burglar: "You shall expiate your crime upon the scaffold." And he would have done, too, only, after all, Frankie was not dead, he had only fainted away and was not hurt at all, not the least little bit.

"Damn my heart!" Mr. Sands huskily said. "But that boy acted very remarkable well."

"Of course," Mr. Febery intimated, "it wasn't a boy at all, it was a gal dressed up in boy's clothes."

"I felt perhaps it was," agreed Sands. "No boy could act so noble as that. It ain't in 'em. Later on, a man if you like, but not a boy, no. Well, that was a marvellous good piece o' drama, like life itself, very enjoyable. It moved you, Albert."

"Oh, ah!" said Mr. Febery.

"It did *me,* anyhow."

Cheery sat between them, smitten with dumb wonder as the grandeurs of Thespian art unfolded themselves before his eyes. Filled with immensity, with inexplicable emotions, he wanted at once to be the boy with the triangle, to roll his marvellous drum. He wanted to be Frankie, to be stabbed, to lie down, to die for ever, and then rise again to confound the wickedness of man. But the last piece was now preparing. The curtain rolled up, revealing an empty stage with a white sheet, and on the sheet a circle of light shone with dazzling splendour in the paramount darkness.

"Magic lanterns," whispered Blandford's father.

A pretty picture appeared on the sheet, of some fields and cattle with a thin moon rising; a bell boomed solemnly far off.

"Curfew," Febery whispered.

And then Blandford became aware that the great Caesar Truman was on the stage. He emerged mysteriously from darkness, and now a light followed him wherever he moved. Melodiously his great vibrating voice began to thrill the soul of young Febery with the words of the poem he had read upon the bill. And how beautiful they sounded!

"*The ploughman homeward plods his weary way.*" With what infinite weariness that line was intoned!

"*And leaves the world to darkness,*" declaimed Caesar Truman. There was a long pause of surprise ere the great tragedian added in a soft whisper: "*and to me.*"

Then, after the actor had burst forth again into: "*Now fades the glimmering landscape on the sight,*" he spread his arms wide, hissing with bated breath: "*And all the air a solemn stillness holds.*"

Behind him on the screen the pictures were withdrawn and changed. There was an owl, a churchyard, a farm, men ploughing or reaping or chopping down trees, and then the churchyard again. But few were mindful of these, for the great Caesar Truman had cast them all under his spell. Not least the boy, in whom the voice of the old tragedian was arousing strange incommunicable recognitions. To declare that the uncomely Blandford Febery was never the same again would be no more than saying "Heaven is high" or "The sea is wide." He had not lived till then; the creature we are to know was born in that hour.

The show being over, the two men went across to Tumble Down Dick's to share a quart of ale. George Sands then mounted his saddle cob and rode away. Febery lit his two gig lamps, led out his harnessed mare, and backed her into the gig, while Cheery brought the little pony and tied its halter to a ring on the tailboard. Silently they drove out of town, but Febery, half-way across the dark heath, bent to his son. "That was a rum come-up, Cheery, eh!"

"We didn't see any ghosts," the boy sullenly responded.

"Naw, we didn't neither! Better luck next time, eh!"

At that moment they saw a green light ahead of them, strangely swaying.

"What's that, in the name of God!" Mr. Febery sat bolt upright and pulled guardedly at the reins. An old bearded man carrying a lantern and leading a white mule came stalking out of the bracken.

"It's only old Barnaby; my God, I thought—"

The man with the mule waved his lantern as they drove past him.

"Good night, Ginger!" Mr. Febery yelled, and turned to see if the pony was still securely hitched to the cart tail.

"I'm going to be an actor," said the boy suddenly.

"Are you?" gurgled his father. "You'll make a fine actor, upon my soul you will. Oh, ah!"

II

The boy was robust enough, no illness molested him, but he had never displayed any relish for the work of the farm and after his momentous visit to the theatre he manifested a deep dislike.

Although he did not care much for school he now became studious, made himself a proficient reader, and was generally found with his head stuck in some book or other, any sort of book, borrowed from anybody. It annoyed his father.

"All that truck will make a fool of him! It's nonsense. He'll never be able to turn his hand to any darn thing!"

"Leave him alone," said Mrs. Febery, "he's got a headpiece, and that's what he wants."

But the father was unconvinced. "Susan, it's folly, you know that well. Your headpiece is good and all for the sense that may be in it, but your feet must be set firm afield and your hands guiding the plough. What all can he get from this here *Pilgrim's Progress* and that Shakespeare?"

"Give him a chance, Albert!" protested Susan. "He's young yet."

"At fourteen years of age! Young! Why, my grandfather was married then!"

"Don't lie so, Albert!"

"Well, he was—very nearly! And I started work myself when I was ten. But him! Oh no, I can't make anything out of him."

But at last he made him a corn chandler, and for four or five years Blandford Febery worked in the office of some millers in the market town, lodging during the week with some relations who also dwelt there.

On market days Albert would pop into the office and greet his son, but Blandford derived little pleasure from the visits; he disliked being kissed so childishly in front of his fellow clerks, and was restless until his chattering father said: "Well, so long, Cheery; see you Sunday." And on Sundays Cheery would trudge over the heath to the farm for the day, to kiss his mother and eat mighty meals and be driven back in the gig by his father at night.

After a year, however, he did not visit the farm so often; he was still madly reading, spending all his leisure on book after book. And what for?—what for? some people would privately ask, and answer themselves with a "God knows!"

By the time he was twenty the morose youth had begun to emerge from his uncouthness into the style of a carefully dressed and not unconfident young man. There were rather sullen eyes in his palish face, his lips were unpleasantly thick, and despite his contact with a variety of people he seemed unable to cotton on to any acquaintance, male or female, of more than passing note. But on a sudden—it was during the Boer War—he resigned his post at the millers' office, wrote to his mother saying that he was off to seek his fortune—and disappeared! His mother took the news with fortitude, his brother and sister grew up, his father went on ploughing and sowing and reaping.

Cheery never saw any of them again, he never went back. They thought he had gone off to fight the Boers, but it was not so; he was journeying around the north country with a circus! Knowing something of horses and forage, he was given a job, but he developed an unsuspected talent for announcing the performances of the circus, and so his scope was enlarged. He was not the ring master, he was the gentleman in a tall silk hat who with whip in hand strutted on the platform outside the great tent and harangued the hesitating mob in a picturesque rodomontade that was impressive, and therefore convincing. His perorations commonly produced a rush to the pay-box. This phase did not last a year, for he found an opportunity to join a travelling theatre company and Blandford Febery became an actor, an actor in plays of the kind that the great Caesar Truman himself had once adorned. His rise was rapid indeed; in a year or two he became a line on the bills of the play; soon he became the top line. Then a whole bill was given up to him until you might have thought the play itself was Febery, and nothing but him. Good God, what impossible changes this world does contrive—as if a toad could turn into a giraffe! That taciturn exterior had been harbouring a muffled but burning magniloquence, whose liberation made Blandford Febery.

"A youth to fortune and to fame unknown," the idol of provincial audiences. And the man himself changed with his fortunes. No longer merely a dumb observer and reader, eloquence flowed from his person in gestures as in speech; he was the eccentric, the admired, the envied comrade of his fellow players.

Though not exactly witty, he was stimulating, and often there was a gush of mystical inspiration from him that awed them. Pity it was that he could not retain their pleased regard, but envy accrued against him, and all too soon, conscious of their misjudgment, he grew overbearing, dictatorial, a passionate cantankerous fellow who could flay the rest of the company with contemptuous criticisms. And the company had to suffer him; they thought him a poseur—but a genius none the less; he was a spoiled ass, but a golden one at that. Yet in truth it was not merely success that had turned Blandford Febery's head; not that alone. He was a creature freed who had once been caged, and he was intoxicated by this realization. Having found a talent long buried in a napkin, he imagined that all had talents that they kept secretly hidden, or were too stupid to seek for, still creeping in their cages, wilfully unfree. He wanted something of them, but they could not understand what he wanted, any more than he could understand their want of understanding.

Perhaps he wanted them to be better than they were, better as actors and better as men, for he swore that only by becoming good actors could they become good men. Hoots! Toots! they would answer; they were all as good as good could be! Once Febery felt a violent urge, a quite burning desire, to call them the miserable drunkards, cowards, gamblers, and fornicators he supposed them to be, but he modified the extreme indictment: they were merely liars and shameful toadies! Whereat the oldest member of the company, a man with harsh eyes and turbulent lips who oft-times played Polonius, rebuked him:

"That won't do, Mr. Febery. All the world's a stage, and we have to play the play. In my time," said Polonius, "I have played many parts. I don't mean as an actor but as a citizen of the world, Mr. Febery. Each part gave me an inkling about the truth, and I took my cue from it. My own father used to exhort me when I was a boy at school: 'Never be ashamed to speak the truth.' He told me, instructed me, and impressed it upon me, never to be ashamed of truth. But I soon found that it was the one thing that *did* profoundly shame me! I took my cue from that, I did. D'you understand? To tell lies shamed me to myself perhaps, but that was far, far better than shaming myself to other people, or shaming them. I soon gave it up. Yes, and whatever I said I stuck to as long as it was necessary—it was never very long. So I say what I say now, true or false, devil or no, simply because it suits me best, pleases them, and injures nobody."

Febery sighed, helpless before such abasement.

Pride goes before a fall, it is said, but you must not blame pride for the disaster; Blandford Febery's downfall was due to other causes. One night he got a little tipsy at a leave-taking party—someone was off to America—and Febery fell into a dock at Liverpool, damaging one of his feet so hideously that it could not be properly repaired. Febery was an extremely abstemious man, he had never been drunk before; if one believed in omens and signs it was indeed a warning. As it turned out, the leave-taking party might have served him for his own, for in hospital he was soon made to realize that he would never again be able to strut heroically before the footlights; never any more. Hamlet with a club-foot and a walking-stick was unthinkable. Never any more. Farewell to the stage. The company resigned him, with tears, with sincere lamentations, with good wishes, and the company passed on. Febery never encountered his old actor friends again, for his life seemed to divide itself into segments having no relation to anything that had gone before.

After a sorry spell of months in hospital he endured a month or two of crutches; then, with a stick and the fanciful cloak he always wore, he obtained a temporary lodging at the house of a successful nonconformist draper, one Scrowncer, who had a nonconformist mission in life. In heart Mr. Scrowncer was a kind, kind creature, but in the tactics of conversion he was a regular Mahomet for militancy and yearned to put the devil and all his minions to the edge of the battleaxe of song and salvation.

Mr. Scrowncer knew his man, realized his predicament, and found a use for his unimpaired gift of eloquence. Febery was taken by him to some very emotional services and soon became profoundly meditative. Paying scrupulous attention to Mr. Scrowncer's suggestions—for he was now confronted by a serious monetary dilemma—he appeared at a chapel entertainment and recited Gray's *Elegy* with miraculous effect. Oh, what an instrument for holy work! The draper declared his conviction that the Lord had put Blandford Febery into his hands for His peculiar purpose, and when Mr. Scrowncer outlined that purpose to him Blandford Febery began to believe it too, and was soon put to the proof by Mr. Scrowncer.

Febery was one of those to whom the sensations of things, rather than their meanings, were important. Inspired by occasions that yielded his cherished gift to eloquence a grander scope than ever, he exhorted with the sombre fire and fearful passion so necessary to bring sinners to their penitential knees until the draper was no longer merely certain. Miracles and marvels were to be wrought! It was a divine appointment! Blandford Febery was an angel and minister of grace!

"What do you require of me?" asked Febery.

And Mr. Scrowncer cried: "To speak the truth, and shame the devil!"

The devil! Shame the devil! Some features of oblivion must have rolled over Mr. Febery. Thrilled by his own emotions, he could believe that he himself believed.

"When I was a boy," he said impressively, "my father always exhorted me to speak the truth. He told me, instructed me, and impressed it on me; never to be ashamed of truth. I will, to the best of my power, do what you wish."

In short, he embarked upon the career of a revivalist preacher under the direction of Abner Scrowncer, whose organizing powers as to gimp, cotton flannel, and hairpins were as nothing compared to his genius in such a tremendous Cause. Not at all unmindful of Febery's theatrical renown, Mr. Scrowncer caused the circuits to blaze with posters announcing the new evangelist. Febery did his part with a degree of secular skill not less than his admonitory gifts. It was no uncommon thing for him to appear at midday in the square of some market town uttering the weird incantation:

"Ring the bells of heaven! Reuben Ranzo's gone! Follow me!"

There was plenty to mock at in his appearance, a slightly unshorn, slightly dissolute-looking man. Aided by a stick, he limped along in a curious black cloak. He wore no hat, and his thin sandy hair hung down to his collar. The eyes gleamed and the lips were heavy and thick, there always seemed to be some saliva on them as though some demon possessed him. But there were few that mocked.

"Give way there! By your leave," he would cry, raising a histrionic hand. Open-mouthed the housewives gazed at his fantastic figure, the children shrank, the cattle-drover paused with uplifted stick as Febery went by, and crowds would follow him to an appointed place in the open air to listen to his denunciation of their godless state:

"Listen to me. Do you suppose for one moment that you are the result of some conscious call into the world? You are *not!* It is true that you stand here now—in a bowler hat and corduroy trousers, with a cotton shirt and a moustache copied from a comedian—but do you suppose that *that* was the figure explicit or implicit in the glow of procreative ardour from which you were begotten? It was *not!* All nature grins at you. Nobody, not one, that knew you when you were born could recognize you now. Nobody could imagine the beginning who sees this curious culmination. We are the result of evil tuition, evil environment, and a faculty for imitation. And now," he would quote with soft irony, *"now on this spot we stand with our robust souls."* With both arms menacingly raised he would cry: "All nature grins at you! Here are we, in the midst of teeming life, clinging to existence like a barnacle on a ship's bottom, without a care for our divine meaning. All of us doing business; one way and another, business; some chopping suet, others selling beans. But I will tell you this about your business: one man's meat is another man's poison, one man's evil is another man's good, what profits some is a fraud to many. From its innocent beginning in Eden, our world has turned into a topsy-turvy world. Sometimes it is comically so, but more often it is tragic, and tears arise, and there seems no consolation possible; we feel tender towards our poor silly fellow creatures."

Febery paused, adjusted his cloak, and shifted his stick from the left hand to the right.

"But you must pardon me, you people, if I seem to treat you as though you were simple little children. For you are *not!* We are none of us innocent now, not you, not I, none. We are all black-guards, one time or another, and all responsible for the measure of evil we create. What is to be the issue of it? How shall we escape from this damnation? You say you are helpless in the toils, that life uses us in this way; you tell me that the devil tempted you. Bah! I tell you: every heart conceives its own sin."

"It's true, it's true!" murmured some of the elderly hearers, and though the younger were silent and perturbed, they seemed to agree.

"Do not come whining that the devil tempted you. Don't try to hang your misdeeds on *that* hook—it is overloaded already! You are merely robbing Peter in order to pay Paul. The gospel of redemption may never find the devil, but it *can* find you! Let me tell you a story:

"There was once a rich man who had received many favours from the Enemy of Mankind, and when in the fullness of time he was brought to bed of a sickness, he sent for a notary to make him a will. The notary got out his pen and his ink-horn. 'Sir, what have you got to dispose of?' The man said he desired to leave his body to corruption, his good works to the devil, and his soul to God. 'But—er—you can't make a will like *that!*' said the notary. 'Not! Why not?' asked the sick man. The notary hummed and haaed, and said it was the first time he had ever heard of such a request. 'That's nothing to the point,' the sick man said, 'it's the first time I've had to die, isn't it? Do as I bid you.' So the notary, not daring to enrage the man in his precarious state, wrote out the will and it was properly attested. The man then bade farewell to all his friends and died soon after, and was buried amid great lamentations. But when the will came to be read—my goodness! The fat was in the fire! His friends exclaimed against it, the family declared against it, and everyone said it was scandalous. Long and bitterly they disputed. They swore it was all a machination of the devil, and determined to bring the devil to book about it, they carried the matter to law. But when the judge and jury took the case in hand it was learnt that the devil was not present in court, and what was more—he never *would* be! 'Why, what is this?' the judge asked very sternly; 'has he not been cited to appear?' 'My lord,' said the clerk, 'we have tried to notify him, but it has been found that you can't serve a writ against the devil.' The judge took a peep into his register and saw that this was truly the law of the land. 'So,' said he, 'the will must stand as a good and proper will. His soul must go to God—nobody will deny him that. His body must go to corruption—nobody can dispute it—while his good works must go to the devil; I do not see what can prevent it, anyway! *Fiat justitia,*' he said, 'you can't serve writs against the devil.'"

Although dubiously swayed, the listening crowd was absorbed in him; as the harangue moved on, his denunciations ceased and were exchanged for promises of mystical bliss. "Oh, blessed are the pure in heart." There came a dying fall, and he spoke with tender urgency of a heaven that opened at the gates of Belief, filled with everlasting beauty, the sports of angels, the delight of kings, and every joy familiar as Eve's paradise.

The man's success as a religious orator was as striking as his success as an actor; it spread over an even wider range, curving like a meteor in evangelical orbits from Milford Haven to The Wash, from Carlisle to Canterbury. People flocked to hear him and were straightway smitten with a hysteria in which miracles and marvels indeed were wrought. Nobody was ever cured of a sickness by him—Blandford Febery never attempted that—but he undeniably did influence the lives of thousands of people, ordinary everyday people, those lambs who had no thought of evil until Blandford Febery expounded it, and thereafter no hope of mercy until he came to save them. Even others, some of the notoriously evil, became unnerved, voluntarily confessed their crimes, and went to prison; while a few of the notoriously good, hopeless of attaining any further sanctification, simply went mad and were conveyed to the appropriate asylums. The Scrowncer fraternity revered him as a creature of ultra-human destiny—prophet, saint, perhaps even an archangel! A long period of proselytizing triumphs inspired Mr. Scrowncer with the colossal ambition of founding a new church with a new iconoclastic creed, but Blandford Febery was not so eager.

"No, friend, no; don't make a church of me!" he cried. "I'd rather go psalm-singing in the tropics. Every church, you know, contains the seeds of its own infamy, snares for its own delusion. The way of the Church is to proselytize, to organize, to subsidize; and then, while it stuffs itself with metaphysical mendacities, it suffers its holy inspiration to sicken and die. Do you not see that? Do you not realize that in a short time the sap perishes and the trunk alone is fostered and cherished? It becomes a valuable property—oh, they must keep it in good repair! It becomes a golden casket indeed, though it has never a gem inside! For that is the fate of all organizations, whether of law, religion, politics, patriotism, or commerce; to play the felon Jacob to its brother Esau, over and over again. The idolaters are worshipping a crown, a cross, a button, or a flag. Bah! No churches for me; I'll beat the highways and the hedges."

III

One autumn night, in the Town Hall of a south-coast town where a thousand people had thronged to hear him, he received a new summons. In the forefront of the hall sat an attractive young woman, with another girl beside her not so attractive. Throughout his discourse the pretty girl observed him with a rapt attention that was possibly not entirely devotional, and her appearance, simple, sweet, and perplexed, was just as magnetic to Febery. His eyes constantly encountered her eyes, confronting him with an appeal he had hitherto scarcely allowed himself to recognize. The choir from the local brotherhood broke into his address at designed stages with hymns. At the singing of *Rock of Ages* a stout widower stumbled weeping from the hall, overcome at the remembrances aroused by the hymn, which had been sung at his late wife's funeral. The massed sympathy of the audience flamed into massed worship, and Febery called aloud for penitents. With closed eyes he waited, one skirt of his cloak cast over one shoulder, leaning both hands heavily upon his stick in exhaustion. Moment after moment ticked by; the hesitant people sobbed, groaned, and sighed; no one responded to his call.

Suddenly he beckoned with his finger in the direction of the pretty girl: "Come, lady; come!" At once she rose. There was a slight scuffle with her companion, who tried to retain her, but with averted head she walked to the little room set apart for those who desired the preacher's private intercession. And there, alone, at the close of the meeting Febery found her awaiting him.

Her name was Marie Shutler and her eyes were beautiful. The room was odd as to shape, having the design of a harp, and odd as to its furniture, which was a big table with a red cloth upon it and coconut matting under it. One wall had a brass bracket with a gas lamp, and on the other were old oil paintings of the unknown ancestors of many living sinners. The charming girl stood meekly before him, answering his questions. She was—well—perhaps twenty-one or twenty-two. On one of her clasped fingers was an engagement ring with pearl stones. Febery closed his eyes, the girl did the same, and they stood immobile as though awaiting some pentecostal sign. Yet while still communing the girl peeped at him. At last he asked:

"Do you feel happiness now?"

"No," said the girl.

Febery asked her if there was anything she didn't understand, and the girl began to rack her brains, right and left, but
could think of nothing to say—she could *not!*

"Sister," he entreated, "let—"

At that moment there came a knock upon the door and a
stout bonneted, corseted, beaded dame bustled in.

"Marie! What ever is the matter? Everybody has gone home,
long ago. You must come now." And turning to Febery she continued with a wry smile: "I must tell you, sir, that my daughter
is already converted—aren't you, dear? Long ago, ever since
childhood, she always has been. And I am, too, and so is my
husband—all of us! I can't think what made her do this. What
ever will people think of us, Marie! It is quite a mistake, sir, she
is a really good girl, and she is going to be married soon to a
sound Christian man. Come along now, Marie, we must go. I'm
sorry she has troubled you, sir. Quite unnecessary!"

And seizing the pretty penitent firmly by the arm, Mrs. Shutler led her daughter away. Febery was conscious of something
very much like annoyance—not with the girl; even her pusil-
lanimity was charming!—but with the mother. The bugbear!
the bugaboo!

The mission was continuing for a week, and on the following day, as Febery was limping along under a sunless sky,
he saw the girl sitting on a bench above the sea wall. He was
thrilled to meet her there, though not with surprise: love has
no surprises commensurate with its anticipations. He sat down
with her.

"What made you respond last night?"

She did not reply at first, but he insisted:

"Why? You must tell me why."

The girl answered: "I do not know what made me do it."

"But," he said sternly, "you *must* know!"

"It was silly of me, I was all wrought up," she lamely explained. "And I told my friend not to let me go if I felt like that, and I did not think I should want to, but somehow, after all, I *did* want to, and I really don't know why. She tried to stop me—"

"I saw that," he interjected. "You snatched your hand away."

"It was wrong of me," said the girl.

"Why wrong?"

"I was all wrought up," she had no other interpretation, and sat watching the mild little waves splashing on sad little stones, and people throwing sticks for mad little dogs. Her eyes were beautiful. At length she burst out with: "I hate being good!"

It was Febery's turn to be puzzled.

"Just as much as I hate being bad," Marie continued.

"Those who hatreds cancel each other!" he exclaimed.

She shook her head decidedly. "No."

"Then what is it you want to do, or be?"

It appeared she hardly knew, but she thought she would like to go out into the wide, wide world and study art.

"Art!"

She loved art; it all had such immense significance, didn't he think?

"I have not studied it," he mused. "I have looked at it, some of it, and some of it I like; but I can't understand how one can like it because it is art."

Oh, but *she* understood that perfectly! And then she plied him with so many questions about his old theatrical career that the morning wore away and she had to hurry home.

They met again, they met daily throughout his stay and talked, recklessly, of things that had no connection with the object of the mission. About her approaching marriage, for instance, to the young flourishing ironmonger.

"I do not really want to marry him," the girl confessed.

"But you are engaged!" said the preacher.

"Yes, I suppose I must."

"It is wrong of you."

"I hate being good."

"That is no reason for marrying *him*—marry me!" the preacher said.

For days he had been ruminating angrily about her marriage to the ironmonger, pious though he was said to be, and although he, Febery, was pious too—in fact, all three of them!—his thoughts insidiously dwelt upon marriage, marriage, marriage, and in the company of the girl his mind was conscious of proprieties that his body demurred at. And Marie, too, was tempted, but: "No," she sadly said. "It would not do, it is too late now, I can't now; I hate being bad."

He implored, he wooed, they wrangled. "No, no, no. It is silly of me," she sighed. But at their final good-bye she kissed him fondly.

Away went Febery on his endless mission, and from the far-off towns he was reviving, still deeply impassioned, he importuned her in numerous letters. But Marie was obdurate, tenderly, even pleadingly, so; her vow to the ironmonger had completely enmeshed her timid soul. Or was it the old disparity of youth and age, Febery being now about thirty-five? Or was it that insubstantial fear which, in the guise of steadfastness, rules so many lives? She hated to be bad, and in a few months she married her ironmonger.

Still, the correspondence continued. Her part was affectionate while his, though more formal now, was deeply flattering to a feminine heart. After a year she grew mysteriously unwell and became a partial invalid. He gave her consoling tittle-tattle of the far-off towns he visited, while she wrote to him of her bathchair. None the less she was still acutely disturbing to him. Alas, there were other disturbances in Blandford Febery now. He had begun to doubt—well, everything: the message he had to preach; the validity of the penitence he could so easily evoke; the minds, wills, and habits of the sheep who so soon relapsed into the old rank pastures; and, saddest reflection of all, he doubted even himself until he was less concerned about ultimate truths, or the truths of other people, than with the black truth about Blandford Febery. It was a figure stuffed into a false heroic semblance! These flashing gleams that stirred the multitudes no longer stirred *him*. They portended a holy fire, but the fire was never seen, and none knew better than he that it had never flamed in him, but had burned out of vapours that he conjured for a fee—it was but a mirage. Not love, not righteousness, moved them at all—it was fear! Without the fear of annihilation there could be no religion, and the fear had seduced and subdued mankind. What it had seduced them from did not matter the toss of a ha'penny!—it had seduced them. For its own ends religion, that social flunkey, had traded upon man's fear of extinction and had promised him an eternal reward for a temporary conformity. Not for the sake of being good was goodness wrought, but from fear of everlasting punishment. Faugh! What reality could ever arise from such Thespian fudge!

It was not long before he was at loggerheads with the fraternity in general and with Mr. Scrowncer in particular. Blandford Febery was indisputably the head and front of their great spiritual revival, but Scrowncer was the alloy that shaped it, the hidden plinth of its structure, the provider of the means whereby it throve, and Scrowner had grown uneasy, become alarmed, and at last appalled, at Febery's recusancy. He pleaded, he protested, he argued, he demonstrated clearly that even an ordinary clergyman could confute these new dogmas with one twist of his cloven tongue. He stormed, he ridiculed, he forbade; but Febery believed, and believed violently, that no one saw things as clearly as himself, or felt so deeply as he. Fortitude, he claimed, was his prime virtue. The truth! The truth alone! He would shame the devil still, though it brought him to the stake!

"The devil!" Mr. Scrowncer said. "You do not shame the devil, my poor man, you only shame us all!"

"Well, if the cap fits," roared Febery, "wear it!"

"God forgive you, Febery," then said Mr. Scrowncer, "this is the end. We have come to the parting of the ways."

They had indeed, and Febery was cast out of the fraternity. Sadly the circuits were notified, meetings were cancelled, and the great mission for the time being came to an end. In the numerous windows of the Scrowncer emporiums, amid their displays of the latest things in linoleum blankets and lingerie, appeared the announcement:

SPECIAL NOTICE
I HAVE NOTHING MORE TO DO WITH
BLANDFORD FEBERY.
(*SIGNED*) A SCROWNCER

His fall was complete.

Hard upon this debacle there came the saddest news from Marie, still suffering from her long-standing malady. It had been thought that marriage would effect a cure, but it had not done so, and now, after four years of wedlock, she was despairing and begged to see him once again—it might be for the last time. Without an hour's delay he went off by train to her seaside town. Bright was the day; the summer had been long and dry, yet seemed in no mood to change, mellow breezes were crimping the blue water of the streams, and as he journeyed Febery felt as elated as the pilgrim who had thrown a burden from his back. At times he was ashamed of this joy, but he continued to rejoice. From the station he limped out to the villa where Marie dwelt, with a sardonic smile upon his heavy face, for the long-haired "ginger" preacher was known to many of the passers-by and his cloaked appearance brought caustic comments from others more staidly clothed than he.

Her house had a garden in front with a tennis lawn and a dell under some trees. There was a summer hammock strung up in the dell, but the garden and the hammock were empty. The window blinds were drawn. "She may be away, or gone out," thought Febery as he gave a gentle knock upon the door.

It opened immediately. Her husband and his brother came out, and the door was shut quietly behind them.

"She is sleeping," muttered the husband, while his brother groped in a nook under the windows and brought out three folding chairs, which they opened and stood upon the lawn.

"She is very ill," her husband said moodily, "but she will not take to her bed as she ought now. She is lying down in the room there. Sit down, please, or is it too hot here?"

They sat down and talked of her condition in low tones. Was she so ill! It seemed to Febery that they were disinclined to let him see her again. Of course he had written to her about his loss of faith and his disagreement with Scrowncer, and she had sympathized, she had praised him, but it was clear that her husband deeply disapproved and was antagonistic. Marie had sent for him, a pathetic invitation, and he had flown in response to her. So this was her husband, the successful tradesman! His expensive clothes somehow hung cheaply upon him, and his pale sour face oppressed the visitor. Ten sombre minutes had passed when the door opened quietly and she herself stood there, her soft eyes blinking in the sharp sunlight, her mouth curved in a wry smile. Her dress was creased upon her, for she had been lying down. Malignant Time! How she had changed! Illness had scooped into her beauty, the contours of her face were angular now, and her hair hung in wispy locks. But the prime design was still there, it was beauty in a cloud—Febery's beauty. She walked slowly up to him as he rose, and they exchanged timid greetings.

Quickly her husband led her out of the sunlight to the dell under the trees, and as she sank down into the hammock she bade Febery bring his chair. He did so. The husband and his brother—partners in ironmongery—did not rejoin them, they went strolling up and down the far side of the lawn as though by intention leaving the two friends together. The dell was screened by its trees, the hammock hidden by them.

"Do you like him?" Marie whispered.

"Who?" he asked doubtfully.

"My husband," she said.

Febery made a shrugging gesture.

"You do not like him!" She smiled as though it were no matter.

"Because you married him," he ventured, "and I still love you."

Marie stared at him. Then she groped for his hand and pressed it fondly. She closed her eyes and turned her face away.

"Ha ha ha!" laughed her husband, and "He he he!" his brother tittered in echo. They were apparently telling each other peculiar stories. With a glance at them through the screen of leaves, Febery bent over Marie and kissed her. She opened her eyes.

"Too late," she whispered. All her graceful frailness smote him with grief and longing. There was a small spider running across her bosom; it had jade-green legs and a lemon-coloured body with a brown disk upon it. Febery brushed it away and let his hand glide along her hip.

"Too late," she murmured again. "And I hate being good!"

"Ah, but when you are well?" he said softly, "when you recover—!"

"No use," she sighed. "I'm done for. Can't last much longer. They're only waiting for me to die. Quick, kiss me again—I don't care!"

They heard her husband chortling across the lawn: "Oh dear! Oh dear!" and his brother replying: "That's good, *very* good!"

The stupefied Febery stared over the back of his chair at the scorched grass of the lawn; the tennis net had slackened, the air was full of gnats. Sweat hung upon Febery's brow. How incredible it was! Of course it *could* not be true! What vital men those two looked prancing over there, though their clothes seemed to sag upon them and their shoes were dusty! Marie was wearing slippers of blue leather with white fur on the edges; her stockings were of silk to the knee, and a little beyond. It was piteous, it was impossible, she *could* not be dying—now!

"Tell me," she said. "What you are going to do now you have broken with old Scrowncer?"

"I have no plans," he answered, "I can think only of you."

"And there'll be no more plans for me, either." She spoke with a gay rally. "Lord, I have done nothing, been nothing, seen nothing—and there's Paris, and all those Alps, and the Kremlin, and the Suez Canal!"

He wanted to comfort her with kisses but feared to excite the frail sick woman and sat on despairingly by her side, wondering whether the predicament of Tantalus was not after all said and done more applicable to her than to him.

"You will not go preaching again?"

"Never any more," he said.

"I am glad of that!"

"I feel no gladness, Marie," he averred. "Far from it."

"Ah, don't fail me now, my dear." She smiled, but added ruthlessly: "I never believed in you as a preacher!"

"Not?"

"Of course not."

"I believed in myself."

"As a preacher of the truth! But you don't now, do you?"

What *was* it he *did* believe, or had *once* believed, or could ever believe again? How explain to her, dying as she was, that he had found out he had been preaching—oh, vanity of vanities!—to God and not to man! It was too piteous now to disturb her simple faith. Not now, not now.

"You don't believe in it now?" she iterated urgently, as though a paramount consolation hung upon his expected answer; and moved by her insistence, he conceded:

"I have no—what you call—beliefs, but—"

"Neither have I!" she interjected triumphantly. "Never. I supposed I had—till I met you. Then I knew I had none. They know it too," she whispered.

"Who?"

She nodded towards the lawn. "I am tired of it all. He worries me. He knows I am fond of you and think just as you think, and he wants me to believe now and be good—good!"

"Then why not, Marie?"

She was startled and half rose from the hammock.

"What! Why do you say that—now?"

Febery hesitated; again she urged him: "Why?"

The miserable man said: "You have nothing to lose—now—if—if—"

"You mean now I am dying?" She turned her face away, murmuring: "Yes, I know that. But it would be mean, now, don't you think?"

"Pooh!" he exclaimed.

"Ah, don't fail me now!" she protested with damnable caressing archness. "You have no faith, you never had any at all."

He could not bring himself to utter a reply, but she understood his silence; it confirmed her.

"Nor have I," she said. "I can't have. What is the use of pretending now? I'm just sorry."

Later in the afternoon Febery went away into the town and took a lodging. Her husband did not ask him to stay with them, and indeed Febery shrank from lingering there. He promised

Marie that he would call every day, every day—until—yes, he would come every day.

He called the next day, but she was not to be seen, she was sleeping. Again he called, but she was sleeping, sleeping; her husband almost shooed him away. For three days he hung around the closed house. Then she died.

IV

For months Febery drifted about like a dead leaf at the will of the winds, limping on foot from town to town, doing little or nothing, until he was reduced to beggary and the winter days came on.

"It is time now," said he, "to take my fate in hand." And he thought and thought and went on thinking until his brains were woolly and the soles of his boots worn thin. Forlorn and unshaven, he was no longer fitted for business, from acting he was bitterly resigned, and religion had cast him out. "Is there nothing to which I can turn my hand?" he mournfully mused. "Am I only a spouter of hyperbole and fudge?"

Well, on a Sunday morning he tramped into a little town. By the grace of God it was a fine day, with no sharpness wherever the sunlight lay, and where it lay brightest and best was on a small green common with an old gibbet conserved in its centre. There were men idling about there, plenty of men waiting for the taverns to open, so Febery walked up to the gibbet, took a stand upon its knoll, and began calling the men to come listen to him. And when they came he began to preach to them of the virtues of temperance and the sin of indulgence in strong drink.

Having sworn vows against it ever since he had broken his foot in the dock at Liverpool, no drop of the evil had again passed his stubborn lips. Inspired now by necessity rather than any moral urge, he harangued so passionately, so despairingly, and yet so amusingly that his hearers were moved to applaud him. It was not his theme that arrested and impressed them so much as his appearance; they were enlivened by his gestures and tickled by his style, so that his appeal for a collection at the close met with a generous response, and he left the common with a new hope in his breast while they left it mostly for the purpose of whetting the whistle with an ironical relish. That was one to Febery; he had preached temperance, and the intemperate had paid him jovially. Well, it was no use preaching to the temperate!

He came to another town at evening and again attracted a large audience for his sermon on the evils of drink, with still more profitable results. There was something hoarsely commanding about the man; wild-eyed and with uplifted hands, he seemed to denounce the whole world in most hearty fashion, and the spittle came spurting from his lips.

Some of his hearers were impressed, others were visibly moved, but all were fascinated. When they flung questions at him his repartee delighted them—oh, they liked to be bullied!—and into a handkerchief he had spread on the ground before him their pence fell like showers of leaves on windy autumn days. It was a long, long time before Febery realized that this largesse was not the reward of virtue communicated or acclaimed, but was bestowed upon him because he was a most impressive *amusement*. By then, however, he was launched upon his new career and, uncontrolled by any executives, spoke wherever he happened to be, in any fashion he chose, and with a lugubrious philosophy that deepened as the months rolled by. Now and again offers were made to him by wealthy societies who required him to lecture for them, but he declined, roughly, rudely. Disliking organizations, he chose to live in haphazard fashion on his itinerant alms. That made a hard life of it, and to the wandering man it seemed as though winter would never pass away. Yet neither spring nor summer brought any ease to the sorrow that laboured in his heart, a sorrow that was often mingled with a mysterious resentment. Poor Marie! It was sad—poor baffled woman! She was—good Lord above—she was—well—she had been born a romantic, a romantic without wings! She had had the flame in her breast, but not the wit to fly!

It was not alone the loss of Marie that fretted and consumed him: there was something within *himself,* loneliness and intolerance, that also consumed, that was all of a piece with his strange appearance. The glitter of heaven had dulled, it was no longer desirable; he was of the world, and yet the world disgusted him; he wanted to love it, love it madly, yet he could take no part in it at all. He was cast out, he too was baffled, and his despairing isolation fumed and quavered at his speeches:

"One enters a tavern at night—Stop! Why have you entered here? The mind stammers at the question; it knows there is a subtle answer, but it cannot enunciate it. To drink, to talk, to rest? Bah! Not these alone! One's journey is long, with an end no man knows, from a beginning that none remembers, and on either hand the Green Dragons and the Black Lions and the Pink Ptarmigans blazon their foolish symbols. One enters a tavern at night—to lounge over a bar counter and be absorbed. Absorbed! What do you mean? Absorbed in what? Well, in a twist of harmonious chaos, minute parochial chaos, torn from immensities of isolation. But what are these figures standing here or sitting there, babbling incessantly in gay tones? There is beer before them on the tables. They have hats on. Their faces are ruddy or sallow. They are arrayed in suits with soiled handkerchiefs in the pockets, matches, tobacco, money, and all the intimate revelations of a gnat. They discourse of work, wenching, and horseracing, or they are immersed in mysteries to which I have no clue. It is a world of shirt-button joys, and griefs that would drown in a single tear. How fatuous! What waste, what profanation! I hear a voice that cries: 'Begone! You may not enter here!' Yet the heart pleads for some charity that the soul ever denies, and I long to enter there, to merge myself humbly with these, and be one with its cheap oblivion. 'Begone! Begone! You may not enter here!'

"The world is my tavern. Am I excluded, or is it I that exclude myself? Are there cherubin at the gate of that paradise from which I have known neither expulsion or exclusion, or is that flaming sword merely my own? I know, I know, for it scorches my hand and heart!"

TWO WINTERS FOLLOWED TWO SUMMERS, AND CARELESS of personal welfare, Febery slept often in barns or among the heather, but in the end his self-consuming flame and the quite needless privations he incurred did their work: he was stricken with a fever and carried helpless into a hospital attached to a convent. A convent! There was no escape for Febery, he was dying. The quiet nuns besought him to take the final consolation. Febery declined. There was bliss in all this restful illness, the small white ward, the immaculate nuns, the comfort, the soft passage of the daylight hours. It was a community of gentle women, sisters of mercy indeed. But the nights were full of mortal anguish and fear of what might lie ahead when there were nights no more. A young monk came to sit by his bedside and spoke earnestly. He too seemed to be lit with gleams of that urgent holy rapture that had once been Febery's joy, and the mind of the sick man faltered under his persuasions; at the core of his dying heart an ash of warmth began again to flicker. What beauteous visions still hung in that curious creed! And he had only to submit himself, to cast away his human pride, and say simply and humbly—yes! The word sang in his heart and had almost trembled from his lips when the voice of poor dead Marie came murmuring to his ears:

"Ah, do not fail me now!"

And Febery remembered. He had led her from the cross; they had agreed! Despite everlasting hell he *could* not fail her now. He dared not. With a grim gurgle he recalled an incident at one of the great Scrowncer revivals. A shoemaker on crutches, with both of his legs partially paralysed, had shuffled up to them, a derelict ugly outcast.

"Tell me this," said the poor wretch to a lady helper. "If I get to heaven at last, shall I have a good pair of legs?"

"Oh yes," she answered with gay conviction. "You will have a good pair of legs. You will be hale and hearty and clean and you'll live for ten thousand years."

"And," said the poor shoemaker, cogitating wistfully, "will there be any gals up there?"

The devout young monk spoke on, hopefully, consolingly,

but Febery's life was ebbing away in dreams of heaths with windmills on them, and green marshes with blue brooks and old wooden bridges; of a day when a small boy rode on a black pony into market with a basket of plums or something, and his father had taken him to a theatre.

Polly Oliver (1935)

Olive and Camilla

❧

THEY HAD LIVED AND TRAVELLED TOGETHER FOR twenty years, and this is a part of their history: not much, but all that matters. Ever since reaching marriageable age they had been together, and so neither had married, though Olive had had her two or three occasions of perilous inducement. Being women, they were critical of each other, inseparably critical; being spinsters, they were huffy, tender, sullen, and demure and had quarrelled with each other ten thousand times in a hundred different places during their "wanderings up and down Europe." That was the phrase Camilla used in relating their maidenly Odyssey, which had comprised a multitude of sojourns in the pensions of Belgium, Switzerland, Italy, and France. They quarrelled in Naples and repented in Rome; exploded in anger at Arles, were embittered at Interlaken, parted for ever at Lake Garda, Taormina, and Bruges; but running water never fouls, they had never really been apart, not anywhere. Olive was like that, and so was her friend; such natures could nowise be changed. Camilla Hobbs, slight and prim, had a tiny tinkling mind that tinkled all day long; she was all things to little nothings. The other, Olive Sharples, the portly one, had a mind like a cuckoo-clock; something came out and cried "Cuckoo" now and again, quite sharply, and was done with it. They were moulded thus, one supposes, by the hand of Providence; it could be neither evaded nor altered, it could not even be mitigated, for in Camilla's prim mind and manner there was a prim deprecation of Olive's boorish nature, and for her part Olive resented Camilla's assumption of a superior disposition. Saving a precious month or two in Olive's favour they were both now of a sad age, an age when the path of years slopes downwards to a yawning inexplicable gulf.

"Just fancy!" Camilla said on her forty-fifth birthday—they were at Chamonix then—"We are ninety between us!"

Olive glowered at her friend, though a couple of months really is nothing. "When I am fifty," she declared, "I shall kill myself."

"But why?" Camilla was so interested.

"God, I don't know!" returned Olive.

Camilla brightly brooded for a few moments. "You'll find it very hard to commit suicide; it's not easy, you know, not at all. I've heard time and time again that it's most difficult . . ."

"Pooh!" snorted Olive.

"But I tell you! I tell you I knew a cook at Leamington who swallowed ground glass in her porridge, pounds and pounds, and nothing came of it."

"Pooh!" Olive was contemptuous. "Never say die."

"Well, that's just what people say who can't do it!"

The stream of their companionship was far from being a rill of peaceful water, but it flowed, more and more like a cataract it flowed, and was like to flow on as it had for those twenty years. Otherwise they were friendless! Olive had had enough money to do as she modestly liked, for though she was impulsive her desires were frugal, but Camilla had had nothing except a grandmother. In the beginning of their friendship Olive had carried the penurious Camilla off to Paris, where they mildly studied art and ardently pursued the practice of water-colour painting. Olive, it might be said, transacted doorways and alleys, very shadowy and grim, but otherwise quite nice; and Camilla did streams with bending willow and cow on bank, really sweet. In a year or two Camilla's grandmother died of dropsy and left her a fortune, much larger than Olive's, in bank stock, insurance stock, distillery, coal—oh, a mass of money! And when something tragical happened to half of Olive's property—it was in salt shares or jute shares, such unstable friable material—it became the little fluttering Camilla's joy to play the fairy godmother in her turn. So there they were in a bondage less sentimental than appeared, but more sentimental than was known.

They returned to England for George V's coronation. In the train from Chamonix a siphon of soda-water that Camilla imported into the carriage—it was an inexplicable thing, that bottle of soda-water, as Olive said after the catastrophe: God alone knew why she had bought it—Camilla's siphon, what with the jolting of the train and its own gasobility, burst on the rack. Just burst! A handsome young Frenchwoman travelling in their compartment was almost convulsed with mirth, but Olive, sitting just below the bottle, was drenched, she declared, to the midriff. Camilla lightly deprecated the coarseness of the expression. How could *she* help it if a bottle took it into its head to burst like that! In abrupt savage tones Olive merely repeated that she was soaked to the midriff, and to Camilla's horror she began to divest herself of some of her clothing. Camilla rushed to the windows, pulled down the blinds, and locked the corridor door. The young Frenchwoman sat smiling while Olive removed her corsets and her wetted linen; Camilla rummaged so feverishly in Olive's suitcase that the compartment began to look as if arranged for a jumble sale; there were garments and furbelows strewn everywhere. But at last Olive completed her toilet, the train stopped at a station, the young Frenchwoman got out. Later in the day, when they were nearing Paris, Olive's corsets could not be found.

"What did you do with them?" Olive asked Camilla.

"But I don't think I touched them, Olive. After you took them off I did not see them again. Where do you think you put them? Can't you remember?"

She helped Olive unpack the suitcase, but the stays were not there. And she helped Olive to repack.

"What am I to do?" asked Olive.

Camilla firmly declared that the young Frenchwoman who had travelled with them in the morning must have stolen them.

"What for?" asked Olive.

"Well, what do people steal things for?" There was an air of pellucid reason in Camilla's question, but Olive was scornful.

"Corsets!" she exclaimed.

"I knew a cripple once," declared Olive, "who stole an ear-trumpet."

"That French girl wasn't a cripple."

"No," said Camilla, "but she was married—at least, she wore a wedding ring. She looked as deep as the sea. I am positive she was up to no good."

"Bosh!" said Olive. "What the devil are you talking about?"

"Well, you should not throw your things about as you do."

"Soda-water," snapped Olive, with ferocious dignity, "is no place for a railway carriage."

"You mean—?" asked Camilla with the darling sweetness of a maid of twenty.

"I mean just what I say."

"Oh no, you don't," purred the triumphant one; and she repeated Olive's topsy-turvy phrase. "Ha, ha, that's what you said."

"I did not! Camilla, why are you such a liar? You know it annoys me."

"But I tell you, Olive—"

"I did not! It's absurd. You're a fool."

Well, they got to England and in a few days it began to appear to them as the most lovely country they had ever seen. It was not only that, it was their homeland. Why have we stayed away so long? Why did we not come back before? It was so marvellously much better than anything else in the world, they were sure of that. So much better, too, than their youthful recollection of it, so much improved; and the cleanness! Why did we never come back? Why have we stayed away so long? They did not know; it was astonishing to find your homeland so lovely. Both felt that they could not bear to leave England again; they would settle down and build a house, it was time; their joint age was ninety! But, alas, it was difficult, it was impossible, to dovetail their idea of a house into one agreeable abode.

"I want," said Olive Sharples, "just an English country cottage with a few conveniences. That's all I can afford and all I want."

So she bought an acre of land at the foot of a green hill in the Chilterns and gave orders for the erection of the house of her dreams. Truly it was a charming spot, pasture and park and glebe and spinney and stream, *deliciously* remote, quite half a mile from *any* village, and only to be reached by a *mere* lane. No sooner had her friend made this decision than Camilla too bought land there, half a dozen acres adjoining Olive's, and began to build the house of *her* dreams, a roomy house with a loggia and a balcony, planting her land with fruit trees. The two houses were built close together, by the same men, and Camilla could call out greetings to Olive from her bedroom window before Olive was up in the morning, and Olive could hear her—though she did not always reply. Had Olive suffered herself to peer steadily into her secret thoughts in order to discover her present feeling about Camilla, she would have been perplexed; she might even have been ashamed, but for the comfort of old acquaintance such telescopic introspection was denied her. The new cottage brought her felicity, halcyon days; even her bedroom contented her, so small and clean and bare it was. Beyond bed, washing-stand, mirror, and rug there was almost nothing, and yet she felt that if she were not exceedingly careful she would break something. The ceiling was virgin white, the walls the colour of butter, the floor the colour of chocolate. The grate had never had a fire in it; not a shovelful of ashes had ever been taken from it, and, please God—so it seemed to indicate—never would be. But the bed was soft and reposeful. Oh, heavenly sleep!

The two friends dwelt thus in isolation; there they were, perhaps this was happiness. The isolation was tempered by the usual rural society, a squire who drank, a magistrate who was mad, and a lime-burner whose daughters had been to college and swore like seamen. There was the agreeable Mr. Kippax, a retired fell-monger, in whom Camilla divined a desire to wed somebody—Olive perhaps. He was sixty and played on the violoncello. Often Olive accompanied him on Camilla's grand piano. Crump, crump, he would go; and primp, primp, Olive would reply. He was a serious man, and once when they were alone he asked Olive why she was always so sad.

"I don't know. Am I?"

"Surely," he said, grinning, running his fingers through his long grey hair. "Why are you?"

And Olive thought and thought. "I suppose I want impossible things."

"Such as—?" he interrogated.

"I do not know. I only know that I shall never find them."

Then there were the vicarage people, a young vicar with a passionate complexion who had once been an actor and was now something of an invalid, having had a number of his ribs removed for some unpleasant purpose; charming Mrs. Vicar and a tiny baby. Oh, and Mrs. Lassiter, the wife of a sea captain far away on the seas; yet she was content, and so by inference was the sea captain, for he never came home. There was a dearth of colour in her cheeks, it had crowded into her lips, her hair, her eyes. So young, so beautiful, so trite, there was a fragrant imbecility about her.

Olive and Camilla seldom went out together: the possession of a house is often as much of a judgment as a joy, and as full of ardours as of raptures. Gardens, servants, and tradespeople were not automata that behaved like eight-day clocks, by no means. Olive had an eight-day clock, a small competent little thing; it had to be small to suit her room, but Camilla had three—three eight-day clocks. And on the top of the one in the drawing-room—and really Camilla's house seemed a positive little mansion, all crystal and mirror and white pillars and soft carpets, but it wasn't a mansion any more than Olive's was a cottage—well, on the mantelpiece of the drawing-room, on top of Camilla's largest eight-day clock, there stood the bronze image of a dear belligerent little lion copied in miniature from a Roman antique. The most adorable creature it was, looking as if it were about to mew, for it was no bigger than a kitten although a grown-up lion with a mane and an expression of annoyance as if it had been insulted by an ox—a toy ox. The sweep of its tail was august; the pads of its feet were beautiful crumpled cushions, with claws (like the hooks of a tiny ship) laid on the cushions. Simply ecstatic with anger, most adorable, and Olive loved it as it raged there on Camilla's eight-day clock. But clocks are not like servants. No servant would stay there for long, the place was so lonely, they said, dreadful! And in wet weather the surroundings and approach—there was only a green lane, and half a mile of that—were so muddy, dreadful mud; and when the moon was gone everything was steeped in darkness, and that was dreadful too! As neither Camilla nor Olive could mitigate these natural but unpleasing features—they were, of course, the gifts of Providence—the two ladies, Camilla at any rate, suffered from an ever recurrent domestic Hail and Farewell. What, Camilla would inquire, *did* the servants want? There was the village, barely a mile away; if you climbed the hill you could see it spendidly, a fine meek little village; the woods, the hills, the fields, positively thrust their greenness upon it, bathed it as if in a prism—so that the brown chimney-pots looked red and the yellow ones blue. And the church was new, or so nearly new that you might call it a good second-hand; it was made of brown bricks. Although it had no tower, or even what you might call a belfry, it had got a little square fat chimney over the front gable with a cross of yellow bricks worked into the face of the chimney, while just below that was a bell cupboard stuffed with sparrows' nests. And there were unusual advantages in the village—watercress, for instance. But Camilla's servants came and went, only Olive's Quincy Pugh remained. She was a dark young woman with a white amiable face, amiable curves to her body, the elixir of amiability in her blood, and it was clear to Camilla that *she* only remained because of Luke Feedy. He was the gardener, chiefly employed by Camilla, but he also undertook the work of Olive's plot. Unfortunately Olive's portion was situated immediately under the hill and, fence it how they would, the rabbits always burrowed in and stole Olive's vegetables. They never seemed to attack Camilla's more abundant acreage.

Close beside their houses there was a public footway, but seldom used, leading up into the hills. Solemn steep hills they were, covered with long fawn-hued grass that was never cropped or grazed, and dotted with thousands of pert little juniper bushes, very dark, and a few whitebeam trees whose foliage when tossed by the wind shook on the hillside like bushes of entangled stars. Half-way up the hill path was a bulging bank that tempted climbers to rest, and here, all unknown to Camilla, Olive caused an iron bench to be fixed so that tired persons could recline in comfort and view the grand country that rolled away before them. Even at midsummer it was cool on that height, just as in winter it took the sunbeams warmly. The air roving through the long fawn-hued grass had a soft caressing movement. Darkly green at the foot of the hill began the trees and hedges that diminished in the pastoral infinity of the vale, farther and farther yet, so very far and wide. At times Olive would sit on her iron bench in clear sunlight and watch a shower swilling over half a dozen towns while beyond them, seen through the inundating curtain, very remote indeed lay the last hills of all, brightly glowing and contented. Often Olive would climb to her high seat and bask in the delight, but soon Camilla discovered that the bench was the public gift of Olive. Thereupon lower down the hill Camilla caused a splendid ornate bench of teak with a foot-rest to be installed in a jolly nook surrounded by tall juniper bushes like cypresses, and she planted three or four trailing roses thereby. Whenever Camilla had visitors she would take them up the hill to sit on her splendid bench; even Olive's visitors preferred Camilla's bench and remarked upon its superior charm. So much more handsome it was, and yet Olive could not bear to sit there at all, never alone. And soon she gave up going even to the iron one.

Thus they lived in their rather solitary houses, supporting the infirmities of the domestic spirit by mutual commiseration, and coming to date occasions by the names of those servants—Georgina, Rose, Elizabeth, Sue—whoever happened to be with them when such and such an event occurred. These were not remarkable in any way. The name of Emma Tooting, for instance, only recalled a catastrophe to the parrot. One day she had actually shut the cockatoo—it was a stupid bird, always like a parson nosing about in places where it was not wanted—she had accidentally shut the cockatoo in the oven. The fire had not long been lit, the oven was not hot, Emma Tooting was brushing it out, the cockatoo was watching. Emma Tooting was called away for a few moments by the baker in the yard, came back, saw the door open, slammed it to with her foot, pulled out blower, went upstairs to make bed, came down later to make fire, heard most horrible noises in kitchen, couldn't tell where, didn't know they came from the oven, thought it was the devil, swooned straight away—and the cockatoo was baked. The whole thing completely unnerved Emma Tooting and she gave notice. Such a good cook, too. Mrs. Lassiter and the lime-burner—that was a mysterious business—were thought to have been imprudent in Minnie Hopplecock's time; at any rate, suspicion was giddily engendered then.

"I shouldn't be surprised," Camilla had declared, "if they were all the way, myself. Of course, I don't know, but it would not surprise me one bit. You see, we've only instinct to go upon, suspicion, but what else has anyone ever to go upon in such matters? She is so deep, she's deep as the sea; and as for men—! No, I've only my intuitions, but they are sufficient, otherwise what is the use of an intuition? And what *is* the good of shutting your eyes to the plain facts of life?"

"But why him?" inquired Olive brusquely.

"I suspect him, Olive." Camilla, calmly adjusting a hair-slide, peered at her yellow carpet, which had a design in it, a hundred times repeated, of a spool of cord in red and a shuttlecock in blue. "I suspect him, just as I suspect the man who quotes Plato to me."

Mr. Kippax that is—thought Olive. "But isn't that what Plato's for?" she asked.

"I really don't know what Plato is for, Olive; I have never read Plato; in fact I don't read him at all; I can't read him with enjoyment. Poetry, now, is a thing I can enjoy—like a bath—but I can't talk about it. Can you? I never talk about the things that are precious to me; it's natural to be reserved and secretive. I don't blame Maude Lassiter for that; I don't blame her at all, but she'll be lucky if she gets out of this with a whole skin: it will only be by the skin of her teeth."

"I'd always be content," Olive said, "if I could have the skin of my teeth for a means of escape."

"Quite so," agreed Camilla, "I'm entirely with you. Oh, yes."

Among gardeners Luke Feedy was certainly the pearl. He had come from far away, a man of thirty or thirty-five, without a wife or a home in the world, and now he lodged in the village at Mrs. Thrupcott's cottage; the thatch of her roof was the colour of shag tobacco; her husband cut your hair in his vegetable garden for twopence a time. Luke was tall and powerful, fair and red. All the gardening was done by him, both Olive's and Camilla's, and all the odd and difficult jobs from firewood down to the dynamo for electric light that coughed in Camilla's shed. Bluff but comely, a pleasant man, a very conversational man, and a very attractable man; the maids were always uncommon friendly to him. And so even was Olive, Camilla observed, for she had actually bought him a gun to keep the rabbits out of the garden. Of course a gun was no use for that—Luke said so—yet, morning or evening, Olive would perambulate with the gun, inside or outside the gardens, while Luke Feedy taught her the use of it, until one October day, when it was drawing on to evening—bang!—Olive had killed a rabbit. Camilla had rushed to her balcony. "What is it?" she cried in alarm, for the gun had not often been fired before and the explosion was terrifying. Fifty yards away, with her back towards her, Olive in short black fur jacket, red skirt, and the Cossack boots she wore, was standing quite still holding the gun across her breast. The gardener stalked towards a bush at the foot of the hill, picked up a limp contorted bundle by its long ears, and brought it back to Olive. She had no hat on, her hair was ruffled, her face had gone white. The gardener held up the rabbit, a small soft thing, dead, but its eyes still stared, and its forefeet drooped in a gesture that seemed to beseech pity. Olive swayed away, the hills began to twirl, the house turned upside down, the gun fell from her hands. "Hullo!" cried Luke Feedy, catching the swooning woman against his shoulder. Camilla saw it all and flew to their aid, but by the time she had got down to the garden Feedy was there too, carrying Olive to her own door. Quincy ran for a glass of water, Camilla petted her, and soon all was well. The gardener stood in the room holding his hat against his chest with both hands. A huge fellow he looked in Olive's small apartment. He wore breeches and leggings and a grey shirt with the sleeves uprolled, a pleasant comely man, very powerful, his voice seemed to excite a quiver in the air.

"What a fool I am!" said Olive disgustedly.

"Oh, no," commented the gardener. "Oh no, ma'am; it stands to reason—" He turned to go about his business, but said: "I should have a sip o' brandy now, ma'am, if you'll excuse me mentioning it."

"Cognac!" urged Camilla.

"Don't go, Luke," Olive cried.

"I'll fetch that gun in, ma'am, I fancy it's going to rain." He stalked away, found his coat and put it on (for it was time to go home), and then he fetched in the gun. Camilla had gone.

"Take it away, please," cried Olive. "I never want to see it again. Keep it. Do what you like, it's yours."

"Thank you, ma'am," said the imperturbable Feedy. Two small glasses of cognac and a long slim bottle stood upon a table in the alcove. Olive, still a little wan, pushed one towards him.

"Your very good health, ma'am." Feedy tipped the thimbleful of brandy into his mouth, closed his lips, pursed them, gazed at the ceiling, and sighed. Olive now switched on the light, for the room was growing dimmer every moment. Then she sat down on the settee that faced the fire. An elegant little settee in black satin with crimson piping. The big man stood by the shut door and stared at the walls; he could not tell whether they were blue or green or grey, but the skirting was white and the fireplace was tiled with white tiles. Old and dark the furniture was, though, and the mirror over the mantel was egg-shaped in a black frame. In the alcove made by the bow window stood the round table on crinkled legs, and the alcove itself was lined with a bench of tawny velvet cushions. Feedy put his empty glass upon the table.

"Do have some more; help yourself," said Olive, and Luke refilled the glass and drank again amid silence. Olive did not face him—she was staring into the fire—but she could feel his immense presence. There was an aroma, something of earth, something of man, about him, strange and exciting. A shower of rain dashed at the windows.

"You had better sit down until the rain stops." Olive poked a tall hassock to the fireplace with her foot, and Luke, squatting upon it, his huge boots covering quite a large piece of the rug there, twirled the half-empty glass between his finger and thumb.

"Last time I drunk brandy," he mused, "was with a lady in her room, just this way."

Olive could stare at him now.

"She was mad," he explained.

"Oh," said Olive, as if disappointed.

"She's dead now," continued Luke, sipping.

Olive, without uttering a word, seemed to encourage his reminiscence.

"A Yorkshire lady she was, used to live in the manor house, near where I was then; a lonely place. Her brother had bought it because it was lonely, and sent her there to keep her quiet because she had been crossed in love, as they say, and took to drink for the sorrow of it; rich family, bankers, Croxton the name, if you ever heard of them?"

Olive, lolling back and sipping brandy, shook her head.

"A middling-size lady, about forty-five she was, but very nice to look at—you'd never think she was daft—and used to live at the big house with only a lot of servants and a butler in charge of her, name of Scrivens. None of her family ever came near her, nobody ever came to visit her. There was a big motor-car and they kept some horses, but she always liked to be tramping about alone; everybody knew her, poor daft thing, and called her Miss Mary, 'stead of by her surname, Croxton, a rich family; bankers they were. Quite daft. One morning I was going to my work—I was faggoting then in Hanging Copse—and I'd got my bill-hook, my axe, and my saw in a bag on my back, when I see Miss Mary coming down the road towards me. 'Twas a bright spring morning and cold 'cause 'twas rather early; a rare wind on, and blew sharp enough to shave you; it blew the very pigeons out the trees, but she'd got neither jacket or hat and her hair was wild. 'Good morning, miss,' I said, and she said: 'Good morning,' and stopped. So I stopped, too; I didn't quite know what to be at, so I said: 'Do you know where you are going?'"

"Look here," interrupted Olive, glancing vacantly around the room. "It's still raining; light your pipe."

"Thank you, ma'am," Luke began to prepare his pipe. "'Do you know where you're going?' I asked her, 'No,' she says. 'I've lost my way; where am I?' and she put"—Luke paused to strike a match and ignite the tobacco—"Put her arm in my arm and said: 'Take me home.' 'You're walking away from home,' I said, so she turned back with me and we started off to her home. Two miles away or more it was. 'It is kind of you,' she says, and she kept on chattering as if we were two cousins, you might say. 'You ought to be more careful and have your jacket on,' I said to her. 'I didn't think, I can't help it,' she says; 'it's the time o' love; as soon as the elder leaf is as big as a mouse's ear I want to be blown about the world,' she says. Of course she was thinking to find someone as she'd lost. She dropped a few tears. 'You must take care of yourself these rough mornings,' I said, 'or you'll be catching the inflammation.' Then we come to a public-house, The Bank of England's the name of it, and Miss Mary asks me if we could get some refreshment there. 'That you can't,' I said ('cause I knew about her drinking), 'it's shut,' so on we went as far as Bernard's Bridge. She had to stop a few minutes there to look over in the river, all very blue and crimped with the wind; and there was a boat-house there, and a new boat cocked upside down on some trestles on the landing, and a chap laying on his back blowing in the boat with a pair of bellows. Well, on we goes, and presently she pulls out her purse. 'I'm putting you to a lot of trouble,' she says. 'Not at all, miss,' I said, but she give me a sovereign, then and there, she give me a sovereign."

Olive was staring at the man's hands; the garden soil was chalky, and his hands were covered with fine milky dust that left the skin smooth and the markings very plain.

"I didn't want to take the money, ma'am, but I had to, of course; her being such a grand lady it wasn't my place to refuse."

Olive had heard of such munificence before; the invariable outcome, the denouement of Feedy's stories, the crown, the peak, the apex of them all was that somebody, at some point or other, gave him a sovereign. Neither more nor less. Never anything else. Olive thought it unusual for so *many* people . . .

"—and I says: 'I'm very pleased, miss, to be a help to anyone in trouble.' 'That's most good of you,' she said to me. 'That's most good of you; it's the time of year I must go about the world, or I'd die,' she says. By and by we come to the manor house and we marched arm in arm right up to the front door and I rong the bell. I was just turning away to leave her there, but she laid hold of my arm again. 'I want you to stop,' she says, 'you've been so kind to me.' It was a bright fresh morning, and I rong the bell. 'I want you to stop,' she says. Then the butler opened the door. 'Scrivens,' she says, 'this man has been very kind to me; give him a sovereign, will you.' Scrivens looked very straight at me, but I gave him as good as he sent, and the lady stepped into the hall. I had to follow her. 'Come in,' she says, and there was I in the dining-room, while Scrivens nipped off somewhere to get the money. Well, I had to set down on a chair while she popped out at another door. I hadn't hardly set down when in she come again with a lighted candle in one hand and a silver teapot in the other. She held the teapot up and says: 'Have some?' and then she got two little cups and saucers out of a chiffonier and set them on the table and filled them out of the silver teapot.

'There you are,' she says, and she up with her cup and dronk it right off. I couldn't see no milk and no sugar and I was a bit flabbergasted, but I takes a swig—and what do you think? It was brandy, just raw brandy; nearly made the tears come out of my eyes, 'specially that first cup. All of a sudden she dropped on a sofy and went straight off to sleep, and there was I left with that candle burning on the table in broad daylight. Course I blew it out, and the butler came in and gave me the other sovereign, and I went off to my work. Rare good-hearted lady, ma'am. Pity," sighed the gardener. He sat hunched on the hassock, staring into the fire, and puffing smoke. There was attraction in the lines of his figure squatting beside her hearth, a sort of huge power. Olive wondered if she might sketch him some time, but she had not sketched for years now. He said that the rain had stopped, and got up to go. Glancing at the window Olive saw it was quite dark; the panes were crowded on the outside with moths trying to get in to the light.

"What a lot of mawths there be!" said Luke.

Olive went to the window to watch them. Swarms of fat brown furry moths with large heads pattered and fluttered silently about the shut panes, forming themselves into a kind of curtain on the black window. Now and then one of their eyes would catch a reflection from the light and it would burn with a fiery crimson glow.

"Good night, ma'am," the gardener said, taking the gun away with him. Outside, he picked up the dead rabbit and put it in his pocket. Olive drew the curtains; she did not like the moths' eyes, they were demons' eyes, and they filled her with melancholy. She took the tall brandy bottle from the table and went to replace it in a cabinet. In the cabinet she saw her little silver teapot, a silver teapot on a silver tray with a bowl and a jug. Something impelled her to fill the teapot from the long slim bottle. She poured out a cup and drank it quickly. Another. Then she switched out the light, stumbled to the couch, and fell upon it, laughing stupidly and kicking her heels with playful fury.

That was the beginning of Olive's graceless decline, her pitiable lapse into intemperance. Camilla one May evening had trotted across to Olive's cottage; afterwards she could recall every detail of that tiniest of journeys; rain had fallen and left a sort of crisp humidity in the gloomy air; on the pathway to Olive's door she nearly stepped on a large hairy caterpillar solemnly confronting a sleek nude slug. That lovely tree by Olive's door was desolated, she remembered; the blossoms had fallen from the flowering cherry tree so wonderfully bloomed; its virginal bridal had left only a litter and a breath of despair. And then inside Olive's hall was the absurd old blunderbuss hanging on a strap, its barrel so large that you could slip an egg into it. Camilla fluttered into her friend's drawing-room. "Olive could you lend me your gridiron?" And there was Olive lounging on the settee simply incredibly drunk! In daylight! It was about six o'clock of a May day. And Olive was so indecently jovial that Camilla, smitten with grief, burst into tears and rushed away home again.

She came back of course; she never ceased coming back, hour by hour, day after day; never would she leave Olive alone to her wretched debauches. Camilla was drenched with compunction, filled with divine energy; until she had dragged Olive from her trough, had taken her to live with her again under her own cherishing wings, she would have no rest. But Olive was not always tipsy, and though moved by Camilla's solicitude, she refused to budge, or "make an effort," or do any of the troublesome things so dear to the heart of a friend. Fond as she was of Camilla, she had a disinclination—of course she was fond of her, there was nothing she would not do for Camilla Hobbs—a disinclination to reside with her again. What if they had lived together for twenty years? It is a great nuisance that one's loves are determined not by judgment but by the feelings. There are two simple tests of any friendly relationship: can you happily share your bed with your friend, and can you, without unease, watch him or her partake of food? If you can do either of these things with amiability, to say nothing of joy, it is well between you; if you can do both it is a sign that your affection is rooted in immortal soil. Now, Olive was forthright about food; she just ate it, that was what it was for. But she knew that even at breakfast Camilla would cut her bread into little cubes or little diamonds; if she had been able to she would surely have cut it into little lozenges or little marbles; in fact, the butter was patted into balls the same as you had in restaurants. Every shred of fat would be laboriously shaved from the rasher and discarded. The cube or the diamond would be rolled in what Camilla called the "jewse"—for her to swallow the grease but not the fat was a horrible mortification to Olive—rolled and rolled and then impaled by the fork. Snip off a wafer of bacon, impale it; a triangle of white egg, impale that; plunge the whole into the yolk. Then, so carefully, with such desperate care, a granule of salt, the merest breath of pepper. Now the knife must pursue with infinite patience one or two minuscular crumbs idling in the plate and at last wipe them gloatingly upon the mass. With her fork lavishly furnished and elegantly poised, Camilla would then bend to peer at sentences in her correspondence and perhaps briskly inquire:

"Why are you so glum this morning, Olive?"

Of course Olive would not answer.

"Aren't you feeling well, dear?" Camilla would exasperatingly persist, still toying with her letters.

"What?" Olive would say.

Camilla would pop the loaded fork into her mouth, her lips would close tightly upon it, and when she drew the fork slowly from her encompassing lips it would be empty, quite empty and quite clean. Repulsive!

"Why are you so glum?"

"I'm not!"

"Sure? Aren't you?" Camilla would impound another little cube or diamond and glance smilingly at her letters. On that count alone Olive could not possibly resume life with her.

As for sleeping with Camilla—not that it was suggested that she should, but it was the test—Olive's distaste for sharing a bed was ineradicable. In the whole of her life Olive had never known a woman with whom it would have been anything but an intensely unpleasant experience, neither decent nor comfortable. Olive was deeply virginal. And yet there had been two or three men who, perhaps, if it had not been for Camilla—such a prude, such a killjoy—she might—well, goodness only knew. But Camilla had been a jealous harpy, always fond, Olive was certain, of the very men who had been fond of Olive. Even Edgar Salter, who had dallied with them one whole spring in Venice. Why, there was one day in a hayfield on the Lido when the grass was mown in May—it was, oh, fifteen years ago. And before that, in Paris, Hector Dubonnel, and Willie Macmaster! Camilla had been such a lynx, such a collar-round-the-neck, that Olive had found the implications, the necessities of romance quite beyond her grasp. Or, perhaps, the men themselves—they were not at all like the bold men you read about, they were only like the oafs you meet and meet and meet. Years later, in fact not ten years ago, there was the little Italian count in Rouen. They were all dead now, yes, perhaps they were dead. Or married. What was the use? What did it all matter?

Olive would lie abed till midday in torpor and vacancy, and in the afternoon she would mope and mourn in dissolute melancholy. The soul loves to rehearse painful occasions. At evening the shadows cast by the down-going sun would begin to lie aslant the hills and then she would look out of her window, and seeing the bold curves bathed in the last light, she would exclaim upon her folly. "I have not been out in the sunlight all day; it would be nice to go and stand on the hill now and feel the warmth just once." No, she was too weary to climb the hill, but she would certainly go tomorrow, early, and catch the light coming from the opposite heaven. Now it was too late, or too damp, and she was very dull. The weeks idled by until August came with the rattle of the harvest reapers, and then September with the boom of the sportsman's gun in the hollow coombs. Camilla one evening was sitting with her, Camilla who had become a most tender friend, who had realized her extremity, her inexplicable grief; Camilla who was a nuisance, a bore, who knew she was not to be trusted alone with her monstrous weakness for liquor, who constantly urged her to cross the garden and live in peace with her. No, no, she would not. "I should get up in the night and creep away," she thought to herself, "and leave her to hell and the judgment," but all she would reply to

Camilla was: "Enjoy your own life, and I'll do mine. Don't want to burden yourself with a drunken old fool like me."

"Olive! Olive! What are you saying?"

"Drunken fool," repeated Olive sourly. "Don't badger me any more, let me alone, leave me as I am. I—I'll—I dunno—perhaps I'll marry Feedy."

"Nonsense," cried Camilla shrilly. She turned on the light and drew the blinds over the alcove window. "Nonsense," she cried again over her shoulder. "Nonsense."

"You let me alone, I ask you," commanded her friend. "Do as I like."

"But you can't—you can't think—why, don't be stupid!"

"I might. Why shouldn't I? He's a proper man; teach me a lot of things."

Camilla shuddered. "But you can't. You can't, he is going to marry somebody else."

"What's that?" sighed Olive. "Who? Oh God, you're not thinking to marry him yourself, are you? You're not going—"

"Stuff! He's going to marry Quincy. He told me so himself. I'd noticed them for some time, and then, once, I came upon them suddenly, and really—! Honest love-making is all very well, but, of course, one has a responsibility to one's servants. I spoke to him most severely, and he told me."

"Told you what?"

"That they were engaged to be married, so what—"

"Quincy?"

"Yes, so what can one do?"

"Do? God above!" cried Olive. She touched a bell and Quincy came in answer. "Is this true?"

Quincy looked blankly at Miss Sharples.

"Are you going to marry Mr. Feedy?"

"Yes'm."

"When are you going to marry Mr. Feedy?" Olive had risen on unsteady legs.

"As soon as we can get a house, ma'am."

"When will that be?"

The girl smiled. She did not know; there were no houses to be had.

"I won't have it!" shouted Olive suddenly, swaying. "But no, I won't, I won't! You wretched devil! Go away, go off. I won't have you whoring about with that man, I tell you. Go off, off with you; pack your box!"

The flushing girl turned savagely and went out, slamming the door.

"Oh, I'm drunk," moaned Olive, falling to the couch again. "I'm sodden. Camilla, what shall I do?"

"Olive, listen! Olive! Now you *must* come to live with me; you won't be able to replace her. What's the good? Shut up the house and let me take care of you."

"No, stupid wretch I am. Don't want to burden yourself with a stupid wretch." With her knuckle Olive brushed a tear from her haggard eyes.

"Nonsense, darling!" cried her friend. "I want you immensely. Just as we once were, when we were so fond of each other. Aren't you fond of me still, Olive? You'll come, and we'll be so happy again. Shall we go abroad?"

Olive fondled her friend's hand with bemused caresses. "You're too good, Camilla, and I ought to adore you. I do, I do, and I'm a beast."

"No, no, listen."

"Yes, I am. I'm a beast. I tell you I have wicked envious feelings about you, and sneer at you, and despise you in a low secret way. And yet you are, oh, Camilla, yes, you are true and honest and kind, and I know it, I know it." She broke off and stared tragically at her friend. "Camilla, were you ever in love?"

The question startled Camilla.

"Were you?" repeated Olive. "I've never known you to be. Were you ever in love?"

"Oh—sometimes—yes—sometimes."

Olive stared for a moment with a look of silent contempt, then almost guffawed.

"Bah! Sometimes! Good Lord, Camilla. Oh no, no, you've never been in love. Oh no, no."

"But yes, of course," Camilla persisted, with a faint giggle.

"Who? Who with?"

"Why, yes, of course, twenty times at least," admitted the astonishing Camilla.

"But listen, tell me," cried Olive, sitting up eagerly as her friend sat down beside her on the couch. "Tell me—it's you and I—tell me. Really in love?"

"Everybody is in love," said Camilla slowly, "some time or another, and I was very solemnly in love—well—four times. Olive, you mustn't reproach yourself for—for all this. I've been—I've been bad, too."

"Four times! Four times! Perhaps you will understand me, Camilla, now. I've been in love all my life. Any man could have had me, but none did, not one."

"Never mind, dear. I was more foolish than you, that's all, Olive."

"Foolish! But how? It never went very far?"

"As far as I could go."

Olive eyed her friend, the mournful, repentant, drooping Camilla.

"What do you mean? How far?"

Camilla shrugged her shoulders. "As far as love takes you," she said.

"Yes, but—" pursued Olive, "do you mean—?"

"I could go no further," Camilla explained quickly.

"But how—what—were you ever really and truly a lover?"

"If you must know—that is what I mean."

"Four times!"

Camilla nodded.

"But I mean, Camilla, were you really, really, a mistress?"

"Olive, only for a very little while. Oh, my dear," she declined on Olive's breast, "you see, you see, I've been worse, much worse than you. And it's all over. And you'll come back and be good too?"

But her friend's eagerness would suffer no caresses; Olive was sobered and alert. "But—this, I can't understand—while we were together—inseparable we were. Who—did I know them? Who were they?"

Camilla, unexpectedly, again fairly giggled. "Well, then, I wonder if you can remember the young man we knew at Venice—?"

"Edgar Salter, was it?" Olive snapped at the name.

"Yes."

"And the others? Willie Macmaster and Hercules and Count Filippo!" Olive was now fairly raging. Camilla sat with folded hands. "Camilla Hobbs, you're a fiend," screamed Olive, "a fiend, a fiend, an impertinent immoral fool. Oh, how I loathe you!"

"Miss Sharples," said Camilla, rising primly, "I can only say I despise you."

"A fool!" shrieked Olive, burying her face in the couch; "an extraordinary person with a horrible temper and intolerant as a—yes, you are. Oh, intolerable beast!"

"I can hardly expect you to realize, in your present state," returned Camilla, walking to the door, "how disgusting you are to me. You are like a dog that barks at every passer."

"There are people whose minds are as brutal as their words. Will you cease annoying me, Camilla!"

"You imagine"—Camilla wrenched open the door—"You imagine that I'm trying to annoy you. How strange!"

"Oh, you've a poisonous tongue and a poisonous manner; I'm dreadfully ashamed of you."

"Indeed." Camilla stopped and faced her friend challengingly.

"Yes." Olive sat up, nodding wrathfully. "I'm ashamed and deceived and disappointed. You've a coarse soul. Oh," she groaned. "I want kindness, friendship, pity, pity, pity, pity, most of all, pity. I cannot bear it." She flung herself again to the couch and sobbed forlornly.

"Very well, Olive, I will leave you. Good night."

Olive did not reply and Camilla passed out of the room to the front door and opened that. Then: "Oh," she said, "how beautiful, Olive!" She came back into Olive's room and stood with one hand grasping the edge of the door, looking timidly at her friend. "There's a new moon and a big star and a thin fog over the barley field. Come and see."

She went out again to the porch and Olive rose and followed her. "See," cried Camilla, "the barley is goosenecked now, it is ripe for cutting."

Olive stood staring out long and silently. It was exquisite as an Eden evening, with a sleek young moon curled in the fondling clouds; it floated into her melancholy heart. Sweet light, shadows, the moon, the seat, the long hills, the barley field, they twirled in her heart with disastrous memories of Willie Macmaster, Edgar Salter, Hercules, and Count Filippo. All lost, all gone now, and Quincy Pugh was going to marry the gardener.

"Shall I come with you, Camilla? Yes, I can't bear it any longer; I'll come with you now, Camilla, if you'll have me."

Camilla's response was tender and solicitous.

"I'll tell Quincy," said Olive. "She and Luke can have this cottage, just as it is. I shan't want it ever again! They can get married at once." Camilla was ecstatic. "And then will you tell me, Camilla," said Olive, taking her friend's arm, "all about—all about—those men!"

"I will, darling; yes, yes, I will," cried Camilla. "Oh, come along."

The Field of Mustard (1926)

Ninepenny Flute

❦

HARRY DUNNING SOLD ME HIS FLUTE FOR NINEPENCE. I
didn't pay him the money all at once because at that time I was
working for two horrible blokes and they didn't do me right.
One was a Scotchman, and very Scotch, and the other a Jew, one
of these 'ere Jews, and a credit to his race I must say. So I give
Harry Dunning a tanner down and promised him the other as
soon as I could. And this flute—I mean it was a fife—had a little
crack in it near the top, only Harry Dunning said that didn't in-
jure the tune at all because the crack was above the mouth-hole
and the noise had to come out the bottom end. He said he'd get
me into his fife and drum band if I bought it, and as it was no
good him getting me in the band if I hadn't got any flute, I said
I'd give him all the ninepence as soon as I could. So that's how
I began to get real musical. My ma was very musical and after
our dad pegged out she used to sing in the streets along of the
Salvation Army. I didn't care much about that but she wanted
me to get musical too, so I bought this fife and practised on *The*

Wild Scottish Bluebells till Harry Dunning took me one night to the instructor's class in Scrase's basement, after I'd paid him twopence more off the ninepence.

Mrs. Scrase always used to go out on the practice nights. She was a fat woman and their sitting-room wasn't very big and when old Scrase got the big drum in there she said it overpowered her. I suppose that's only woman-like, but all the same I really reckon it was because she didn't care much about music; in fact, I don't think she liked it. Well, there was about a dozen of us there besides old Scrase; one of 'em had a kettledrum all polished up like gold and a lot of little screw taps on it to screw the skin up tighter or not. But it cost a fearful lot and it was only such chaps as Hubert Fossdyke could go in for a drum, his father being a master butcher as sold his own meat and cooked sheep's heads and had a horse and cart. Old Scrase instructed Hubert some way I couldn't get the gauge of. "Daddy—mummy" he used to keep on saying to him, "daddy—mummy," and Hubert would make a roll on the kettledrum that blooming near deafened you. Daddy meant tap it one way with one stick and mummy meant tap it some other way—I couldn't cotton on to it—and it was a treat to hear. I'd much rather have had a kettledrum, they've got more dash than these flutes, only they cost such a fearful lot. And it's Eyes Front for drummers, always, none of your looking to the right or left—Eyes Front! The fifers had little brass gadgets to fit on the flutes and put the music cards in, and old Scrase comes up to me. He was a paperhanger by trade, with a cast in his eye. Not half the size of his missus and he'd got a medal pinned on his lapel for life-saving somebody out of the sea that was drowning, and I made up my mind I'd have a go at learning to swim too, because it's healthy for you and I like medals. There's something about medals, especially when you've got four or five all in a row. And Scrase says to me:

"Can't you read music?"

"I ought to," I says, "I was in a church choir once."

"Yah, but can you *play* it? Let's hear you."

I had a go at some card he give me, but as a matter of fact I was absolutely bamfoozled, because as a matter of fact I never could make anything of this old notation. So I told him I could really play anything if only I heard it once or twice. I'd a good ear for music.

"Oh!" he says; "how'd you get in the church choir if you couldn't read music?"

"I got in all right," I told him.

"Yes, but how?"

"I dunno—I did. But it's this flute, I can't do with it yet, not properly."

"No," he says, "you can't."

"I never played before."

"No," he says, "you ain't."

All the same, after about an hour, off we all goes out for a route march slap up the High Street playing hallelujah on the *Wild Scottish Bluebells*, Hubert in front blurring away on his kettledrum (grand it was) and old Scrase bringing up the rear— whump, whump—on the big 'un. Half the time I didn't know what else we was playing, but I give 'em *Bluebells*, and we kept in step, everybody on the pavements stopping and staring at us and some bits of kids stepping out behind whistling the tune.

I dunno what it is, but there's something in a band makes you want to sock anybody that sauces you, and there was a couple of chaps as gave us a nasty bit of lip. They did; but you mustn't step out of the ranks when you're playing on the march, not without orders. You're all together, doing your best, and you get no thanks for it, no thanks at all. There was these two chaps I made a note of—I know 'em—and when I sees 'em again—! I wonder what they'll have to say then! I shall stipulate for one at a time, of course.

After we had done our route march we finished up outside Scrase's and he give us the dismiss.

"But step inside a minute, boys, will you?" he said. "Just a minute, I'm not satisfied; there's something wrong tonight."

So in we goes. "Shan't keep you a minute," he says, and we all tumbled after him down the basement stairs, and there was Mrs. Scrase frying something hot for supper.

"My God!" she says. "Albert, you ain't going to bring that ruddy drum in here again, are you?"

"No," he says, "I ain't going to do that, Min." And half of us was already in the sitting-room when she says: "What's all these blooming mohawks want here for?"

It was enough to make poor old Albert set about her, but he only said: "They don't want anything to eat, Min. There was something not quite all si-garney about 'em tonight, and I'm just a-trying 'em. Now, boys, I want a bar or two of *The Wild Scottish Bluebells*."

So we ups and tootles a few.

Poor old Albert shook his blooming head. "Damme, whatever is it? Play it again, right through."

We does so.

"God!" he says then. "Play it singly."

So Fashy played it by himself, and Billy Wigg played it, and then it came to my turn and I played it.

"Ar! I thought so!" says Albert. "It's you, is it!"

And so it was. My flute was a different pitch to theirn; not much, only half a note or so, but it properly upset Albert. He grabbed hold of my flute and unscrewed it.

"It's cracked!" he said. "Where'd you get this thing?"

I told him I bought it off Harry Dunning. Harry Dunning said it was quite all right when he sold it to me. I said no it wasn't. "It was cracked," I said, "and you said that didn't matter as I could play alto on it." But Harry Dunning denied that; he denied it. And it surprised me a lot and I didn't like him any the more. I never did like him much, he was only a plasterer's boy though he always made out to be apprenticed to a mason, and I never did like the shape of his nose, it looked bad somehow. He denied it.

"Well, it's no good," Albert said. "Don't you come here with that thing any more."

I tell you, I went red in the face about it, and then, when we got outside again, Harry Dunning asked me for the penny I still owed him on it.

"Not much!" I says. "It's broke, it's out of tune, and Albert says it's no good—you heard him."

"That flute's all right," Harry Dunning says. "Only you can't play it yet."

"I could play it," I says, "if it was a good 'un."

He said: "No, you couldn't do that even. And what do you expect for eight penn'orth?"

"You take it," I says, "and give me back my eightpence."

"Gives nothing," he says. "It cost two and ninepence original— what could you have better than that? Two bob I'm giving you! The flute's perfect. All you got to do is poke a bit of wood up in the top of the mouthpiece part and that will make the pitch same as all ours."

Of course I didn't like him at all, but he was bigger than me. Next day I cut out a round piece of wood and shoved it up in the top of the mouthpiece part. It sounded worse than awful. I must have put up too much. And the worst of it was I couldn't get it down again, so there I was, dished. But I didn't give Harry Dunning the penny I owed him. Not me!

I couldn't afford no more on fifes and drums then, so I didn't go again, I give it up, but my ma was struck more than ever on me getting musical ideas. She even wanted me to be confirmed, but that was the doings of some old priest called Father Isinglass. She'd gone up very high-church all of a sudden and chucked the Salvation Army for the Roman Catholics because she liked confessing her sins. Well, I don't, but she did—only she was very forgetful. She wrote out what she was going to tell Father Isinglass on a little bit of paper, just to remind herself at the end of the week, only she would leave this bit of paper knocking about all over the room, and when I used to read it I couldn't help laughing. Poor old ma! I'm blessed if she didn't forget to take it with her sometimes!

So she wanted me to be confirmed and she wanted me to get some musical ideas, but I said I couldn't contend with 'em both. She said I ought to do one or the other, and I said music was as good as confirmation any day. She said it wasn't *quite* as good, but still it *was* very good and so she let me off being confirmed. To tell you the truth, I did not much care for this holy father she was struck on; his breath smelt rotten, and he brought us some Jerusalem artichokes once that nearly did me in. I got rather keen on the volunteers, only I wasn't grown up enough to join them. They used to go round about our town lugging four great cannons behind some horses and chaps on 'em dressed up like soldiers. They didn't look *quite* like soldiers, not quite, but the drivers had whips and helmets and jackboots with spurs on; and there'd be a squad of volunteers on foot, all dressed up like soldiers, only as it happened our town was a garrison town and had a barracks full of regulars like the Inniskilling Dragoons or the Lancers, and you couldn't help noticing the difference. Especially on Sunday mornings when the proper army turned out from the barracks to go to St. Martin's Church for the service, with the band playing. Hundreds of 'em, all of 'em with swords and spurs and tight trousers with yellow stripes down the leg, dead in step from the front rank to the back one—plonk, plonk, plonk, plonk! When you watched 'em sideways from behind, it looked like one long scorpion with thousands of legs. Going under the railway arch by the pill factory you couldn't hear yourself speak, especially if there was a train going over. And when any of 'em died they did have some grand funerals. Grand and solemn, the poor corpse on the gun carriage leading the regiment for the only time, Union Jack on the corpse, his helmet on top of that, and his old horse walking behind him without a rider. Ma always cried when she saw the horse. There'd be all the regiment following, very slow step, carbines upside down, and the "Dead March." Lord, it made you feel good! And when they'd finished burying him in the cemetery on the hill, they'd fire a few shots up in the air and blow on the bugles. So long, old pal, so long. Then they'd all turn home again, quick march, quick as you like now, with the band playing something lively, like *Biddy McGrah*:

> *Biddy McGrah, the colonel said,*
> *Would you like a soldier made of your son Fred,*
> *With a sword by his side and a fine cocked hat—*
> *Biddy McGrah, how would you like that?*

and everybody would be laughing—nearly everybody—whistling and laughing and jolly like.

Still, the volunteers was quite nice. They was all right. One of the volunteers' wives (he was a sergeant) knew my ma and knew I was musical, so her husband asked us if I would like to join them as a bugle boy. Course, there wasn't any chance of ever going to any wars—I shouldn't have cared a lot for that sort of thing—but I thought it 'ud be grand to have red stripes and a bugle with white cord and tassels. My! So I told my ma to say as I wouldn't mind being a bugler boy as long as there wasn't anything to pay, because I tell you straight you can't keep on for ever buying, buying, buying these here instruments. So this sergeant comes along one evening and takes me with him down to the drill hall to try and see how I could get on with bugles. It was a big hall where these four cannon was kept, but the sergeant took me up some wooden steps to a loft where the practice was going on and set me down on a box and left me there among a lot of chaps dressed anyhow in their ordinary clothes, but they had all got helmets on and I watched 'em blowing on bugles enough to deafen a Greek. Then they had a go on some trumpets made of brass, larger than the bugles and very pretty. I liked 'em much better; there's more music in a trumpet, you know; it makes a nicer kind of noise, much grander and looks more nice. It's the proper thing you have to blow before the King when he goes out, or these judges when they go to assizes, not like these fat little bugles which only give a kind of a moo—there's no comparison.

After about an hour the bandmaster come up to me and asked me what I wanted. Of course, I didn't really know, because the sergeant hadn't told me what to say—they do mess you about, these chaps, and all for nothing. This bandmaster was a posh fellow, all got up with black braid on his tunic and a quiff. Well, I told him something, and he says:

"You're not very big."

"But I'm tough," I says.

"How old are you?"

I told him, and he said I wasn't old enough, but anyway he went and fetched me a bugle to try on. I wasn't half surprised when I found I couldn't blow the thing at all, not a sound, not in five minutes! I hurt my face trying. So then he gets me a trumpet, and the trumpet was no better than the bugle—not for me. And it looked so easy! Well, the result was he said I was too young (of course I knew that already) and too little, and said I should have to eat a lot more pudden for a year or two and then try again. I tell you, I was ashamed about the whole blessed lot of these volunteers. I was quite angry, too. It gets you that way, messing about over sizes and ages when you been left school and out to work for nearly two years. If a chap's old enough to go out to work he's old enough to go bugling. I should say so, and you couldn't expect a nipper like me to play *Annie Lorry* on the thing the very first time. I should say not. Anyhow, I gives him a salute and says: "Good night, sir."

I couldn't find the sergeant, he'd mizzled, so I started off home by myself. It was dark outside and the gas lamps were all alight. Mind you, I was in a great wax, but it somehow made me feel as if I wanted to cry. My ma's a bit that way too, only she cries about nothing at all. This drill hall was in a quiet street, but not far off I sees a crowd where there was a row on. I like a bit of a shindy so I wedges my way in. The row was over a couple of drunken soldiers out in the middle of the road challenging anyone to fight, and nobody 'ud take 'em on! There they was, the crowd all standing on the pavement each side, and the two soldiers prancing up and down the middle of the road offering to pay anyone who'd fight 'em. They'd got forage caps on and spurs and canes in their hands, both of 'em half canned, but one of 'em a bit more mad than the other. He kept on yelling out:

"Come on, ye bastards, I'm the ten-stone champion of Belfast! Forty men I've killed and I've eaten tigers alive!"

Not a soul in that crowd said a word or blinked an eye—he sounded too awful. The second soldier walked behind the other and kept swishing his own leg with his cane and asking everybody very quiet-like: "D'ye want to fight? D'ye want to fight? He's the cock of the world."

As if they would! But it made you feel angry though, it does make you get angry, that kind of thing. I could feel my savage blood surging up, but I thought I'd better keep quiet. Nobody wanted to tackle this champion and he got angrier and angrier, going up to fellows and grabbing them by the lapel of their coats.

"Come on, come on," he said, "it'll do ye the world of good." But the chaps all dodged away from him.

"Almighty God!" the soldier yells, "I must kill somebody. Come on, ye yeller guts, all of ye!" And he picked hold of another chap and spit in his face. Then the people in the back of the crowd started calling out: "Send for the picket. Where's the police?" And I'm blessed if this champion didn't come up to me and say: "D'ye want a bit of a brish?"

I thought to myself: "Lord, shall I have just one good sock at his eye!" but before I knew what I was thinking of I said: "No, thank you, sir," and he passed on to someone else. We all stood silent there like a flock of sheep waiting to be pole-axed and not daring to say a word. I was ashamed, but still, if anyone had tried to move away he'd 'a' been pounced on by this soldier and corpsed straight there. And this pal of his kept swishing his own leg with his cane: "D'ye want to fight? He's the cock of the world."

Now, standing just by the crowd was a deaf and dumb bloke known as Dummy—but I didn't know his right name. Everybody knew him because he *was* dumb and couldn't speak or hear, but these two soldiers didn't know him. Old Dummy stood there with his bowler hat on, but he couldn't 'a' known much about what was going on, being deaf, and anyway he couldn't say anything 'cause he couldn't speak, and this fighting soldier seemed to take a regular fancy to Old Dummy.

"Come on," he roars out at him; "come on, you'll do!" and prances in front of him, wagging his fists. Old Dummy never said a thing—well, he couldn't, you see. But this soldier didn't know that and kept prancing at him till some woman at the back shrieks out:

"Don't you hit him! He's dumb, he is. Let him alone, you dirty coward!"

When the soldier heard that he stopped still and looked all over the crowd. Everybody shivered in their shoes, you could 'a' heard a pin drop.

"What did I hear? Me? Who said that? Who said it?" And he

didn't half swear. He chucked his cane to his pal and marched right into the crowd and banged poor Dummy's hat hard down on his ears.

"Will ye fight?" he says, and poked his ugly face out to Dummy and tells him: "Come on, hit me, hit me here."

Old Dummy could only make a funny noise with his mouth—"Mum . . . um . . . um . . . um . . . um"—and he put up his hands to save his hat. That only made the soldier madder still. He rushed at Dummy and fetched him a terrible slosh across the jaw with his right and followed it up with another biff in the neck with his left. Talk about wallop, I never seen anything like it—and really, there's something grand about this scientific art of boxing. Poor Old Dummy went down like a sow, full stretch on his side with his nose in the gutter. The blood was coming out of his face. He didn't move and he didn't say a word—well, of course, he couldn't. And that did seem to stir up one or two of these people. They began shouting at the soldiers and some picked Dummy up and carried him across into a pub called the Corporation Arms—I could see its gold letters shining sideways because of the gas lamp farther up. When the two soldiers saw the damage they done and the crowd getting so threatening, they went to clear off. The champion got his cane from his pal and marched away like a lord, but his pal stopped to argue with some of the people, and while he was arguing who should come out of the Corporation Arms but Arthur Lark! He was a tough nut, was Arthur Lark, a carriage-cleaner up at the railway; only just left off work, because he still had his uniform on, green corduroys, and was having a drink when they took Dummy in the pub where Arthur was. He come walking up to the crowd very quiet and says: "Is this him?"

They says: "That's one of 'em," they says, and without any more ado Arthur knocked the soldier's pal senseless with one punch. Oh gosh!

"Where's the other?" says Arthur.

Of course he'd gone off, but we all pelted after him, this champion one, and except for a couple of women no one took any notice of that blooming soldier lying in the road like a dead 'un. We soon saw the champion of Belfast staggering along and wagging his cane about, but just then a bobby pops round a corner, sees our crowd, and steps in the road and stops us. A big chap, fifteen stone I bet he was, and I could tell you his number only that wouldn't do! Stops us: "What's all this? What's going on here?"

Arthur Lark never budged an inch. He up and told the bobby what was on and what had happened, what the soldier had done to Dummy. The bobby said: "I'll run the bleeder in."

"That's no good, no," says Arthur, "what's the use a doing that! Soon as you got him the picket 'ull come and fetch him away! You let me have a word or two with him now, just five minutes. Shan't want any more. You turn your eyes another way, you go on up the street for a walk, it's a nice evening, ain't it?"

I can see old Arthur now, a fine bloke with a funny bent face. After a bit more palaver the bobby did a grin. "All right, go on," he says, "but hurry up, and don't forget—I ain't *seen* you, I ain't seen *anything!*"

We went off with a whoop again, and the bobby shouted: "Not so much noise there, please!"

Coughdrop, he was.

When that soldier heard us all coming after him he turned and gave one look and then bolted for his life. We youngsters headed him off a side turning. Arthur got up with him at the bottom of the street, where there's a row of houses with gardens and iron railings facing you. The soldier didn't know whether to run to the right or the left, and Arthur caught him wallop in the gutter. I never saw such a blow in my life, right in the guts, and lifted him fair across the pavement bang into the iron railings. And so help me God, the railings cracked and broke, fair crumbled up, and when the soldier fell the bits fell all over him. He lay down there quiet as a lamb. We gathered round and picked up the bits of iron railing.

"Get up!" says Arthur.

But the soldier wouldn't get up, he said he couldn't, he said it was a foul blow: "It's damn near killed me!"

"Foul!" Arthur says, and he shoved his fist right in front of this soldier's nose: "D'ye see that! Was it a foul blow? Was it?"

"You let me alone," the soldier said, "or you'll be sorry for it." And you could see he was real bad.

"You got that for striking a harmless dumb man what couldn't help hisself," said Arthur.

"How did I know he was dumb?" the soldier said.

"How did you *know!* Couldn't you *see* it? And deaf, too!"

"How did I know he was deaf?" the swaddy said. He was sweating like a stoker and his face was the colour of suet. Anyone could see he was real bad. So Arthur said: "Here, some of you chaps, just fold him up and put him in a tram for the barracks. With my compliments, say." And off goes Arthur as calm as a cucumber! He left us to it. That's what I liked so much about Arthur; so quiet with his old bent face, and no fuss; he just put this soldier out of mess and left us to it. Presently we saw the policeman coming towards us again.

"Come on, soldier," we says, "here's a rozzer coming, you better get up now."

He managed to sit up all right after a bit, and then he says: "Go away or I'll blind the lot of ye to hell!" So we mooched off and left him, because of this rozzer. But I think he was all right—anyways I never heard no more about him nor any of 'em. I suppose he must have been all right, because you don't half cop it for killing a soldier. He was supposed to be the true champion of Belfast, but he didn't like the way Arthur cooked his eggs for him. My God! But there's no doubt about it, boxing is the most patriotic thing after all. To my mind it's absolutely noble. I mean what's the good of these here bugles, blowing your insides out? Give me a pair of dukes like Arthur Lark.

Well, after all my blooming trouble this musical business didn't come to anything again, so I give up the idea altogether. Somebody showed me a pipe called a oboe, but it cost a fearful lot. Besides, I couldn't make any sound come out of it. I dunno why everything you wants to go in for costs so much. I can't make it out and I can't stand it neither, so I give up these musical ideas and bought a rabbit off a fellow as said he was going to learn me all the doings of the noble art of self-defence.

Ninepenny Flute (1937)

A Little Boy Lost

❦

"THE BOY OUGHT TO HAVE A CRICKET BAT, TOM," SAID
Eva Grieve to her husband one summer evening. He was a farm
labourer, very industrious, very poor, and both were so proud
of their only child that they sometimes quarrelled about him.
They all lived together in a tiny field that was shaped like a
harp and full of sweet grass. There was an ash tree in it, a water
splash, a garden with green things, and currant bushes in corners; and of course their little cottage.

"He can't play cricket," Tom Grieve replied.

"Not without a bat, he can't; he ought to have a bat, like
other boys."

"Well, I can't buy him no cricket bats and so he can't have
it," said Tom.

"Why, you mean wretch—" began Eva with maternal bel-
ligerence.

"For one thing," continued her mate, "he ain't old enough—
only five; and for another thing, I can't afford no cricket bat."

"If you had the true spirit of a father"—very scornful Eva was—"You'd make him one, yourself."

So Tom chopped a cricket bat out of a slice of willow bough and presented it to his son. The child hardly looked at it.

"Course not," snapped Eva to her sarcastic husband, "he wants a ball, too, don't he?"

"You'll be wanting some flannel duds for him next."

"I'll make him a ball," cried Eva.

Eva went into the fields and collected wisps of sheep's wool off the briars for her firstborn and bound them firmly into a ball with pieces of twine. But the child hardly looked at that either. His mother tossed the ball to him, but he let it fall. She pelted him playfully with it, and it made his nose bleed.

"He's got no one to play with," explained Eva, so she cut three sticks for a wicket, and in the evenings she and Tom would take the child out into the harp-shaped field. But the tiny Grieve did not care for cricket; it was not timid, it simply did not care. So Eva and Tom would play while David stood watching them with grave eyes; and at last Tom became very proficient indeed, and so enamoured of the game of cricket that he went and joined the village club and no longer played with Eva; and the child wouldn't, so she was unhappy.

"He likes looking at things, but he doesn't want to *do* anything himself. What he ought to have is a telescope," said Eva. But how to get a telescope? She did not know. The village store had stocks of hobnailed boots and shovels and peppermint drops, but optical instruments were not in demand, and Eva might for ever have indulged in dreams—as she constantly did—of telescopes that brought the interior of heaven itself close up to you as clear as Crystal Palace. But one day she went to a farm auction, and there had the luck to meet a great strapper of a gypsy man, with a husky voice, a long ragged coat, and a depressed bowler hat, who had bought a bucketful of crockery and coathooks and odds and ends, including a little telescope.

"Here," Eva approached the gaunt man, "is that telescope a good one?"

"Good!" he growled. "Course it's a good 'un, and when I say it's a good 'un I mean the gentleman's gone to Canada, ain't he? And he don't want it. Ho, ho!" he yelled, extending the instrument and tilting it against his solemn eye. "Ho, ho! I give you my oath it's good. I can see right clean into the insides of that cow over there!" Forty people turned to observe that animal, even the auctioneer and his clerk and his myrmidons. "I can see his liver, I can. Ho, what a liver he has got—I never see such a liver in my life! Here"—he dropped the glass into Eva's hand—"Two shillings."

Eva turned it over and over. It looked perfect. "Have a squint at me!"

Eva was too dashed in public to do any such thing.

"How much do you want?"

"Look here, ma'am, no talk for talk's sake. Two bob."

Eva quickly gave him back the telescope.

"Eighteenpence, then," wailed he.

She turned away.

"Come here, a shilling."

Eva took the telescope and gave the gypsy a shilling. Home she went, and David received the telescope on his birthday. It occupied him for an hour, but he did not seem able to focus it properly, and so he only cared to look through it from the wrong end. He would sit on one side of the table and stare through the cylinder at his mother on the other side. She seemed miles away, and that appeared to amuse him. But Eva was always taking peeps with it and carried it with her wherever she went. She would look at the trees or the neighbouring hill and discover that those grey bushes were really whitebeam; or tell you what old woman had been tiggling after firewood in the hanging copse and was bringing a burden home; or who that man was riding on the slow horse through the shocks of barley. Once when she surveyed the moon she saw a big hole in the planet that no one had ever mentioned to her before; and there wasn't a man in the moon at all. But David could not contrive to see any of these wonders, and after a while the telescope was laid by.

A singularly disinterested child was David; not exactly morose, and certainly never peevish, but how quiet he was! Quiet as an old cat. "He'll twine away!" sighed his mother. Gay patient Eva would take him into the spring woods to gather flowers, but he never picked a bloom and only waited silent for her.

"Look at this, I declare!" cried she, kneeling down in a timber lane before a strange plant. When its green shoots had first peered into light they pushed themselves up through a hole in a dead leaf that had lain upon them. They had grown up now to four or five inches, but they still carried the dead constricting leaf as if it were a collar that bound them together; it made them bulge underneath it, like a lettuce tied with bast, only it was much smaller. Eva pulled at the dead leaf; it split, and behold! the five released spears shot apart and stretched themselves flat on the ground.

"They're so pleased now," cried she. "It's a bluebell plant."

And Eva, singular woman, delighted in slugs! At a threat of rain the grass path in the harplike field would be strewn with them, great fat creatures, ivory or black, with such delicate horns. Eva liked the black ones most.

"See!" she would say to her son. "It's got a hole in its neck, that little white hole, you can see right into it. There!" And she would take a stalk of grass and tickle the slug. At once the hole would disappear and the horns collapse. "That's where it breathes." She would trot about tickling slugs to make them shut those curious valves. David was neither disgusted nor bored; he just did not care for such things, neither flowers, nor herbs, nor fine weather, nor the bloom of trees.

One day they met a sharp little man with grey eyebrows that reminded you of a goat's horns. There was a white tie to his collar, shiny brown gaiters to his legs, and an umbrella slanted through his arm as if it were a gun.

"How is your cherry tree doing this year, Mr. Barnaby?"

Mr. Barnaby wagged his head and gazed critically down at Eva's son.

"There was a mazing lot of bloom, Eva; it hung on the tree like—like fury, till it come a cold wind and a sniggling frost. That coopered it. A nightingale used to sing there; my word it could sing, it didn't half used to chop it off!" Then he addressed the lad. "Ever you see a nightingale part its hair?"

David gazed stolidly at Mr. Barnaby.

"Say no," commanded Eva, shaking him.

The boy only shook his head.

"No, you wouldn't," concluded the man.

"There's no life in him. I'm feared he'll twine away," said Eva.

For David's ninth birthday she procured him a box of paints and a book with outlines of pigs and wheelbarrows and such things, to be coloured. David fiddled about with them for a while and then put them aside. It was Eva who filled up the book with magnificent wheelbarrows and cherubic pigs. She coloured a black-and-white engraving of *The Miraculous Draught of Fishes,* every fish of a different hue, in a monstrous gamboge ocean; a coloured portrait of David himself was accomplished, which made her husband weep with laughter; and a text, extravagantly illuminated, *I am the Way, the Truth, and the Life,* which was hung above David's bed. To what ambitious lengths this art might have carried her it is impossible to say, the intervention of another birthday effecting a complete diversion. This time the lad was given a small melodeon by his fond parents, but its harmonic complications embarrassed him, baffled him; even the interpretations of *All hail the power* or *My Highland Laddie* which Eva wrung from its desperate bosom were enough to unhinge the mind of a dog, let alone poor David.

David seemed to be a good scholar, he was obedient and clean, and by the time he was due to leave school at the age of fourteen he had won the right to a free apprenticeship with an engineer who specialized in steam-rollers. How proud Eva was! Tom too, how proud!

Yet he had not been at work three months when he was stricken with a spinal infirmity that obliged him to take to his bed. There he remained a long time. The doctor prescribed rest, and David rested and rested and rested, but he did not get better. At the end of a year he was still as helpless. There was no painful manifestation of disease, but it seemed as if his will were paralysed, as if he had surrendered a claim on life which he did not care to press. Two years, three years rolled on, and four years went by. The long thin youth, prematurely nipped, and helpless, was a burden like the young cuckoo that usurps a dunnock's nest. But even the cuckoo flits, and David Grieve did not. For seven years thus he lay. There were ill-speaking folk who hinted that he was less ill than lazy, that his parents were too easy with him, that he wanted not rest but a stick. At times Tom, who had begun to feel the heavy burden of years, seemed to agree, for there was nothing the brooding invalid was interested in save brandy in lieu of medicine, and a long row of bottles in Eva's kitchen testified that the treatment had been generous. It had, to the point of sacrifice. Decent steady-going people the Grieves had been, with the most innocent vices—for vice comes to all—but at last Tom had to sink the remnant of his savings in a specialist doctor from London. To the joy of the devoted parents the doctor declared that a certain operation might effect a cure.

So David was bundled off to the county hospital and operated upon. For a while Eva breathed with gaiety, an incubus was gone; it was almost as if she herself had been successfully operated upon. But soon, like a plant that flourishes best in shade, she began to miss not only David but the fixed order his poor life had imposed on her. His twenty-second birthday occurred as he was beginning to recover, and so they sent him a brand-new suit of clothes, the first he had had since boyhood.

Dear Son, [Eva wrote to him]

We are pleased to hear of you getting so well thank God we are very pleased and miss you a lot but cant expect no other you being our only little pipit. Your father has bought you

*a suit for you to ware when you get up and you can walk a
drak serge like himself, what a tof. And will send them by the
parcel post off next week. Look careful in the pockets.*

And God bless love from

Tom and Eva

He looked careful in the pockets—and found a halfcrown.

It was on an April day that he returned to his parents, very
much enfeebled, neither man nor child. Seven years of youth he
had forgone, his large bones seemed too cumbersome for him,
and adult thoughts still hung beyond his undeveloped flight.
But even to him the absence had taught something: his mother
had lost her sprightly bloom, his father was setting towards the
sere. Both of them kissed him with joy, and Eva hung upon his
neck in an ecstasy of tears that made him gasp and stagger to
a chair.

Restoration to vigour was still far off. Sometimes a villager
would come in of an evening and chat with him, or invite him
to a party or a "do" of some sort, but David did not go; he was
frail, and as it were immobile. He was on his feet again, but
hardly more than enough to convey him about the harplike
field. Restless and irritable he grew; his life was empty, quite
empty, totally irremediably empty. The weather, too, also un-
manned him; summer though it was, the storms of rain were
unending and he would sit and sigh.

"What is that you're saying?" asks Eva.

"Rain again!"

"Oh lord," says his mother, "so it is. Well!"

The grass was lush in the field, the corn grew green and

high, but the bloom of the flowering trees was scattered and squandered. Whole locks of laburnum would lie in the lane, the blossomy cream of the quicken trees was consumed, and the chestnut flowers were no more than rusty cages.

But on one brighter eve he suddenly took a stick and hobbled off for to take a walk. The wrath of the morning had gone like the anger of a good woman. The sky was not wholly clear, but what was seen was radiant, and the shadows were august. Trees hummed in the bright glow, bees scoured the blooms without sound, and a tiny bird uttered its one appealing note—Please! For half an hour he strolled along a road amid woods and hills; then the sky overdarkened quickly again, and he waited under a thick tree to watch a storm pass over. Clouds seemed to embrace the hills, and the woods reeled in a desperate envy. Rain fell across the meads in drooping curtains, and died to nothing. Then, in a vast surprise, heaven's blue waves rocked upon a reef all gold, and with a rainbow's coming the hills shone, so silent, while the trees shone and sung.

There was no song in the heart of the desolate man; his life was empty, and even its emptiness had a weight, a huge pressure; it was a fearful burden—the burden of nothingness. Grieve turned back, and when he came to an inn he entered and drank some brandy. Others there who knew him offered him ale, and he sat with them until his sorrow fell away. But when he got up to go, the world too seemed to fall away, his legs could not support him, nor his mind guide him. Two companions took him and with his arms around their necks conveyed him home.

"He's drunk, then?" uttered Tom harshly.

"No, it's the weakness," cried Eva.

"That's it," corrected one of the men. "That beer at the Drover ain't worth gut room. If you has five or six pints you be giddy as a goose."

For a week David could not rise from his bed, but as soon as he was up he went out again, and as often as he went out, he was carried home, tipsy. Tom took his money away from him, but that did not cure him.

"He's mad," said the father, and at last Tom took the suit of clothes, too, rolled them into a bundle, and went and sold them to a neighbour.

So David Grieve lies on his bed, and his mother cherishes him. Sometimes he talks to her of his childhood and of school-treats he remembers on days that smelt—so he says—like coconut. Eva has ransacked her cupboards and found a melodeon and a box of paints and a telescope. The sick man watches for her to come and feed him, and then he sleeps; or, propped against a pillow, he hugs the melodeon to his breast and puffs mad airs. Or he takes the telescope and through the reverse end stares at a world that is not so far away as it looks. Eva has taught him to paint inscriptions, but he repeats himself and never does any other than *Lead Kindly Light,* because it is easy to do, and the letters are mostly straight ones.

Fishmonger's Fiddle (1925)

The Hurly Burly

❧

I

The Weetmans—mother, son, and daughter—lived on a thriving farm. It was small enough, God knows; but it had always been a turbulent place of abode. For the servant it was "Phemy, do this," or "Phemy, have you done that?" from dawn to dark, and even from dark to dawn there was a hovering of unrest. The Widow Weetman, a partial invalid, was the only figure that manifested any semblance of tranquility; and it was a misleading one, for she sat day after day on her large hams, knitting and nodding, and lifting her grey face only to grumble, her spectacled eyes transfixing the culprit with a basilisk glare. And her daughter, Alice, the housekeeper, who had a large face, a dominating face, in some respects she was all face, was like a blast in a corridor with her "Maize for the hens, Phemy!—More firewood, Phemy!—Who has set the trap in the harness room?—Come along!—Have you scoured the skimming-pans?—Why not?—Where are you idling?—Come along, Phemy, I have no time to waste this morning; you really must help me!" It was not only in the house that this cataract of industry flowed; outside there was activity enough for a regiment. A master farmer's work consists largely in a series of conversations with other master farmers, a long-winded way of doing long-headed things; but Glastonbury Weetman, the son, was not like that at all; he was the incarnation of energy, always doing and doing, chock-full of orders, adjurations, objurgatives, blame, and blasphemy. That was the kind of place Phemy Madigan worked at. No one could rest on laurels there. The farm and the home possessed everybody, lock, stock, and barrel; work was like a tiger, it ate you up implacably. The Weetmans did not mind—they liked being eaten by such a tiger.

After six or seven years of this, Alice went back to marry an old sweetheart in Canada, where the Weetmans had originally come from; but Phemy's burden was in no way lessened thereby. There were as many things to wash and sew and darn; there was always a cart of churns about to dash for a train it could not possibly catch, or a horse to shoe that could not possibly be spared. Weetman hated to see his people merely walking. "Run over to the barn for that hayfork!" or "Slip across to the ricks, quick, now!" he would cry; and if ever an unwary hen hampered his path it only did so once—and no more. His labourers were mere things of flesh and blood, but they occasionally resented his ceaseless flagellations. Glas Weetman did not like to be impeded or controverted; one day in a rage he had smashed that lumbering loon of a carter called Gathercole. For this he was sent to jail for a month.

The day after he had been sentenced Phemy Madigan, alone in the house with Mrs. Weetman, had waked at the usual early hour. It was a foggy September morning; Sampson and his boy Daniel were clattering pails in the dairy shed. The girl felt sick and gloomy as she dressed; it was a wretched house to work in, crickets in the kitchen, cockroaches in the garret, spiders and mice everywhere. It was an old long low house; she knew that when she descended the stairs the walls would be stained with autumnal dampness, the banisters and rails oozing with moisture. She wished she was a lady and married, and living in a palace fifteen stories high.

It was fortunate that she was big and strong, though she had only been a charity girl taken from the workhouse by the Weetmans, when she was fourteen years old. That was seven years ago. It was fortunate that she was fed well at the farm, very well indeed; it was the one virtue of the place. But her meals did not counterbalance things; that farm ate up the body and blood of people. And at times the pressure was charged with a special excitation, as if a taut elastic thong had been plucked and released with a reverberating ping.

It was so on this morning. Mrs. Weetman was dead in her bed.

At that crisis a new sense descended upon the girl, a sense of responsibility. She was not in fear, she felt no grief or surprise. It concerned her in some way, but she herself was unconcerned, and she slid without effort into the position of mistress of the farm. She opened a window and looked out of doors. A little way off a boy with a red scarf stood by an open gate.

"Oi—oi, kup, kup, kup!" he cried to the cows in that field. Some of the cows, having got up, stared amiably at him, others sat on ignoring his hail, while one or two plodded deliberately towards him. "Oi—oi, kup, kup, kup!"

"Lazy rascal, that boy," remarked Phemy; "we shall have to get rid of him. Dan'l! Come here, Dan'l!" she screamed, waving her arm wildly. "Quick!"

She sent him away for police and doctor. At the inquest there were no relatives in England who could be called upon, no other witnesses than Phemy. After the funeral she wrote a letter to Glastonbury Weetman in jail, informing him of his bereavement, but to this he made no reply. Meanwhile the work of the farm was pressed forward under her control; for though she was revelling in her personal release from the torment, she would not permit others to share her intermission. She had got Mrs. Weetman's keys and her box of money. She paid the two men and the boy their wages week by week. The last of the barley was reaped, the oats stacked, the roots hoed, the churns sent daily under her supervision. And always she was bustling the men.

"Oh dear me, these lazy rogues!" she would complain to the empty rooms. "They waste time, so it's robbery—it *is* robbery. You may wear yourself to the bone, and what does it signify to such as them? All the responsibility too! They would take your skin if they could get it off you—and they can't!"

She kept such a sharp eye on the corn and meal and eggs that Sampson grew surly. She placated him by handing him Mr. Weetman's gun and a few cartridges, saying: "Just shoot me a couple of rabbits over in the warren when you get time." At the end of the day Mr. Sampson had not succeeded in killing a rabbit, so he kept the gun and the cartridges many more days. Phemy was really happy. The gloom of the farm had disappeared. The farm and everything about it looked beautiful, beautiful indeed with its yard full of ricks, the pond full of ducks, the fields full of sheep and cattle, and the trees still full of leaves and birds. She flung maize about the yard; the hens scampered towards it and the young pigs galloped, quarrelling over the grains which they groped and snuffled for, grinding each one separately in their iron jaws, while the white pullets stalked delicately among them, picked up the maize seeds— one, two, three—and swallowed them like ladies. Sometimes on cold mornings she would go outside and give an apple to the fat bay pony when he galloped back from the station. He would stand puffing with a kind of rapture, the wind from his nostrils discharging in the frosty air vague shapes like smoky trumpets. Presently, upon his hide, a little ball of liquid mysteriously suspired, grew, slid, dropped from his flanks into the road. And then drops would begin to come from all parts of him until the road beneath was dabbled by a shower from his dew-distilling outline. Phemy would say:

"The wretches! They were so late they drove him near distracted, poor thing. Lazy rogues, but wait till master comes back, they'd better be careful!"

And if any friendly person in the village asked her: "How are you getting on up there, Phemy?" she would reply: "Oh, as well as you can expect with so much to be done—and such men!" The interlocutor might hint that there was no occasion in the circumstances to distress oneself, but then Phemy would be vexed. To her, honesty was as holy as the Sabbath to a little child. Behind her back they jested about her foolishness; but, after all, wisdom isn't a process, it's a result, it's the fruit of the tree. One can't be wise, one can only be fortunate.

On the last day of her elysium the workhouse master and the chaplain had stalked over the farm, shooting partridges. In the afternoon she met them and asked for a couple of birds for Weetman's return on the morrow. The workhouse was not far away, it was on a hill facing west, and at sunset-time its windows would often catch the glare so powerfully that the whole building seemed to burn like a box of contained and smokeless fire. Very beautiful it looked to Phemy.

II

The men had come to work punctually, and Phemy herself found so much to do that she had no time to give the pony an apple. She cleared the kitchen once and for all of the pails, guns, harness, and implements that so hampered its domestic intention, and there were abundant signs elsewhere of a new impulse at work in the establishment. She did not know at what hour to expect the prisoner, so she often went to the garden gate and glanced up the road. The night had been wild with windy rain, but morn was sparklingly clear though breezy still. Crisp leaves rustled along the road where the polished chestnuts beside the parted husks lay in numbers, mixed with coral buds of the yews. The sycamore leaves were black rags, but the delicate elm foliage fluttered down like yellow stars. There was a brown field neatly adorned with white coned heaps of turnips, behind it a small upland of deeply green lucerne, behind that nothing but blue sky and rolling cloud. The turnips, washed by the rain, were creamy polished globes.

When at last he appeared she scarcely knew him. Glas Weetman was a big, though not fleshy, man of thirty, with a large boyish face and a flat bald head. Now he had a thick dark beard.

He was hungry, but his first desire was to be shaved. He stood before the kitchen mirror, first clipping the beard away with scissors, and as he lathered the remainder he said:

"Well, it's a bad state of things, this—my sister dead and my mother gone to America. What shall us do?"

He perceived in the glass that she was smiling.

"There's nought funny in it, my comic gal!" he bawled indignantly. "What are you laughing at?"

"I wer'n't laughing. It's your mother that's dead."

"My mother that's dead, I know."

"And Miss Alice that's gone to America."

"To America, I know, I know, so you can stop making your bullock's eyes and get me something to eat. What's been going on here?"

She gave him an outline of affairs. He looked at her sternly when he asked her about his sweetheart.

"Has Rosa Beauchamp been along here?"

"No," said Phemy, and he was silent. She was surprised at the question. The Beauchamps were such respectable high-up people that to Phemy's simple mind they could not possibly favour an alliance now with a man that had been in prison; it was absurd, but she did not say so to him. And she was bewildered to find that her conviction was wrong, for Rosa came along later in the day and everything between her master and his sweetheart was just as before; Phemy had not divined so much love and forgiveness in high-up people.

It was the same with everything else. The old harsh rushing life was resumed, Weetman turned to his farm with an accelerated vigour to make up for lost time, and the girl's golden week or two of ease became an unforgotten dream. The pails, the guns, the harness crept back into the kitchen. Spiders, cock-roaches, and mice were more noticeable than ever before, and Weetman himself seemed embittered, harsher. Time alone could never still him, there was a force in his frame, a buzzing in his blood. But there was a difference between them now; Phemy no longer feared him. She obeyed him, it is true, with eagerness, she worked in the house like a woman and in the fields like a man. They ate their meals together, and from this dissonant comradeship the girl, in a dumb kind of way, began to love him.

One April evening, on coming in from the fields, he found her lying on the couch beneath the window, dead plumb fast asleep, with no meal ready at all. He flung his bundle of harness to the flags and bawled angrily to her. To his surprise she did not stir. He was somewhat abashed; he stepped over to look at her. She was lying on her side. There was a large rent in her bodice between sleeve and shoulder; her flesh looked soft and agreeable to him. Her shoes had slipped off to the floor; her lips were folded in a pout.

"Why, she's quite a pretty cob," he murmured. "She's all right, she's just tired, the Lord above knows what for."

But he could not rouse the sluggard. Then a fancy moved him to lift her in his arms; he carried her from the kitchen and, staggering up the stairs, laid the sleeping girl on her own bed. He then went downstairs and ate pie and drank beer in the candlelight, guffawing once or twice: "A pretty cob, rather." As he stretched himself after the meal a new notion amused him: he put a plateful of food upon a tray, together with a mug of beer and the candle. Doffing his heavy boots and leggings, he car-ried the tray into Phemy's room. And he stopped there.

III

The new circumstance that thus slipped into her life did not effect any noticeable alteration of its general contour and progress. Weetman did not change towards her. Phemy accepted his mastership not alone because she loved him, but because her powerful sense of loyalty covered all the possible opprobrium. She did not seem to mind his continued relations with Rosa.

Towards midsummer one evening Glastonbury came in in the late dusk. Phemy was there in the darkened kitchen. "Master!" she said immediately he entered. He stopped before her. She continued: "Something's happened."

"Huh, while the world goes popping round something shall always happen!"

"It's me—I'm took—a baby, master," she said. He stood chock-still. His back was to the light, she could not see the expression on his face, perhaps he wanted to embrace her.

"Let's have a light, sharp," he said in his brusque way. "The supper smells good, but I can't see what I'm smelling, and I can only fancy what I be looking at."

She lit the candles and they ate supper in silence. Afterwards he sat away from the table with his legs outstretched and crossed, hands sunk into pockets, pondering while the girl cleared the table. Soon he put his powerful arm around her waist and drew her to sit on his knees.

"Are you sure o' that?" he demanded.

She was sure.

"Quite?"

She was quite sure.

"Ah, well, then," he sighed conclusively, "we'll be married!"

The girl sprang to her feet. "No, no, no! How can you be married? You don't mean that—not married—there's Miss Beauchamp!" She paused and added a little unsteadily: "She's your true love, master."

"Ay, but I'll not wed her!" he cried sternly. "If there's no gainsaying this that's come on you I'll stand to my guns. It's right and proper for we to have a marriage."

His great thick-fingered hands rested upon his knees; the candles threw a wash of light upon his polished leggings; he stared into the fireless grate.

"But we do not want to do that," said the girl dully and doubtfully. "You have given your ring to her, you've given her your word. I don't want you to do this for me. It's all right, master, it's all right."

"Are ye daft?" he cried. "I tell you we'll wed. Don't keep clacking about Rosa—I'll stand to my guns." He paused before adding, "She'd gimme the rightabout, fine now—don't you see, stupid—but I'll not give her the chance."

Her eyes were lowered. "She's your true love, master."

"What would become of you and your child? Ye couldn't bide here!"

"No," said the trembling girl.

"I'm telling you what we must do, modest and proper; there's naught else to be done, and I'm middling glad of it, I am. Life's a seesaw affair. I'm middling glad of this."

So, soon, without a warning to anyone, least of all to Rosa Beauchamp, they were married by the registrar. The change in her domestic status produced no other change; in marrying Weetman she but married all his ardour, she was swept into its current. She helped to milk cows, she boiled nauseating messes for pigs, chopped mangolds, mixed meal, and sometimes drove a harrow in his windy fields. Though they slept together, she was still his servant. Sometimes he called her his "pretty little cob," and then she knew he was fond of her. But in general his custom was disillusioning. His way with her was his way with his beasts; he knew what he wanted, it was easy to get. If for a brief space a little romantic flower began to bud in her breast it was frozen as a bud, and the vague longing disappeared at length from her eyes. And she became aware that Rosa Beauchamp was not yet done with; somewhere in the darkness of the fields Glastonbury still met her. Phemy did not mind.

In the new year she bore him a son that died as it came to life. Glas was angry at that, as angry as if he had lost a horse. He felt that he had been duped, that the marriage had been a stupid sacrifice, and in this he was savagely supported by Rosa. And yet Phemy did not mind; the farm had got its grip upon her, it was consuming her body and blood.

Weetman was just going to drive into town; he sat fuming in the trap behind the fat bay pony.

"Bring me that whip from the passage!" he shouted. "There's never a dam thing handy!"

Phemy appeared with the whip. "Take me with you," she said.

"God-a-mighty! What for? I be comen back in an hour. They ducks want looking over, and you've all the taties to grade."

She stared at him irresolutely.

"And whose to look after the house? You know it won't lock up—the key's lost. Get up there!"

He cracked his whip in the air as the pony dashed away.

In the summer Phemy fell sick, her arm swelled enormously. The doctor came again and again. It was blood-poisoning, caught from a diseased cow that she had milked with a cut finger. A nurse arrived, but Phemy knew she was doomed, and though tortured with pain she was for once vexed and protestant. For it was a June night, soft and nubile, with a marvellous moon; a nightingale threw its impetuous garland into the air. She lay listening to it and thinking with sad pleasure of the time when Glastonbury was in prison, how grand she was in her solitude, ordering everything for the best and working superbly. She wanted to go on and on for evermore, though she knew she had never known peace in maidenhood or marriage. The troubled waters of the world never ceased to flow; in the night there was no rest—only darkness. Nothing could emerge now. She was leaving it all to Rosa Beauchamp. Glastonbury was gone out somewhere—perhaps to meet Rosa in the fields. There was the nightingale, and it was very bright outside.

"Nurse," moaned the dying girl, "what was I born into the world at all for?"

Clorinda Walks in Heaven (1922)

The Field of Mustard

~

ON A WINDY AFTERNOON IN NOVEMBER THEY WERE gathering kindling in the Black Wood, Dinah Lock, Amy Hardwick, and Rose Olliver, three sere disvirgined women from Pollock's Cross. Mrs. Lock wore clothes of dull butcher's blue, with a short jacket that affirmed her plumpness, but Rose and Amy had on long grey ulsters. All of them were about forty years old, and the wind and twigs had tousled their gaunt locks, for none had a hat upon her head. They did not go far beyond the margin of the wood, for the forest ahead of them swept high over a hill and was gloomy; behind them the slim trunks of beech, set in a sweet ruin of hoar and scattered leaf, and green briar nimbly fluttering made a sort of palisade against the light of the open, which was grey, and a wide field of mustard, which was yellow. The three women peered up into the trees for dead branches, and when they found any Dinah Lock, the vivacious woman full of shrill laughter, with a bosom as massive as her haunches, would heave up a rope with an iron bolt tied to one end. The bolted end would twine itself around the dead branch, the three women would tug, and after a sharp crack the quarry would fall; as often as not the women would topple over too. By and by they met an old hedger with a round belly belted low, and thin legs tied at each knee, who told them the time by his ancient watch, a stout timepiece which the women sportively admired.

"Come Christmas I'll have me a watch like that!" Mrs. Lock called out. The old man looked a little dazed as he fumblingly replaced his chronometer. "I will," she continued, "if the Lord spares me and the pig don't pine."

"You—you don't know what you're talking about," he said. "That watch was my uncle's watch."

"Who was he? I'd like one like it."

"Was a sergeant-major in the lancers, fought under Sir Garnet Wolseley, and it was given to him."

"What for?"

The hedger stopped and turned on them. "Doing of his duty."

"That all?" cried Dinah Lock. "Well, I never got no watch for that a-much. Do you know what I see when I went to London? I see'd a watch in a bowl of water, it was glass, and there was a fish swimming round it . . ."

"I don't believe it."

"There was a fish swimming round it . . ."

"I tell you I don't believe it . . ."

"And the little hand was going on like Clackford Mill. That's the sort of watch I'll have me; none of your Sir Garney Wolsey's!"

"He was a noble Christian man, that was."

"Ah! I suppose he slept wid Jesus?" yawped Dinah.

"No, he didn't," the old man disdainfully spluttered. "He never did. What a God's the matter wid ye?" Dinah cackled with laughter. "Pah!" he cried, going away, "great fat thing! Can't tell your guts from your elbows."

Fifty yards farther on he turned and shouted some obscenity back at them, but they did not heed him; they had begun to make three faggots of the wood they had collected, so he put his fingers to his nose at them and shambled out to the road.

By the time Rose and Dinah were ready, Amy Hardwick, a small, slow, silent woman, had not finished bundling her faggot together.

"Come on, Amy," urged Rose.

"Come on," Dinah said.

"All right, wait a minute," she replied listlessly.

"Oh God, that's death!" cried Dinah Lock, and heaving a great faggot to her shoulders she trudged off, followed by Rose with a like burden. Soon they were out of the wood, and crossing a highway they entered a footpath that strayed in a diagonal wriggle to the far corner of the field of mustard. In silence they journeyed until they came to that far corner, where there was a hedged bank. Here they flung their faggots down and sat upon them to wait for Amy Hardwick.

In front of them lay the field they had crossed, a sour scent rising faintly from its yellow blooms, which quivered in the wind. Day was dull, the air chill, and the place most solitary. Beyond the field of mustard the eye could see little but forest. There were hills there, a vast curving trunk, but the Black Wood heaved itself effortlessly upon them and lay like a dark pall over the outline of a corpse. Huge and gloomy, the purple woods

draped it all completely. A white necklace of a road curved below, where a score of telegraph poles, each crossed with a multitude of white florets, were dwarfed by the hugeness to effigies
that resembled hyacinths. Dinah Lock gazed upon this scene
whose melancholy, and not its grandeur, had suddenly invaded
her; with elbows sunk in her fat thighs, and nursing her cheeks
in her hands, she puffed the gloomy air, saying:

"Oh God, cradle and grave is all there is for we."

"Where's Amy got to?" asked Rose.

"I could never make a companion of her, you know," Dinah
declared.

"Nor I," said Rose, "she's too sour and slow."

"Her disposition's too serious. Of course, your friends are
never what you want them to be, Rose. Sometimes they're
better—most often they're worse. But it's such a mercy to have
a friend at all; I like you, Rose; I wish you was a man."

"I might just as well ha' been," returned the other woman.

"Well, you'd ha' done better; but if you had a tidy little family like me you'd wish you hadn't got 'em."

"And if you'd never had 'em you'd ha' wished you had."

"Rose, that's the cussedness of nature, it makes a mock of
you. I don't believe it's the Almighty at all, Rose. I'm sure it's
the devil, Rose. Dear heart, my corn's a-giving me what-for; I
wonder what that bodes."

"It's restless weather," said Rose. She was dark, tall, and not
unbeautiful still, though her skin was harsh and her limbs angular. "Get another month or two over—there's so many of these
long dreary hours."

"Ah, your time's too long, or it's too short, or it's just right

but you're too old. Cradle and grave's my portion. Fat old thing!
he called me."

Dinah's brown hair was ruffled across her pleasant face and
she looked a little forlorn, but corpulence dispossessed her of
tragedy. "I be thin enough a-summer-times, for I lives light and
sweats like a bridesmaid, but winters I'm fat as a hog."

"What all have you to grumble at, then?" asked Rose, who
had slid to the ground and lay on her stomach staring up at her
friend.

"My heart's young, Rose."

"You've your husband."

"He's no man at all since he was ill. A long time ill, he was.
When he coughed, you know, his insides come up out of him
like coffee grouts. Can you ever understand the meaning of that?
Coffee! I'm growing old, but my heart's young."

"So is mine, too; but you got a family, four children grown
or growing." Rose had snapped off a sprig of the mustard flower
and was pressing and pulling the bloom in and out of her mouth.
"I've none, and never will have." Suddenly she sat up, fumbled in
her pocket, and produced her purse. She slipped the elastic band
from it, and it gaped open. There were a few coins there and a
scrap of paper folded. Rose took out the paper and smoothed it
open under Dinah's curious gaze. "I found something lying about
at home the other day, and I cut this bit out of it." In soft tones
she began to read:

The day was void, vapid; time itself seemed empty.
Come evening it rained softly. I sat by my fire turning
over the leaves of a book, and I was dejected, until I

came upon a little old-fashioned engraving at the bottom of a page. It imaged a procession of some angelic children in a garden, little placidly-naked substantial babes, with tiny bird-wings. One carried a bow, others a horn of plenty, or a hamper of fruit, or a set of reed-pipes. They were garlanded and full of grave joys. And at the sight of them a strange bliss flowed into me such as I had never known, and I thought this world was all a garden, though its light was hidden and its children not yet born.

Rose did not fold the paper up; she crushed it in her hand and lay down again without a word.

"Huh, I tell you, Rose, a family's a torment. I never wanted mine. God love, Rose, I'd lay down my life for 'em; I'd cut myself into fourpenny pieces so they shouldn't come to harm; if one of 'em was to die I'd sorrow to my grave. But I know, I know, I know I never wanted 'em, they were not for me, I was just an excuse for their blundering into the world. Somehow I've been duped, and every woman born is duped so, one ways or another in the end. I had my sport with my man, but I ought never to have married. Now I'd love to begin all over again, and as God's my maker, if it weren't for those children, I'd be gone off out into the world again tomorrow, Rose. But I dunno what 'ud become o' me."

The wind blew strongly athwart the yellow field, and the odour of mustard rushed upon the brooding women. Protestingly the breeze flung itself upon the forest; there was a gliding cry among the rocking pinions as of some lost wave seeking a forgotten shore. The angular faggot under Dinah Lock had

begun to vex her; she too sunk to the ground and lay beside
Rose Olliver, who asked:

"And what 'ud become of your old man?"

For a few moments Dinah Lock paused. She too took a sprig
of the mustard and fondled it with her lips. "He's no man now,
the illness feebled him, and the virtue's gone; no man at all since
two years, and bald as a piece of cheese—I like a hairy man,
like—do you remember Rufus Blackthorn, used to be gamekeeper here?"

Rose stopped playing with her flower. "Yes, I knew Rufus
Blackthorn."

"A fine bold man that was! Never another like him here-
abouts, not in England neither; not in the whole world—though
I've heard some queer talk of those foreigners, Australians,
Chinymen. Well!"

"Well?" said Rose.

"He was a devil." Dinah Lock began to whisper. "A perfect
devil; I can't say no fairer than that. I wish I could, but I can't."

"Oh come," protested Rose, "he was a kind man. He'd never
see anybody want for a thing."

"No," there was playful scorn in Dinah's voice; "he'd shut
his eyes first!"

"Not to a woman he wouldn't, Dinah."

"Ah! Well—perhaps—he was good to women."

"I could tell you things as would surprise you," murmured
Rose.

"You! But—well—no, no. I could tell *you* things as you
wouldn't believe. Me and Rufus! We was—oh my—yes!"

"He *was* handsome."

"Oh, a pretty man!" Dinah acceded warmly. "Black as coal

and bold as a fox. I'd been married nigh on ten years when he first set foot in these parts. I'd got three children then. He used to give me a saucy word whenever he saw me, for I liked him and he knew it. One Whitsun Monday I was home all alone, the children were gone somewheres, and Tom was away boozing. I was putting some plants in our garden—I loved a good flower in those days—I wish the world was all a garden, but now my Tom he digs 'em up, digs everything up proper and never puts 'em back. Why, we had a crocus once! And as I was doing that planting someone walked by the garden in such a hurry. I looked up and there was Rufus, all dressed up to the nines, and something made me call out to him. 'Where be you off to in that flaming hurry?' I says. 'Going to a wedding,' says he. 'Shall I come with 'ee?' I says. 'Ah yes,' he says, very glad; 'but hurry up, for I be sharp set and all.' So I run in-a-doors and popped on my things and off we went to Jim Pickering's wedding over at Clackford Mill. When Jim brought the bride home from church that Rufus got hold of a gun and fired it off up chimney, and down come the soot, bushels of it! All over the room, and a chimney-pot burst and rattled down the tiles into a prambulator. What a rumbullion that was! But no one got angry—there was plenty of drink and we danced all the afternoon. Then we come home together again through the woods. Oh lord, I said to myself, I shan't come out with you ever again, and that's what I said to Rufus Blackthorn. But I did, you know! I woke up in bed that night, and the moon shone on me dreadful—I thought the place was afire. But there was Tom snoring, and I lay and thought of me and Rufus in the wood, till I could have jumped out into the moonlight, stark, and flown over the chimney. I didn't sleep any more. And I saw Rufus the next night, and the night after that, often, often. Whenever I went out I left Tom the cupboardful—that's all he troubled about. I was mad after Rufus, and while that caper was on I couldn't love my husband. No."

"No?" queried Rose.

"Well, I pretended I was ill, and I took my young Katey to sleep with me, and give Tom her bed. He didn't seem to mind, but after a while I found he was gallivanting after other women. Course, I soon put a stopper on that. And then—what do you think? Bless me if Rufus weren't up to the same tricks! Deep as the sea, that man. Faithless, you know, but such a bold one."

Rose lay silent, plucking wisps of grass; there was a wry smile on her face.

"Did ever he tell you the story of the man who was drowned?" she asked at length. Dinah shook her head. Rose continued. "Before he came here he was keeper over in that Oxfordshire, where the river goes right through the woods, and he slept in a boathouse moored to the bank. Some gentleman was drowned near there, an accident it was, but they couldn't find the body. So they offered a reward of ten pound for it to be found."

"Ten, ten pounds!"

"Yes. Well, all the watermen said the body wouldn't come up for ten days."

"No, more they do."

"It didn't. And so late one night—it was moonlight—some men in a boat kept on hauling and poking round the house where Rufus was, and he heard 'em say: 'It must be here, it must be here,' and Rufus shouts out to them: 'Course he's here! I got him in bed with me!'"

"Aw!" chuckled Dinah.

"Yes, and next day he got the ten pounds, because he *had* found the body and hidden it away."

"Feared nothing," said Dinah, "nothing at all; he'd have been rude to Satan. But he was very delicate with his hands, sewing and things like that. I used to say to him: 'Come, let me mend your coat,' or whatever it was, but he never would, always did such things of himself. 'I don't allow no female to patch my clothes,' he'd say, ''cos they works with a red-hot needle and a burning thread.' And he used to make fine little slippers out of reeds."

"Yes," Rose concurred, "he made me a pair."

"You!" Dinah cried. "What—were you—?"

Rose turned her head away. "We was all cheap to him," she said softly, "cheap as old rags; we was like chaff before him."

Dinah Lock lay still, very still, ruminating; but whether in old grief or new rancour Rose was not aware, and she probed no further. Both were quiet, voiceless, recalling the past delirium. They shivered, but did not rise. The wind increased in the forest, its hoarse breath sorrowed in the yellow field, and swift masses of cloud flowed and twirled in a sky without end and full of gloom.

"Hallo!" cried a voice, and there was Amy beside them, with a faggot almost overwhelming her. "Shan't stop now," she said, "for I've got this faggot perched just right, and I shouldn't ever get it up again. I found a shilling in the 'ood, you," she continued shrilly and gleefully. "Come along to my house after tea, and we'll have a quart of stout."

"A shilling, Amy!" cried Rose.

"Yes," called Mrs. Hardwick, trudging steadily on. "I tried

to find the fellow to it, but no more luck. Come and wet it after tea!"

"Rose," said Dinah, "come on." She and Rose with much circumstance heaved up their faggots and tottered after, but by then Amy had turned out of sight down the little lane to Pollock's Cross.

"Your children will be home," said Rose as they went along, "they'll be looking out for you."

"Ah, they'll want their bellies filling!"

"It must be lovely a-winter's nights, you setting round your fire with 'em, telling tales, and brushing their hair."

"Ain't you got a fire of your own indoors?" grumbled Dinah.

"Yes."

"Well, why don't you set by it then!" Dinah's faggot caught the briars of a hedge that overhung, and she tilted round with a mild oath. A covey of partridges feeding beyond scurried away with ruckling cries. One foolish bird dashed into the telegraph wires and dropped dead.

"They're good children, Dinah, yours are. And they make you a valentine, and give you a ribbon on your birthday, I expect?"

"They're naught but a racket from cockcrow till the old man snores—and then it's worse!"

"Oh, but the creatures, Dinah!"

"You—you got your quiet trim house, and only your man to look after, a kind man, and you'll set with him in the evenings and play your dominoes or your draughts, and he'll look at you—the nice man—over the board, and stroke your hand now and again."

The wind hustled the two women close together, and as they stumbled under their burdens Dinah Lock stretched out a hand

and touched the other woman's arm. "I like you, Rose, I wish you was a man."

Rose did not reply. Again they were quiet, voiceless, and thus in fading light they came to their homes. But how windy, dispossessed, and ravaged roved the darkening world! Clouds were borne frantically across the heavens, as if in a rout of battle, and the lovely earth seemed to sigh in grief at some calamity all unknown to men.

The Field of Mustard (1926)

The Watercress Girl

I

When Mary McDowall was brought to the assize court the place was crowded, Mr. O'Kane said, "inside out." It was a serious trial, as everybody—even the prisoner—well knew; twelve tons of straw had been thrown down on the roads outside the hall to deaden the noise of carts passing and suchlike pandemoniums, and when the judge drove up in his coach with jockeys on the horses, a couple of young trumpeters from the barracks stiffened on the steps and blew a terrible fanfare up into heaven. "For a sort of a warning, I should think," said Mr. O'Kane.

The prisoner's father, having been kicked by a horse, was unable to attend the trial, and so he had enlisted Mr. O'Kane to go and fetch him the news of it; and Mr. O'Kane in obliging his friend suffered annoyances and was abused in the court itself by a great fat geezer of a fellow with a long staff. "If you remained on your haunches when the judge came in," complained Mr. O'Kane, "you were poked up, and if you stood up to get a look at the prisoner when *she* came in you were poked down. Surely to God we didn't go to look at the judge!"

Short was her trial, for the evidence was clear, and the guilt not denied. Prisoner neither sorrowed for her crime nor bemoaned her fate; passive and casual she stood there at the willing of the court for a thing she had done, and there were no tears now in Mary McDowall. Most always she dressed in black, and she was in black then, with masses of black hair; a pale face with a dark mole on the chin, and rich red lips; a big girl of twenty-five, not coarsely big, and you could guess she was strong. A passionate girl, caring nothing or not much for this justice; unimpressed by the solemn court, nor moved to smile at its absurdities; for all that passion concerns with is love—or its absence—love that gives its only gift by giving all. If you could have read her mind, not now but in its calm before the stress of her misfortune, you would have learned this much, although she herself could not have formulated it: I will give to love all it is in me to give; I shall desire of love all I can ever dream of and receive.

And because another woman had taken what Mary McDowall wanted, Mary had flung a corrosive acid in the face of her enemy, and Elizabeth Plantney's good looks were gone, gone for certain and for ever. So here was Mary McDowall and over there was Frank Oppidan; not a very fine one to mislead the handsome girl in the dock, but he had done it, and he too had suffered and the women in court had pity for him, and the men—envy. Tall, with light oiled hair and pink sleepy features (a pink heart, too, you might think, though you could not see it), he gave evidence against her in a nasal tone with a confident manner, and she did not waste a look on him. A wood-turner he was, and for about four years had "kept company" with the prisoner, who lived near a village a mile or two away from his home. He had often urged her to marry him, but she would not, so a little while ago he told her he was going to marry Elizabeth Plantney. A few evenings later he had been strolling with Elizabeth Plantney on the road outside the town. It was not yet dark, about eight o'clock, but they had not observed the prisoner, who must have been dogging them, for she came slyly up and passed by them, turned, splashed something in his companion's face, and then walked on. She didn't run; at first they thought it was some stupid joke, and he was for going after the prisoner, whom he had recognized.

"I was mad angry," declared Oppidan, "I could have choked her. But Miss Plantney began to scream that she was blinded and burning, and I had to carry and drag her some ways back along the road until we came to the first house, Mr. Blackfriar's, where they took her in and I ran off for the doctor." The witness added savagely: "I wish I *had* choked her."

There was full corroboration, prisoner had admitted guilt, and the counsel briefed by her father could only plead for a lenient sentence. A big man he was with a drooping yellow moustache and terrific teeth; his cheeks and hands were pink as salmon.

"Accused," he said, "is the only child of Fergus McDowall. She lives with her father, a respectable widower, at a somewhat retired cottage in the valley of Trinkel, assisting him in the conduct of his business—a small holding by the river where he cultivates watercress, and keeps bees and hens and things of that kind. The witness Oppidan had been in the habit of cycling from his town to the McDowalls' home to buy bunches of watercress, a delicacy of which, in season, he seems to have been—um—inordinately fond, for he would go twice, thrice, and often four times a week. His visits were not confined to the purchase of watercress, and he seems to have made himself agreeable to the daughter of the house; but I am in possession of no information as to the nature of their intercourse beyond that tendered by the witness Oppidan. Against my advice the prisoner, who is a very reticent, even a remarkable, woman, has insisted on pleading guilty and accepting her punishment without any—um—chance of mitigation, in a spirit, I hope, of contrition, which is not—um—entirely unadmirable. My lord, I trust . . ."

While the brutal story was being recounted, the prisoner had stood with closed eyes, leaning her hands upon the rail of the dock; stood and dreamed of what she had not revealed:

Of her father, Fergus McDowall; his child she was, although he had never married. That much she knew, but who her mother had been he never told her, and it did not seem to matter; she guessed rather than knew that at her birth she had died, or soon afterwards, and the man had fostered her. He and she had always been together, alone, ever since she could remember, always together, always happy, he was so kind; and so splendid in the great boots that drew up to his thighs when he worked in the watercress beds, cutting bunches deftly or cleaning the weeds from the water. And there were her beehives, her flock of hens, the young pigs, and a calf that knelt and rubbed its neck on the rich mead with a lavishing movement just as the ducks did when the grass was dewy. She had seen the young pigs, no bigger than rabbits, race across the patch of greensward to the blue-roan calf standing nodding in the shade; they would prowl beneath the calf, clustering round its feet, and begin to gnaw the calf's hoof until, full of patience, she would gently lift her leg and shake it, but would not move away. Save for a wildness of mood that sometimes flashed through her, Mary was content, and loved the life that she could not know was lonely with her father beside the watercress streams. He was uncommunicative, like Mary, but as he worked he hummed to himself or whistled the soft tunes that at night he played on the clarinet. Tall and strong, a handsome man. Sometimes he would put his arms around her and say: "Well, my dear." And she would kiss him. She had vowed to herself that she would never leave him, but then—Frank had come. In this mortal conflict we seek not only that pleasure may not divide us from duty, but that duty may not detach us from life. He was not the first man or youth she could or would have loved, but he was the one who had wooed her; first-love's enlightening delight, in the long summer eyes, in those enticing fields! How easily she was won! All his offers of marriage she had put off with the answer: "No, it would never do for me," or "I shall never marry," but then, if he angrily swore or accused her of not loving him enough, her fire and freedom would awe him almost as much as it enchanted. And she might have married Frank if she could only have told him of her dubious origin, but whether from some vagrant modesty, loyalty to her father, or some reason whatever, she could not bring herself to do that. Often these steady refusals enraged her lover, and after such occasions he would not seek her again for weeks, but in the end he always returned, although his absences grew longer as their friendship lengthened. Ah, when the way to your lover is long, there's but a short cut to the end. Came a time when he

did not return at all and then, soon, Mary found she was going to have a child. "Oh, I wondered where you were, Frank,
and why you were there, wherever it was, instead of where I
could find you." But the fact was portentous enough to depose
her grief at his fickleness, and after a while she took no further
care or thought for Oppidan, for she feared that like her own
mother she would die of her child. Soon these fears left her
and she rejoiced. Certainly she need not scruple to tell him of
her own origin now, he could never reproach her now. Had he
come once more, had he come then, she would have married
him. But although he might have been hers for the lifting of a
finger, as they say, her pride kept her from calling him into the
trouble, and she did not call him and he never sought her again.
When her father realized her condition he merely said "Frank?"
and she nodded.

The child was early born, and she was not prepared; it came
and died. Her father took it and buried it in the garden. It was
a boy, dead. No one else knew, not even Frank, but when she
was recovered, her pride wavered and she wrote a loving letter
to him, still keeping her secret. Not until she had written three
times did she hear from him, and then he only answered that
he should not see her any more. He did not tell her why, but she
knew. He was going to marry Elizabeth Plantney, whose parents had died and left her five hundred pounds. To Mary's mind
that presented itself as a treachery to their child, the tiny body
buried under a beehive in the garden. That Frank was unaware
made no difference to the girl's fierce mood; it was treachery.
Maternal anger stormed in her breast, it could only be allayed by
an injury, a deep admonishing injury to that treacherous man.
In her sleepless nights the little crumpled corpse seemed to

plead for this much, and her own heart clamoured, just as those bees murmured against him day by day.

So then she got some vitriol. Rushing past her old lover on the night of the crime, she turned upon him with the lifted jar, but the sudden confrontation dazed and tormented her; in momentary hesitation she had dashed the acid, not into *his* faithless eyes, but at the prim creature linked to his arm. Walking away, she heard the crying of the wounded girl. After a while she had turned back to the town and given herself up to the police.

To her mind, as she stood leaning against the dock rail, it was all huddled and contorted, but that was her story set in its order. The trial went droning on beside her remembered grief like a dull stream neighbouring a clear one, two parallel streams that would meet in the end, were meeting now, surely, as the judge began to speak. And at the crisis, as if in exculpation, she suffered a whisper to escape her lips, though none heard it.

"'Twas him made me a parent, but he was never a man himself. He took advantage; it was mean, I love Christianity." She heard the judge deliver her sentence: for six calendar months she was to be locked in a jail. "Oh Christ!" she breathed, for it was the lovely spring; lilac, laburnum, and father wading the brooks in those boots drawn up to his thighs to rake the dark sprigs and comb out the green scum.

They took her away. "I wanted to come out then," said Mr. O'Kane, "for the next case was only about a contractor defrauding the corporation—good luck to him, but he got three years—and I tried to get out of it, but if I did that geezer with the stick poked me down and said I'd not to stir out of it till the court rose. I said to him I'd kill him, but there was a lot of peelers about so I suppose he didn't hear it."

II

Towards the end of the year Oppidan had made up his mind
what he would do to Mary McDowall when she came out of
prison. Poor Liz was marred for life, spoiled, cut off from the
joys they had intended together. Not for all the world would
he marry her now; he had tried to bring himself to that issue
of chivalry, of decency, but it was impossible; he had failed in
the point of grace. No man could love Elizabeth Plantney now,
Frank could not visit her without shuddering, and she herself,
poor generous wretch, had given him back his promise. Apart
from his ruined fondness for her, they had planned to do much
with the five hundred pounds; it was to have set him up in a
secure and easy way of trade, they would have been established
in a year or two as solid as a rock. All that chance was gone, no
such chance ever came twice in a man's lifetime, and he was
left with Liz upon his conscience. He would have to be kind
to her for as long as he could stand it. That was a disgust to
his mind, for he wanted to be faithful. Even the most unstable
man wishes he had been faithful—but to which woman he is
never quite sure. And then that bitch Mary McDowall would
come out of her prison and be a mockery to him of what he had
forgone, of what he had been deprived. Savagely he believed in
the balance wrought by an act of vengeance—he, too!—eye for
eye, tooth for tooth; it had a threefold charm, simplicity, relief, triumph. The McDowall girl, so his fierce meditations ran,
miked in prison for six months and then came out no worse
than when she went in. It was no punishment at all, they did
no hurt to women in prison; the court hadn't set wrong right

at all, it never did; and he was a loser whichever way he turned. But there was still a thing he could do (Jove had slumbered, he would steal Jove's lightning) and a project lay troubling his mind like a gnat in the eye, he would have no peace until it was wiped away.

On an October evening, then, about a week after Mary Mc-Dowall's release, Oppidan set off towards Trinkel. Through Trinkel he went and a furlong past it until he came to their lane. Down the lane too, and then he could hear the water ruttling over the cataracts of the cress-beds. Not yet in winter, the year's decline was harbouring splendour everywhere. Whitebeam was a dissolute tangle of rags covering ruby drops, the service trees were sallow as lemons, the oak resisted decay, but most confident of all the tender-tressed ashes. The man walked quietly to a point where, unobserved, he could view the McDowall dwelling, with its overbowering walnut tree littering the yard with husks and leaves, its small adjacent field with banks that stooped in the glazed water. The house was heavy and small, but there were signs of grace in the garden, of thrift in the orderly painted sheds. The conical peak of a tiny stack was pitched in the afterglow, the elms sighed like tired old matrons, wisdom and content lingered here. Oppidan crept along the hedges until he was in a field at the back of the house, a hedge still hiding him. He was trembling. There was a light already in the back window; one leaf of the window stood open and he saw their black cat jump down from it into the garden and slink away under some shrubs. From his standpoint he could not see into the lighted room, but he knew enough of Fergus's habits to be sure he was not within; it was his day for driving into the town. Thus it could only be Mary who had lit that lamp. Trembling still! Just beyond him was a heap of dung from the stable, and a cock was standing silent on the dunghill while two hens, a white one and a black, bickered around him over some voided grains. Presently the cock seized the black hen, and the white scurried away; but though his grasp was fierce and he bit at her red comb, the black hen went on gobbling morsels from the manure heap, and when at last he released her she did not intermit her steady pecking. Then Oppidan was startled by a flock of starlings that slid across the evening with the steady movement of a cloud; the noise of their wings was like showers of rain upon trees.

"Wait till it's darker," he muttered, and skulking back to the lane he walked sharply for half a mile. Then, slowly, he returned. Unseen, he reached the grass that grew under the lighted window, and stooped warily against the wall; one hand rested on the wall, the other in his pocket. For some time he hesitated but he knew what he had to do and what did it matter! He stepped in front of the window.

In a moment, and for several moments longer, he was rigid with surprise. It was Mary all right (the bitch!), washing her hair, drying it in front of the kitchen fire, the thick locks pouring over her face as she knelt with her hands resting on her thighs. So long was their black flow that the ends lay in a small heap inside the fender. Her bodice hung on the back of a chair beside her, and her only upper clothing was a loose and disarrayed chemise that did not hide her bosom. Then, gathering the hair in her hands, she held the tresses closer to the fire, her face peeped through, and to herself she was smiling. Dazzling fair were her arms and the one breast he astonishingly saw. It was Mary; but not the Mary, dull ugly creature, whom his long rancour had conjured for him. Lord, what had he forgotten! Absence and resentment had pared away her loveliness from his recollection, but this was the old Mary of their passionate days, transfigured and marvellous.

Stepping back from the window into shadow again, he could feel his heart pound like a frantic hammer; every pulse was hurrying at the summons. In those breathless moments Oppidan gazed as it were at himself, or at his mad intention, gazed wonderingly, ashamed and awed. Fingering the thing in his pocket, turning it over as a coin whose toss has deceived him, he was aware of a revulsion; gone revenge, gone rancour, gone all thought of Elizabeth, and there was left in his soul what had not gone and could never go. A brute she had been—it was bloody cruelty—but, but—but what? Seen thus, in her innocent occupation, the grim fact of her crime had somehow thrown a conquering glamour over her hair, the pale pride of her face, the intimacy of her bosom. Her very punishment was a triumph; on what account had she suffered if not for love of him? He could feel that chastening distinction melting now; she had suffered for his love.

There and then shrill cries burst upon them. The cat leaped from the garden to the window-sill; there was a thrush in its mouth, shrieking. The cat paused on the sill, furtive and hesitant. Without a thought Oppidan plunged forward, seized the cat, and with his free hand clutched what he could of the thrush. In a second the cat released it and dropped into the room, while the crushed bird fluttered away to the darkened shrubs, leaving its tail feathers in the hand of the man.

Mary sprang up and rushed to the window. "Is it you?" was all she said. Hastily she left the window, and Oppidan with a grin saw her shuffling into her bodice. One hand fumbled at the buttons, the other unlatched the door. "Frank." There was neither surprise nor elation. He walked in. Only then did he open his fist and the thrush's feathers floated in the air and idled to the floor. Neither of them remembered any more of the cat or the bird.

In silence they stood, not looking at each other.

"What do you want?" at length she asked. "You're hindering me."

"Am I?" He grinned. His face was pink and shaven, his hair was almost as smooth as a brass bowl. "Well, I'll tell you." His hat was cumbering his hands, so he put it carefully on the table.

"I come here wanting to do a bad thing, I own up to that. I had it in my mind to serve you same as you served her—you know who I mean. Directly I knew you had come home, that's what I meant to do. I been waiting about out there a good while until I saw you. And then I saw you. I hadn't seen you for a long, long time, and somehow, I dunno, when I saw you—"

Mary was standing with her hands on her hips; the black cascades of her hair rolled over her arms; some of the strands were gathered under her fingers, looped to her waist; dark weeping hair.

"I didn't mean to harm her!" she burst out. "I never meant that for her, not what I did. Something happened to me that I'd not told you of then, and it doesn't matter now, and I shall never tell you. It was you I wanted to put a mark on, but directly I was in front of you I went all swavy, and I couldn't. But I had to throw it, I had to throw it."

He sat down on a chair, and she stared at him across the table. "All along it was meant for you, and that's God's truth."

"Why?" he asked. She did not give him an answer then, but stood rubbing the fingers of one hand on the finely scrubbed boards of the table, tracing circles and watching them vacantly. At last she put a question:

"Did you get married soon?"

"No," he said.

"Aren't you? But of course it's no business of mine."

"I'm not going to marry her."

"Not?"

"No, I tell you I wouldn't marry her for five thousand pounds, nor for fifty thousand, I wouldn't." He got up and walked up and down before the fire. "She's—aw! You don't know, you don't know what you done to her! She'd frighten you. It's rotten, like a leper. A veil on indoors and out, has to wear it always. She don't often go out, but whether or no, she must wear it. Ah, it's cruel."

There was a shock of horror as well as the throb of tears in her passionate compunction. "And you're not marrying her!"

"No," he said bluntly, "I'm not marrying her."

Mary covered her face with her hands and stood quivering under her dark weeping hair.

"God forgive me, how pitiful I'm shamed!" Her voice rose in a sharp cry. "Marry her, Frank! Oh, you marry her now, you must!"

"Not for a million, I'd sooner be in my grave."

"Frank Oppidan, you're no man, no man at all. You never had the courage to be strong, nor the courage to be evil; you've only the strength to be mean."

"Oh, dry up!" he said testily; but something overpowered

her and she went leaning her head sobbing against the chimney-piece.

"Come on, girl!" he was instantly tender, his arms were around her, he had kissed her.

"Go your ways!" She was loudly resentful. "I want no more of you."

"It's all right, Mary. Mary, I'm coming to you again, just as I used to."

"You . . ." She swung out of his embrace. "What for? D'ye think I want you now? Go off to Elizabeth Plantney . . ." She faltered. "Poor thing, poor thing, it shames me pitiful; I'd sooner have done it to myself. Oh, I wish I had."

With a meek grin Oppidan took from his pocket a bottle with a glass stopper. "Do you know what that is?"

It looked like a flask of scent. Mary did not answer. "Sulphuric," continued he, "same as you threw at her."

The girl silently stared while he moved his hand as if he were weighing the bottle. "When I saw what a mess you'd made of her, I reckoned you'd got off too light, it ought to have been seven years for you. I only saw it once, and my inside turned right over, you've no idea. And I thought: there's she—done for. Nobody could marry her, less he was blind. And there's you, just a six months and out you come right as ever. That's how I thought and I wanted to get even with you then, for her sake, not for mine, so I got this, the same stuff, and I came thinking to give you a touch of it."

Mary drew herself up with a sharp breath. "You mean—throw it at me?"

"That's what I meant, honour bright, but I couldn't—not now." He went on weighing the bottle in his hand.

"Oh, throw it, throw it!" she cried in bitter grief, but covering her face with her hands—perhaps in shame, perhaps fear.

"No, no, no, no." He slipped the bottle back into his pocket. "But why did you do it? She wouldn't hurt a fly. What good could it do you?"

"Throw it," she screamed, "throw it, Frank, let it blast me!"

"Easy, easy now. I wouldn't even throw it at a rat. See!" he cried. The bottle was in his hand again as he went to the open window and withdrew the stopper. He held it outside while the fluid bubbled to the grass; the empty bottle he tossed into the shrubs.

He sat down, his head bowed in his hands, and for some time neither spoke. Then he was aware that she had come to him, was standing there, waiting. "Frank," she said softly, "there's something I got to tell you." And she told him about the babe.

At first he was incredulous. No, no, that was too much for him to stomach! Very stupid and ironical he was until the girl's pale sincerity glowed through the darkness of his unbelief: "You don't believe! How could it not be true!"

"But I can't make heads or tails of it yet, Mary. You a mother, and I were a father!" Eagerly and yet mournfully he brooded. "If I'd 'a' known—I can't hardly believe it, Mary—so help me God, if I'd 'a' known—"

"You could done nothing, Frank."

"Ah, but I'd 'a' known! A man's never a man till that's come to him."

"Nor a woman's a woman, neither; that's true, I'm different now."

"I'd 'a' been his father, I tell you. Now I'm nothing. I didn't know of his coming, I never see, and I didn't know of his going, so I'm nothing still."

"You kept away from me. I was afraid at first and I wanted you, but you was no help to me, you kept away."

"I'd a right to know, didn't I? You could 'a' wrote and told me."

"I did write to you."

"But you didn't tell me nothing."

"You could 'a' come and see me," she returned austerely, "then you'd known. How could I write down a thing like that in a letter as anybody might open? Any dog or devil could play tricks with it when you was boozed or something."

"I ought 'a' bin told, I ought 'a' bin told." Stubbornly he maintained it. "'Twasn't fair, you."

"'Twasn't kind, you. You ought to 'a' come; I asked you, but you was sick o' me, Frank, sick o' me and mine. I didn't want any help, neither, 'twasn't that I wanted."

"Would you 'a' married me then?" Sharply but persuasively he probed for what she neither admitted nor denied. "Yes, yes, you would, Mary. 'Twould 'a' bin a scandal if I'd gone and married someone else."

When at last the truth about her own birth came out between them, oh, how ironically protestant he was! "God a'mighty, girl, what did you take me for! There's no sense in you. I'll marry you now, for good and all (this minute if we could), honour bright, and you know it, for I love you always and always. You were his mother, Mary, and I were his father! What was he like, that little son?"

Sadly the girl mused. "It was very small."

"Light hair?"

"No, like mine, dark it was."

"What colour eyes?"

She drew her fingers down through the long streams of hair.

"It never opened its eyes." And her voice moved him so that he cried out: "My love, my love, life's before us; there's a many good fish in the sea. When shall us marry?"

"Let me go, Frank. And you'd better go now, you're hindering me, and father will be coming in, and—and—the cakes are burning!"

Snatching up a cloth, she opened the oven door and an odour of caraway rushed into the air. Inside the oven was a shelf full of little cakes in pans.

"Give us one," he begged, "and then I'll be off."

"You shall have two," she said, kneeling down by the oven. "One for you—mind, it's hot!" He seized it from the cloth and quickly dropped it into his pocket. "And another, from me," continued Mary. Taking the second cake, he knelt down and embraced the huddled girl.

"I wants another one," he whispered.

A quick intelligence swam in her eyes: "For?"

"Ah, for what's between us, dear Mary."

The third cake was given him, and they stood up. They moved towards the door. She lifted the latch.

"Good night, my love." Passively she received his kiss. "I'll come again tomorrow."

"No, Frank, don't ever come any more."

"Aw, I'm coming right enough," he cried cheerily and confidently as he stepped away.

And I suppose we must conclude that he did.

Fishmonger's Fiddle (1925)

Fifty Pounds

❧

AFTER TEA PHILLIP REPTON AND EULALIA BURNES DIS-
cussed their gloomy circumstances. Repton was the precarious
sort of London journalist, a dark deliberating man, lean and
drooping, full of genteel unprosperity, who wrote articles about
Single Tax, Diet and Reason, The Futility of this that and the
other, or The Significance of the other that and this; all done
with a bleak care and signed P. Stick Repton. Eulalia was brown-
haired and hardy, undeliberating and intuitive; she had been
milliner, clerk, domestic help, and something in a canteen; and
P. Stick Repton had, as one commonly says, picked her up at a
time when she was drifting about London without a penny in
her purse, without even a purse, and he had not yet put her down.

"I can't understand! It's sickening, monstrous!" Lally was
fumbling with a match before the penny gas fire, for when it
was evening, in September, it always got chilly on a floor so high
up. Their flat was a fourth-floor one and there was—oh, fifteen
thousand stairs! Out of the window and beyond the chimney

you could see the long glare from lights in High Holborn and hear the hums and hoots of buses. And that was a comfort.

"Lower! Turn it lower!" yelled Phillip. The gas had ignited with an astounding thump; the kneeling Lally had thrown up her hands and dropped the matchbox saying "Damn" in the same tone as one might say good morning to a milkman.

"You shouldn't do it, you know," grumbled Repton. "You'll blow us to the deuce." And that was just like Lally, that was Lally all over, always: the gas, the nobs of sugar in his tea, the way she . . . and the, the . . . oh dear, dear! In their early life together, begun so abruptly and illicitly six months before, her simple hidden beauties had delighted him by their surprises; they had peered and shone brighter, had waned and recurred; she was less the one star in his universe than a faint galaxy.

This room of theirs was a dingy room, very small but very high. A lanky gas tube swooped from the middle of the ceiling towards the middle of the tablecloth as if burning to discover whether that was pink or saffron or fawn—and it *was* hard to tell—but on perceiving that the cloth, whatever its tint, was disturbingly spangled with dozens of cup-stains and several large envelopes, the gas tube in the violence of its disappointment contorted itself abruptly, assumed a lateral bend, and put out its tongue of flame at an oleograph of Mona Lisa which hung above the fireplace.

Those envelopes were the torment to Lally; they were the sickening monstrous manifestations which she could not understand. There were always some of them lying there, or about the room, bulging with manuscripts that no editors— they *couldn't* have perused them—wanted; and so it had come to the desperate point when, as Lally was saying, something had to be done about things. Repton had done all *he* could; he wrote unceasingly, all day, all night, but all his projects insolvently withered, and morning, noon, and evening brought his manuscripts back as unwanted as snow in summer. He was depressed and baffled and weary. And there was simply nothing else he could do, nothing in the world. Apart from his own wonderful gift he was useless, Lally knew, and he was being steadily and stupidly murdered by those editors. It was weeks since they had eaten a proper meal. Whenever they obtained any real nice food now, they sat down to it silently, intently, and destructively. As far as Lally could tell, there seemed to be no prospect of any such meals again in life or time, and the worst of it all was Phillip's pride—he was actually too proud to ask anyone for assistance! Not that he would be too proud to accept help if it were offered to him: oh no, if it came he would rejoice at it! But still, he had that nervous shrinking pride that coiled upon itself, and he would not ask; he was like a wounded animal that hid its woe far away from the rest of the world. Only Lally knew his need, but why could not other people see it—those villainous editors! His own wants were so modest and he had a generous mind.

"Phil," Lally said, seating herself at the table. Repton was lolling in a wicker armchair beside the gas fire. "I'm not going on waiting and waiting any longer, I must go and get a job. Yes, I must. We get poorer and poorer. We can't go on like it any longer, there's no use, and I can't bear it."

"No, no, I can't have that, my dear . . ."

"But I will!" she cried. "Oh, why are you so proud?"

"Proud! Proud!" He stared into the gas fire, his tired arms hanging limp over the arms of the chair. "You don't understand.

There are things the flesh has to endure, and things the spirit too must endure . . ." Lally loved to hear him talk like that; and it was just as well, for Repton was much given to such discoursing. Deep in her mind was the conviction that he had simple access to profound, almost unimaginable wisdom. "It isn't pride, it is just that there is a certain order in life, in my life, that it would not do for. I could not bear it, I could never rest; I can't explain that, but just believe it, Lally." His head was empty but unbowed; he spoke quickly and finished almost angrily. "If only I had money! It's not for myself. I can stand all this, any amount of it. I've done so before, and I shall do so again and again I've no doubt. But I have to think of you."

That was fiercely annoying. Lally got up and went and stood over him.

"Why are you so stupid? I can think for myself and fend for myself. I'm not married to you. You have your pride, but I can't starve for it. And I've a pride, too. I'm a burden to you. If you won't let me work now while we're together, then I must leave you and work for myself."

"Leave! Leave me now? When things are so bad?" His white face gleamed his perturbation up at her. "Oh well, go, go." But then, mournfully moved, he took her hands and fondled them. "Don't be a fool, Lally; it's only a passing depression, this. I've known worse before, and it never lasts long, something turns up, always does. There's good and bad in it all, but there's more goodness than anything else. You see."

"I don't want to wait for ever, even for goodness. I don't believe in it, I never see it, never feel it, it is no use to me. I could go and steal, or walk the streets, or do any dirty thing—easily. What's the good of goodness if it isn't any use?"

"But, but," Repton stammered, "what's the use of bad, if it isn't any better?"

"I mean—" began Lally.

"You don't mean anything, my dear girl."

"I mean, when you haven't any choice it's no use talking moral, or having pride; it's stupid. Oh, my darling"—she slid down to him and lay against his breast—"It's not you, you are everything to me; that's why it angers me so, this treatment of you, all hard blows and no comfort. It will never be any different. I feel it will never be different now, and it terrifies me."

"Pooh!" Repton kissed her and comforted her: she was his beloved. "When things are wrong with us our fancies take their tone from our misfortunes, badness, evil. I sometimes have a queer stray feeling that one day I shall be hanged. Yes, I don't know what for, what *could* I be hanged for? And, do you know, at other times I've had a kind of intuition that one day I shall be— what do you think?—Prime Minister of the country! Yes, well, you can't reason against such things. I know what I should do, I've my plans, I've even made a list of the men for my Cabinet. Yes, well, there you are."

But Lally had made up her mind to leave him; she would leave him for a while and earn her own living. When things took a turn for the better she would join him again. She told him this. She had friends who were going to get her some work.

"But what are you going to do, Lally? I—"

"I'm going away to Glasgow," said she.

"Glasgow?" He had heard things about Glasgow! "Good heavens!"

"I've some friends there," the girl went on steadily. She had got up and was sitting on the arm of his chair. "I wrote to them last week. They can get me a job almost any when, and I can stay with them. They want me to go—they've sent the money for my fare. I think I shall have to go."

"You don't love me, then!" said the man.

Lally kissed him.

"But *do* you? Tell me!"

"Yes, my dear," said Lally, "of course."

An uneasiness possessed him; he released her moodily. Where was their wild passion flown to? She was staring at him intently, then she tenderly said: "My love, don't you be melancholy, don't take it to heart so. I'd cross the world to find you a pin."

"No, no, you mustn't do that," he exclaimed idiotically. At her indulgent smile he grimly laughed too, and then sank back in his chair. The girl stood up and went about the room doing vague nothings, until he spoke again.

"So you are tired of me?"

Lally went to him steadily and knelt down by his chair. "If I was tired of you, Phil, I'd kill myself."

Moodily he ignored her. "I suppose it had to end like this. But I've loved you desperately." Lally was now weeping on his shoulder and he began to twirl a lock of her rich brown hair absently with his fingers as if it were a seal on a watch-chain. "I'd been thinking that we might as well get married, as soon as things had turned round."

"I'll come back, Phil"—she clasped him so tenderly—"As soon as you want me."

"But you are not really going?"

"Yes," said Lally.

"You're not to go!"

"I wouldn't go if—if anything—if you had any luck. But as we are now I must go away, to give you a chance. You see that, darling Phil?"

"You're not to go; I object. I just love you, Lally, that's all, and of course I want to keep you here."

"Then what are we to do?"

"I—don't—know. Things drop out of the sky, but we must be together. You're not to go."

Lally sighed: he was stupid. And Repton began to turn over in his mind the dismal knowledge that she had taken this step in secret, she had not told him while she was trying to get to Glasgow. Now here she was with the fare, and as good as gone! Yes, it was all over.

"When do you propose to go?"

"Not for a few days, nearly a fortnight."

"Good God," he moaned. Yes, it was all over, then. He had never dreamed that this would be the end, that she would be the first to break away. He had always envisaged a tender scene in which he could tell her, with dignity and gentle humour that—Well, he never had quite hit upon the words he would use, but that was the kind of setting. And now here she was with her fare to Glasgow, her heart towards Glasgow, and she as good as gone to Glasgow! No dignity, no gentle humour—in fact he was enraged—sullen but enraged, he boiled furtively. But he said with mournful calm:

"I've so many misfortunes, I suppose I can bear this too."

Gloomy and tragic he was.

"Dear, darling Phil, it's for your own sake I'm going."

Repton sniffed derisively. "We are always mistaken in the reasons for our commonest actions; Nature derides us all. You are sick of me; I can't blame you."

Eulalia was so moved that she could only weep again. Nevertheless she wrote to her friends in Glasgow promising to be with them by a stated date.

TOWARDS THE EVENING OF THE FOLLOWING DAY, AT A time when she was alone, a letter arrived addressed to herself. It was from a firm of solicitors in Cornhill inviting her to call upon them. A flame leaped up in Lally's heart: it might mean the offer of some work that would keep her in London after all! If only it were so she would accept it on the spot, and Phillip would have to be made to see the reasonability of it. But at the office in Cornhill a more astonishing outcome awaited her. There she showed her letter to a little office boy with scarcely any fingernails and very little nose, and he took it to an elderly man who had a superabundance of both. Smiling affably, the long-nosed man led her upstairs into the sombre den of a gentleman who had some white hair and a lumpy yellow complexion. Having put to her a number of questions relating to her family history, and appearing to be satisfied and not at all surprised by her answers, this gentleman revealed to Lally the overpowering tidings that she was entitled to a legacy of eighty pounds by the will of a forgotten and recently deceased aunt. Subject to certain formalities, proofs of identity and so forth, he promised Lally the possession of the money within about a week.

Lally's descent to the street, her emergence into the clamouring atmosphere, her walk along to Holborn, were accomplished in a state of blessedness and trance, a trance in which life became a thousand times aerially enlarged, movement was a delight, and thought a rapture. She would give all the money to Phillip, and if he very much wanted it she would even marry him now. Perhaps, though, she would save ten pounds of it for herself. The other seventy would keep them for . . . it was impossible to say how long it would keep them. They could have a little holiday somewhere in the country together, he was so worn and weary. Perhaps she had better not tell Phillip anything at all about it until her lovely money was really in her hand. Nothing in life, at least nothing about money, was ever certain; something horrible might happen at the crucial moment and the money be snatched from her very fingers. Oh, she would go mad then! So for some days she kept her wonderful secret.

Their imminent separation had given Repton a tender sadness that was very moving. "Eulalia," he would say, for he had suddenly adopted the formal version of her name; "Eulalia, we've had a great time together, a wonderful time, there will never be anything like it again." She often shed tears, but she kept the grand secret still locked in her heart. Indeed, it occurred to her very forcibly that even now his stupid pride might cause him to reject her money altogether. Silly, silly Phillip! Of course, it would have been different if they had married; he would naturally have taken it then, and really it would have *been* his. She would have to think out some dodge to overcome his scruples. Scruples were *such* a nuisance, but then it was very noble of him: there were not many men who wouldn't take money from a girl they were living with.

Well, a week later she was summoned again to the office in Cornhill and received from the white-haired gentleman a cheque for eighty pounds drawn on the Bank of England to the order of Eulalia Burnes. Miss Burnes desired to cash the cheque straightway, so the large-nosed elderly clerk was deputed to accompany her to the Bank of England close by and assist in procuring the money.

"A very nice errand!" exclaimed that gentleman as they crossed to Threadneedle Street past the Royal Exchange. Miss Burnes smiled her acknowledgment, and he began to tell her of other windfalls that had been disbursed in his time—but vast sums, very great persons—until she began to infer that Blackbean, Carp & Ransome were universal dispensers of largesse.

"Yes, but," said the clerk, hawking a good deal from an affliction of catarrh, "I never got any myself, and never will. If I did, do you know what I would do with it?" But at that moment they entered the portals of the bank, and in the excitement of the business Miss Burnes forgot to ask the clerk how he would use a legacy, and thus she possibly lost a most valuable slice of knowledge. With one fifty-pound note and six five-pound notes clasped in her handbag she bade good-bye to the long-nosed clerk, who shook her fervently by the hand and assured her that Blackbean, Carp & Ransome would be delighted at all times to undertake any commissions on her behalf. Then she fled along the pavement, blithe as a bird, until she was breathless with her flight. Presently she came opposite the window of a typewriter agency. Tripping airily into its office, she laid a scrap of paper before a lovely Hebe who was typing there.

"I want this typed, if you please," said Lally.

The beautiful typist read the words of the scrap of paper and stared at the heiress.

"I don't want any address to appear," said Lally. "Just a plain sheet, please."

A few moments later she received a neatly typed page folded in an envelope, and after paying the charge she hurried off to a district messenger office. Here she addressed the envelope in a disguised hand to P. Stick Repton, Esq., at the address in Holborn. She read the typed letter through again:

Dear Sir,

In common with many others I entertain the greatest admiration for your literary abilities, and I therefore beg you to accept this tangible expression of that admiration from a constant reader of your articles, who for purely private reasons, desires to remain anonymous.

Your very sincere

Wellwisher

Placing the fifty-pound note upon the letter Lally carefully folded them together and put them both into the envelope. The attendant then gave it to a uniformed lad, who sauntered off whistling very casually, somewhat to Lally's alarm—he looked so small and careless to be entrusted with fifty pounds. Then Lally went out, changed one of her five-pound notes, and had a lunch—half a crown, but it was worth it. Oh, how enchanting and exciting London was! In two days more she would have been gone; now she would have to write off at once to her Glasgow friends and tell them she had changed her mind, that she was now settled in London. Oh, how enchanting and delightful! And tonight he would take her out to dine in some fine restaurant, and they would do a theatre. She did not really want to marry Phil, they had got on so well without it, but if he wanted that too she did not mind—much. They would go away into the country for a whole week. What money would do! Marvellous! And looking round the restaurant she felt sure that no other woman there, no matter how well-dressed, had as much as thirty pounds in her handbag.

Returning home in the afternoon she became conscious of her own betraying radiance; very demure and subdued and usual she would have to be, or he might guess the cause of it. Though she danced up the long flight of stairs, she entered their room quietly, but the sight of Repton staring out of the window, forlorn as a drowsy horse, overcame her and she rushed to embrace him, crying: "Darling!"

"Hullo, hullo!" he smiled.

"I'm so fond of you, Phil dear."

"But—but you're deserting me!"

"Oh, no," she cried archly; "I'm not—not deserting you."

"All right." Repton shrugged his shoulders, but he seemed happier. He did not mention the fifty pounds then; perhaps it had not come yet—or perhaps he was thinking to surprise her.

"Let's go for a walk, it's a screaming lovely day," said Lally.

"Oh, I dunno," he yawned and stretched. "Nearly tea-time, isn't it?"

"Well, we—" Lally was about to suggest having tea out somewhere, but she bethought herself in time. "I suppose it is. Yes, it is."

So they stayed in for tea. No sooner was tea over than Repton remarked that he had an engagement somewhere. Off he went, leaving Lally disturbed and anxious. Why had he not mentioned the fifty pounds? Surely it had not gone to the wrong address? This suspicion once formed, Lally soon became certain, tragically sure, that she had misaddressed the envelope herself. A conviction that she had put No. 17 instead of No. 71 was almost overpowering, and she fancied that she hadn't even put London on the envelope—but Glasgow. That was impossible, though, but—oh, the horror!—somebody else was enjoying their fifty pounds. The girl's fears were not allayed by the running visit she paid to the messengers' office that evening, for the rash imp who had been entrusted with her letter had gone home and therefore could not be interrogated until the morrow. By now she was sure that he had blundered; he had been so casual with an important letter like that! Lally never did, and never would again, trust any little boys who wore their hats so much on one side, were so glossy with hair-oil, and went about whistling just to madden you. She burned to ask where the boy lived but in spite of her desperate desire she could not do so. She dared not, it would expose her to—to something or other she could only feel, not name; you had to keep cool, to let nothing, not even curiosity, master you.

Hurrying home again, though hurrying was not her custom and there was no occasion for it, she wrote the letter to her Glasgow friends. Then it crossed her mind that it would be wiser not to post the letter that night; better wait until the morning, after she had discovered what the horrible little messenger had done with her letter. Bed was a poor refuge from her thoughts, but she accepted it, and when Phil came home she was not sleeping. While he undressed he told her of the lecture he had been to, something about Agrarian Depopulation it was, but even after he had stretched himself beside her, he did not speak about the fifty pounds. Nothing, not even curiosity, should master her, and she calmed herself, and in time fitfully slept.

At breakfast next morning he asked her what she was going to do that day.

"Oh," replied Lally offhandedly, "I've a lot of things to see to, you know; I must go out. I'm sorry the porridge is so awful this morning, Phil, but—"

"Awful?" he broke in. "But it's nicer than usual! Where are you going? I thought—our last day, you know—we might go out somewhere together."

"Dear Phil!" Lovingly she stretched out a hand to be caressed across the table. "But I've several things to do. I'll come back early, eh?" She got up and hurried round to embrace him.

"All right," he said. "Don't be long."

Off went Lally to the messenger office, at first as happy as a bird, but on approaching the building the old tremors assailed her. Inside the room was the cocky little boy who bade her "Good morning" with laconic assurance. Lally at once questioned him, and when he triumphantly produced a delivery book she grew limp with her suppressed fear, one fear above all others. For a moment she did not want to look at it: truth hung by a hair, and as long as it so hung she might swear it was a lie. But there it was, written right across the page, an entry of a letter delivered, signed for in the well-known hand, P. Stick Repton. There was no more doubt, only a sharp indignant agony as though she had been stabbed with a dagger of ice.

"Oh yes, thank you," said Lally calmly. "Did you hand it to him yourself?"

"Yes'm," replied the boy, and he described Phillip.

"Did he open the letter?"

"Yes'm."

"There was no answer?"

"No'm."

"All right." Fumbling in her bag, she added: "I think I've got a sixpence for you."

Out in the street again she tremblingly chuckled to herself. "So that is what he is like, after all. Cruel and mean! He was going to let her go and keep the money in secret to himself!" How despicable! Cruel and mean, cruel and mean! She hummed it to herself. "Cruel and mean, cruel and mean!" It eased her tortured bosom. "Cruel and mean!" And he was waiting at home for her, waiting with a smile for their last day together. It would *have* to be their last day. She tore up the letter to her Glasgow friends, for now she *must* go to them. So cruel and mean! Let him wait! A bus stopped beside her, and she stepped on to it, climbing to the top and sitting there while the air chilled her burning features. The bus made a long journey to Plaistow. She knew nothing of Plaistow, she wanted to know nothing of Plaistow, but she did not care where the bus took her; she only wanted to keep moving and moving away, as far away as possible from Holborn and from him, and not once let those hovering tears down fall.

From Plaistow she turned and walked back as far as the Mile End Road. Thereabouts wherever she went she met clergymen, dozens of them. There must be a conference, about charity or something, Lally thought. With a vague desire to confide her trouble to someone, she observed them; it would relieve the strain. But there was none she could tell her sorrow to, and failing that, when she came to a neat restaurant she entered it and consumed a fish. Just beyond her, three sleek parsons were lunching, sleek and pink; bald, affable, consoling men, all very much alike.

"I saw Carter yesterday," she heard one say. Lally liked listening to the conversation of strangers, and she had often wondered what clergymen talked about among themselves.

"What, Carter! Indeed. Nice fellow, Carter. How was he?"

"Carter loves preaching, you know!" cried the third.

"Oh yes, he loves preaching!"

"Ha, ha, ha, yes."

"Ha, ha, ha, oom."

"Awf'ly good preacher, though."

"Yes, awf'ly good."

"And he's awf'ly good at comic songs, too."

"Yes?"

"Yes!"

Three glasses of water, a crumbling of bread, a silence suggestive of prayer.

"How long has he been married?"

"Twelve years," returned the cleric who had met Carter.

"Oh, twelve years!"

"I've only been married twelve years myself," said the oldest of them.

"Indeed!"

"Yes, I tarried very long."

"Ha, ha, ha, yes."

"Ha, ha, ha, oom."

"Er—have you any family?"

"No."

Very delicate and dainty in handling their food they were; very delicate and dainty.

"My rectory is a magnificent old house," continued the recently married one. "Built originally 1700. Burnt down. Rebuilt 1784."

"Indeed!"

"Humph!"

"Seventeen bedrooms and two delightful tennis courts."

"Oh, well done!" the others cried, and then they all fell with genteel gusto upon a pale blancmange.

From the restaurant the girl sauntered about for a while, and then there was a cinema wherein, seated warm and comfortable in the twitching darkness, she partially stilled her misery. Some nervous fancy kept her roaming in that district for most of the evening. She knew that if she left it she would go home, and she did not want to go home. The naphtha lamps of the booths at Mile End were bright and distracting, and the hum of the evening business was good despite the smell. A man was weaving sweetstuffs from a pliant roll of warm toffee that he wrestled with as the athlete wrestles with the python. There were stalls with things of iron, with fruit or fish, pots and pans, leather, string, nails. Watches for use—or for ornament—what d'ye lack? A sailor told naughty stories while selling bunches of green grapes out of barrels of cork dust which he swore he had stolen from the Queen of Honolulu. People clamoured for them both. You could buy back numbers of the comic papers at four a penny, rolls of linoleum for very little more—and use either for the other's purpose.

"At thrippence per foot, mesdames," cried the sweating cheapjack, lashing himself into ecstatic furies, "that's a piece of fabric weft and woven with triple-strength Andalusian jute, double-hot-pressed with rubber from the island of Pagama, and stencilled by an artist as poisoned his grandfather's cook.

That's a piece of fabric, mesdames, as the king of heaven himself wouldn't mind to put down in his parlour—if he had the chance. Do I ask thrippence a foot for that piece of fabric? Mesdames, I was never a daring chap."

Lally watched it all, she looked and listened; then looked and did not see, listened and did not hear. Her misery was not the mere disappointment of love, not that kind of misery alone; it was the crushing of an ideal in which love had had its home, a treachery cruel and mean. The sky of night, so smooth, so bestarred, looked wrinkled through her screen of unshed tears; her sorrow was a wild cloud that troubled the moon with darkness.

In miserable desultory wanderings she had spent her day, their last day, and now, returning to Holborn in the late evening, she suddenly began to hurry, for a new possibility had come to lighten her dejection. Perhaps, after all, so whimsical he was, he was keeping his "revelation" until the last day, or even the last hour, when (nothing being known to her, as he imagined) all hopes being gone and they had come to the last kiss, he would take her in his arms and laughingly kill all grief, waving the succour of a flimsy bank-note like a flag of triumph. Perhaps even, in fact surely, that was why he wanted to take her out today! Oh, what a blind, wicked, stupid girl she was, and in a perfect frenzy of bubbling faith she panted homewards for his revealing sign.

From the pavement below she could see that their room was lit. Weakly she climbed the stairs and opened the door. Phil was standing up, staring so strangely at her. Helplessly and half-guilty she began to smile. Without a word said he came quickly to her and crushed her in his arms, her burning silent man, loving and exciting her. Lying against his breast in that constraining embrace, their passionate disaster was gone, her doubts were flown; all perception of the feud was torn from her and deeply drowned in a gulf of bliss. She was aware only of the consoling delight of their reunion, of his amorous kisses, of his tongue tingling the soft down on her upper lip that she disliked and he admired. All the soft wanton endearments that she so loved to hear him speak were singing in her ears, and then he suddenly swung and lifted her up, snapped out the gaslight, and carried her off to bed.

Life that is born of love feeds on love; if the wherewithal be hidden, how shall we stay our hunger? The galaxy may grow dim, or the stars drop in a wandering void; you can neither keep them in your hands nor crumble them in your mind.

What was it Phil had once called her? Numskull! After all it was his own fifty pounds, she had given it to him freely, it was his to do as he liked with. A gift was a gift, it was poor spirit to send money to anyone with the covetous expectation that it would return to you. She would surely go tomorrow.

The next morning he awoke her early and kissed her.

"What time does your train go?" said he.

"Train!" Lally scrambled from his arms and out of bed.

A fine day, a glowing day. Oh, bright, sharp air! Quickly she dressed and went into the other room to prepare their breakfast. Soon he followed, and they ate silently together, although whenever they were near each other he caressed her tenderly. Afterwards she went into the bedroom and packed her bag; there was nothing more to be done, he was beyond hope. No woman waits to be sacrificed, least of all those who sacrifice themselves with courage and a quiet mind. When she was ready to go she took her portmanteau into the sitting-room; he, too, made to put on his hat and coat.

"No," murmured Lally, "you're not to come with me."

"Pooh, my dear!" he protested; "nonsense!"

"I won't have you come," cried Lally with an asperity that impressed him.

"But you can't carry that bag to the station by yourself!"

"I shall take a taxi." She buttoned her gloves.

"My dear!" His humorous deprecation annoyed her.

"Oh, bosh!" Putting her gloved hands around his neck she kissed him coolly. "Good-bye. Write to me often. Let me know how you thrive, won't you, Phil? And"—a little wavering—"Love me always." She stared queerly at the two dimples in his cheeks; each dimple was a nest of hair that could never be shaved.

"Lally, darling, beloved girl! I never loved you more than now, this moment. You are more precious than ever to me!"

At that, she knew her moment of sardonic revelation had come—but she dared not use it, she let it go. She could not so deeply humiliate him by revealing her knowledge of his perfidy. A compassionate divinity smiles at our puny sins. She knew his perfidy, but to triumph in it would defeat her own pride. Let him keep his gracious, mournful airs to the last, false though they were. It was better to part so, better from such a figure than from an abject scarecrow, even though both were the same inside. And something capriciously reminded her, for a flying moment, of elephants she had seen swaying with the grand movement of tidal water—and groping for monkey nuts.

Lally tripped down the stairs alone. At the end of the street she turned for a last glance. There he was, high up in the window, waving good-byes. And she waved back at him.

The Field of Mustard (1926)